STOP THEM DEAD

Peter James is a UK number one bestselling author, best known for his Detective Superintendent Roy Grace series, now a hit ITV drama starring John Simm as the troubled Brighton copper.

Much loved by crime and thriller fans for his fast-paced page-turners full of unexpected plot twists, sinister characters and accurate portrayals of modern-day policing, Peter has won over forty awards for his work, including the WHSmith Best Crime Author of All Time Award and the Crime Writers' Association Diamond Dagger.

To date, Peter has written an impressive total of nineteen *Sunday Times* number ones, has sold over 21 million copies worldwide and has been translated into thirty-eight languages. His books are also often adapted for the stage, with his six stage shows up to now grossing over £17 million at the box office.

www.peterjames.com
 @peterjamesuk
 @peterjames.roygrace
 @peterjamesuk
You Tube Peter James TV

WANT YOU DEAD

Who knew online dating could be so deadly?

YOU ARE DEAD

Brighton falls victim to its first serial killer in eighty years.

LOVE YOU DEAD

A deadly black widow is on the hunt for her next husband.

NEED YOU DEAD

Every killer makes a mistake somewhere. You just have to find it.

DEAD IF YOU DON'T

A kidnapping triggers a parent's worst nightmare and a race against time for Roy Grace.

DEAD AT FIRST SIGHT

Roy Grace exposes the lethal side of online identity fraud.

FIND THEM DEAD

A ruthless Brighton gangster is on trial and will do anything to walk free.

LEFT YOU DEAD

When a woman in Brighton vanishes without a trace, Roy Grace is called in to investigate.

PICTURE YOU DEAD

Not all windfalls are lucky. Some can lead to murder . . .

STOP THEM DEAD

A senseless murder hides a multitude of other crimes.

STOP THEM DEAD

PETER JAMES

PAN BOOKS

First published 2023 by Macmillan

This paperback edition first published 2024 by Pan Books
an imprint of Pan Macmillan
The Smithson, 6 Briset Street, London EC1M 5NR
EU representative: Macmillan Publishers Ireland Ltd, 1st Floor,
The Liffey Trust Centre, 117–126 Sheriff Street Upper,
Dublin 1, D01 YC43
Associated companies throughout the world
www.panmacmillan.com

ISBN 978-1-5290-8998-1

1 3 5 7 9 8 6 4 2

A CIP catalogue record for this book is available from the British Library.

Map artwork by ML Design
Contains OS data © Crown copyright and database right (2023)

Typeset by Palimpsest Book Production Ltd, Falkirk, Stirlingshire
Printed and bound by CPI Group (UK) Ltd, Croydon, CR0 4YY

Visit **www.panmacmillan.com** to read more about all our books
and to buy them. You will also find features, author interviews and
news of any author events, and you can sign up for e-newsletters
so that you're always first to hear about our new releases.

To all our canine friends who have been,
or still are, victims of the illegal trade in dogs.
I hope this helps give you a voice.

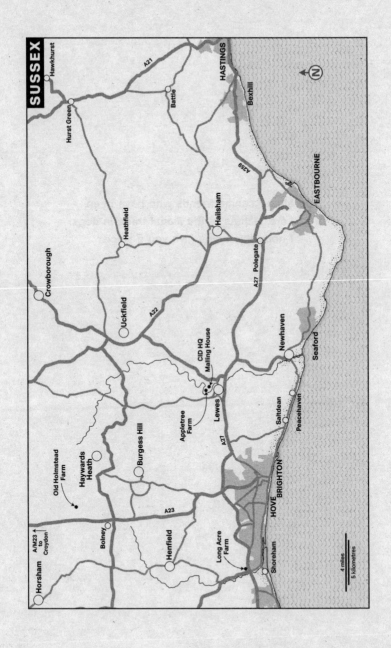

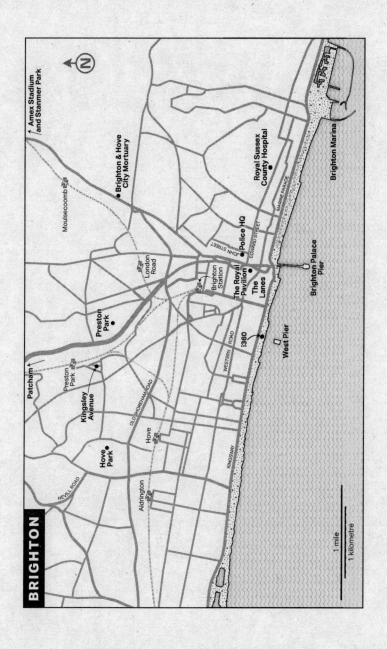

AUTHOR'S NOTE

Although the time period of this novel is set when the world was suffering from the effects of the Covid pandemic, this is a work of fiction. I hope, dear reader, you will forgive me for taking the liberty of making amendments to some events, dates and timings that would have been affected by the government restrictions.

1

Tim Ruddle was a reluctant disciple of Winston Churchill's maxim that success is the ability to go from failure to failure with no loss of enthusiasm. And if failure had been an Olympic sport, he could have taken gold countless times over, he rued as he lay in bed unable to sleep on this stormy late March night, unlike his wife, Sharon, who was as usual lost to the world beside him. She could sleep for England and if sleeping was an Olympic sport, she would sure as hell be on that podium.

He so envied her that ability. He could not remember when he'd last had a good night's sleep, a night when he hadn't lain awake worrying about this latest chapter in their life, then needed to get up and pee. Once, moving to the countryside and buying a farm had been their dream. The good life. Their two kids brought up away from all the violence and the other crap that London threw at you. Back to nature. The idyll that existed only in the pages of books. Not the grim reality of a farmer's life. The regulations. The subsidies that everyone else seemed eligible for except themselves.

They'd tried diversifying, opening a farm shop, and had recently been granted planning application to create a petting zoo and cafe. Both of them loved animals and had created a small revenue stream from alpaca-walking. But so far their biggest source of income from Old Homestead Farm was quite by accident and a very welcome surprise. Thanks to the massive rise in demand for dogs due to the lockdowns, the blue French bulldog

1

puppies their beloved pet, Brayley, had given birth to just seven weeks ago, were worth a staggering £3,000 each.

In breeding her, it had originally been their intention to keep at least one of the puppies, but the injection of badly needed cash they would get from the sales would help considerably with their new project. The five puppies were awaiting collection by their new owners in a week's time, after their inoculations.

Outside in the barn across the farmyard below their bedroom window, Rudi, the proud father, had begun barking. Rudi regularly barked at the wind, at rustling leaves, and most of all at Enemy No. 1, the aircraft that regularly flew overhead on their flight path to Gatwick Airport whenever the wind was blowing from the east, as it was tonight. Sharon frequently joked that Rudi was pretty effective: during the year they had been here not a single aeroplane had landed on their fields!

But Rudi's bark was different tonight. Ferocious, as if he was genuinely troubled by something out there in the darkness. And after a few moments, Sally, their female Labrador, who rarely ever made a sound – as if she had a mute button permanently pressed – started up too.

Worried the noise would wake their kids, Tim slipped out of bed and padded, naked, across to the window, parted the curtains and peered out into the darkness. As he did so he heard a sound, faint but distinct. The rumble of a diesel engine. One, or was it two? He glanced at his watch: 1.23 a.m.

Their farm was down a track, over a mile from the road – and that was just a quiet country lane. They had never been troubled by cold callers and no one ever drove up the rutted, potholed track by mistake. Anyone who came here had a reason and the last nocturnal visitors, a couple of months ago, had been a bunch of youths from a nearby caravan site, lamping rabbits.

Norris Denning, their elderly farmhand, who had come with the farm as a long-time employee – and had been a godsend to them – lived with his wife in the former gamekeeper's cottage, a few hundred yards back down the track. He'd sent the lampers packing.

The sound of the engines became louder. Nearer. And as it did so the barking of the dogs became more manic. Then Tim saw the silhouette of an off-roader vehicle, with no lights on, enter his farmyard. It was followed by another, a pickup truck.

He felt a stab of fear. What the hell was going on? These weren't lampers.

Then he saw the flare of a flashlight behind them. Heard a shout, an angry shout. Norris's voice. 'HEY!' the farmhand shouted.

Sharon stirred. 'Was going on?' she murmured sleepily.

'Call the police,' Tim said, quietly and urgently. 'Call 999 and say we have intruders.'

He pulled on some jeans and a sweatshirt, hurried downstairs, and shoved his feet into his wellingtons. Then he grabbed his Barbour jacket and the large torch from the shelf above the boot rack by the front door, switched it on, opened the door and shone the powerful beam ahead.

And stared in bewilderment, anger momentarily masking his fear. In the beam he saw Norris standing, feet planted, torch crooked under one arm and pointing a shotgun at the intruders. 'What the hell do you think you are doing?' he yelled in his Sussex burr. 'You clear off right away, you hear me?'

'Fuck off, Grandad, go back to bed,' one of them jeered at the elderly farmhand. Then he grabbed the shotgun by the barrel and ripped it out of Norris's hands.

2

Through the blustery drizzle, behind the man now holding Norris's shotgun, Tim saw the barn doors were open, and figures were moving around inside. Parked outside, engines still running, were an old Range Rover with its tailgate up and a Ford Ranger pickup in front of it. Two dogs, Rudi and Brayley, were barking furiously.

Striding forward, Tim called out more assuredly than he felt right now, 'Norris, it's all right, I can handle this.' Turning to the man with the shotgun, he shouted, 'What do you want?' As he did so, two men came out of the barn, holding a net full of wriggling creatures. The puppies, Tim saw to his horror. 'Those are my dogs, what do you think you're doing?' he demanded, his voice masking his fear and sense of utter helplessness.

Over to his left he saw Norris's jigging flashlight and a moment later heard him shout, 'No, Tim, leave this to me, I'll stop them.' Norris, who walked with a limp from a tractor accident years back, hobbled forward several paces. 'Give me my gun back and clear off NOW, the bloody lot of you!'

Tim felt momentarily helpless and terrified, as if he was trapped in one of those nightmares he sometimes had where he wanted to run but his legs wouldn't work and couldn't get any traction. His brain was spinning. He had a shotgun and a rifle, but they were locked in a cabinet down in the cellar. If Sharon had called the police, it would be a good while before they got here, far too long.

4

'YOU!' Norris yelled, lumbering towards the Range Rover as one of the men closed the tailgate then jumped into the back of the car. The engines of both vehicles were gunning now. Norris, wielding his flashlight, hurried to the front of the Range Rover and stood resolutely in front of it, shining the beam straight into the eyes of the driver.

Tim heard the roar of an engine and the slithering of tyres spinning. Horrified, he could see what was about to happen. Not even thinking about his own safely, the former rugby player hurled himself at the farmhand and with all his considerable strength shoved him away to the side, watching him fall clear of the vehicle, the torch clattering to the ground beside him.

Then he turned and, standing between its glaring headlights, faced the Range Rover, putting his arms up in furious defiance, shining the torch straight through the windscreen at two ugly, scowling faces. 'You stop right there!' he shouted.

From somewhere behind him he heard Sharon scream, 'Tim, no! Tim, no! The police are on their way!'

Before he had time to react, and to his shocked disbelief, the Range Rover began moving forward, striking him firmly, with the force of a concrete wall, in the midriff. Were they seriously trying to run him over? As the vehicle slowly picked up speed, pushing him backwards faster and faster, he panicked. This could not be happening, not here in this beautiful sanctuary. Please God. There was no way he could jump clear. In desperation, he pressed his hands on the warm bonnet, frantically trying to get a grip on the metal surface and running backwards, faster and faster to try to stay upright and not go under the front bumper. Faster.

The torch fell from his hands.

Faster.

He could not keep it up. He was going – going to go – falling—

Then his back struck something hard. Sharp edges against his calves and his back. The Ford Ranger pickup, he realized.

'No!' he screamed. 'NO!'

And heard Sharon's scream, too.

The Range Rover crushed his midriff agonizingly, jetting all the air out of his lungs, as searing flames of pain burned up through his chest and down through his whole body.

He stared in agony and disbelief as the vehicle began backing away now. The headlights were no longer dazzling. As if the batteries in them were exhausted and giving out. No brighter than two candles now. His legs were no longer supporting him. He flailed with his arms, falling, falling. It seemed to be an age before he landed on his face in the mud.

Again he heard his wife's voice. A torchlight momentarily shone in his eyes, blinding him. Then he heard Sharon's screaming. 'Oh God, no. Stay with me, Tim.'

'I'm – I'm OK, he said, but was struggling through the pain to speak. 'I feel a – a bit – faint.'

He was dimly aware she was kneeling beside him, opening his coat. He heard her say, as if she were somewhere in the distance, 'I can't see any blood, that's good.'

'That's good,' he gasped weakly.

'I've called the police,' she repeated. 'They're on the way. I'm calling an ambulance.'

'Ambulance,' he echoed. And dimly heard three pips. She was dialling, he realized.

'Open your eyes, darling,' he heard. And felt a faint squeeze on his hand. Heard her say, 'Ambulance.' And then some moments later, 'Hello, please, we need an ambulance – I just called the police who are on their way and we need an ambulance urgently, please.'

'Ambulance,' he murmured. He heard Sharon give the address and directions. Heard her say, 'Crushed between two vehicles.'

Her voice was getting fainter.

'He's breathing, but he's pale and very clammy.'

'I'll – I'll be OK,' he wheezed. 'Just a bit – a bit—'

'Yes, I'll get a blanket, keep him warm. No, I won't, I won't try to move him, but it's cold. Please ask them to hurry.'

'I love you,' he rasped.

'I love you. Stay strong, you're OK, the ambulance is on its way.'

Her voice was faint now. Somewhere in the distance. So faint. Fading.

The pain, at least, was fading now too.

3

Eldhos Matthew had wanted to be a police officer since he was nine years old and had watched a reality cop show on television. He'd been glued to the screen as two officers had pursued a stolen car across a city – he could not remember where; he just remembered the excitement as the stolen car had driven on the wrong side of the road, against the oncoming traffic and then out into a dark rural road, and listening, enthralled, to the voices of the police over the radios.

The pursuit had continued with a helicopter watching the chase through a night vision camera, before the car had crashed on a bend, and two shadowy figures had leaped from the vehicle and were chased on foot, under the glare of the helicopter's searchlight, and each brought to the ground.

That's what I want to do! he had thought right then. And from then on, until his mid-teens, pretty much the only television programmes he watched were cop shows – real-life or drama. When his parents or brothers and sisters wanted to watch something else, he retreated to his room in the family home in Brighton and watched them on his laptop. While all his school friends were absorbed in gaming in their free time, he just binge-watched anything that had police in it.

At some point his interest switched from the officers carrying out traffic stops, pursuits, drugs raids, to those solving murders, especially dramas like *Line Of Duty*, *CSI* and *Endeavour*. He found he had a natural talent for getting ahead of the detectives in most of the dramas.

He'd always loved solving puzzles, and his mother, a psychotherapist who worked as a marriage guidance counsellor, told him he had a sharp brain. From an early age he regularly played chess with his father, a mortgage broker, who had taught him, and from around the age of twelve Eldhos began beating him regularly. At fifteen he had become chess champion of the Dorothy Stringer school, and when he had the time, between schoolwork and the endless detective shows, he played chess on the internet with several opponents around the world.

But neither of his parents were enamoured by the notion, as he approached school leaving age, of his joining the police. His mother feared for his safety; his father, a pragmatic man, who had brought his family to England from their native India in search of a more prosperous life, was unhappy with his eldest son's ambition. In a heart-to-heart conversation he warned Eldhos he would never become rich working for the police, and in an organization that in his opinion was still institutionally racist, he would always struggle for promotion.

Eldhos had replied that he wasn't interested in becoming rich, that what he wanted was a career where he could make a difference to the world, and he genuinely believed he could make a difference. As to the racism, he could deal with that if it happened, and it seemed all of those prejudices were changing, and he was determined to play a part in that.

He was now, at twenty-one, two years and three weeks into his career with Sussex Police. Just three weeks out of his probationary period, and due to several members of his section being off with Covid, he was single crewed in a response car, based out of Haywards Heath. He had already put in his application for a transfer to CID and at the moment, with a shortage of detectives in the force, the future for his chosen path was looking good.

And on this drizzly March night, as he cruised the dark, silent streets of the small county town ten or so miles north of the city of Brighton and Hove, he was waiting, as he did every night he was on patrol, for a shout from the Control Room to send him off on the kind of action he craved, but which rarely happened.

So far tonight he had stopped a car with a tail-light out, and leaned in to smell the driver's breath for alcohol, but there was no trace. The young woman, a shift worker, was heading home from Gatwick Airport. He politely told her to get the bulb replaced and allowed her on her way without breathalysing her. Then he'd had a short Grade One blue light run, after a report of two men acting suspiciously outside a computer store in the High Street, where a burglar alarm was ringing. But when he got there, it turned out to be a fault and the manager and a work colleague were trying to deactivate it.

Eldhos had just made up his mind to head back to the nick for a coffee and to eat the chicken salad and chocolate bar that he'd brought along for his supper, when he heard the calm voice of a controller over the radio.

'Whisky Mike One-Seven-One.'

He clicked the button on his mic and responded with pride, 'Whisky Mike One-Seven-One.'

'Whisky Mike One-Seven-One, we have a report of intruders at Old Homestead Farm, Balcombe. We have the caller on the line and she's very frightened.'

'Old Homestead Farm, Balcombe?' He pulled over.

'Do you know the location?'

'No.'

'I'll give you the What3Words location.' She read them out.

Eldhos repeated them, pulling his phone from his chest cradle and tapping the words into the app. Instantly the location came to life on a map. 'OK, got it, I'm about five miles away.'

'Please attend, Grade One. I'll have backup for you but they are twenty minutes away.'

'En route now.' He entered an approximate address into the car's satnav system. He hadn't yet completed the pursuit driving course, but he held an amber ticket, which qualified him to drive to a scene on blue lights and siren. Excitedly, for only the third time since getting this permit, he leaned forward and punched a button on the dash-mounted control panel. Instantly, shards of blue strobed the dark country road around him. As he accelerated away hard, he debated whether to switch on the siren. Would it scare off the intruders? Would he have a better chance of catching them if he approached silently?

That was his decision, he realized, feeling apprehensive suddenly and wishing he had an experienced officer beside him. He decided against the siren. The countdown to the location reduced rapidly. Four minutes. Three. Two. Headlamps flared ahead of him then passed. The ANPR – Automatic Number Plate Recognition – cameras readout on his dash display gave the registration but did not indicate anything wrong with the BMW saloon. It was the same with a second vehicle, a Mazda, a few seconds later.

One minute.

He slowed right down, peering out at the narrow country lane. Again, he wished for a crewmate who could shine a torch. Shortly ahead he saw a small, tatty sign.

OLD HOMESTEAD FARM.

He turned into the driveway, a potholed cart track.

4

Molly Elizabeth Margaret Grace was nearly sixteen months old and so far, unlike her three-and-a-half-year-old brother Noah, she was generally a good sleeper. Cleo breast-fed her last thing at night, and she would normally sleep through until 5 a.m., only very occasionally waking during the intervening hours.

Except tonight, when they were both woken repeatedly by her crying. Their deal was that Cleo got up for Molly, who slept in a cot in their bedroom, and Roy for Noah, who was in his bedroom along the landing of their cottage. And this week it hadn't been such a great deal for Roy, who had been woken by the sound of Noah crying, on the monitor by his bed, twice during each night. Which entailed him getting up and heading through the cold air into Noah's room, holding his hand and soothing him until he was asleep again.

It seemed only moments had passed since he'd drowsed off, after getting up for the second time for his son at 2.30 a.m., when the ringtone of his job phone snapped him awake again. He reached out a hand and answered quietly and groggily. 'Roy Grace.'

To his dismay he heard the voice of one of his least favourite police officers, Andy *Panicking* Anakin, who made every incident sound like an Armageddon-category emergency. Anakin had recently been moved to the role of Detective Inspector for West Sussex Division. A classic example, in Grace's view, of the

Peter principle, which states that sooner or later, in every hierarchy, people get promoted to the level of their incompetence.

'Roy!' he shrieked. 'We have an incident. Do you need a few minutes to wake up?'

'I'm fine, I'm awake.'

As Head of Crime for the Surrey and Sussex Major Crime Team, Detective Superintendent Roy Grace had a team of four Senior Investigating Officers and a further four Deputy SIOs to deal with the average of twenty-four murders each year across the two counties. If needed during a particularly busy period, he had a further pool of four SIOs currently deployed in other areas that he could draft in. But he liked to remain hands-on, which was why, once every six weeks, he did a spell as the on-call SIO himself – which he was for this week.

From long experience in this role, he knew he was unlikely to get through many nights during these on-call weeks when his job phone did not ring. But mostly it would be something he could deal with without leaving home – last night it had been a case of the Duty DI at Brighton police station needing guidance on handling a death that had all the hallmarks of a tragic suicide.

'Hold a sec, Andy,' he said, slipping out of bed and, holding the phone to his ear, walked over to the ensuite bathroom, closed the door behind him and switched on the light. 'Tell me?'

As he listened to Anakin relate the still sketchy details of the unfolding story, he felt the familiar rush of adrenaline. It was the same that all SIOs he'd ever talked to got, when they had to drop everything. The buzz. But tainted with the knowledge that their best days at work would all too often be the worst day of someone's life.

All need of sleep forgotten, he told the DI he would be there in about an hour. Five minutes later, dressed and ready, he hurried down into the kitchen to make himself a quick double espresso and checked on his laptop for the log of the call handler who had answered the 999 call. He requested the call to be downloaded right away so he could listen to both the caller and the handler, to get chapter and verse of the situation.

Sipping the hot coffee, he pulled up Google Earth and had a quick look at the location and the topography. As soon as he had done that he gave the Control Room a series of urgent actions relating to resourcing, cordoning off roads and vehicle stop-checks. Then he called his colleague – and close friend – Glenn Branson.

The DI answered, clearly as sleepy as Grace had felt five minutes ago. 'What's up? You suffering from insomnia?'

'Yep, thought I'd share it with you.'

'You're all heart.'

'Meet me in the car park of The Plough at Pyecombe in twenty minutes.'

'We going somewhere nice?'

'We're going farming.'

'Arable or dairy?'

5

Thursday 25 March

'So, how's life as a country bumpkin this week then with your herd of hens?' Glenn Branson said, driving the unmarked Mondeo. They were heading north on the A23 shortly after 3.50 a.m.

'It's a *brood* of hens,' Roy Grace corrected him. 'Best eggs ever,' he added.

The DI kept just under the 70 mph speed limit, wipers clouting away the fine drizzle, the headlights picking out the road ahead. The satnav indicated to take the slip road coming up.

'Now listen,' Grace continued. 'I had an update yesterday from Alison Vosper, she said our old friend Cassian Pewe's trial should be coming up at the Old Bailey sometime this summer. She also tried to tap me up again to join her in the Met as a Commander, but I like what we're doing too much.'

'Perhaps at last Pewe will get what he deserves,' Branson replied.

'He'll never get what he deserves, but anything will be a bonus,' Grace said with a trace of bitterness.

They bantered in between the constant calls Grace was making to the 24/7 intel team, to check all traffic movement in the surrounding area through the National ANPR Service – NAS – and to alert the media team of a potential major crime investigation. Additionally, he made sure Hannah Robinson, the ACC, was updated so she wouldn't hear the news as a surprise from another source.

'What's going to be next, Farmer Roy? Pigs, geese, horses?'

'A dog.'

'Really? A baby and another dog? You're a glutton for punishment.'

'We know what we're up against! Anyhow, we already have Humphrey so one more won't make much difference. It'll be good for Noah to have a younger dog that he can help train – a dog of his own. We want the kids being brought up comfortable with animals, and Humphrey will love a playmate – help keep him young and all that.' Humphrey was Cleo's rescue six-year-old Labrador cross – and Roy Grace's regular early morning jogging companion.

'Getting another rescue?'

'That's what we are thinking. Maybe some type of spaniel.'

'They're gun dogs, aren't they?' Branson grinned. 'See, you're getting all rural, all hunting, shooting, fishing. Get you!'

'They have a nice nature,' Grace replied. 'They're very gentle dogs.'

'Unless you happen to be a pheasant.'

Grace did not respond for some moments, he was concentrating on the task in hand as they headed along a twisting country lane, their destination just two miles away now. Then he turned to Branson and said, 'Why are you smiling so much at this hour of the morning?'

After Glenn's long on–off engagement to Siobhan Sheldrake, a reporter on the local newspaper, the *Argus*, and with all their plans for a big local wedding with Grace as best man put on hold, in the end the couple had jetted off to Las Vegas over Christmas and married on a whim in a wedding chapel there.

'I'm living the dream, Roy! No, seriously, I do wake up happy these days. I try to be grateful and enjoy my life, we both know how life can be turned in a flash. We have a lot to be thankful for, right? Do you feel that, even after Bruno's death? It must be hard some days when everyone else has moved on and you still feel sad.'

'Yeah, it is hard, he's forever there in my thoughts. I'm not sure you ever get over the death of a child. Hey, I'm glad to hear you are enjoying life though, you deserve it,' Grace replied. And he was genuinely glad for this big-hearted and brilliant detective who had in recent years become his closest friend.

'I keep meaning to ask, have you done anything about that last text message to Bruno – do you know who sent it or if it's of any significance?'

'No, there was no subscriber to that number and I haven't bothered to follow it up, just doesn't seem any point.'

The satnav announced they would arrive at their destination in half a mile. Both detectives fell silent, and Roy Grace wondered if Glenn Branson was feeling the same niggling apprehension he always felt approaching a crime scene. About what you were going to find and the responsibility of making all the right decisions once you got there. Making the most of the so-called Golden Hour. That crucial time period for securing evidence, gathering witnesses, and sometimes sealing off as wide an area as you could justify with roadblocks. But along with advice from colleagues he'd already ruled out the latter, after studying a map of the area around the reported crime scene and calculating the time.

The 999 call from the farmer's wife had been logged at 1.27 a.m. It was now coming up to 4 a.m. The suspects could be anywhere by now, and besides they had only sketchy descriptions of them, and equally of their vehicles, possibly a Ford Ranger pickup and an old model Range Rover with possibly a J and a 2 in its registration plate.

Fortunately, the drizzle was subsiding, not turning into pelting rain – the enemy of forensics, as it reduced the chance of getting identifiable footprints and washed away hair and clothing fibres. The forty-something-year-old male victim had been certified dead by a First Responder at 2.15 a.m.

As Glenn turned into an adjacent field next to the sign for Old Homestead Farm, which was designated a holding area for police vehicles, to avoid them driving over the offenders' tracks and risking destroying evidence, Grace was thinking about his next wave of priority actions. He was already satisfied enough from Anakin's report that he had a murder enquiry on his hands and had arranged for calls to be made to the key members of his team to assemble at the Major Crime Team conference room at 8 a.m. ready for the 8.30 a.m. briefing.

They pulled out the protective white suits and wormed their way into them, pulling up the hoods, then pushed their feet into the overshoes and each grabbed a torch and approached the farmyard on foot along the common-approach path that the Crime Scene Manager had established. Beyond them there was a line of blue and white crime scene tape across the track, with a uniformed police officer, on duty as scene guard, standing steadfast in front, accompanied by a very young officer.

The scene guard, PC Dave Simmons, who Roy knew, walked towards them, holding a clipboard. 'Hello, gentlemen,' he said breezily.

Roy Grace remembered from his own experience in his early days as a uniformed probationer that guarding a crime scene was sometimes one of the shittiest jobs you could land. Especially in winter, at night, in the rain, although at least the rain had stopped. Hours of unremitting boredom, but from the broad smile on his face this officer wasn't showing it.

'What do you have?' Grace asked.

'This officer was first on scene here,' Simmons replied. The two detectives turned towards him.

'I'm a Response officer, PC Eldhos Matthew. When I saw the victim, I immediately asked for a tarpaulin, as large as possible, which I laid over him to preserve as much of the scene as I could, then I instructed everyone who has come subsequently to walk in one single line to and from the body.'

'Nice work,' Grace said.

The young officer said, 'You are Detective Superintendent Roy Grace, Head of Major Crime?'

'I am, yes.'

'Not the right time, I know, but I would love one day to serve under you. I'm applying to be a detective. If there is ever a chance to work with your team, please think of me. I would work very hard for you and I think you'd find me potentially a good detective, sir.'

Grace smiled, impressed by the young man. 'I will, you seem to have initiative.' He mentally noted the ID on his uniform.

'Oh yes, sir, thank you. I promise you I have initiative.'

'So what exactly did you find?'

'It's nasty, sir. A husband and wife, Timothy and Sharon Ruddle, are the farmers. From what Mrs Ruddle told me, they were woken at around 1.15 a.m. by the sound of their dogs barking – they had five French bulldog puppies, all sold and waiting for another week before going to their new owners – and saw two vehicles and a bunch of strangers in the farmyard apparently trying to steal the puppies and the parent dogs. Mr Ruddle went down to confront them, along with their farmhand, Norris Denning.

'When I arrived, I saw a man – Mr Ruddle – lying in the farmyard in a Barbour jacket, bleeding from his mouth, nose and midriff, with his wife kneeling beside him, in a hysterical state. Mr Denning was on the phone to the ambulance service, receiving directions on CPR, but from the gentleman's injuries I was pretty sure he was dead. This was confirmed by the medic who arrived ahead of the ambulance. That was when I asked Mr Denning for a tarpaulin to protect the victim and area around him as much as possible from the weather.'

'Good,' Grace said, again impressed. Not every officer who

was first on the scene of a murder had such presence of mind. 'Eldhos Matthew?' he said, checking.

He nodded. 'Yes, sir. I'm waiting to take my detective's exams.'

'When you've passed, let me know, OK?'

Eldhos beamed with delight. 'I will, sir, Detective Superintendent. I will absolutely!'

'So, who is here?'

'This is the outer cordon, sir. I thought I should protect as big an area as possible. There is the second cordon two hundred yards up the track. At the present time there is DI Anakin, my supervisor, a second scene guard and two CSIs, with more due to arrive shortly. I should tell you, sir, that DI Anakin was not impressed I would not let him drive up to the scene. And that I had to remind him to put on a forensic suit.'

It was the duty of the first police officer at the location of a murder to protect that scene. They were empowered to let no one through, not even the Chief Constable, without wearing protective clothing – both to avoid contaminating the area and to restrict the number of people. Grace grinned at the thought of this spirited young officer standing his ground with Anakin. 'Excellent!' he said. 'Is the paramedic still here?'

'No, sir, he was called away to an RTC.'

Two minutes later, they were greeted in the shadowy darkness by the identically clad figure of Anakin. 'It's not looking good, boss, not good at all.'

Deaths generally didn't look good, Grace thought, but didn't say. Instead he asked, 'Tell me what we have?'

6

'I don't know how to put it, Mr Fairfax,' the meek sixty-seven-year-old man said in a small voice, and blushed. He sat on his chair, hunched, like a dormouse in a human frame, the solicitor thought.

'I'm a family lawyer,' Chris Fairfax replied. 'You can tell me anything.' And he meant it. There was nothing, absolutely nothing he hadn't heard, in his office at Fairfax Law in Brighton's Ship Street, a wedding ring's throw from the seafront. All the things that demented people say about their partners, often little more than annoying habits which corroded and ultimately destroyed their relationships. And the acts of bitterness that followed – fights over child custody being among the worst. Heartbreaks over adoptions that didn't work out. Harsh pre-nups leaving one of the loving couple in tears. Bitterness and greed over wills. As Chris had once remarked wryly to his wife, 'Where there's a will there's a lawyer.'

'I heard Graham Norton on the radio – I like his show,' Noel Dudley said, and wrung his bony hands. 'Last Saturday he commented that he would prefer to live alone than with someone who folded the towels the wrong way. That's what Deirdre does. She folds them the wrong blooming way!' He held his clenched fists in the air, his eyes gleaming with an almost messianic fervour – and rage. Real rage.

The forty-year-old solicitor was neatly suited, lean and tall, with a shock of dark curly hair and round tortoiseshell glasses. A good listener, he exuded empathy, with a warm smile that made all his clients feel that he cared about them – which he genuinely did. He was still youthful enough not to have become jaded by the endless procession of people that came through the door of his family legal practice, which he and his wife, Katy, had established nine years ago as joint partners, to share the private details of their family with them.

Although it was only a couple of nights ago, over a glass of wine with their evening meal, after a particularly grim day, he'd complained to Katy that not many clients ever came to them because they were happy.

It was 9.10 a.m. and Noel Dudley, a draughtsman, was the first of what looked from his diary to be a rammed morning of client meetings. It was a school inset day and this afternoon was booked out to take his seven-year-old daughter, Bluebell, swimming and then to go and see and – *maybe* – buy a golden doodle puppy she had set her heart on. Chris had his notebook in front of him and held a fountain pen in his hand.

Dudley wore an old-fashioned charcoal suit which might once have fitted him but now looked a size too big, as did his shirt collar, which hung loose around his turkey neck, and a limp, green tie with a massive knot that hung a good inch south of his top button. His grey hair was neatly brushed and his eyes, behind large, old-fashioned spectacles, were rheumy and sad. He looked every inch a man crushed by life, a man beaten into a mouse.

'How long have you been married, Mr Dudley?' the solicitor asked.

'Forty-seven years,' he replied.

Chris smiled. 'And you are absolutely certain you don't want to remain with your wife?'

Dudley nodded vehemently. 'Like I said, enough is enough.'

'So you really want to divorce your wife and start anew at your age – no disrespect meant?'

'I dunno about starting anew. I just want to be able to enjoy my remaining years, you know?'

Chris Fairfax did know. During his years of practising family law, he'd seen far too many couples who fitted exactly Thoreau's quote about the mass of people living lives of quiet desperation. Couples in their seventies, eighties and even their nineties who had grown to hate each other and had left it too late to separate and find happiness in their twilight years. He felt a little empathy towards this sad diminutive man.

'Apart from folding your towels the wrong way, what are your other reasons for wanting a divorce?'

'I can't stand her,' Noel Dudley said. 'I don't think she can stand me either. I could have retired twelve years ago, but we became empty nesters a year before I came up for retirement, and I realized it would be just me and her. She's a control freak if you want to know the truth.'

'In what way?'

'We have to eat together every night at the dining table even though we don't have anything to say to each other. She always makes soup for a starter and she sits there slurping it with a noise like a dog licking his bollocks.'

Chris tried not to grin, but when he saw his client smile, he couldn't help it. 'OK, so she folds towels in a way that annoys you and she eats her soup noisily. Anything else?'

'We never agree on what to watch on television. I want to watch the footy, rugby, golf. All she ever wants to watch are soaps and cookery programmes.'

'Couldn't you get two televisions?'

'Are you on my side or hers?' Noel Dudley asked him sharply.

'I'm asking you questions a judge might ask.'

'There's no way she'd allow me to buy a second television.

I'm not allowed to spend money on anything. She goes through our bank statement and credit card bills every month. I have to explain every item.'

'Does Deirdre have a career?'

'She used to work part-time in a bookshop – City Books.'

The solicitor raised his eyebrows. 'I know it, great bookshop – I've been going there for years.'

'I just feel trapped. If she got ill, suddenly, how could I leave? What if she became an invalid and I had to spend the next twenty years caring for someone I hated?'

Chris nodded, aware that he was liking his client less and less. 'I understand. But you need to consider the financial arrangements between yourself and your wife. Generally under English divorce law the wife will get an equal share of the assets. Do you have many?'

'The house. The mortgage is paid off.' Noel Dudley began shaking his head. 'I don't care what she gets. She can have it all, I just can't take it any more.' He lowered his face into his hands and began sobbing.

7

Thursday 25 March

Roy Grace sat in the briefing room of the Major Crime Suite at Sussex Police HQ, trying to warm up. He had spent much of the past four hours outside at Old Homestead Farm in the freezing cold.

But it wasn't just the pre-dawn cold that had chilled him to the marrow, it was what had happened at the farm that had touched him deeply in a way that few violent crimes in his career, to date, had. It was the sheer senseless brutality that had so destructively invaded the lives of such a seemingly decent family that was getting to him.

An expression he had once heard, from a now long-retired SIO, was lodged in his mind like the needle of an old vinyl record stuck in the groove, repeating one refrain over and over.

Fishermen of greed.

A farmer crushed to death between two vehicles by greedy, vicious criminals for doing what any normal, decent person would do – trying to protect his livelihood. The result was a family destroyed, leaving a widow and two fatherless children.

Feeling a surge of anger at the people who had done this, further fuelled by his own personal love of dogs, he sipped a stewed-to-death coffee and munched an equally vile and soggy all-day breakfast sandwich he'd bought from a petrol station on his way in from the crime scene, where he had been until forty minutes ago. He had no appetite but knew he needed fuel for the very long hours he faced ahead.

Glenn Branson, who normally chided him for his penchant for unhealthy food, sat opposite him at the oval table, and held up his identical sandwich with a frown of distaste. 'Know what Michael Caine said about the traditional full-English breakfast?'

'No, but I'm guessing I'm about to learn.'

'He said it was a *heart attack on a plate.*' Then he wolfed his down in four large bites.

'So we've probably each shortened our lives by about three minutes eating these.'

Branson pursed his lips into a smile.

The room was starting to fill for the 8.30 a.m. briefing Grace had called. DS Jo Dillon, the new Office Manager, had set up four whiteboards on easels. On the first she had pinned two photographs of the dead man, supplied by his wife, on the second two Intelligence Profiles, one for the victim and another for the suspects – as and when they had any – and the third contained an Ordnance Survey map of Old Homestead Farm and the immediate surrounding area, with the murder scene marked with a red pin. The fourth contained photographs of several dog breeds.

Next in – new to the team – was Michelle Boshoff, a motivated and highly experienced Exhibits Officer who would be responsible for all material evidence gathered. She had long fair hair, large black-rimmed glasses and a penchant for loud blouses. She was followed by DCs Nick Nicholl, Velvet Wilde and Emma-Jane Boutwood, Financial Investigator Emily Denyer, DS Jack Alexander, Chris Gee the Crime Scene Manager, Luke Stanstead and Vanessa Blackmore – the researchers – and several other investigators on the team, including Polly Sweeney. The last to enter, perspiring as if he'd been running, was DS Norman Potting, sporting a black eye and a strip of plaster across the bridge of his nose.

As Potting sat down at the oval table, with a grunt, Velvet turned to him and in her Belfast accent asked him cheekily, 'Another successful date last night, eh Norman?'

Everyone around the table smiled.

'Kind of you to ask, Velvet, but it was actually a date with a slippery shower tray and a soap dish,' Potting replied.

'You need to be careful, Norman,' Glenn Branson said. 'Only old people fall over in showers.'

'Talking from experience, are we?' Potting retorted.

'All right, children,' Roy Grace said. 'Let's save the banter for the playground break, shall we?'

After a brief pause he continued. 'This is the first briefing of Operation Brush, the investigation into the murder of Timothy Edward Ruddle, co-owner with his wife, Sharon, of the Old Homestead Farm, two miles from the village of Balcombe. From what we know so far, the murder is linked to the theft of five French bulldog puppies valued at three thousand pounds each and two adult dogs, an un-neutered male and an un-spayed bitch, of potentially very much higher value from this property.

'Tim Ruddle, aided by his farmhand Norris Denning, was trying to prevent the thieves from making off with these dogs, and it seems he was deliberately and callously killed for his efforts, by being run down and crushed between two vehicles. We will know the full extent of his injuries when the postmortem takes place later today.'

He paused to sip his coffee and noticed his hand was shaking. He felt dreadful, he realized, tired and still cold, upset and angry.

Potting raised a hand.

'Yes, Norman?'

'I've been reading some crime statistics on puppy farming, dog theft and illegal importing of dogs. Some organized crime gangs here in the UK are apparently making more money from this than from drugs – and with far lower sentences if they're caught.'

Grace nodded. 'You're well informed, Norman. I understand, for example, that the type of *blue* French bulldogs stolen from the Ruddles, can go – with the right colouring – for as much as twenty-five thousand pounds on the black market. That may give us some sense of the scale of what we might be dealing with here. The only way these thieves can be given much longer sentences is if they can be arrested on charges of conspiracy to traffic dogs, and that's what we will be looking for.'

Polly Sweeney raised her hand.

'Yes, Polly?' Grace said.

'I've started my work on the victim profile. I've checked the backgrounds of the Ruddles and Norris Denning. None of them have any criminal record; the only thing on file is a speeding ticket for Tim Ruddle, three years ago, doing 52 mph in a 40 limit. Then I ran a search on reported dog crimes, sir,' she said. 'There are a number of recent crimes in the county involving dogs that show up. The first is a raid last week by the RSPCA on a car park in Eastbourne where a number of puppies were found in a caravan, emaciated and in a bad way. They are currently still in the care of the charity.'

'Good work, Polly,' Grace said.

Polly then brought up a facial image on her laptop. As the man's picture appeared, she said, 'The facial image is unclear but we can see it is a male. His technique is pretty ugly. According to witnesses, he pushed over an elderly lady walking her pug in St Ann's Well Gardens last week and ran off with the dog. Two days later a male, matching his description, punched an elderly gentleman in the stomach in Preston Park and ran off with the Cavalier King Charles spaniel he was walking for his granddaughter. This same aggressive person is linked with four other dog thefts in the city in the last ten days.

'I'm linking with both the Rural Crimes Unit and the RSPCA; they are working hand-in-hand on the current crimewave over dogs, both theft and illegal farming and importation.'

'Keep on it,' Grace said.

'I will, sir. There was an incident with a break-in at boarding kennels near Lewes, where eight dogs were stolen – two Labrador retrievers, three cocker spaniels and three springer spaniels – all under two years old and sought-after breeds. It looks like these dogs were specifically targeted. Then, there was a van with RSPCA markings on the side that turned up at a well-known breeder's home in East Sussex, and two men, using what turned out to be fake IDs, posing as RSPCA inspectors, seized five poodle puppies, and their parents, under the pretext that the dogs did not appear to have been properly cared for. The breeder, a highly reputable lady, who is also a Crufts judge, immediately called the police. The dogs were chipped, and she believes they would be easily traceable.'

'Not so,' Norman Potting interrupted. 'I've been speaking to Sergeant Tom Cartwright, based at Midhurst, who runs the force Rural Crimes Unit. He told me that there are a number of highly professional gangs, equipped with chipping equipment, who can implant a new chip, either over the original one – which means a scan picks up the new one – or after ripping out the original one.' Potting paused as several members of the team groaned and winced. 'Yep, brutal. Sergeant Cartwright is tied up this morning but has offered to attend our next briefing if we feel that would be helpful.'

'Thank you, Norman,' Grace said. 'I've also spoken to Tom. If you could get back to him and ask him if he could attend this evening's briefing at 6 p.m.'

'No problem, chief.'

'In advance of that, he's working on known intelligence relating to crime gangs he is aware of who are dealing in dogs, as well as any individuals.'

Grace glanced down. In front of him, he had his investigator's notebook and his laptop, on which was now an electronic version of his Policy Book, replacing the old, pale blue bound paper version. The Policy Book was every Senior Investigating Officer's insurance – as well as potentially their poisoned chalice. SIOs wrote down all their decisions in it, which would then be looked at during the subsequent regular reviews. Every review was a stomach-churning moment, Grace knew, in which all his ability – or incompetence – was laid bare.

He stood up and walked over to the whiteboard with the pictures of dog breeds. He pointed at one, a photograph of a puppy whose stubby body was grey-blue, with pointy, sticking-up ears above a cute, expressive, wrinkled face. The dog, its paws planted firmly on the ground, looked so confident, as if it was ready to take on the world.

'Five lovely puppies, looking like this, and two adults were stolen at approximately 1.15 a.m. today and the farmer who had bred them was crushed to death between two vehicles when he tried to stop the thieves. We have an exceptionally nasty murder on our hands, and we are going to find those who did this, every damned one of them, and lock them up for a very long time.'

He looked around his team. No one was smiling any more. They were all feeling something of the outrage that was burning inside him.

Potting raised a hand.

'Yes, Norman?'

'Sergeant Cartwright did say some travellers have been suspects when it comes to dog theft and puppy farming, chief.'

'I agree that local traveller sites should be part of our enquiry,' Grace said. 'But only a small part. I want us to look beyond that into the bigger picture of the major crime gangs operating in Sussex, in the key towns and cities – Brighton, Hastings, Eastbourne, Worthing – and beyond. We should not be preju-diced or led by stereotypes we might see or hear in the press.'

Potting nodded.

At that moment Grace's phone rang. Raising an apologetic hand, he answered with a curt, 'Roy Grace'. Then immediately changed his tone to a polite, 'Good morning, ma'am,' as he recognized the voice of Lesley Manning, the Chief Constable of Sussex Police.

'If you could hold just one moment, ma'am,' he asked, and hastily stepped out of the room.

8

Thursday 25 March

They called him Gecko. He'd had the name for so long most people didn't know him by anything else, and he was fine with that. Pretty proud, in fact. It was his mum who'd first called him that, some decades back, when he was five years old. She had said he looked like one of the wide-eyed lizards, but it wasn't only that fact that had secured his moniker.

He had freaked his mum out by running up to her while she was in the kitchen cooking his tea, and opened his mouth to reveal a large spider, alive and crawling around on his tongue.

She'd screamed and dropped the saucepan full of baked beans on the floor. He'd closed his mouth, grinning, chewed and swallowed the creature. And from then on it had been his party trick, grossing out his classmates and freaking out his teachers throughout his school years.

Mostly the other kids kept their distance from him. Some chanted, *Weirdo! Freak!* Others shouted, *Ugly little wart!* The only ones who befriended him were a couple of the older boys, Tommy Skinner and Darryl Gillespie, because he made himself useful to them. They ran the drugs supply into the school, and Gecko didn't mind bunking off classes to take the train to London, entrusted with a wodge of cash, to go and score weed for them from a dude in Brixton. For the first time in his life, he had felt wanted. Felt he had a value.

A big life lesson learned early. People wouldn't care how you looked if you could make yourself useful to them. This was important because he had found life difficult. But this discovery made life a little easier.

Make yourself useful, be helpful, always say yes, he would murmur to himself whenever he felt stressed.

Then the three of them were kicked out of West Brighton School at sixteen, for running a drugs supply network on behalf of Clifford Keele, the scion of one of Brighton's major crime families. A few months later they were moved from running drugs to stealing older-style cars, to be cut and shut – and clocked – for one of Keele's dealerships, used for laundering his firm's drugs money.

Later, at eighteen, during his first spell in prison, after a long chase – and bad crash – in a stolen car, Gecko had found that by opening his mouth to reveal a spider in there, other inmates would give him a wide berth. The short, tattooed man, with his swaggering walk, tapered crew cut and big, slow eyes too far apart, like the lizard's, ready to take a painful swing at anyone who messed with him and spit a half-chewed spider at their face, was left well alone.

Truth was, Gecko liked spiders. He enjoyed the sensation of them crawling around inside his mouth, and he liked the soft crunch as he bit into them – the bigger the better, the more crunch! He really enjoyed that. He was aware that his appearance made him different to other people, but he didn't care. Enough people had already told him he was different to normal folk, with his hyperthyroid bulging eyes, tiny height and pale skin he'd masked in places with tattoos. But a few years ago he'd watched a television show called *The Undateables*. And became addicted to it. There, on that show, were people like he imagined he was. Differently handsome; differently gifted; differently attractive.

Differently beautiful.

Like Elvira Polkinhorne.

They'd met on a dating site for lovers of arachnoids and had been seeing each other for three months now, and he was madly in love with her. In love for the first time in his life. She had two dozen spiders in glass cages in her adorable little house where he often stayed over. Up until Elvira, the only sex he'd had was with sullen, mostly Eastern European, prostitutes in some of Brighton's cheap brothels. But with Elvira it was – wow! A total awakening! Every time he dated her, he took her presents, flowers mostly, flowers with strong scents she could enjoy – because she could barely see them. She had been losing her eyesight since the age of seven through macular degeneration, and her vision these days was extremely limited.

Now, shortly after 9.30 a.m., as he cruised the van slowly along Goldstone Crescent, looking at Hove Park to his left, one hand on the wheel, the other rolling a cigarette, he watched the morning dog walkers, heads bowed against the rain, some keeping their mutts on leads, others letting them run free. One lady with a baby in a pram with a plastic rain cover and a small terrier of some sort tied to it, running along taking many steps to its owner's few, and a tall, elderly man with a tiny dachshund.

He pulled into a parking space, finished rolling his cigarette by licking the sticky strip on the paper, put it in his mouth and lit it with a match he again struck one-handed. Then he concentrated on the job he was paid to do.

His white van was emblazoned with the name JASON PLUNKETT PUMPS AND DRAINS, in orange and black, applied with magnetic stickers. Jason Plunkett Pumps and Drains did not exist. Nor did any of the other company names he stuck to the side of the van, regularly, before taking it out of his boss's depot. Trade vans were good cover, just like hi-vis jackets and clipboards. No one took any notice of a van parked up, the driver having a fag break.

But Gecko was taking notice of everyone in the park. He watched a woman in a green anorak being dragged across the damp grass by an Irish wolfhound. The dog was running the show.

If Gecko were in a position to dictate who could own a dog and who couldn't, he would tell green anorak she was too stupid to own a dog. But he wasn't in that position.

An elderly man rode past on a sit-up-and-beg bicycle, with a forlorn-looking mongrel attached to a lead, trotting beside him. *Cruel lazy bastard*, Gecko thought. Moments later he saw what looked like a professional dog walker, a tall, lean, bald man with military posture, holding a clutch of six different breeds on leads.

Then he saw a potential. Definitely. A woman in one of those stupid cagoules, bright red, a plastic rain hat and white wellington boots, who was bending down to let her dog off the lead. A black and white poodle. Young. No more than a year old. He quickly checked the photographs on his phone. A match. Definitely a match!

The dog raced off excitedly, heading straight in his direction. He saw Red Cagoule shout at the dog, but it wasn't hearing her, it had reached Baldie's six dogs, and was barking excitedly at them. Baldie tried to shoo the poodle away, as all the dogs kicked off. The woman yelled again, then again. He could hear the name. *Zulu.* Was that seriously the dog's name?

'Zulu!' she shouted. 'Zulu! Come here! Come back! ZULU!'

The leads of all Baldie's dogs were now in a right old tangle, and Gecko smiled at the absurdity, as the man kneeled, trying to disentangle six barking dogs with one hand and shoo off the unwelcome poodle with the other.

Grabbing the opportunity of the distraction, he raised his binoculars and focused on the dog. It was a male. Perfect! Even more perfect if he wasn't neutered. He lowered the binoculars. A definite possibility. His boss would be mightily pleased with him, if he could deliver exactly what he'd requested so quickly. He patted his anorak pocket, which was full of treats, pondering his move.

Then it all fell into his lap.

Before the woman reached the dog walker, the poodle darted playfully away and dashed across the grass.

Straight in his direction!

Oh yes!

Come to Daddy!

9

Immediately after ending his call Roy Grace went back into the briefing room. 'That was the Chief,' he announced. 'I gave her an update on our investigation She's also very worried about the rising wave of criminality in the canine world, both in our county and in others. We both feel there may be a connection. You may also know there are over forty Chief Constables in the UK and for their term of office each selects responsibility for reducing a particular area of crime. Ours, Lesley Manning, has elected the growing challenge of animal criminality and as a dog lover is deeply passionate about it. And that means with Operation Brush that we are properly in the spotlight.'

He paused to let that sink in as he took his seat, then said, 'Blowflies can smell a dead body five miles away. But news reporters can smell one much further away than that, and far faster. Comms have already fielded calls from the local and regional press, and supplied them with my holding press release, and it's only 9.30 a.m., for God's sake! This is clearly going to be a major news story and the Chief will have the other Chief Officers watching with acute interest. You are all in this room with me because I've personally chosen you, because you're the best.' He looked around his team and saw several smiles and nods.

'Right, so during the course of today, Polly, you'll continue with your action in identifying dog theft crimes in Sussex and in all our neighbouring counties of Kent, Hampshire, Surrey.'

She nodded.

'I'd like you also to get me a list of all online sites where dogs are advertised for sale. There's also a very respected dog breeder, who runs kennels near Lewes, called Janet Oliver – we've lodged our dog with her a couple of times when we've been away. It would be worth speaking to her, to see if she's heard anything she's suspicious of.'

'I will do, boss.'

Grace continued. 'All the information we have so far about the offenders is that there were possibly four or more males, in two vehicles, one of which may have been a Ford Ranger pickup and the other an old model Range Rover, with possibly a J and a 2 in its registration plate.' He turned to DC Emma-Jane Boutwood. 'EJ, I'm giving you the action of liaising with the Intelligence Team, checking the ANPR for any possible matches with these two specific vehicles. I did request earlier a list of all vehicles pinging ANPR cameras in the vicinity around the time of the murder, which Jack is working on. As it was in the small hours there shouldn't be too many, which will make our task a bit easier. I suggest starting with a thirty-mile radius covering an hour each side of the time of Mrs Ruddle's 999 call.' ANPR cameras covered all major arteries in the county. But of course, as Grace well knew, smart villains could avoid most of them by taking back roads. Although sooner or later they would have to join a main road.

He turned to DS Alexander. 'Jack, we need a witness trawl. As we have it so far, there are just two, Sharon Ruddle and Norris Denning. We need to eliminate both of them as suspects. I'm pretty confident Mrs Ruddle is not involved, but we can't be completely sure. The farmhand is an unknown quantity. Could he have had a grievance? Or be in collusion with the offenders? We need to eliminate both of them – or not.'

'Absolutely, sir.'

'And, Jack, I need you to arrange a House-to-House Team to cover all the Ruddles' neighbours, see if any of them have seen or heard anything, or had any attempted break-ins themselves. Let me know if they come up with anything and we can get one of your team to follow up and revisit the property to obtain full details.'

He turned to the Financial Investigator. 'Emily, I need you to look into the finances.'

'I'll look for proof of deposits in any bank account that would indicate unusual payments, and the farmer's general finances, sir,' she replied. 'To ensure this wasn't a put-up job that went wrong.'

'Smart thinking, Emily,' he said.

Next, he turned to DS Potting, then DC Wilde. 'Brief Alec Butler, our Witness Coordinator, who is organizing the video recorded cognitive interviews this morning. I'd like you both to interview Sharon Ruddle, as soon as she is up to it, to fill in the association chart of all the people she and her husband have had dealings with in the last three months, as well as all their relatives and friends. Ask her for a list of all the individuals who had put down a deposit on one of the puppies, and check out their backgrounds. Then the same with Norris Denning. I need you also to contact the RSPCA in Sussex and see what other incidents of dog theft might have been reported to them, but not to the police.'

He allocated a number of other tasks to the rest of the team. Next, he turned to the Crime Scene Manager. 'Chris, see if we can get any identifiable tyre tread marks. Also see if the Forensic Gait Analyst, Haydn Kelly, is available. There are a lot of footprints around the crime scene and hopefully the rain hasn't washed everything away. It would be very useful to have him take a good look there. Jack, we should put up a drone and do a survey of all the surrounding area. Did the offenders approach the property via the main driveway, or did they use another entrance?'

'I'm already on the drone, sir,' Jack said. 'I've had a drone operator out there since first light. We're waiting on the footage that was captured this morning.'

'I'll call Professor Kelly right away,' Chris Gee said. 'I will also look for any loose vehicle parts, glass, or paint transfer for later comparison. Does the pathologist want to view the body in situ?'

Grace shook his head. 'I've spoken to Nadiuska De Sancha who's been assigned this – thank God for small mercies.'

Several of the team smiled, knowing that the alternative to Nadiuska was Dr Frazer Theobald. Nadiuska was every bit as efficient and three times as fast. 'She says she doesn't need to see the body at the crime scene, so I've arranged for it to be recovered to the mortuary. The postmortem will commence early this afternoon – DI Branson and I will attend.'

There was a time, before he had met and fallen in love with Cleo who ran the mortuary, when Roy Grace considered attending postmortems to be the worst part of his job. But now, while he did not exactly relish them, he enjoyed being able to work with his wife. Although he sometimes wondered how many couples would find it normal to be discussing intricate details of an eviscerated cadaver over the kitchen table.

'Finally, I have asked a digital media investigator to go to the farmhouse to download the router and try to get a hardware address and any other details about phones trying to connect to the broadband. It is a slim shot but worth trying. Does anyone have anything to add? Any bases we've not covered?' he asked.

Several members of the team shook their heads. No one had anything else.

'OK, good. I'm going to liaise with the Assistant Chief Constable and Comms to set up a press conference tomorrow morning. I want to get the message out to as wide a reach as possible, that anyone looking to buy a blue French bulldog needs to check the dog's owner with the Kennel Club to ensure they're not buying one of the dogs stolen last night, or an illegal import. That they should see a vet's report, especially on the dog's hip and elbow scores, and they need to see the vaccination certificates. We'll meet here again at 6 p.m.'

10

Thursday 25 March

'*ZULU!*' Sara Gurner shrieked the name, running on the wet grass as fast as she could in her gum boots. The large mutt, shooed away from the dog walker's group, was now running excitedly towards a vizsla that was having a dump, its owner pulling a plastic bag from her pocket.

Enjoying the great game of *Bark at Every Dog*, Zulu ran on, in search of the next one, his owner lagging, tiring, some hundred yards behind him.

Zulu was the substitute for everything Sara Gurner did not have in her life – her job, working part-time as a receptionist in a Brighton medical practice, was hanging by a thread due to yet another reorganization, she had yet again failed her driving test, and her current social life was non-existent. She utterly doted on this wilful, gorgeous creature.

Zulu had replaced her adored Dalmatian, Belle, who had been her constant companion for nine years, before sadly passing away from a tumour. Sara Gurner had gone for a boy second time around for a change.

'ZULU!' she commanded, imperiously and uselessly.

A grey terrier, off its lead, was racing towards Zulu and barking – ferociously or playfully, it was hard to tell. Zulu took one look, then hared away, to Sara's horror, making straight for the road, as if in some kind of blind panic.

'*ZULU!*' she yelled and ran as fast as her boots and the soggy grass would let her. But the dog was now a good two to three hundred yards ahead, racing through the trees and towards the pavement.

'*NO!*' she screamed in horror.

Oh God.

A steady stream of cars drove along the road in both directions. Large, detached houses were on the far side. A bus trundled past.

There was a van parked at the kerb, and suddenly a small man, in an anorak and woollen hat, jumped out and grabbed the dog by the collar.

Relief surged through her. 'THANK YOU!' she yelled. 'Thank you so much!'

But then, as she got nearer, the man lifted Zulu up, hurled him in through the driver's door and jumped in, slamming the door shut behind him.

'Hey! It's my dog, it's my dog!'

Zulu was barking.

Closing the gap, reaching the pavement, Sara Gurner heard the engine start. In desperation she ran to the front of the van, waving her arms frantically. 'It's OK, it's my dog. Stop, stop!'

She saw the man's face through the windscreen. His big, round bulging eyes.

'It's my dog!' she screamed at him. 'It's my dog! I'm the owner!'

She could have sworn he was grinning at her as he reversed then drove off past her at reckless speed, almost clipping her arm with a wing mirror.

She was too shaken to think of writing down the number plate. She just stood in the middle of the road, shouting at the disappearing van, and crying.

A bell tinged, and a Lycra-clad cyclist swerved past her shouting, 'Get off the road, you stupid woman!'

11

Even at the height of summer, the chilled air and pervading grey light made it feel like winter here in the mortuary – or the *Hotel du Mort* as Norman Potting called it.

And at 2 p.m. on a cold, drizzly March day, it was about as grim as it got. And yet, the team of three who worked here, Cleo, Darren and their new assistant, Kevin Jones, seemed impervious to it, and were mostly unremittingly cheerful.

To them it was just another day in the office. And the actual office Roy Grace was sitting in, which used to be a sickly pink colour, had recently been refurbished, along with the rest of the building. Now, with its grey walls hung with framed certificates and modern art, its speckled black worktop, charcoal carpet, comfortable chairs and up-to-date computer technology, it could have been the office of almost any profession.

Apart from the smell.

That persistently noxious odour that came through the open door into the hallway. The reek of disinfectant and decaying human bodies which had been part of the fabric of this building for as far back as he could remember.

The West Sussex coroner had asked that the postmortem be carried out at Brighton and Hove Mortuary for logistical reasons. Darren, Cleo's deputy, a youthful-looking man in his late twenties, lightly bearded and with a warm, friendly face, dressed in a collarless blue shirt, jeans and work boots, chatty and gregarious, could have been front of house in a cool restaurant. Kevin, tall and more fully bearded, also in jeans and work boots, was quieter but no less friendly. At this moment, Cleo was in one of the mortuary's two main postmortem rooms with the Home Office pathologist Dr Nadiuska De Sancha, Glenn Branson, CSI James Gartrell, who was photographing and videoing every step of the process, and the Coroner's Officer, Michelle Websdale.

Before joining Glenn and Cleo, Grace was having a catch-up chat over a mug of tea with Darren and Kevin, who had attended the crime scene earlier that morning to recover Tim Ruddle's body. In his early days as a homicide detective, the Home Office pathologist would always attend the body in situ at the scene. But in more recent times, now paid per job and not per hour, unless there were compelling reasons to visit the crime scene, most, like Nadiuska today, opted to go straight to the mortuary.

The key role of the mortuary team was to safely recover the body, including any potential forensic evidence which could then be assessed at the mortuary. Their skills were another chance to glean any nuggets of information that those, including himself, who had attended the crime scene earlier, might have missed.

But neither of them had noticed anything that did not fit the report from the two witnesses of what had happened. Other than bruising around the victim's misshapen abdomen, there were no other signs of injury to his body, and very little blood on the body or at the scene. Darren reported overhearing one of the attending police officers saying the First Responder took half an hour to arrive, and if he had come quicker, maybe they could have done something. The victim's wife, apparently, said her husband was still breathing until minutes before the paramedic arrived.

Finishing their tea, they gowned up in the changing room, and Grace, waddling in a pair of white wellingtons a size too big, followed them through into the fridge-lined corridor, where the recent arrivals briefly resided – and some, those as yet unidentified, stayed much longer. Building up their loyalty points, he thought grimly. For an upgrade on their next visit. Except this was one hotel where residents never got rewards.

Most of the fridges, all numbered, were racked for four bodies. But in the recent refurbishment, accommodation had been provided for the growing numbers of morbidly overweight members of the community, and those extra-wide fridges were just two deep. As he passed them, Grace couldn't help shaking his head in sad bewilderment at the story Darren had just told him, of the body of a man who'd been brought in, weighing forty-two stone, whose coffin was so heavy it had to be carried to his grave by a JCB bulldozer.

As they entered the postmortem room with its brown and cream speckled terrazzo tile floor, stark overhead fluorescents and the male body on the steel table, he looked around at all the green-gowned people, and for an instant it reminded him of his terror, being in the operating theatre, sixteen months ago, watching the birth of their daughter Molly by C-section. And desperately worried for Cleo. This so soon after his elder son Bruno had died tragically in a road traffic accident.

Then he tried to put that out of his mind to focus on why he was here. Molly was a healthy, happy baby, who had brought much joy back into their lives. The dead, broken corpse on the steel table had been, less than twelve hours ago, the father of two children. Now they would never see their daddy again. A husband who would never hold his wife again. Would never kiss her again. Would never tell her how much he loved her again.

All of them were in this room firstly to establish the cause of death, and to see what clues, if any, the victim's body would reveal to help them find the killers who had murdered him.

And they would. Four offenders. Four would never get away with it. One killer acting solo would stand a better chance. But not *four*. One of them would talk, one day, to someone. One of them would brag, or, after remorse brought on by a few pints, tell someone. And the moment they told one person, they would have told the whole world. It was the unwritten law of getting away with crime, Grace knew from long experience:

Don't have an accomplice. Never tell a soul.

12

'Hey, turtle!'

Bluebell, in her turquoise bathing costume and goggles, broke the surface smiling and swam energetically towards her father. There were other kids in the pool and other parents, but Chris Fairfax was oblivious to them. Standing waist-deep in the warm water of Brighton's King Alfred swimming pool, he looked adoringly at his seven-year-old daughter, her blonde ringlets darkened by the water, her face the absolute picture of happiness that was, at this moment, melting his heart, and making him forget a woeful morning, filled with an entire week's worth of client problems. One after another. Starting with poor, sad and bitter Noel Dudley.

But right now, all that was forgotten as Bluebell swam into his arms and he raised her in the air. 'That was brilliant, turtle!' He kissed the tip of her tiny nose.

'I'm not a turtle,' she said indignantly. 'I'm a girl!'

'Of course you are! But in the water you're a *turtle*.'

She giggled. He loved looking at her tiny, perfect teeth, her big happy smile, holding her body so full of wriggling energy. This creature so very precious to him and Katy. This human life they'd tried for so many years to bring into the world – and ironically, just months after they'd given up with IVF and had begun seriously to consider adoption, Katy had become pregnant.

'Can I do it again, Daddy?' She pointed up at the blue water chute she'd just hurtled down.

He glanced at his sports watch. 'We really need to get out.'

'Just one more, please!' she shrieked, then giggled again.

'Just once more, then we'll have go get changed – unless,' he teased, 'you'd like to forget about seeing the puppy and stay here all afternoon?'

'Nooooooo!' She looked at him hard, as if examining his face to see if he was serious. 'I have a name for her!'

'You do? What is it?'

'Not telling, it's a secret.'

She wriggled out of his arms and splashed her way over to the side of the pool. Chris watched her climb out and run, in her frilly costume, along to the steps up to the chute. God, he loved her so much. He watched the top of the chute for her to appear. The sheer joy of her being in his life – in his and Katy's life. Then he felt a flash of darkness. How many other parents before him had stared with this kind of love at their child, only to watch them grow up to become like the broken people who came into his office with so much anger?

But you won't ever turn out like that, my darling. You will always be happy. You will have the happiest childhood in the world. Your mummy and I will make sure of that.

He saw her now, up there. She waved at him, and he waved back. Then he saw her little body shooting down the tube, and moments later break surface, beaming again.

His heart did a back-flip.

Moments later, she was splashing towards him. 'Can you pick me up again, Daddy?'

'Once more, darling, then we have to go.'

She took a deep breath, and he raised her up out of the water.

'That was so high, Daddy!'

'I know! Now it's puppy time.'

'Yayyyyyyy!'

13

The man on the steel table in the postmortem room looked, from a distance, as if he had just popped in here for a cheeky snooze. He lay on his back in jeans, sweatshirt and green wellington boots, his brown hair dishevelled, a large bald patch around his crown. His Barbour had been the single item of clothing removed because he had been pronounced dead almost immediately after the paramedics had arrived and therefore any life-saving procedures had been unnecessary. Only the colour of his skin, a cold, marble white, indicated he wasn't ever going to be waking up.

Tim Ruddle was forty-one, his wife, Sharon, had told Roy Grace tearfully. A decent, hardworking man, who should have been out milking their cows earlier this morning and then on his tractor harvesting the winter crop of kale they'd been experimenting with. Grace looked for some moments at his big hands and grimy fingernails, several badly bitten.

It reminded him uncomfortably of visiting his own father, Jack, a few days after he had died. He'd lain in his pyjamas, in the little enclosed room at the funeral parlour, emaciated from the cancer that had killed him. But what he remembered most about that visit was his dad's fingernails, all gnawed to the quick. His dad bit his nails and the skin around them constantly. His mum used to chide him, even playfully slapping his hand sometimes, but he had never stopped. Roy Grace always thought of that whenever he'd been about to chew his own nails and it had always prevented him. It was a ridiculous thought, he knew, but he didn't want his own children coming to pay their last respects when his turn came, and taking away the memory that their dad was lying there with bitten nails.

The CSI officer finished her painstaking tapings of the farmer's clothes and boots, and the exposed parts of his flesh, in the hope that under lab analysis there might be something from which they could obtain DNA that would lead them to his killers – hairs, skin cells, clothing fibres – although the drizzle that had fallen, before the first officer attending had a chance to cover him with a tarpaulin, would have reduced the chances of that.

Under De Sancha's instructions, Darren and Kevin lifted the body, to enable Cleo to remove the clothing. Then, when Ruddle was laid back down, naked, she pulled off his gum boots and they were bagged and sealed along with all the other items of clothing. Other than extensive black and brown bruising around his lower abdomen and shins, the dead man did not appear to have a mark on the rest of his muscular body.

As James Gartrell moved efficiently around, recording Ruddle from all angles, the pathologist, holding her dictating machine, turned to Grace and Branson. 'What I'm seeing is consistent with the information I have been given about how this man may have died,' she said in her very endearing accent. She'd been in the country for many years, after leaving her native Spain to marry her husband, a plastic surgeon, but had never fully lost that accent. 'You can see the contusions and bruising around the pelvis.'

Grace could see what she meant. It did look misshapen, sagging unnaturally to one side. Normally he would have expected to see the hip bones clearly delineated and protruding. But he could see no sign of either, just a sloppy mass of bruised flesh like a fat man's belly. Except Ruddle was lean, not an ounce of fat on his body.

'We will know for sure when I open him up,' she said. 'But I understand he was crushed between two vehicles and was conscious for a short while afterwards?'

'Correct,' Grace confirmed.

She pointed a gloved finger. 'At the back of the pelvis are veins and arteries that run around, supplying all the blood to the legs, bottom and bladder. The pelvis, as you will have seen before, is almost circular, with a hole in the centre – like a Polo mint!' There was a smile in her eyes above her mask.

Grace winced at the analogy. He used to like Polos but hadn't eaten one in years. As a younger detective, on the advice of his dad, he used to suck on a mint when attending postmortems, as well as rubbing Vicks VapoRub under his nose, to mitigate the odours. But he was long used to them now.

'It is a strong bone,' she continued. 'But if it is broken or crushed from the front, the person will start to exsanguinate – bleed out – all the veins becoming a complete mush, as I expect we will see shortly. It is possible, if the victim is taken to hospital in time, to repair ruptured arteries, but not veins, they can't be repaired, and they just ooze.'

'Are you saying he could have been alive for some time after he was crushed by these vehicles?' Branson asked. 'But there was nothing anyone could have done to save him? Not even if the ambulance had arrived sooner, or if he had been airlifted to hospital?'

'You are right, Glenn, he would have been conscious but in a lot of pain and steadily getting weaker – that's what I'm specu-lating. If I'm correct, that injury would not have been survivable. But let's not get ahead of ourselves. We need to see if he has any other underlying health conditions that might have contributed to his death.'

Roy Grace had handled a recent murder case where the victim turned out to have a weak heart, and he knew that when the defendants came to court, the defence counsel would have a field day if the victim had had any pre-existing health issues. He silently hoped that the farmer lying in front of him now had been in rude health, because he wanted to nail each of the individuals who had done this to the poor guy.

Having fully examined the abdomen area where the main injuries to the body were, the pathologist then began the invasive part of the postmortem, starting with the removal of the skull cap. Grace and Branson stepped back from the mortuary table, to let her get on with the job.

An hour later, Tim Ruddle was looking very different to when they had first seen him, and on the whiteboard on the wall behind him were written in black marker pen the weights of his brain, heart, lungs, liver and kidneys.

'So far,' De Sancha said, 'I've not found any anomalies to indicate the deceased had any underlying health issues. Very little calcification in his arteries and no sign of any brain damage or heart disease, or any abnormalities with any of his other internal organs. I will be taking samples of his bloods and fluids and have analysis done on these, but from what I can see so far, he appears to have been a man in – how do you call it – rude health?'

'Well, that's good news, if you can call it that,' Grace replied. 'We can confirm that the reason for his death is as a result of his injuries and not by way of natural causes.'

14

The dog didn't like him. And the feeling was entirely mutual. Gecko held it by the collar with his left hand, on the passenger seat beside him, steering the van with his right, and the poodle was constantly twisting and turning and trying to pull away from him. As well as barking at everything they drove past – cars, pedestrians, other dogs, and a horse peering over the gate of a field.

Its curly black and white fur made it look like it was wearing an ill-fitting hand-me-down coat from an older relative. The name tag on the collar said *Zulu*, along with a phone number. Stupid name for a dog owned by a stupid woman. It was now barking at a retriever in the back of a stationary Volvo estate in front of them.

'ZULU!' he shouted. 'Shut it!' He tried bribing it with yet another from the diminishing supply of treats in his pocket. The dog gobbled it down and immediately began barking again at a passing cyclist.

If all had been well, he would have delivered the creature over half an hour ago, but all was not well. He was stuck in this shitfest of a traffic jam. Stuck with a dog who seemed to think it had been put on this planet for the sole purpose of barking. He tapped on his phone for a traffic report and was told to expect delays of up to thirty minutes due to emergency roadworks. He gave the dog another treat, which silenced it for all of two seconds, before the biscuit went down its gullet seemingly without touching the sides.

Why am I stealing yappy dogs for a living? he wondered. Although he knew the answer. Mr Jim. Mr *Gentleman* Jim, they all called him, paid him good money.

Zulu began barking again at the retriever.

'Shut up!' Gecko yelled.

He felt panicky. All the time he was stuck here, with the false ID on the van and the dog with him, he was a sitting duck. If anyone had reported him, he could get nicked. And that would mean a night or longer in custody. And that could not happen. It was Elvira's birthday tonight and he'd arranged a big surprise for her, taking her for funfair rides on Brighton's Palace Pier and then a fish and chip supper – her favourite – at Palm Court.

And with the money Mr Jim would pay him on receipt of this dog, he'd be able to go out and buy a present for her. She'd already dropped a hint that she'd like a talking watch, and he'd found a shop in Brighton that sold them. The money Mr Jim would pay him was going to more than cover the cost of it, and that of their evening on the pier tonight.

Suddenly the traffic was moving again.

He drove through deep water across the road, the source of the problem, a burst water main. Then headed on towards Hailsham and Appletree Farm.

Not that he'd ever seen an apple tree there. Only dogs, horses and pigs. The people who worked in this place were here to look after the dogs. And the pigs were here to eat anyone who upset Mr Jim, or his wife, Rula, so the rumour was. In the three months he'd worked for them, he made sure to please Mr Jim most of all. Mrs Jim was only slightly less menacing than Mr Jim, and she terrified him, too. The only seemingly nice person was Mrs Jim's daughter, Darcy, a friendly girl in her late twenties who was into ponies. He liked her very much. He once saw Mr Jim about to stamp on a spider and she'd screamed at him and rescued it. She always smiled at him when he saw her.

Twenty minutes later he turned off the main road onto the rutted, potholed track, with fields of crops on either side, and then, reaching the five-bar gate to the farm itself, halted, jumped out, opened the gate, drove through and closed it behind him, knowing from previous experience that Mr Jim, who had it all covered with CCTV, would bollock him if he left it open.

After lurching across the rough cart track for another half-mile, now with barren fields on either side, and the green hills of the South Downs in the distance, he reached the tall, spiked steel security gate, put down his window and punched in the code on the panel, aware of the camera looking down at him.

The gate swung open. He drove through, then stopped, watching in his rear-view mirror, as Mr Jim insisted, until it closed behind him. Then he drove on, the dog sitting sullen now, with nothing to bark at. Rounding a curve, he saw the familiar ventilated concrete kennels ahead. And now, even with the windows up, he could hear the cacophony of barking.

Zulu joined the chorus, barking crazily again. The buildings they passed, Gecko knew, contained multiple litters of puppies.

He halted, gave Zulu the last treat in his pocket to shut it up again, parked the van and walked across to a locked gate which secured the breeding pens and pressed the single button on the entryphone panel.

After a moment a male voice replied, deep, guttural and sharp as a gunshot. 'Yes?'

Mr Jim.

'It's Gecko,' he said nervously. '*Make yourself useful, be helpful, always say yes,*' he murmured to himself.

The gate began to open.

15

Back in his office, having left Glenn Branson at the mortuary to finalize the postmortem paperwork, Roy Grace scanned through his email mountain for anything important. He responded to one about a police rugby fixture against a team of inmates at Lewes Prison – a charity initiative he was involved with, but which would need careful handling, both the game itself and the potential media fallout.

He made a note to ensure Arron Hendy, the editor of the influential local paper, the *Argus*, was properly briefed about the fixture by the Comms team, remembering the time when police officers were able to simply pick up the phone to friendly journalists, or have a drink with them in a pub.

He had a meeting in twenty minutes to brief the ACC on Operation Brush, prior to the press conference he would attend with her tomorrow. But before making a list of the key points, he had a quick look through the serials – the ongoing log of all reported incidents in the county, and any updates. One caught his eye. It was a report of a dog theft from Hove Park. Snatched by a man who had driven off in a van.

Here was another example of the growing crime wave in dog theft. There had been several briefing notes on the topic issued by the Rural Crimes Unit, pointing out what they had discussed in the morning's briefing, that some local Sussex crime gangs were making more money out of these avenues than from drugs, and facing only minuscule sentences if caught.

One report he'd read only a few days ago, from Sergeant Tom Cartwright, based at Midhurst, suggested that the national lock-downs for the Covid-19 virus had prompted a wave of panic buying of dogs for companions – pushing the prices up dramatically and playing into the hands of the criminals.

He picked up the phone and asked the controller to see if he could locate the officer. Moments later Grace was connected to the Sergeant, who was out on an operation. Cartwright proved to be a mine of information.

Most valuable of all was the list of names of Sussex and Surrey crime gangs known to be involved in the illegal trafficking of dogs. The Sergeant finished his litany by saying, 'I'm currently in Hastings, sir. We've had a tip-off about some illegal puppy breeding on an estate. We don't have specific information where yet. Would you like me to keep you updated, sir?'

'Very definitely, Tom,' Grace replied. 'Any intel on any area of puppy farming or dog theft, please call me right away.'

Tom Cartwright assured him he would.

16

After pulling the gate closed behind him, Gecko drew the van up outside the black front door, behind Mr Jim's massive American pickup truck.

After a few moments, the door opened and Mr Jim came out, walking in his usual swaggering stride. He was dressed the way Gecko had always seen him, shirtless despite the season, in baggy jogging bottoms and gum boots. A big man, with a shaven head, both arms heavily tattooed, and sporting several gold earrings, his bare chest was flabby, nothing to be proud of, Gecko thought.

He did not have any idea of Mr Jim's age, but had long guessed him to be around sixty. He lowered the window as he approached the passenger side of the van, but to his surprise, Mr Jim walked straight past and entered a long corrugated-iron shed to his left. A moment later, Mrs Jim strode imperiously out of the front door and straight towards him, her daughter, Darcy, not far behind, keeping a low profile.

Dressed in a hacking jacket over a roll-neck pullover, jeans and riding boots, Rula Jim was a similar age to her husband but a good foot shorter, with a pinched weather-beaten face carrying a permanently angry expression. Her short hair, the colour of motor oil, looked like she styled it by ironing it, a forelock hanging low to one side over her forehead, just above her left eye.

She approached the van and peered in, looking first at the

barking dog then at Gecko. Then more closely again at the dog. Her eyes were the colour of dangerous ice on a pond.

The dog, sensing something, maybe hope, maybe malevolence, suddenly stopped barking and instead gave a little whine.

'What is this thing, Marion?' she asked in her deep voice.

Gecko cringed. He hated his name. His mother, obsessed with John Wayne, whose birth name was Marion Robert Morrison, had christened him Marion in one of her many moments of being off her head on drugs. It had been a constant source of embarrassment and teasing at school. But Mr and Mrs Jim insisted on calling him by his real name instead of Gecko, the one he had adopted to hide his shame.

'It's what you ordered me to get, Mrs Jim,' Gecko said, trembling and perspiring. But even as he spoke, he could tell his paymaster was less than impressed.

'We requested you to bring a male poodle. This is just a mutt, a mongrel. Are you a complete idiot?'

The dog barked at Mrs Jim. It had decided it didn't like her any more than Gecko did.

'I – I thought – I checked against the photographs you gave me, Mrs Jim.' His hands felt clammy.

'Are you a total moron?' she asked, ignoring the barking. 'Get out of the van.'

Make yourself useful, be helpful, always say yes, Gecko murmured silently, terrified. Terrified he might be taken to the pigs.

'Get out!' Mrs Jim raised her voice. 'Are you deaf as well?'

Gecko put the window up and got out of the van, leaving the dog inside it, barking.

'Wait there,' she instructed before shouting, 'Terry, I need you here, please. Terry!'

Barely able to speak through his fear, he blurted, 'Really, Mrs Jim, I was sure – I checked the photographs so carefully. I thought he was a poodle, just like you wanted. I—'

'Terry!' she yelled again just as he reappeared from the shed. 'Have a word with this idiot will yer, luv?'

'Mum,' Darcy said, reluctantly getting involved. 'Leave it, for God's sake just leave it. I hate that you do this.'

'What seems to be the problem?' Terry Jim said angrily as he reached them, elbowing Darcy out of his way. 'What's this prick done now?'

Mrs Jim strode on powerfully ahead, seemingly as oblivious to the rain as she was to the conversation, entered the breeding compound and stopped at the next shed along. Gecko and Mr Jim followed. She slid open the door and ushered them inside, into the stench of urine and faeces and the sound of piercing yapping.

Gecko stared through the bars of the rows of tiny cages as he followed Mrs Jim past each of them, all containing various-sized puppies on a concrete floor thinly covered in soiled straw. At the far end in a cage on its own, as if in solitary confinement, sat a forlorn-looking adult male, surrounded by excrement, some fresh, some desiccated. It didn't look like its cage had been cleaned in days.

'Marion, take a very good look at this schnauzer. He won Best of Breed at Crufts two years ago. We're talking quality. All you had to do was to find either a mate for him or for the poodle over there and you failed, you stupid man. You've brought us a doodle, a bloody doodle!' She turned and her upper lip slid up to reveal a row of yellow teeth. She was smiling, Gecko realized, but it was a smile of anger like a crevice that had opened in her face. He'd once kept a crevice spider as a pet, but he'd never put it in his mouth because he knew it was poisonous, and he hadn't wanted it biting him. She looked over to Terry, encouraging him to take over.

'Listen, prick. Do you want to keep finding dogs for us, or would you rather help feed our pigs?'

Gecko shook nervously. 'I – I want to keep working for you, Mr Jim, sir.'

Terry Jim lifted Gecko up against the wall by his throat, almost choking the pale, gangly man, and held him there.

'Can't you leave him alone?' Darcy muttered at Terry, disgusted. Then to her mother, who completely ignored her, 'Mum, stop him, get him to stop!'

'Listen, young lady,' Terry Jim snapped, his pointed finger inches from his stepdaughter's face. 'You better remember whose side you are on here, and where you sleep at night. Quit your namby-pamby woke bully nonsense. I've heard enough of it. I suggest you fuck off back to shovelling the shit out of the kennels. And leave us adults to sort this out. Rula, tell her, for fuck's sake. Get her out of here. NOW.'

'Darcy, luv, go on, you heard him. There's nothing here for you to do.'

Terry drew closer to Gecko and tightened his grip.

'Get. Rid. Of. This. Rubbish. And bring me something I want. A poodle. Male. Entire. Or a schnauzer. Female. You know, one that's going to make me some proper money. It's not that hard, is it? Better still, bring me both. Or do you want to get acquainted with sty number 9, you complete fucking waste of space?'

'I – I understand, how do you suggest I get rid of that one, Mr Jim?' Catching his breath as Terry released his neck.

He gave him a withering glare, but seemed, at least, a little calmer. 'Whatever, I don't care, it's your problem.'

'OK, I'll take it back to Brighton and throw it out.' He hesitated. 'It's my girlfriend's birthday. I have to buy her a present. Would you – could you – sort of pay me – you know – sort of in advance?'

'For fuck's sake, Marion, you think I give a shit about that? How very sweet she is, having a birthday. If you need money to buy her a present, then bring us what we want.' He looked at his watch. 'You have plenty of time. Shops don't shut until at least 5 p.m. Now fuck off.'

Then as if to reinforce it and stamp her authority, Rula added, 'You heard, Marion, off you fuck.' She smiled again and this time there was real warmth. Like steam from the crater of a volcano.

17

Thursday 25 March

'Are we nearly there yet?' Bluebell, strapped in the rear of the Audi, asked. She wore a pink hooded anorak, jeans cut off just below the knees that she had recently insisted on wearing, along with her beloved trainers with black uppers and thick white soles.

'Are we really sure about this, Chris?' Katy asked.

Checking the satnav, then glancing in the rear-view mirror, Chris Fairfax called out to his daughter, 'Ten minutes, darling!'

He glanced at the car clock. It was 4.15 p.m. They were heading on the A24 dual carriageway, north of Horsham, on schedule for their rendezvous.

'Ten minutes, ten minutes!'

'I am having big doubts,' Katy said. 'We don't know anything about this puppy.'

Trying to laugh off her concerns, he said, 'Look, we've got this far, darling, we can't go back now. I'm sure it's all good.'

'Only,' she said dubiously, 'all that stuff I've been reading online and in the papers, about unscrupulous gangs trading in puppies – that's exactly what we're doing now.'

'Doing what – what do you mean?' he asked.

'That whole piece I read out to you last weekend, in the *Sunday Times*, you weren't really listening, were you? You said you'd read it later, but you didn't, right?'

'I'm sorry, no, but I will read it.'

'It talks about meeting breeders in lay-bys and other places.

I was looking at one puppy forum and it said you should always visit the home and meet the parents of the puppy – and assess the conditions there.'

'Yup, well, we know that, and we discussed that's a little easier said than done right now. We've been looking for a doodle puppy for over a month now – all of them were sold before we even contacted the breeders. And at insane prices – we'd have saved a fortune if we'd bought one a year ago, before the pandemic got going.'

'Well, we didn't, and that's an awful way to look at it,' Katy said.

'This puppy Bluebell likes has been bred in South Wales – that's a six-hour drive each way. We've Zoomed the breeders and the couple seem like really nice, genuine people. They showed us the parents and the whole litter and they look like they're well cared for. And Bluebell likes her.'

'I LOVE her!' Bluebell said excitedly.

Chris and Katy looked at each other and smiled. He shrugged. 'So, what's the worst that could happen? We buy a dog that's not the mix of doodle we thought – does that matter? We're not interested in showing her – we just want a family pet that we love.'

'I've already named her!' Bluebell shouted.

'You told me in the pool you have! But we all need to agree on it. What is your suggestion?'

'Moose!'

'Um, no, my love,' Katy said.

'Yes, Mummy. Please. Because she's got big eyes and ears! Please, please, please!'

'I quite like Moose actually,' Chris said.

'You do?' Katy quizzed.

He shrugged. 'It's different. And if Bluebell likes it – hey, why not?'

'MOOSE!!!' shouted Bluebell. 'MOOSE! MOOSE! MOOSE!'

'OK, OK, Moose it is. If . . .' his wife cautioned.

'If what, Mummy?'

'If we are happy with her, OK? If Mummy and Daddy feel there's something not right and we're not happy with her, then we'll find another puppy, all right?'

'We *will* be happy with her. I will love her!'

Chris, concentrating on the directions, barely heard her. The turn-off was coming up in under a mile. He tuned his wife and daughter out, pulling over into the left lane, and slowing as the satnav counted down. Even so he nearly missed the turning, braking sharply and swinging left.

'Do you have to drive so fast?' Katy admonished.

He bit his tongue. With nine points on her licence for speeding, she was a fine one to talk. 'Sorry.'

They were heading down a twisty lane. They passed a sign to a farm shop, then a couple of cottages and immediately ahead he saw a pub sign to the right. *The Dragon.*

He braked and turned into the forecourt, looking for a grey van. He drove slowly past rows of parked cars, and then through into the overflow parking area at the rear, and saw what he thought might be it, a silver Volkswagen van parked up against a fence onto farmland. The driver was sitting behind the wheel smoking a cigarette, which he tossed out of his window as Chris pulled up alongside.

The three of them climbed out of the Audi and a man in his fifties, with a shock of unnatural-looking silver curly hair, dressed in dungarees and a Shetland sweater, came around to greet them, all smiles. He held out a meaty hand with grimy nails and in a strong Welsh accent said, 'Mr and Mrs Fairfax, it is very nice to meet you in the flesh, as it were! I am John Peat.' Then he kneeled and charmed Bluebell by shaking her hand and saying, 'Now you must be the boss of the family. I am right to think that?'

'I am!' she said. 'I am the boss.'

'Of course you are! And the boss will have the prettiest puppy I've ever seen. Good as gold these puppies are, and they slept all the way. I don't think you'll ever find a better one. All the parents have really lovely temperaments.'

'I'm going to call mine Moose,' Bluebell told him.

'That's a great name,' Peat said. 'Let's have a look at them, shall we?'

He slid open the side door of the van. Bluebell climbed excitedly inside, followed by her parents. Chris wrinkled his nose at the smell of damp fur mixed with a faint whiff of urine.

There were six cages, three of them empty. One contained a blonde ball of fluff. The puppy immediately jumped up, putting its paws against the bars and whining.

'This is the golden doodle,' Peat said.

'Awwww!' Bluebell exclaimed.

In the next cage was a brown dachshund, looking up gloomily. 'She's taken, I'm delivering her later today,' he said.

In the third cage along was a tiny Staffordshire bull terrier puppy, jumping up and down, throwing itself against the wide cage bars and yapping excitedly.

Bluebell kneeled in front of it. 'Hello!' she said. 'You are lovely, aren't you!'

'Would you like to hold her?' Peat asked. 'She's still available too.'

Bluebell nodded vigorously.

He opened the cage, grabbed the wriggling puppy, and placed it in Bluebell's arms.

She looked down at it and, an instant later, the puppy bit her on the nose.

'Owwwww!' Bluebell yelped.

The breeder stepped forward, grabbed the puppy from her and put it back in its cage.

'Owwwwww!' Bluebell yelped again. A tiny ribbon of blood trickled down from the bridge of her nose. Katy immediately dabbed it with her handkerchief, put some spittle on it and dabbed again.

'Naughty dog!' Bluebell admonished, pulling away from her mother's attempt to dab her nose again and turning back to the cage with the blonde ball of fur. 'Can I hold her?' she asked Peat.

'Of course, poppet!'

As Katy dabbed her daughter's nose again, Peat lifted the golden doodle puppy from its cage and handed it to Bluebell.

'Hello,' she said, hugging and stroking the soft fur.

The puppy opened a droopy eye and, as Bluebell held it to her face, a tiny pink tongue shot out and licked her lips. She giggled in delight.

Chris Fairfax looked at his wife. She smiled and raised her eyebrows and he knew exactly what that meant. Then he patted the breast pocket of his sleeveless puffer jacket. Checking he could feel the two thousand five hundred pounds of banknotes he had stashed in there.

'Moose!' Bluebell said.

Neither of them had ever seen their daughter look so happy.

'I've brought along some food for her,' Peat said. 'Enough for the next three days or so. And I have her vaccination certificate. She's a beautiful puppy, so friendly. I'm sorry to be saying goodbye to her, honestly I am. I think I told you over the phone that my wife has been very torn about letting her go – and I have too. But you seem good people, so we are comfortable with that. And now I've met you I'll be able to tell her that she has gone to a really good home, a truly loving home.'

Chris looked at his wife and saw her shrug. Her *OK* shrug.

He pulled the cash from his pocket.

18

After ending his call with Tom Cartwright, Roy Grace got himself another coffee, then returned to his office. When he started any homicide investigation, one of his first considerations would be to pose himself three questions – which he had done earlier today as he stood in the farmyard looking at Tim Ruddle's body.

Why him?
Why here?
Why now?

He took a sip of the coffee, knowing he was overdosing on caffeine, but after his almost total lack of sleep, he reckoned he was going to need plenty of the stuff to get him through the rest of the day.

He wrote in his investigator's notebook, *Why him?* And thought hard about that question. Could Ruddle simply have been the wrong place, wrong time victim of a random burglary, or was there more to it? It was more likely the farm had been targeted. He also needed to ensure that the couple had not become involved in any criminal activity. From his conversation with the man's wife, Sharon, he felt it unlikely. She came across as a decent person and he got the impression that she and her husband were simply trying to make a living, diversifying their farm and adding other income streams to help make ends meet.

But as he well knew, if people became desperate, they would sometimes take dangerous risks. Emily Denyer was looking into the Ruddles' finances and, if there was anything that raised a warning flag, he was pretty confident she would find it. He jotted down a summary of his thoughts then turned to the next question.

Why here? On the surface, the answer was obvious, because that's where the dogs were. Again, he needed to see what Emily Denyer came up with.

Why now? Most likely because the thieves knew they had to take the puppies before they had all been collected by their new owners, which was due to happen the following week. But how did they know that? Guesswork that most puppies get picked up at eight weeks old, or had they been watching the place? Or did they have insider information – and if so from whom? One of the customers? Where had they been advertised? The seventy-one-year-old farmhand, Norris Denning, was the only employee. But, as had been established at the briefing, he had no previous criminal record. That did not rule Denning out, but in Grace's view it made him unlikely to be a suspect.

Until today, crimes involving dogs, whether theft or unlicensed puppy farming or importation, would not have been considered serious enough for his Major Crime Team to become involved, but Ruddle's murder was a game changer. It had become his top priority, and not just because the Chief Constable was now taking a personal interest. Roy Grace hated any form of cruelty to animals, and he especially loved dogs, both for the amazing creatures so many of them were, and for all they meant to the people who owned and loved them.

In the space of just a few hours, three separate incidents involving dogs had been reported in Sussex. In addition to Ruddle, there was the tip-off Tom Cartwright had of a van containing puppies found in Hastings, as well as the serial he had read earlier of the woman in Hove Park whose dog had been stolen.

The latter was seemingly the least significant. But, as he had often discovered during his past investigations into murders carried out by crime gangs, that old phrase, *a chain is only as strong as its weakest link*, so often proved true. With drugs, the street runners were the low-hanging fruit, the easiest people to arrest – mostly young, dispensable people, they carried the risk, while the overlords sat safely out of sight and in the belief they were out of reach. Except, occasionally, a runner would squeal in exchange for a reduced sentence, and arrests could start to be made much higher up the chain, in a kind of domino effect, as more scumbags – none of them principled – were prepared to rat on their masters when they realized the length of sentences they were facing.

Maybe it was the same with dog-snatchers, he pondered. Some lowlife given a list of dogs to look out for by an active gang? If he could find them, maybe it would take him higher up the chain. To Tim Ruddle's killers?

He called Stanstead, who answered immediately.

'Luke, I read on the serials an incident of a woman who reported her dog stolen in Hove Park earlier today – around 10 a.m. We need to action a visit to her.'

'Yes, boss.'

As he ended the call, an alert on his private phone indicated an incoming text. He looked at it and saw it was from Cleo's sister, Charlie. A photograph of a bunch of cute chocolate brown and white puppies with huge floppy ears. Beneath was her message.

> **Roy, look at these spaniels! You told us you were looking at getting another dog. I know you were thinking a rescue dog but these are the cutest! I found them on the internet, and they look like they're really well cared for by a nice breeder – I just spoke to her, a lovely lady. They're near Bournemouth. Would be ideal for you and Cleo. She's asking £2.5k, a good price at the moment –**

some charge up to £4k. Could you get any time off to see them? She says they will go quickly! I'll be free later. XX

Grace winced at the price, but he knew just how much the cost of dogs had shot up recently – and was still rising. He had been wanting a spaniel type for some time, because of their temperament – they were supposed to be particularly good with children. He and Cleo had both wanted a rescue dog ideally. But, given the current investigation, he thought it might be worth going to see how it was all set up to help him understand that world better. Immerse himself in the detail and gain some insights. There was no way he could take time out today. Nor tomorrow; he needed to focus one hundred per cent on Operation Brush. He texted back:

Can you ping me the details, I'll make an appt for the weekend? xx

As he sent the text he reflected, sadly, that his football team, Brighton and Hove Albion, were playing a home match on Saturday. When his son Bruno had been alive, he would have moved heaven and earth to have been able to attend a game with him. But since his tragic death, much though he loved the team, he hadn't wanted to go to the Amex stadium – not yet anyway, it brought back too many painful memories.

Charlie texted back the details.

As he took another sip of his coffee, his phone rang. It was Luke Stanstead, with the name, address and mobile phone number of the woman whose dog had been stolen in Hove Park this morning, Sara Gurner.

Thanking Stanstead, he glanced at his watch. He needed to prepare for the press conference with the ACC, but he had enough time. He dialled Sara Gurney's number. It rang for some moments, then went to voicemail. He left a message asking her to call him back as soon as it was convenient.

19

'Moose is so gorgeous. I LOVE HER!' Bluebell squealed.

Chris Fairfax, driving along the country road back towards Brighton, glanced in the rear-view mirror at his daughter, on the back seat, cradling the little ball of blonde fur to her face. She looked so happy, so utterly rapt, and he felt a deep, incredible wave of love for her. He reached out his left hand and squeezed Katy's, shot her a glance and smiled. Although she squeezed his hand back, he saw the doubt beneath the veil of her thin smile. 'I thought he was a nice guy, that breeder, didn't you? Genuine.'

'He *genuinely* knew how to charge.'

'That's the going price for these puppies now, we know that. But he didn't seem like one of those rogue puppy farmers or importers we've read about.'

'If you say so,' she replied, sounding unconvinced. Then she turned round to face her daughter and was relieved to see the bleeding from the nip on her nose had stopped. 'She's your responsibility now, you know that, don't you? You'll have to feed her before you go to school and then again after you get home. And after she's had her second set of vaccinations, we'll have to take her out for walks every day.'

'I know that, Mummy!' Bluebell said, sounding quite indignant. 'And I will, of course I will – oooooh, she's just licked the end of my nose!'

Turning back to her husband, Katy exchanged another glance with Chris, grinning. *Yep, sure*, they were both thinking. Just like Bluebell had promised to look after her gerbils, Snuffle and Sniffle, then had got bored of them after a few months. The same with her rabbit, Tipsy, and the same with her budgie, Rocky. It had fallen to them both to feed the creatures and clean out their cages while they were alive, and no doubt in a couple of months or so, when Bluebell moved on to something else she wanted, they'd be the ones feeding and walking Moose.

But for now, Chris's heart was so filled with love for his daughter, he didn't mind, he really didn't. She brought them such happiness and contentment, and all he wanted was to make her the happiest little girl in the world. And, hey, it would be great to have a dog in the house again, now they'd all got over their grief at losing their beloved and oh-so-gentle German shepherd, Phoebe, who'd had to be put down just before Christmas.

'Ouch!' Bluebell suddenly cried out, in a kind of mock anger.

'What, darling?' Katy asked.

'She's got very sharp teeth, Mummy! They're so tiny but very sharp!'

'She'll lose those baby teeth and get her grown-up teeth soon enough.' She turned again to face her daughter.

Bluebell raised the puppy's black upper lip with her finger, to reveal a row of tiny white incisors. 'Look at those!'

'They need to be sharp, darling, dogs have to be able to chew meat.'

'Moose's *not* going to eat meat,' she said indignantly. 'She's going to be like me. Anyhow, the man said she likes the dog biscuit food.'

Chris said nothing, concentrating on his driving. Bluebell had been vegetarian for the past six months. His fault, he knew – if he could call it a *fault*. They'd been following a slatted lorry, on foreign plates, crammed with sheep. It was heading towards

Newhaven port and Bluebell had asked if the sheep were going on holiday. Both Chris and Katy firmly believed they should always tell their daughter the truth, so he had told her that no, they weren't going on holiday, they were going to be sold for meat somewhere in Europe.

Bluebell had begun crying, and from that moment on had resolutely refused to eat any kind of meat – and got angry at her parents when they did. So their home had become pescatarian, and increasingly vegetarian and vegan. Katy was quite happy, Chris less so, and although he accepted the regime at home, whenever they went out to dinner he pointedly went for the meat options on the menu, both for starters and mains.

'I think Moose is hungry!' Bluebell announced.

'We're nearly home,' her father said. 'Fifteen minutes.'

'I'll put some Savlon on that bite when we get home.'

'It's fine, Mummy!'

'I read that one of the most poisonous bites in the world – apart from some snakes – is a human one,' Chris said. 'Far worse than a dog bite!'

'Maybe, but we don't know what diseases that puppy might be carrying,' Katy replied.

'Peat said his dogs have had all the vaccinations,' Chris said.

'Let's hope so,' Katy said, eyeing Bluebell's nose yet again.

'What's that meant to mean?'

'You liked him and trusted him, I wasn't convinced.'

'But the puppy's gorgeous, right?'

'I think we should take her to Dr Bradley and get her checked out if she's still local.' Dr Helen Bradley was the vet who had cared for Phoebe and had eventually put her to sleep.

'And spend another three hundred quid on her fees and whatever she gives her?' Chris quizzed. 'Why don't we just see how Moose is over the next few days?'

Katy gave a reluctant nod.

20

Shortly before 4 p.m., Roy Grace ended a call to RSPCA Inspector and case officer Kirsty Withnall. She was providing him with a list of all Persons of Interest they had on their current records in the world of illegal puppy dealing and importing in the counties of Sussex, Surrey, Hampshire and Kent. But also, further afield, she had alerted him to a number of suspect puppy farms in Wales that they currently had firmly on their radar.

As he made notes in preparation for the evening briefing on Operation Brush, his job phone rang, the display showing a number he didn't recognize.

'Roy Grace,' he answered. And heard the voice of a well-spoken middle-aged woman.

'Detective Superintendent Grace? This is Sara Gurner. You rang me earlier today and I do apologize for only now getting back to you. I've had a terrible day.'

'I can imagine,' he said. 'My wife and I are big dog lovers – and I was shocked when I heard about what happened to your dog.'

'Well,' she replied. 'I'm happy to say that all's well that ends well.'

'Really – tell me?'

'I had a phone call an hour ago from a taxi driver, a very nice gentleman called Mark Tuckwell. He'd seen my labradoodle, Zulu, standing in the middle of the Old Shoreham Road. He swung his taxi across the road, blocking the traffic, jumped out and somehow managed to grab him by the collar and get him into his car. He really deserves a medal! I can't imagine what would have happened if he hadn't done that.'

Grace could imagine and it didn't make pleasant thinking. The Old Shoreham Road was one of the major thoroughfares through the city for any vehicles travelling east or west, especially lorries heading towards Shoreham Harbour or destinations beyond. It claimed the lives of pedestrians and cyclists annually, and a dog would stand little chance. 'That is very good news indeed,' he replied.

'I honestly thought after he was taken this morning, I would never see him again,' she said, sounding quite emotional.

He gave her a moment to compose herself then asked, 'Ms Gurner, can you tell me exactly what happened this morning? Any details at all that you can remember – did you see the person who got out of the van and picked up your dog?'

'Only from a distance,' she replied.

'What were you able to see?'

'He was very pale, not tall – and he had one of those woollen hats on.'

'A beanie?'

'Yes,' she said. 'A *beanie*, that's it.'

'Anything else about him? About the way he walked?'

'Not really, no, it all happened so fast. I – I thought at first what a nice man, he's stopped Zulu from running out into the road. Then I couldn't believe it – he put him in his van and drove off.'

'And that was it?' he asked.

'I – I ran after the van.'

'Can you remember any details about the van?'

'It was white with black and orange lettering. I think it might have had the name of a plumbing company but I can't be sure.'

'Would you know what make it was?'

'No, I'm sorry. It was – you know – a typical van.'

'Did it have windows in the side?'

'Only at the front, I think.'

'So it was a panel van?'

'I honestly don't know.'

'Did it have windows in the rear?'

She hesitated. 'You know, I really can't say. I – I was so shocked.'

'Can you think of any reason why the man who stole him let him go?'

'No, none.'

'Has your dog been neutered?'

'Yes, he has been.'

He thought for a moment. 'Ms Gurner, I'm very happy that you are now reunited with your dog. But your experience could be very valuable to us in preventing further thefts of dogs. If one of my team contacted you, would you be willing to be interviewed in more depth?'

'If it prevents someone else from going through the nightmare I've suffered today, absolutely, Detective Superintendent.'

'Thank you, Ms Gurner. Please give Zulu a hug from me.'

'I will, oh I absolutely will!'

Smiling, Grace made a mental note for her to be formally interviewed. Often, through carefully posed questions, trained cognitive witness interviewers could coax valuable details from a witness's subconscious.

There was silence for a moment. Then he heard Sara Gurner's voice saying, 'Did you hear that, Zulu? Detective Superintendent Grace instructed me to give you a hug!'

As soon as he hung up, he dialled Glenn Branson. When he answered, Grace said, 'I want to take another ride out to see Sharon Ruddle – we'll put the briefing back to 7 p.m. – meet you in the car park in five?'

'I'll be there.'

21

Gecko was freezing his nuts off in his thin leather jacket, in the biting wind, in the middle of Stanmer Park. He was impatient and growing increasingly desperate as he watched the old man being tugged this way and that by the young dog on the extender lead.

He'd been discreetly following the stooped man in his shapeless tweed coat, flat cap and scarf for almost an hour, waiting for the moment when there was no one else around. But there were other dog walkers, joggers, cyclists, as well as a dad who had now appeared with his small child, attempting to fly a kite. The old man was constantly shooing other dogs away. A lot were interested in this schnauzer, and her tail was up very high. She was flagging it from side to side, which indicated she could be trying to disperse her scent and attract these males because she was on heat. Exactly what he was after! He would strike when the old man was back at his car, he decided.

But when? Time was running out. He checked his cheap little watch again. At least, he reflected, Elvira couldn't see it too well, although she could of course feel and smell it. One day he'd have a nice, swanky watch on his wrist, a shiny Rolex, and then he'd let her feel it with pride – and smell that it was gold . . . One day, when his boat came in.

Come on, come on, old man, you shouldn't have a young dog like that, you should have an old one, like yourself.

For the past few hours he had been cruising the city's parks in his van, which was now re-branded Fleming Digital Services. He'd trawled Wild Park, Queen's Park, Preston Park, St Ann's Well Gardens, Hove Lawns and Wish Park. No schnauzer or poodle matching the photograph Mr Jim had given him in any of those. But here, in the vast space of Stanmer Park, he'd finally got lucky. The right dog, he was certain. If he was right and she was a bitch that hadn't been spayed and was on heat, Terry Jim would be very pleased. Perfect!

Except, not quite perfect, as it was now 3.45 p.m., giving him barely an hour and a half to drive the dog over to Appletree Farm, get paid, and dash back to the Brighton Lanes, in rush-hour traffic, in time to buy the talking watch for Elvira before the shop closed. Tight. Stuff could go wrong. Stuff always did go wrong, story of his life.

From his vantage point behind a large oak, he saw the old man pull the dog hard on the extender lead, as another dog ran towards her. The man shouted something, wisps of grey hair batting around either side of his flat cap, as he yanked the handle, pulling the schnauzer back down the sloping grass. God knows why he had such an energetic dog, Gecko wondered. And one not spayed?

Now the schnauzer stopped, squatted on her haunches and was dumping. The old man took an interminable time to bend down with his plastic bag and pick up the mess. Time that was running out, the gauge almost on empty. Gecko checked his watch yet again.

Fucking come on!

Finally, the old man headed down towards a line of parked cars. No other dog walkers in sight. Gecko stiffened, slipped his hand in his pocket, took out the tiny, clear plastic container with the airholes he had punched and looked at the spider he'd captured earlier today. *Amaurobius ferox*. The black lace-weaver.

An inch across, with its bulbous sac, people confused it with the false widow, but this one didn't have a venomous bite. He popped it in his mouth and felt the tickle on his tongue as it scurried around.

He followed the man. The time to strike would be when he was distracted, putting his dog in the car. Gecko planned to walk up to him, open his mouth, and when the man recoiled in shock at the sight of the spider, push him over, grab the lead – good that she was on a lead – and outrun the oldster to his van.

The oldster was heading towards a little mushy-pea-coloured Skoda, and as he approached, he pulled something from his pocket – the key fob, Gecko guessed – and moments later the Skoda's indicators flashed.

Yes! Now!

Striding fast towards the old man and his dog, Gecko was just ten yards away when he saw something moving, out of the corner of his eye.

A police car.

Shit, shit, shit.

Was it looking for him? Or just on routine patrol?

He turned abruptly away and strode off uphill, trying to look nonchalant, like he was just out for a stroll in the park. He didn't stop for a good minute, then when he did look back, he saw the police car had gone and the Skoda was reversing.

No.

He blew the spider out of his mouth, back into the container, closed the lid, then looked at his watch again: 3.50 p.m. No chance of finding another dog now. And even if he did, he'd never get it to the farm in time to be paid and get back to the shop before it closed. He was panicking. And thinking hard. His only credit card was maxed out and had been declined on the last two occasions he'd used it. He had £60 in his wallet, but he needed that to pay for their fish and chip supper tonight and for the rides on the pier.

There was only one option now, his Plan B, and he needed to act before that closed out on him. Jumping into his van, he drove out of the park and headed towards Brighton.

Twenty minutes later he was driving along Hove seafront, passing the Angel of Peace statue – an angel holding an orb and an olive branch, which delineated the border between the old towns of Brighton and Hove, now co-joined into one city since 2001. Almost in desperation, as he drove, he was looking across to his right for people walking their dogs on the upper promenade, although he knew that most of them would be down below, walking on the beach or along by the Arches.

Plan B was still sketchy in his head. As was the local geography. It was 4.40 p.m. He took the slip road at the West Street lights and halted for the red. When they changed, he made a left turn, followed by another, then turned into the Cannon Place car park, found a space and parked the van.

4.45 p.m.

He hurried out of the car park, ran back to West Street, crossed it then walked quickly along an alley that took him into the network of Brighton's historic Lanes district. He navigated the warren of pedestrian alleys, filled with antique and modern jewellers, artisan shops, cafes, restaurants, pubs and bars. He dodged through the dawdling window-shoppers and business folk heading home at the end of the working day. Alarmed at the number of shops already pulling down their metal shutters, he quickened his pace.

Right then left. And, reaching East Street, he breathed a sigh of relief. Ahead, in the fading late afternoon light, Gecko saw the shopfront of the premises he had come to visit, looking still very much open. He stopped a short distance away, in front of an antique jeweller who was in the process of lowering his steel shutters, and pulled his scarf up over the lower part of his face. Happy for the cold weather today. Oh, so happy indeed!

He'd be even happier if it was just the friendly old guy in the shop, and not his disdainful young male assistant who had looked at Gecko last time as if he was something the cat had brought in.

With his beanie pulled low over his forehead and his scarf pulled high over his nose, he was confident that only his eyes were visible, as he entered the door of the Brighton Antique and Modern Watch Co., and approached the glass counter, beneath which was an array of modern watches, and behind which, to his relief, was just the elderly, silver-haired man, wearing a Perspex visor. 'May I help you?' he asked with a smile.

Not wishing to remind the man he had been here before, a couple of days ago, Gecko said, 'I have a lady cousin who is blind, and I wondered if you sell any talking watches?'

'I do indeed, I have a whole range, sir.'

'And which do you consider the best, money no object?'

He saw the proud look in the man's face behind his visor. 'The Verbalise range, sir, no question at all. Elegant and with most clear diction. May I show you the very latest – just in stock this week.'

'You may indeed,' Gecko said. His eyes also fell, greedily, on a display cabinet of pre-owned Rolex watches. He pointed to one with a bevelled edge, a gold face with a date display, and a gold bracelet. 'Would that be an Oyster?'

'It would indeed, sir.'

'I'd like to have a look at that, too.'

'Absolutely, sir!'

But then, to Gecko's dismay, the proprietor turned and called out through an open door at the rear of the shop, 'Toby, I need your help, please!'

The old man opened the display case containing the talking watches with a tiny key then pulled out and held up an elegant, silver-cased watch, its face a pale blue and with a silver bracelet.

'Top of the range, this is radio-controlled, so it is always accurate and is a most elegant timepiece.' He handed it to Gecko, who cradled it in his palm, studying it thoughtfully.

'Very nice,' he said enthusiastically.

'Oh it is, it really is, you honestly could not do better than this! And to make it even more attractive, if it is for a registered blind person, you can claim the VAT back.'

'I can?' he asked.

'Absolutely, sir, I can give you the form to fill in. It will reduce the price from £69.99 to £55.99.'

Gecko nodded, as the assistant, a man in his early twenties, in a sharp suit and with foppish black hair, appeared – and looked at Gecko with a faint, uncertain, hint of recognition.

'Toby, please show the gentleman the vintage gold Rolex.'

Giving Gecko a dubious look, the young assistant unlocked another cabinet, removed the Rolex and handed it to him.

The proprietor said proudly, 'It is a very fine example, in quite beautiful condition and very recently serviced by Rolex themselves. I'm asking nine thousand pounds, but I'm sure we could come to a deal.'

Gecko smiled, studying it for a moment before closing his fist around it, and murmured, 'Oh, I'm sure of that. Does it come in the original box?'

'Yes, yes. Toby, help me find the presentation box.' They fumbled around under the counter. While they were distracted, Gecko turned away and surreptitiously removed the container from his pocket. He then slipped his scarf down and popped the spider back in his mouth, before raising his scarf again.

'And we could offer you a warranty of—'

Before he could finish, Gecko had lowered his scarf and opened his mouth, to reveal the spider crawling around in there.

'Bloody hell!' the old man shrieked, backing away in revulsion. Then, before he could regain his composure, Gecko had turned away, still holding both watches, and was heading towards the door to the street.

The assistant vaulted the counter and grabbed Gecko by his shoulder.

Gecko spun round, punched him full in the face, sending him reeling backwards, and was out the door, running.

22

Thursday 25 March

Most psychologists agreed that there were various stages of grief at the sudden loss of a loved one. Roy Grace knew from personal experience, with the loss of his elder son Bruno, that they were pretty much right. And he had seen it all too often when dealing with the loved ones of a murder victim.

Grief would go through stages of shock or disbelief, denial, anger, bargaining, guilt, depression; before, finally, acceptance and – sometimes – hope.

Each stage lasted only a short while, the first as little as twenty-four hours and, Grace knew, the best time to get information from a bereaved loved one, brutal though it might be, was during this initial period of shock or disbelief, before they went into the denial phase and shut down. Which was why he wanted to try to have another conversation with Sharon Ruddle while she was still in a state of shock; as well as, compassionately, trying to give her some crumbs of comfort.

Glenn Branson turned the Ford onto the rutted track that was the driveway to Old Homestead Farm. As they lurched through the potholes, Grace was thinking hard, both about what he was going to say and about the pieces of the puzzle – those that he had, those that were missing and those that might or might not belong to this particular case. Dots to be joined up, or not.

Ahead, in the failing light of the overcast day, the farm buildings were coming into sight. The blue and white tape of the outer cordon, with the frozen-looking scene guard on the far side, loomed ahead. They turned into the field that was the rendezvous point. The large white Crime Scene Investigator's van was in there, along with a white Subaru, a marked and a couple of unmarked police vehicles, and a mud-spattered navy-blue C-class Mercedes coupe. Branson pulled the Mondeo up alongside the Mercedes and they climbed out. The rain had stopped and given way to a strong, icy wind.

There were several people in the farmyard, beyond the second, inner cordon, all concentrating intently on their tasks. Three CSIs, in blue oversuits, on their hands and knees, doing a fingertip search of the area around the marked silhouette of where Tim Ruddle's body had lain; the Crime Scene Manager, Chris Gee, also in a blue oversuit; and a man in a white oversuit and overshoes, stepping carefully around, taking photographs on his phone.

Grace and Branson booked in with the scene guard, PC Dave Simmons, then ducked under the tape, which he obligingly held up for them, and walked along the metal track that had been laid on the mud, to create a path with minimal contamination of the scene up to the second cordon, and ducked under that, entering the farmyard, where they were greeted by Gee, who looked as frozen as Simmons. The barn which had been broken into was to his left, the door still open, and the small farmhouse was to his right, lights on in several windows.

'How are we doing, Chris?' Grace asked.

Rubbing his gloved hands across his chest, he replied, 'Making good progress, sir. There's a back entrance to the farmhouse, which the lady, Mrs Ruddle, is able to use to get out and feed the animals without crossing the crime scene. The farmhand has stayed in his cottage most of the day – he's in a state of shock. Looks like the offenders were a clumsy lot – we've recovered a cigarette butt, part of a broken index plate, and Professor Kelly says he already has a lot of good footprints.'

'The professor's here already?'

Gee pointed at the man in the white oversuit. 'Yes, luckily he was in the country and free today.'

'Are you going to be at the briefing this evening?'

'I'm leaving shortly, sir.'

Grace thanked him and walked over to the renowned pioneer of Forensic Gait Analysis, a sturdy, ebullient figure, mask below his chin, who greeted him as ever like a long-lost buddy, as they bumped gloved fists. 'Good to see you, Roy!' Then he bumped fists with Branson. 'And you too, Glenn.'

'Good to see you too, Haydn. Thanks for coming,' Grace said.

'It worked out well for me, I should have been in South Korea this week, but I'm stuck in the UK at the moment. Sounds like a nasty murder.'

'I've yet to come across a nice one,' Grace replied, grimacing.

'Those your wheels back there?' Branson asked. 'The Merc?'

Kelly beamed proudly. 'It's a beast, AMG, 6.3 litre, last of the naturally aspirated ones. Not many years left to have fun on the roads, are there, guys?'

Both detectives shook their heads.

'So business is good, eh?' Grace retorted.

Kelly gave him an impish grin then glanced at Branson. 'You guys are probably too young to remember the late grocery tycoon, Jimmy Goldsmith, right?'

Taking Grace's frown as a yes, Kelly went on, 'Sir James Goldsmith famously declared there are only two kinds of businesses to be in – food and munitions. He said people are always going to have to eat, and they are always going to kill each other.'

'He got that about right,' Grace said, nodding ruefully. Then after a moment he added, 'Maybe the funeral business, too. Had a colleague who retired a few years back and told us all, at his retirement bash, he was planning to start a funeral parlour. He said he was going to call it "Yours Eventually".'

'And did he?'

Grace shook his head. 'The Grim Reaper called his bluff. Dropped dead from a heart attack three days after handing in his ticket.' He shrugged. 'So, tell me, what do you have?'

'Give me a little longer and I'll be able to tell you a fair bit about the offenders. I've got some good, fresh footprints off the wet mud and grass – I need to exclude the farm manager and the deceased, and we'll need to establish who visited this farmyard in the past twenty-four hours, to eliminate them, before I can tell you my estimate of the number of offenders – and vehicles they came in. Oh, and by the way, I've got two very distinct and different tyre treads that don't match any of the farm vehicles. Two vehicles unaccounted for – but this is something you need to get your vehicle people on, after eliminating any legitimate visitors.'

'Are you able to come to our evening briefing, Haydn, and present your findings?' Grace asked.

Kelly shook his head. 'There's heavy rain forecast for later. I'd like to use the remaining daylight to take impressions on the mud and grass to get the shoe sizes and a sense of the people you might be looking for. I've already identified one set, which might be helpful—' He nodded at the barn. 'They look to me like they were made by an endomorph with a limp.'

'Endomorph?' Branson quizzed.

Haydn smiled. 'In plain English, Glenn, a *fat bastard.*'

Grace smiled. 'Best keep that expression to yourself!'

'Humble apologies. Would, a *large bloke, probably very overweight* be more acceptable?'

Grace nodded. 'Yes, it would.'

'I prefer the first description,' Branson smiled.

23

Roy Grace and Glenn Branson left Haydn Kelly to his work and walked along the metal track the CSIs had laid. In front of the farmhouse was an old Land Rover with a canvas rear, and a more modern four-wheel-drive Fiat Panda. They followed the track around to the rear of the farmhouse, passing a plastic toy tractor, a wheely bin and a row of plastic sacks, and came to a conservatory in poor repair, with its door peeling paint.

Through the glass he saw Sharon Ruddle, in dungarees and a big sweater, her hair a mess, slumped head in hands over the kitchen table, and two children on a sofa close by. A brown cat was eating from a red bowl on the floor, beside an Aga, almost at the feet of the Family Liaison Officer, Emma Gallichan. The FLO was occupied stirring the contents of a large, steaming saucepan on top of the range.

Grace knocked on a pane of glass, softly, then louder. Sharon looked up, startled, at the same time as Gallichan looked round. Sharon said something to the FLO and walked towards them, like a zombie. She opened the door and gave a nod of recognition.

'I'm sorry to bother you again, Mrs Ruddle,' Grace said. 'Would it be possible to have another quick word?'

She shrugged. 'Come in – have you – have you found them?'

Grace and Branson walked into the room, which was uncomfortably hot. Just like the houses of so many bereaved people he had visited in the past. It was as if they turned up the heat – and often drew the curtains, too – to exclude the reality of the old world they had once inhabited and which would now, forever, be different in the worst possible way.

Gallichan took the pan off the heat and placed it on the side of the stove before turning round and acknowledging Grace and Branson with a respectful, 'Sir, sir.'

'All OK, Emma?' Grace asked.

'I'm just heating up the children's supper.'

'Please sit down,' Sharon Ruddle said. She raised her right arm, holding it in the air like a limp flag, then dropped it again. 'Would you like a drink? Tea? Coffee?'

'We're fine, thank you,' Grace said, although he could have done with a pint of coffee right now. 'We won't keep you long.' He signalled to Emma to continue with her task, then they joined Ruddle at the kitchen table.

Grace and Branson exchanged a glance. Both of them were aware that she may now be moving from the shock to denial phase. Roy spoke. 'Are you getting all the support you need, Sharon?'

'Yes, I think so. Emma's been brilliant, helping me with the kids, and we've had the chance to sit down and talk about what is happening. She's explained to me what you and your team will be doing and helping me get through this. It's the kids, I just don't know what the future holds for them. What am I going to tell them?' she asked.

'You have just these two, right?' Glenn Branson asked gently.

She looked down fondly at them. 'Felix and Ava. We were going to take them to Florida this summer, to Disney World – that was the plan, anyway.' She shrugged and gave a wan smile. 'We have the tickets booked and everything – did you know you can get them much cheaper by booking a long way ahead? We got such a great deal on them.'

Then she dropped her face into her hands and sobbed.

Without looking up she said, 'Oh shit. What am I going to do? I've lost my husband and . . .' Her voice tailed.

Grace and Branson waited patiently. After a few moments she said, 'Brayley. The kids adore her – she's just the sweetest dog. And Rudi. They keep asking where they are.'

'Have you got anyone who could come and stay with you?' Grace asked. 'Any relative? Parents, sister, brother? A close friend?'

'My sister, Jo, lives in Aberdeen, her husband flies helicopters to oil rigs. He's starting a week's leave so he can look after their kids. She's coming down tomorrow.'

'That's good,' Branson said.

Suddenly a sharp, synthesized voice, sounding like a Dalek, announced, 'Game over!'

Grace looked at the sofa. The little girl was fixed on an iPad. She tapped it again. 'Next level!' it said.

'I'm not being a very good host, am I? I should offer you a drink.'

'You did already, we're fine. Thank you. I've seen your interview from this morning and just wanted to ask, since then have you remembered any more about the vehicles these people came in?' Grace continued. 'You said when we talked earlier that you thought one was a Range Rover and the other some kind of pickup truck.'

'It was dark as I said. Maybe a Range Rover, maybe a pickup – I'm not very good on cars.'

'One more thing, Mrs Ruddle,' Grace asked. 'Had your puppies been microchipped?'

She nodded. 'Last week – I took them to the vet.'

'Game over!' the voice on the sofa said.

Sharon Ruddle stood up, weeping. 'I'd better get the children fed and bathed.'

Grace and Branson shot each other a glance, then also stood up – Grace just in time to catch her arm as she stumbled.

24

Sunset wasn't for another hour, but as Branson and Grace headed back from Old Homestead Farm towards the Police HQ at Lewes, beneath a tombstone sky and through an onslaught of pelting rain, it already felt pretty much like night.

Grace was upset by the grief Sharon Ruddle was suffering. The grief of victims always got to him, more so since he was still grieving Bruno. The darkness outside deepened his gloom, but he could feel the heat of anger burning away inside him. The anger he felt whenever some innocent person had been murdered for no other reason than pure greed, as seemed to be the case here. And he remembered the words of an old Icelandic detective he'd met some years ago when he and Sandy had been on a trip there to a conference. It had been November and even at midday it had felt like dusk. Sandy had asked the old guy how he coped with the lack of sunlight for so many months and he'd replied, 'If you have a light inside you, everything is bright.'

'Bummer, isn't it?' Branson, who was driving, sensed his mood.

'Bummer,' Grace repeated, almost absently, as he thought about the evening briefing ahead, and how he was going to handle the press conference arranged for tomorrow with the ACC. 'Can you do me a favour, mate? Take over from me on Saturday afternoon – Cleo and I are going to see a puppy. You can have Sunday off – would that work?'

'Sure.' Then he added, 'From a legit source, I presume?'

94

Grace gave him a smile. 'Cleo's sister told us about them and has done some pretty thorough research; the breeders look very genuine, a nice set-up. But to be honest, Cleo and I would prefer to get a rescue, and with what we're seeing with this case, it makes me more certain a rescue would be better. We're just going to take a look at them, it's all good research for this investigation anyhow. I'm interested to see how it's done.'

'Yeah, I hear you, but be careful. Not many people just go and *look* at cute puppies and walk away!'

'I know, no doubt they'll suck us in. But we'll try to be strong.'

Branson shot him a sideways look, grinning.

'What?'

'Strong – not when you see a cute little puppy, no way!'

Grace shrugged. 'We've waited over a year since we first thought about a buddy for Humphrey, so we can wait a bit longer for the right dog. As I say, if nothing else it'll be in our interests to hopefully meet a good breeder, someone who does it for all the right reasons. And a nice drive about with a purpose!'

'Fair enough,' Branson said. 'God, I feel so sorry for Sharon Ruddle. I mean, like, what is that poor woman's future? She and her husband bought that farm as their dream, away from all the shit of city life, and they had so many plans for it. Now it's just her and the old farmhand to run it. And at some point she's going to have to explain to her kids why their daddy's never coming home again.'

'All because of the greed of a bunch of scumbags,' Grace said.

'Let me ask you something.'

'Go on,' Grace said.

'You know when you first joined the police – why did you join? Because your dad had been a copper, or for some other reason?'

He thought for some moments, before replying, watching the wipers clouting away the water, which blurred the screen almost instantly again. 'I had a lot of conversations with my dad when he was dying of cancer in the Martlets hospice. We'd never really talked much before. I asked him why he'd become a police officer and he told me it was because he'd wanted to do a job that would make a difference to people – to the world, I guess.' He fell silent for a short while. 'I suppose that made me think, you know, about why we are here. About what life is all about.'

'And you figured it out, right? You figured what life is all about?'

As Grace stared through the windscreen, now blurred even more by the spray of a lorry in front, and at the lights of oncoming vehicles, he said quietly, 'Maybe.'

'Maybe?'

'Uh huh.'

'You going to share it with me?'

'It's a little bit left-field.'

'I do left-field.'

'Probably why I like you.'

'And not because I'm highly intelligent, handsome, charming and always have your back?'

'Maybe that too. Because mediocrity recognizes nothing higher than itself, it takes talent to appreciate genius!'

Branson shook his head, grinning. 'I agree, Mr Modesty!'

Grace glanced at his watch: 5.55 p.m. They would be at the headquarters in ten minutes.

'I asked if you'd figured out life, like what life is about? As left-field as you like.'

Roy Grace shrugged. 'OK. This is what I think – what I *really* think sometimes. You know those Escape Room places you can go and play games?'

Branson nodded. 'Yeah, Siobhan's friends, Dem and Jenn, had an Escape Room party. We all got locked in this room down on the seafront and we had to figure out a bunch of clues to get out.'

'Exactly,' Grace replied.

Branson shot him a glance. 'Meaning?'

'You know I'm not a religious believer. But sometimes, when I try to make sense of existence, I wonder if God – or whatever we want to call Him or Her – didn't create life for us humans as a giant Escape Room. If you can figure out how to live forever, you win; if you die, you lose. So far, in the two hundred and fifty thousand years that humans have been on this planet, there's not been one winner.'

Branson shook his head. 'Seriously? That's what you believe?'

'Look at all these tech billionaires, like Musk and Bezos, all throwing their money at life extension. I read somewhere recently that scientists reckon the first person to live to 200 has already been born.'

'And that's what you'd like – to live forever?'

'I'd like to live long enough to see forensics develop to the point where we can solve every murder. Where we can lock up people like the ones who've just destroyed Sharon Ruddle's life and left her children without a father, within days. If I have a dream, that's it. Do you have a dream?'

Branson looked wistful. 'Not a dream – just an aspiration.' He drove on in silence.

'Tell me?'

'Sammy and Remi think I'm a better person than I really am.' He shrugged. 'I'm constantly trying to improve myself, in order to cushion their eventual disappointment.'

Grace smiled. He hadn't seen Glenn's kids in a while. Then he patted his friend's leg. 'I think you're succeeding. Don't ever stop trying.'

'Yeah,' Branson said, and fell silent again.

25

Aerial footage from a drone camera was playing on the wall-mounted monitor in the conference room, at the evening briefing. It was moving across the Old Homestead Farm and environs, over the ramshackle outbuildings and the fields of cows and sheep. Next to the monitor was a small-scale Ordnance Survey map, pinned to a whiteboard, showing the farm's perimeter marked in red, and the surrounding five-mile radius. The minor roads on the map were highlighted in blue, and the only major road in orange.

Jack Alexander, standing close but out of the way so everyone in the evening briefing could see both clearly, mirrored what the drone was showing with the beam of his laser pen on the map. He indicated the two neighbouring farms, the local villages of Twineham, Bolney and Handcross and the minor and major roads, including the A23 London–Brighton main artery. Two ANPR cameras sited on this section of the road, one northbound, the other southbound, were marked on the map with green crosses.

'We don't know where the offenders came from, nor which roads they took after they left Old Homestead Farm,' Jack said. 'Earlier today I put in a request to the ANPR team to run a check for any vehicles travelling in close proximity to each other between the hours of 12.30 and 2.30 this morning, and they've come up with something that may be of interest.' He pointed the laser beam at the green cross on the A23.

'At approximately 1.10 a.m. – tallying with our time frame – two vehicles were clocked on this northbound camera. One was the registration plate of a 2011 Range Rover and the other, following no more than a hundred yards behind, was the plate of a 2014 Ford Ranger pickup. These same two vehicles were clocked at 1.55 a.m. on the southbound camera at almost the same location on the A23. And again, they were clocked at 2.24 a.m. on the A22 road away from Eastbourne. There were no further sightings of them.'

'Good work, Jack,' Grace said. 'So if these are the offenders' vehicles – and it is only an *if* – it indicates their destination might have been somewhere in East Sussex.'

'There's more, sir,' Jack added. 'The Range Rover has been identified as belonging to a retired Sussex Police officer, Andy Batten.'

Grace frowned. 'What? Andy? I remember him when I was a DC – he was on the Antiques Squad a very long time ago – he's been retired for years.'

Alexander nodded. 'We've eliminated him, sir – his Range Rover has been in a garage at Forest Row, with its engine out, since Tuesday of this week.'

'Cloned plates?' Nick Nicholl questioned.

'Looks like it, Nick,' Jack replied.

'Well, I'll be doggone!' Norman Potting quipped.

There were a few grins and a couple of head shakes.

'And the Ford Ranger, Jack?' Grace asked.

'We have the same thing – it belongs to a builder called Neil Wakeling, who we've confirmed is currently at his holiday home in Como, Italy, with his wife.'

Alexander turned to another, larger-scale OS map on another whiteboard to his right. Almost the entire area of the map was encircled in red. 'I extended the time to 4 a.m. for the ANPR team. If the offenders were heading any further east or north, there is at least one camera they would have almost certainly pinged in either direction, so in my view this puts them within this radius.' He tracked the red circle with his pen beam.

'That's a pretty big area, Jack,' Grace said.

'It is, sir – approximately six hundred square miles.'

'Grid it out,' Grace said. 'And continue with the drone search – see if we can find a pairing of these two vehicles anywhere within that area.'

'I've already started, sir, and will continue at first light tomorrow.'

'Good work.' Grace turned to the Rural Crimes Sergeant, Tom Cartwright. 'Do you have any intel of crime around dogs in that area?' He pointed at the large-scale map.

Cartwright looked like the kind of man who was more at home in the country than in a city. Burly and rugged, in his late thirties, he had an amiable face framed with an unruly mop of dark brown hair. He nodded. 'I do, sir. In case none of the team are familiar with Operation Rake, it's the Sussex Police dedicated response to dog theft and illegal dog breeding, which I am currently running.'

'I think most members of the team here are aware of it to some degree, Tom,' Grace said and looked around. There were several nods of confirmation.

Continuing, Cartwright said, 'Among the dogs currently most valuable to thieves are French bulldogs – the breed stolen from Old Homestead Farm earlier today. We have seven reported incidents across the county in the past two months of dog owners being physically assaulted and their dogs – all popular breeds or cross-breeds – taken. The most recent of which was in Hove Park this morning, when a woman's dog was taken, although I understand the lady has now been reunited with her dog.' He looked at Grace for confirmation.

The Detective Superintendent nodded. 'I spoke to this lady earlier this afternoon, Mrs Sara Gurner. Her dog is a labradoodle and their established mix of poodle and Labrador has become very popular. She acquired it as a rescue from the Brighton RSPCA.'

Cartwright looked pensive. 'Was this lady certain her dog was stolen, and not simply found wandering on a street by someone?'

'From speaking to her, I'm pretty certain it was stolen, Tom,' Grace replied. 'She told me the man who snatched him knew she was calling after him and definitely intended to take the dog.'

'In which case it might have been discarded subsequently, when the thieves realized it wasn't what they wanted. Maybe they were after a pure-bred poodle to use as a stud – it does have strong poodle characteristics. Those might fetch more money.' He looked again at the large-scale map on the whiteboard.

'Those of you familiar with Operation Rake will already be aware of the raid on a caravan in a car park in Eastbourne, a week ago. It contained forty-three puppies, dehydrated and starving, many of them diseased, which we believe came through the Eurotunnel. Four of them have subsequently died from parvovirus, but I'm informed that thanks to the fast work of the RSPCA the rest are doing well. Some are at the Dogs Trust kennels in Shoreham and some temporarily rehomed with foster parent families. From the intel we have, we believe these puppies were illegally imported from Europe.'

'By whom, Tom?' DC Nick Nicholl asked.

'It's my suspicion this caravan is linked to Polegate and Hailsham, where there is known criminal activity, and which is within that radius on your larger-scale map.'

The Sergeant continued, 'We've recently secured poaching convictions on two men residing in a smallholding in Hailsham. They were arrested in possession of an air rifle with a scope, hunting knives, catapults and ball bearings, along with several dead pheasants. My officers conducting the searches reported they heard a lot of barking coming from a number of buildings at the location – indicating a very large quantity of dogs, way beyond what would be normal for domestic pets. I reported their observation to the Sussex RSPCA. Subsequently, the inspector we've been working with, Kirsty Withnall, attempted to visit but was refused access. She has so far been unable to provide grounds for a search warrant.'

'What grounds would she need?' Velvet Wilde asked.

Cartwright replied, 'Evidence either that they are trading in dogs without a licence, or that the animals are being kept in substandard conditions. Past activity at this location includes theft of agricultural machinery, trade in stolen auto parts, as well as various other scams. The weather forecast for tomorrow is clear, and I've requested drone surveillance. It will be carried out at high altitude, so they won't be aware they're being filmed. I'm going to be watching the footage in real time with Kirsty Withnall to see if it is linked to our investigation.'

'Thanks, Tom,' Grace said. 'Anything else to add context for those not up to speed?'

'Yes, a little,' Cartwright replied. 'Breeders are resorting to every trick in the book to fool buyers into thinking they're buying properly cared-for, vaccinated dogs with Kennel Club approved breeder certificates.' He paused to let this sink in.

'The reality is,' he continued, 'that many of these dogs are either illegal imports or bred in appalling conditions, and being sold with all kinds of exaggerated features, diseases and health issues. They are often dirty and malnourished. A lot of people who are conned into buying them suffer their dogs dying, or horrific vet bills – often running into the thousands – and just as often find themselves with animals that have not been socialized and will forever be problem dogs. I only have ten officers and six PCSOs and it's an impossible task to follow up every complaint we get.'

'Where do all these dogs come from, Tom?' Grace asked. 'You said some are illegal imports from Europe, and some from rogue breeders here.'

Cartwright nodded. 'Some are stolen – as already mentioned, we've had a number of reports of dog walkers being mugged. And there has been an explosion of unscrupulous breeders in Wales, for some reason, mostly around the Carmarthen region. Over half the police forces in England have less than two officers dedicated to rural crime, and when they do make arrests, the sentences are a joke. Conspiracy to smuggle or trade illegally is the only offence that carries a punitive jail term – and it's a hard one to prove.'

'Tom,' EJ asked. 'What do you think is likely to happen to the dogs taken from Old Homestead Farm?'

'From what we know, the puppies will be advertised for sale on the popular sites like Facebook, Gumtree and Pets4Homes. The adult male and female will be retained for breeding – they could produce two more litters in the next twelve months.'

'So we should be closely monitoring these sites over the next few days for any French bulldog puppies coming up for sale, Tom?' Grace asked.

'Definitely worth keeping an eye on them – I can give you a full list of all the popular sites – but the problem is these are selling dogs right across the UK, it will be quite a major resourcing task, sir, and will require the Authorizing Officer's authority.'

Grace made a note.

'I'm right that these puppies had all been microchipped?' Cartwright asked.

'Mrs Ruddle said they had – last week,' Glenn Branson replied.

'That's possibly helpful,' the Rural Crimes Sergeant said and turned to Grace. 'You could put out a request to all vets to scan the chip of any French bulldog puppy brought in for the first time. But, as we know, the professionals in the game – and it sounds like these people are – have the kit to put in a second chip above the original – and the scanner may only pick up the top one.'

'What about DNA testing?' Norman Potting asked.

'That would definitely be a good way to establish the provenance of a dog,' Cartwright said, turning to Gee. 'Be a good precaution to ask your CSIs, Chris, to preserve any baskets, rugs and toys the bulldogs had.'

'I already have done,' the Crime Scene Manager replied, looking just a little pleased with himself. He then gave the team a detailed update on the forensic examination of the scene and key items of interest.

'Nice work, Chris,' Roy Grace said, when he had finished. Then, addressing the team, he said, 'OK, not much is likely to happen overnight. I have the press conference in the morning, in which I'll put out an appeal to the public. So, our next briefing will be tomorrow evening.'

26

The ghost train was hurtling towards closed doors. Gecko felt Elvira grip his arm tightly. Could she see them? He was never sure quite how much she could or couldn't see.

BLAM!

She screamed as they burst through them and into pitch darkness. Then both of them screamed as the strands of something brushed their faces. A hideous luminous gargoyle popped out of the darkness ahead and cackled at them.

Elvira screamed again and clutched him even more tightly. He gripped her arm back. They were accelerating again. Towards more closed doors.

BLAM!

Then lights ahead. They were travelling downhill, then levelling out. They came to a halt under the glare of bright lights. She was laughing, her white stick wedged between her legs. 'Oh that was so good! Can we go again?'

'You weren't scared?'

'Just a little. Were you?'

'Me, nah!'

She prodded him with a finger. 'My brave soldier. Go on, let's do it again!'

'We have a dinner reservation.' He said it importantly, like he'd once seen Daniel Craig in a Bond movie say it. And that's how he felt right now, in his dark jacket and white open-neck shirt, beneath his anorak, with this beautiful girl in her pretty grey coat on his arm. He was James Bond!

'Just one more time.'

'I'll go and pay,' he said. 'Need a token.'

Elvira found his face with her hand, and kissed him on the cheek. 'That's my token,' she said. 'My love token.'

Twenty minutes later they were seated side by side at a window table in the large, ornate interior of the Palm Court, a short walk down Brighton's Palace Pier from the ghost train.

'This is nice,' Elvira said.

'You are nice,' Gecko replied.

'You too, Marion.'

He'd felt so good with Elvira that he'd recently confided in her what his real name was, and she told him she loved it. 'You will always be Marion to me,' she had said.

And tonight, seated on the banquette, with the woman he adored beside him and the large plastic menu in his hand, he felt on top of the world, and important, as the waitress stood in front of them with her order pad. 'We are celebrating!' he told her. 'We'll have the cod and chips with champagne meal for two! And bring us extra mushy peas!'

'Mushy peas?' Elvira said.

'Got to have mushy peas,' he replied. 'You don't like them?'

She shrugged. 'Maybe.'

As the waitress smiled and headed off, he looked into Elvira's eyes. One was opaque, completely blind; the other had partial sight. It wasn't important. What mattered was that she was beautiful to him, inside and out, with her shock of dark hair, cute nose and sweet, tiny mouth with a mole just to the left of it. She looked a little like a younger Helena Bonham Carter, only ten times prettier, in his eyes. And she was wearing a sexy dress.

'Happy birthday!' he said. 'I've brought you a present.'

'A present? You shouldn't have!'

'Course I should!' He'd not had any time to buy wrapping paper, so he'd wrapped it in tissues from a box in his bedsit room and bound it with Sellotape. 'I'm not very good at wrapping,' he said, digging it out of his pocket and handing it to her, blushing.

As she tugged away at the sticky tape, their flutes of champagne arrived. He guided her right hand to the stem of hers, then raised his glass. 'Happy birthday to the lady I think I'm falling in love with!'

They clinked glasses. A little spilled from hers, but he didn't mind. She sipped some, put the glass down and he quickly steadied it. Then she removed the tissue, fumbled the box open, peered inside with it inches from her face and squealed with delight. 'Oh my God, oh wow!'

He helped attach the silver strap to her slender wrist, smelling her gorgeous perfume as he did. 'You just tap it!' he said.

She tapped the face. A voice said, 'Eight minutes past eight.'

'Oh wow!' she exclaimed.

'Tap it twice, fast!'

She did so and the voice said, 'Thursday, March the twenty-fifth.'

'I love it!' she said.

'I think I love you.'

'You only *think*?' she chided, with a smile.

'I *know* I love you!'

'And I *know* I love you!' She touched the watch's face again. 'It must have cost you a fortune!' she said.

Out of the corner of his eye he saw a uniformed police officer enter the restaurant. Followed by another.

Shit.

He grabbed her face and kissed her passionately, watching the two officers, warily, out of the corner of his eye. His heart racing. *Not now, please not now!*

Then, to his relief, he saw the restaurant manager lead them to a table and they sat down.

'You OK, my sweet?' Elvira said, drawing back a fraction. 'Something's spooked you?'

'I'm OK,' he said. 'I'm fine.'

The two coppers were studying menus. That was good. 'You haven't told me about your day,' he said. Elvira worked on the helpline of a computer company.

'I had a complete dickhead on the phone. Well – what's the female equivalent?'

'A dickheadess?'

She laughed. 'Yeah, well this was the crown princess of all dickheadesses. She complained that nothing was coming up on her desktop screen. I went through all the checks, then finally asked her to check it was plugged in. She told me she couldn't see, because she was in a room with no windows and there was a power cut!'

Gecko laughed.

'You haven't told me about your day,' she said.

'It was OK,' he replied. 'I think we've found a nice home for a rescue spaniel,' he lied.

'I love what you do, the way you're so dedicated to helping dogs. You're such a good person.'

'I try,' he said.

'I love that you do,' she replied.

He glanced at the two coppers. Then he looked back at Elvira. 'Always,' he said. He glanced at the coppers again. One was looking at him. With a little too much interest. Before turning back to her menu.

'Do you need the toilet?' he asked.

She frowned. 'No.'

'You need the toilet,' he said.

'I don't need the toilet.'

'I'm telling you, you do,' he said urgently. 'Trust me, you need the toilet.'

'My love, what are you talking about?'

'I'm going to pretend to take you to the toilet, then we are going to run. Bring your stick.'

Shaking her head in confusion, Elvira eased out from behind the table, and Gecko reached over to grab her stick. Arms locked, he led her across towards the back of the room and the exit to the toilets. All the time surreptitiously glancing at the female copper, who was still reading her menu.

As soon as they were outside, Gecko said, 'Run! Hold my arm and run!'

'Why? Why, Marion?'

'Do you love me?'

'Yes, yes I love you.'

'Then, just run!'

27

The capacious L-shaped canteen at Sussex Police HQ was often used out of mealtimes for large gatherings, such as on ceremonial occasions, the Chief Constable's welcome speech to a fresh intake of recruits and for press conferences, which for major crimes would be well attended. This morning, press and media reporters occupied the three rows of chairs that had been laid out.

The local BBC, ITV and Latest TV news camera crews as well as BBC Radio Sussex and Siobhan Sheldrake, the *Argus* reporter – and Glenn Branson's wife – were here.

Roy Grace faced them alongside ACC Hannah Robinson and the RSPCA inspector Kirsty Withnall. The conference was being broadcast live on Microsoft Teams by Sussex Police Media and Comms, to enable other journalists and media outlets to participate virtually. And, in particular, they were now involving social media, including Twitter, Facebook and Instagram, in the conference to get as broad a reach as possible.

The forty-three-year-old ACC, fair hair pulled up in a neat bun, was in full dress uniform, and the RSPCA inspector, in her late thirties, with a serious face beneath elegantly styled brown hair, wore a white shirt with dark epaulettes sporting two gold pips, a black tie and black trousers. Roy Grace, aware of always needing to convey to the public the reassuring image expected of an SIO, was dressed in one of his trademark dark suits, white shirt, sober tie, and black shoes with a near-military shine. This latter was something he had learned from his father, that properly polished shoes were a sign of someone you could respect.

Hannah Robinson started the conference by introducing herself, Grace and Withnall confidently, then briefly set the scene. 'In the early hours of yesterday morning, Thursday, Timothy Ruddle, a farmer in Balcombe and a dedicated family man, was murdered, brutally and senselessly. Disturbed from his sleep by a commotion, he went out into his farmyard to see what was going on and found four intruders who were in the process of stealing a litter of French bulldog puppies he and his wife had recently bred, as well as the puppies' parents, and loading them into one of two vehicles they had arrived in. Mr Ruddle died attempting to prevent them from driving off. I will hand over to Detective Superintendent Roy Grace, who has been appointed the Senior Investigating Officer, and who will give you more details.' She sat down.

Grace took a deep breath, as he had long learned it had a calming effect. What he was about to say could have a major impact on the enquiry. In as few words as possible he needed to emotionally engage every member of the public, and hopefully fire their anger at this horrible crime sufficiently to make every single one of them wrack their brains for anything, even the tiniest nugget they might recall, that could be helpful to his enquiry.

'Timothy – Tim – Ruddle was a decent man who wanted nothing more than to provide a good life for his family,' he said, aware of the nervous tremble in his voice before he settled into his stride. 'He and his wife, Sharon, made the decision a few years ago to move from London into the Sussex countryside, giving up their city jobs to become farmers. Their dream was it would provide an idyllic childhood for their children. They found it tougher to make a living off the land than they had planned, but they got an unexpected bonus due to Covid, which brought about a large increase in the value of dogs.'

He then gave a brief summary of the events that took place in the early morning of 25 March culminating in the murder of Tim Ruddle. He concluded by saying, with heartfelt emotion, 'If anyone watching has seen – during the time period I've mentioned, or outside of it – two similar vehicles in convoy, please call the Incident Room for Operation Brush on the number displayed or, completely anonymously, please call Crimestoppers on their number which is also displayed. I'm now going to hand over to Kirsty Withnall, a senior inspector with the RSPCA.'

Kirsty spoke calmly, but with palpable anger in her voice. 'We are all aware of the impact that lockdown had on the price of many popular breeds of dog. In turn this enabled criminals to cash in. These people, unlike respectable breeders, don't care about where their dogs go to. They provide fake vaccination certificates, fake documentation regarding the provenance, age and pedigree of the dogs, and often keep them in appalling conditions.

'Many dogs will be advertised for sale at vastly inflated prices. Farmed puppies bred mostly in Romania, Poland and the Republic of Ireland – but also in Wales and other parts of the UK – are being sold illegally. People desperate for a puppy are paying these inflated prices only to find they have a very sick dog which, if it survives, will have cost them in vet fees many times the original purchase price. I will now hand back to Detective Superintendent Grace.' She turned to him and sat back down.

He stood. 'Operation Brush, as you will now see on your screen, is a significant operation deploying a number of officers, including members of the Rural Crimes Team, in the search for the offenders. Our appeal this morning is to anybody who may have information as to the identity of those involved. We believe they may be local, all wore dark clothing and it appeared there were four of them in total. Two of them were younger, in their late teens or early twenties, and the other two men were older, in their thirties or early forties. They left the scene with a double-barrelled twelve-bore Webley and Scott shotgun they stole from the farmhand.

'The vehicles were described by witnesses as being an old-model Range Rover with a noisy exhaust and a cracked windscreen, and a Ford Ranger, both dark in colour, but no other details have been established to date. Were you in the area at this time, perhaps driving past the location, did you see anything suspicious around the time of the incident or perhaps in the days before? If you think you have anything that may be helpful, as I've said, please call us directly on the number now displayed or anonymously on the Crimestoppers number, also now displayed.' He read them both out. 'I will now hand back to the Assistant Chief Constable.'

Hannah Robinson stood again. 'I would like to repeat that this is a murder enquiry and we need the help of the public. Local and rural officers have been tasked with increasing routine patrols, particularly at night-time, and my message to the public is that if anything similar looks like it is happening on your land or farm, please contact us using 999, or Crimestoppers, anonymously, and do not go out to confront any intruders.' She paused and then said, 'We have time for a couple of questions.'

Several hands shot up and a barrage of shouts came from the reporters. Although he knew he shouldn't really have done, Grace favoured Siobhan Sheldrake first, nodding at her.

'Detective Superintendent,' she said, displaying no signs that she knew him personally, 'the Ruddles advertised their puppies on a number of websites, including Gumtree and Pets4Homes. Do you think it's possible the offenders found out about the Ruddles' dogs this way – and if so how do you advise legitimate dog breeders to protect themselves against this happening to them?'

'In answer to the first part of your question, I think it is highly likely the offenders would have seen the dogs advertised on one or more of these sites. Regarding how legitimate breeders can protect themselves, I would advise all dog breeders to be vigilant, and without causing too much concern, to take every security measure possible, including intruder alarms, CCTV and security lights.'

Grace next nodded at a reporter from Latest Television.

'Detective Superintendent,' the young man said, 'can you confirm that despite Mrs Ruddle dialling 999 the moment they saw the intruders, it took some time for the police to arrive at the scene? And even longer for an ambulance?'

Grace shot a glance at the ACC before responding, aware he could fall into a massive elephant trap here. 'You can rest assured we will be looking into both of these response times.'

'I've a question for the RSPCA inspector,' the BBC TV reporter called out.

Kirsty Withnall acknowledged her.

'Ms Withnall, this horrible trade must have a devastating impact on the animals themselves. What message can you give to members of the public to help protect them from buying puppies from rogue dealers?'

'It's a good question,' she replied. 'I would like to direct anyone interested in buying a puppy to our website, which is now on the screen, displaying the simple tips and advice we have suggested to establish whether you are dealing with a legitimate dog breeder or not.'

Hannah Robinson stood up. 'Thank you everyone for attending, that's all we have time for today.'

An ITV reporter called out, 'How worried are any of you that the offenders made off with a shotgun?'

'As I said earlier,' she replied, 'do not go out and confront anyone. Call 999.'

'And wait an age for an officer to turn up?' the reporter said.

His question was met with a brief, stony silence. 'I'm afraid that's all we have time for,' the ACC said. She stood up and walked out, followed by Roy Grace and Kirsty Withnall.

As he reached the door, Grace heard another voice call out, 'ACC Robinson, can you confirm that Sussex Police makes arrests in just five per cent of the county's recorded burglaries?'

Grace was sorely tempted to respond that this wasn't the fault of his overworked force, that the blame lay with budget cuts, leaving them with just six response cars at that time of night, covering eight hundred square miles of the county. But he said nothing, silently following the two women out, and privately reiterated his determination to do whatever was needed, however hard he had to work and however long it took, to find these four individuals.

If Operation Brush was going to be just one of that five per cent, he was going to make damned sure it was the one that punched above its weight.

28

The longer he practised family law, Chris Fairfax thought, cynically, the more he could understand the reasons why some family members murdered each other, rather than going through the traumas of legal intervention. It really was a lot simpler. On the surface, anyway.

It was 3.45 p.m. on a bright, sunny afternoon. Longer days, lighter evenings, and he was going home earlier than he had planned. The weekend lay ahead, no more warring families to deal with, and tomorrow night they were going to a birthday dinner at his and Katy's favourite Brighton restaurant, the Gingerman, with a group of close friends.

He pulled up behind the queued traffic at the roundabout in front of Brighton's Palace Pier. As he did so a large white lump of seagull shit splattered on the shiny bonnet of his Audi, which he'd only taken through the car wash yesterday. 'Thanks, pal!' he murmured. Gulls were an occupational hazard of seaside living and it didn't dent his good mood. He was so much looking forward to getting home to Katy, who, ever since their daughter had been born, did not work on Fridays, to Bluebell and to their new puppy, Moose. And thanks to an irate Family Law judge, he was getting a bonus extra hour with them this weekend.

As he drove on, navigating the roundabout and then along the seafront, past the Royal Albion Hotel, he shook his head and grinned. Jesus! He'd spent the past five hours, including a lunch break, in chambers with his client Garry Grimes, his wife, Elaine, and her solicitor, in front of an increasingly irascible Judge Bonner.

There were three sticking points on their divorce settlement from which neither side would budge. Their elderly West Highland White Terrier, their Christmas decorations, and Elaine's granny's bone china tea set – which his client was arguing was a wedding present and should be divided equally.

Judge Paul Bonner several times had repeated, 'You need to sort it out, this is ridiculous – and it's costing you both a fortune.'

But they hadn't sorted it out. Finally, the judge, who had a train to catch, had adjourned the hearing to Monday, telling the couple to try and agree something over the weekend, unless they wanted to make their respective lawyers even richer still.

And they married and lived happily ever after! That great myth, Chris thought, as he drove along, squinting against the low sun.

Hey, stop this, I'm happily married, I love my wife, my daughter. My life! Don't ever let us get angry, dull and resentful, please.

And he determined they never would.

His mood improved even more as he made a right turn opposite Hove Lagoon into Wish Road, a pretty street of mock-Tudor houses, some detached and some semis, and a couple of hundred yards up turned left onto the drive of their semi, parking alongside Katy's pink electric Fiat 500, cable running to the charger in the wall.

'I'm home!' he called out as he went in through the front door. Then frowned. Normally at the sound of his voice, Bluebell would come running up to him. But not this afternoon. He could hear the television on in the kitchen, the show *Pointless* that Katy was addicted to.

Chucking his bag and jacket onto the tall hall-porter's chair in the hallway, he strode past the funky black and white sign on the wall which read *LIVE, LAUGH, LOVE*, through into the kitchen, bright from the late afternoon sunlight, and to his slight surprise saw Katy in jeans and a baggy sweater kneeling beside the dog basket, tenderly stroking Moose, who was surrounded by her toys. Katy had a strange expression on her face.

'Hey, babes,' he said, bending down and kissing her. 'All good?'

'Not really,' she said.

'Oh?' Immediately some of his good mood slipped away. 'Why, what's up?'

'Moose hasn't left her bed all day – except to pee and poop on the kitchen floor a couple of times, and she's not eating.'

He shrugged. 'Maybe she's unsettled – it's her first day away from her mummy and her brothers and sisters, it's probably pretty traumatic for her.'

Katy shook her head. 'I've been googling stuff about puppies. Sure they need to sleep a lot, but they should be playful and curious, too. She's neither. I hope she's not ill. And look.' She raised her hand above the puppy's head and the dog flinched, then looked balefully at her. 'Do you think she's been mistreated?'

'I – I wouldn't have thought so – that breeder, John Peat, seemed a pretty caring guy.' He put a hand forward to try to stroke the puppy's head and she flinched again, then closed her eyes.

'She's not right,' Katy said. 'I think we should take her to the vet to get her checked over. I spoke to Kerry and she also uses Helen Bradley who's still based along New Church Road.' Kerry was her best friend and was animal-mad.

'Sure, we need to get her registered anyhow,' he said and again reached to stroke the puppy. This time Moose let him, but gave no reaction back. 'She hasn't been sick?'

'No but her poop was pretty runny.'

'Which reminds me,' he said.

'Reminds you? Of what?'

He stood, removed a plastic bucket from under the sink and

ran water into it from the hot tap. 'Got a direct hit on the bonnet from a seagull. And I had the car cleaned yesterday.'

She grinned. 'Isn't that meant to bring luck?'

He shook his head, squeezing washing-up liquid into the bowl. 'You have some weird superstitions!' He dropped in a sponge and pulled on a pair of rubber gloves. 'I'll be back in a couple of minutes.' Then he hesitated. 'Where's Bluebell? I didn't get my usual hug – is she doing homework?'

Katy shook her head. 'Having a lie-down in her room. She said she wasn't feeling great when I picked her up from school. She's got a birthday party tomorrow that she's really looking forward to, so I'm sure she'll perk up.'

'Not great in what way?'

'She said she feels a bit feverish. Her forehead is a little clammy. I took her temperature and it's just very slightly up – nothing to worry about.'

'Good,' he said. 'I'll go up and see her in a minute. Perhaps we'll take her to the GP just to be sure.'

He went back out through the front door and stopped, staring in dismay. There was a large splatter on the Audi's windscreen and another two on the roof as well as on the driver's door. And Katy's car, which just a few minutes ago had looked pristine, looked like it had suffered an aerial bombardment from an entire squadron of gulls.

Hey-ho, he thought, walking around the side of the house, past the bin store, and grabbing the end of the hose on the reel. *Looks like we're in for years of good luck!*

29

Tomorrow night the clocks went forward for UK daylight saving. This was one of the weekends of the year that Roy Grace loved the most. Waking up on Sunday morning to a day that always felt like the start of spring, even if it was windy and raining. That glorious first week of longer days and lighter evenings always gave him a feeling of optimism, no matter how dark the cases he was dealing with.

He sat at his desk in his shirtsleeves in a pensive mood. He had a lot on his mind at the moment, the most important of which was to get an Easter card and egg for Cleo and some bits for the kids for the following weekend. As well as a giant bag of mini-eggs for his goddaughter Jaye Somers, he thought, guilty he'd not seen her or her family for far too long. When he had been with Sandy, they'd been close friends with the Somers, going on several holidays together, but hey, that was life. Some friends you stayed tight with, others you drifted apart from. He made a note on his long *to-do* list to see if they could go out for a pub supper one evening. Cleo liked them and it would be good to catch up and not lose touch completely.

Then he focused back on work, on his preparation for the 6 p.m. briefing, in one hour's time. As he did so he flicked, habitually, through the serials on his computer screen – the rolling, and constantly updated, log of all incidents in the county attended by the police – looking in particular for anything dog-related. But the reported theft of Sara Gurner's dog – and her subsequent reunion with it – was the only one.

He clocked a snatch-and-grab robbery at a jeweller in Brighton's East Street yesterday afternoon, in which the thief had made off with a high-value Rolex watch and a cheap talking watch for blind people. *Odd*, he thought inconsequentially. *What was that about?* Continuing his scan, he saw nothing other than the usual litany of minor crimes and public order incidents. Just another day in the city he loved so much.

Out of interest he returned to the Sara Gurner report of her dog theft and saw there had been some follow-up before her dog was found wandering on the street later in the day. A house in Goldstone Crescent, opposite the park, had an outward-facing CCTV camera which had apparently recorded a man in a beanie grabbing the dog, putting it into a van and driving off at speed.

He emailed Luke Stanstead to get the footage; it might be worth his Operation Brush team looking at it, and perhaps have the super recognizers that Sussex Police worked with look at it also. This tiny minority of people, mostly civilian volunteers, had powers of recognition way beyond the norm. They could identify someone from a single facial feature, such as the shape of an ear, nose or chin, and match them to known criminals. They could be invaluable when there was no other form of evidence, such as fingerprints or DNA, available. Might turn out to be a lead, or might be nothing.

Next, he turned his attention to the report that had come in from Forensic Gait Analyst Professor Haydn Kelly, and the research that had been done by his team on the footprints he had photographed and taken casts of in the Ruddles' farmyard. The UK National Footwear Reference Collection was a constantly updated resource, providing pattern data on pretty much every shoe sold in shops or online. They also used the National

Footwear Database, which documented shoe prints taken from crime scenes and in custody. From the moment a shoe started being worn, the wear in tread pattern would be unique to the individual wearing them. As unique as their fingerprints.

On his screen in front of him he had images of seven different sets of footprints in the farmyard. Three had already been eliminated by Kelly, as belonging to Ruddle himself, his wife and the farmhand – although they hadn't yet fully eliminated Norris Denning as a suspect. Of the remaining four, because of heavy rain over the past few days, it was likely they were reasonably fresh. They almost certainly, Grace thought, belonged to the offenders.

Taking a moment out, he called the recently promoted Commander of Haywards Heath Police, Chief Inspector Vicky Boarder, a bright officer who had once been a detective on his Major Enquiry Team before going back to uniform.

'Roy!' she answered. 'Great to hear from you, all good?'

'All good – how's life in the sticks?' he teased.

'Haha! Apart from coming into work with muddy boots and chewing straw it's pretty challenging. What can I do for you?'

'You've a PC, Eldhos Matthew, with you, right?'

'Yes, we do.'

'He struck me as a brighter than average spark.'

'He is and very keen. Why? You're not thinking of poaching him from me, are you? I'm short-handed enough as it is.'

Grace waggled a hand in the air, even though she couldn't see it. 'I met him the night before last – on Operation Brush – I liked his energy.'

'Everyone here does – he's very popular.'

'I thought he might be. I had a brief chat with him, and he told me he's ambitious to be a detective.'

'And?'

'Just saying.'

'I know you too well, Roy. I remember when you had eyes on that young DC, Glenn Branson – and look how you've helped him. If you want to talk to PC Matthew, I won't stand in your way.'

'You're a brick.'

'Nah, I'm just a sodding martyr. In fact, I can release him for a few days for him to work with your team. He came on at 3 p.m.'

'That's great. Send him over to the incident room at head-quarters. It'll be good for him, and me too!'

Laughing, he thanked her and hung up. Then he opened the file of the drone footage of the Ruddles' farm and surrounding twenty-square-mile area that had been sent to him earlier today and began fast-forwarding through it. He was looking in particular for known criminal hotspots within close proximity. As the drone radius broadened, he saw a couple of small sites – just a handful of caravans and vehicles, but nothing on a large scale, and no pair of vehicles matching those described by the murder victim's wife.

All the same, he made a note for the Outside Enquiry Team to check them out thoroughly. It was a known scam to park up illegally on farmland, or close to it, steal farm dogs and then ransom them back. But murder was a whole different level.

His thoughts were interrupted by a knock on his door.

'Come in!' he called out.

It was Norman Potting. 'Do you have a moment, chief? Want to ask you something personal – some advice.'

Grace fondly beckoned the old war horse in.

30

Friday 26 March

Lyndsey Cheetham had from earliest childhood wanted to work with animals. She loved all creatures but held a particular soft spot for dogs – pretty much all breeds or mixes. Her ambition had once been to become a vet, but she had failed the tough entry exams to qualify for a university place. Instead, she'd settled quite happily on a veterinary nursing course.

As part of this, she needed to spend some time gaining practical experience working with animals. To her joy – well, at least initial joy – she found work in the kennels of Appletree Farm, a few miles from her parents' home in Chiddingly, East Sussex, where she still lived.

At first it had seemed a dream job. A major part of the business for Mr and Mrs Jim, who owned the farm, was breeding puppies, and with the current demand for lockdown dogs, they had converted two large, concrete-walled outbuildings to house several different breeds of dogs and their litters. There were currently over eighty puppies – all popular breeds and cross-breeds – springer spaniels, cockapoos, golden doodles, Staffies and French bulldogs as well as several adult dogs.

She'd become good friends with her co-worker in charge of the kennels, a fun and outgoing Ukrainian girl a couple of years older than her, Rosalind Esche, who had entered the UK before Brexit. They'd also become friendly with Darcy Jim who, despite her brutal stepfather and fairly cold mother, seemed genuinely kind, and to like them. None of the three young women currently had a boyfriend and Lyndsey and Rosalind had been experimenting – unsuccessfully so far – with internet dating. Darcy listened to their litany of train-crash after train-crash of disastrous dates, dispensing advice with the earnest enthusiasm of a magazine agony aunt.

Over the past months they'd been working in the kennels, during which there was a fast turnover of puppies, with some mysteriously appearing overnight to replace others that had been sold. They had all been increasingly unhappy about the conditions the dogs were kept in. They were only permitted, by the deeply unpleasant Mr Jim, to change the straw in the kennels once a week, but worse was the rations of food. The puppies were all pitifully hungry. Mrs Jim was more amenable – but only to Darcy. She made Lyndsey and Rosalind nervous.

It had got to the point where the girls sneaked in extra bags of food and treats they paid for themselves from their meagre wages. They never saw any visitors to the kennels. As far as they could work out, all sales of the puppies were done online.

On this particular chilly day, the three of them were taking their mid-afternoon tea break outside one of the sheds, as usual, so that Rosalind could smoke a cigarette. None of them was aware that Terry Jim was on the other side of the thin corrugated-iron wall, fixing wiring that mice had chewed through, for the shed's lights.

'Hey,' Lyndsey said. 'Those five blue French bulldog puppies and the two adult ones that have just arrived – do either of you think there could be any connection to that story on the news today about the farmer murdered in Balcombe? Apparently he had French bulldog puppies stolen.'

Darcy, who had long fair hair obscuring much of her face, shook her head. 'No way, it's got to be a coincidence, don't you think?'

'Maybe,' Lyndsey said, sounding unconvinced. 'He's your dad, you'd know best.'

'Stepfather,' Darcy corrected her. 'Look, I know he's a total bastard and a bully. I hate how cruel he is to all the dogs here. But he hasn't anything to do with that. He's not a bloody murderer.'

'You sure? I thought you were scared of him?' Rosalind quizzed her.

'I am, well, a bit, and you should be too,' Darcy said a little anxiously.

'I thought you said your mum knows the real reason he keeps pigs is because they eat everything. Like, *everything*!' Rosalind added.

Lyndsey frowned. 'Meaning?'

'Meaning anyone who pisses him off!' Darcy added.

'You're not serious?'

Darcy shrugged. 'Sort of, I mean he's a horrible man. I know he's tortured people over in Sty 9 – the deep one – to punish them when they piss him off, but he doesn't kill them. I'm certain he hasn't anything to do with that news story. I'd have seen something, heard something.'

'I'm not scared of him; I'm going to ask him outright. I'm sick of the condition these animals are kept in. I want to see how he reacts, if he *squirms*.' Rosalind exaggerated the last word.

'Shushhhhh. Be serious a minute, girl. I'm honestly thinking about tipping off the police about what's going on here, tell them about the bulldogs. What do you both think?' Lyndsey asked, her voice a little hushed.

'I think you should go ahead,' Rosalind said, crushing out the stub of her cigarette and quickly lighting another.

'Yeah, who doesn't want a bit of torture!' Darcy said jokingly. 'Well, don't say I didn't warn you. If I were you, I'd keep zipped. We can help the puppies in a better way. I could try to get Mum to let us clean them out and feed them more.'

'Well, I won't go to the police till after the weekend – if I do. Give us some time to see what's really going on,' Lyndsey said.

On the other side of the wall, Terry Jim had stopped replacing the chewed wire and was listening intently with rising fury. He stepped away and dialled Dallas's number on his phone.

31

Gecko was well aware of the clocks changing this weekend, with twilight being one of his best hunting times. He was cruising slowly in the van now emblazoned with the sign LANDES INTERIORS.

Still nervous after last night's close encounter with the police in the Palm Court restaurant on the pier, he wore his beanie even lower over his forehead, his collar turned up, and dark glasses. His bosses were not happy with him for failing to deliver yesterday and he was now trying extra hard. But at least, he thought happily, Elvira had been delighted with her watch. Like, super delighted, despite the evening having been cut short. He would need to make up for that, he knew, but at least she seemed to believe what he'd told her about why they'd had to run out of the restaurant. His spiel about an old enemy of his having just walked in had sorted that out.

Late afternoon and early evening were when a lot of people took their dogs out for a walk. Guilty office workers hurried home to get back and walk their mutts. Although many were working at home more often these days, they still took that time for walking them in the parks, throwing balls and bending down with their plastic bags to scoop up their poop. During the winter at that time, he was all but invisible. But now, with lighter evenings, it was just a little harder.

He glanced, proudly, at the gold Rolex on his wrist: 5.25 p.m. Thanks to the overcast sky, it already felt like dusk, although sunset was still a good hour away. As he cruised slowly along Shirley Drive, past Hove Recreation Ground, he was looking over to his left, into the large park, at the people walking their dogs. He had a new, additional task today. An instruction to find a short-haired female dachshund puppy. The photograph of one was displayed on his iPhone screen. He was going to get it right this time.

He watched a massive badly trained dog leaping up at its owner's chest – nearly as tall as the man and almost knocking him over. Then, a short distance beyond, he saw a young girl, a goth-type, walking what looked like three unruly dachshund puppies on a lead. And struggling with them.

At that moment a black cat ran across the road right in front of him.

A sign!

Some people thought a black cat crossing their path was bad luck, but his mum had always told him the opposite. He turned sharp left into Hove Park Road and immediately saw a parking space to his left. Oh yes, good luck indeed! His mum was right. She was always right.

He pulled into the space and checked the picture of the dog again. A match for sure. He jumped out of the van, scrambled over a bush and sprinted across the wet grass towards the teenage girl in her studded black jacket, black hair, tight jeans and Doc Martens, trying to untwist the leads of her three dogs from around her legs.

'Hey!' he said. 'Need some help?'

'I'm just trying to help my nan out – these crazy things – I'm not really a dog person.'

'How old are they?' he asked.

'Twelve weeks – this is their first time out – I— Stop it, you little bastard!'

'I'll help you,' he said. 'I used to have dachshunds, I know what they're like – they can be crazy.'

'Oh, thanks.'

'Are they male or female?'

The leads were getting even more twisted around her legs.

'Stop it, calm down! Max, Dufoss, Doris!'

'Doris?' he said.

She pointed at the one attached to a pink lead. It was running crazily around her, winding the leash around her ankles.

'I've got her!' Gecko said, kneeling down and grabbing the dog by its pink collar.

'Thanks. Why are you wearing sunglasses?'

'Yeah, right, I see better with them.'

'What's your name?'

'Darren,' he said, untwisting the pink leash, and walking the dog – Doris – around her twice. There were still the leashes of the other two dogs well twisted around her legs. Then, scooping Doris in his arms – the dog was heavier than he had expected – he sprinted away.

'Hey!' the girl yelled. 'Hey, hey!'

He turned and saw she had fallen flat on her face.

Result! he thought, reaching the van. He clambered in, dumped Doris on the passenger seat, then looked across. The girl was struggling to her feet, totally tangled up in the leads of the other two dogs.

What a result!

A female dachshund, too young to have been spayed. Mr and Mrs Jim would be well pleased with him. He started the engine, checked his mirror and drove off. It was going to be a proper payday. Then he would go to Elvira and make it up to her for the crappy night yesterday.

Thank you, black cat!

32

Norman Potting could have taken retirement on his full pension some years earlier, but he had chosen to stay on and was now in his late fifties. There were plenty of senior colleagues who would have liked to have seen dinosaurs like him gone, but Roy Grace constantly fought his corner.

Sure, Potting was old-fashioned, sometimes his comments were close to the line, but rarely offensive these days and he was a damned good detective. The team accepted him for what he was, and all were more than capable of slapping him down if needed. He was one of the finest detectives Grace had ever worked with, with decades of experience that the younger generation lacked, and he solidly believed the day Potting did hand in his warrant card would be a big loss to the job Sussex Police existed for – *to catch criminals and keep the community safe.*

Not long back, after falling in love with one of his team members, Bella Moy, Potting had gone through a transformation, losing his old comb-over in favour of a more modern style and sharpening up his wardrobe. Ever since Bella's tragic death, Grace had noticed the Detective Sergeant not paying so much attention to his appearance. But he was glad he'd not started smoking again, after he'd recently had a cancer of the larynx scare. Though he did sometimes see him take a sneaky puff on his vape.

'Tell me?' Grace asked, as Potting sat down in front of his desk.

'I need some advice about a young lady, Roy,' he said, a little sheepishly.

Grace smiled sympathetically. Potting had been married four times, three had failed and the other was annulled. He would have married Bella, but she'd died in the line of duty. He would have liked nothing better than to hear that the DS had finally found a new soulmate.

'The thing is,' Potting said in his rural Devon burr, 'I met this lady during chemo. We were both in the hospital together having our treatment. I've rather fallen for her.' He shrugged and fell silent.

'OK,' Grace said, trying not to be distracted by the drone footage of fields and farm buildings on his screen, which he'd paused. 'She feels the same about you?'

'She does, Roy, but life's a bitch, isn't it?'

'Sometimes – you've had more than your fair share of that.'

Potting gave him a wan smile. 'I really care about her, you see. No one will ever replace Bella, but I feel – you know – almost as strongly for Heather as I did for Bella.'

'That's good, isn't it?' Grace said. But he had the feeling there was something else to come.

'Well, Roy, the thing is, after I came through the treatment with an all-clear, I was so elated that day that I invited her out to dinner – and it's been going pretty well since.' His eyes lit up. 'I think I'm in love again.'

Grace stared back at him. God, he was so fond of this old monster. 'I'm very happy for you, Norman.'

Potting shook his head. 'The chemo seems to be working at the moment, but I don't know what the future really holds for her.'

'OK,' Grace said. 'So that's good news the treatment is working, Norman. Focus on the positives.'

'I know, Roy. I love her, I really love her.'

'Tell me more about her – how old is she, has she been married before, does she have kids?'

'She's fifty-eight, two kids, one in Canada and the other in Australia. She's high up in HR at a recruitment firm. Ex is an idiot she's not seen for ten years.'

'What does your heart tell you?'

'She's a keeper. Shit. Did you ever see that old film *Love Story*?'

Grace shook his head and smiled. 'I bet Glenn has, you know he loves a good romance.'

'Saw it when I was a kid. Ryan O'Neal and Ali MacGraw. He falls in love with this girl and then she's diagnosed with terminal cancer. Moved me to tears – now I feel I'm living it.'

'But, Norman, she isn't at that stage yet. I guess if it was me, and I truly loved her, I'd be hoping she makes a full recovery, like you have. In any sense, none of us know how much time we have, do we? I think about that every day myself with Bruno being taken from us so young. But if you really do love her, then make time with her count. I say go and get on with it!'

Potting looked at his watch. 'Thanks, chief. I know we've got the briefing in half an hour. I appreciate your advice. I really do.'

Grace smiled and shook his head. 'My first marriage wasn't exactly textbook perfection, Norman. I read somewhere, once, you have to make choices in life, and live with the consequences not only of your actions, but of your inactions. I don't know if that's of any help.'

Potting nodded thoughtfully.

As he did so, an email pinged in on Grace's computer. Glancing at it, he saw it was from Luke Stanstead. The CCTV footage he'd requested only a short while ago of the dog theft in Hove Park yesterday morning.

Potting stood up. 'Thanks, chief. It's good to be able to talk this through with someone.'

'I don't know that I've been much help.'

'You have,' he replied. 'Hugely.'

'If you'd like to have a drink one day after work and talk more sometime?'

'I would, I'd like that.' Potting thanked him once more and headed for the door.

As soon as the DS had walked out and closed the door behind him, Grace turned his focus back to work. He watched more of the drone video, but it wasn't telling him much more than he already knew about the murder scene and environs. He stopped it and then played the footage Stanstead had just sent.

And watched it with growing interest.

33

According to Luke Stanstead, the owners of the house in Goldstone Crescent, opposite Hove Park, had recently had their almost brand-new Porsche Cayenne stolen from their driveway during the night. As a result they'd installed two outward-facing CCTV cameras, one directed down their driveway, the other, wider-angle, covering the road and the tree-lined border of the park beyond it.

It was this wider-angle footage Roy Grace was looking at, but it was very blurred, as if the lens was misted. Parked across the road was a white Transit panel van with the name, which he could just make out, JASON PLUNKETT PUMPS AND DRAINS emblazoned along the side in orange and black. A short-looking man with a very pale face, in a beanie, was in the driver's seat, the window partly open, but the image was too unclear to make out his features. Grace watched as he appeared to light a cigarette and toss what he presumed was a match out onto the road.

Faintly, Grace heard a shout. It sounded like, '*Zulu!*'

A moment later he heard it again, louder, more high-pitched. 'ZULU!'

The van driver ducked down, out of sight. As he did so, a double-decker bus drove past, momentarily blocking the view. When it had gone, Grace saw the van driver staring in the direction of the park with a pair of binoculars held to his face.

More vehicles passed.

Suddenly the van driver jumped out and ran around to the pavement, out of sight on the far side of the van.

'ZULU!' the cry came again, from somewhere close in the park. It was followed by, 'Thank you, thank you so much!'

Moments later the driver reappeared, holding a struggling black and white dog, with floppy ears, in his arms – a poodle type, Grace recognized from his limited but growing knowledge of dogs. He watched in horror as the man opened the driver's door and threw the dog in, as if it was nothing more than a rugby ball, and jumped in after it, slamming his door.

At that moment a woman in a red cagoule and wellington boots appeared, looking frantic. Sara Gurner, according to Stanstead. She ran to the front of the van as if to try to prevent it from driving off. 'It's my dog!' she screamed. 'I'm the owner!'

The van reversed and then drove off at speed, almost running her over.

Grace watched the distraught woman standing in the road, shouting and gesticulating at the van.

Then a Lycra-clad cyclist swerved past her, shook a fist and shouted something.

He halted the video. Sara Gurner and the kind stranger – *not*, he thought.

He wound the footage back then zoomed in on the van driver's face, but it was just a blur. He frowned. This person had clearly been on the lookout for something and had taken this dog, Zulu, but only to set him free a few hours later. Why?

Sara Gurner had told him the dog had been neutered. Was that the reason? Had the driver been on the lookout for a stud dog he – or whoever he worked for – could breed from? And when he realized this one had been neutered, he'd dumped it?

This was a whole new world of crime he knew so little about. He glanced at his watch – twenty-four minutes to the next briefing.

He spent part of it taking a quick scan through dogs being offered for sale on websites, looking in particular at poodle cross-breeds. Curious, he also looked up the advert for the spaniel puppies he was going to see tomorrow for comparison. They did look adorable, he had to admit. Next he called up the intel on known organized crime gangs operating in the Sussex area and surrounding counties. If he was going to solve the murder of Tim Ruddle quickly, he needed to do a crash course in this whole new – and clearly highly lucrative – world of dog crime.

A world that sickened him.

34

'ZULU!' the cry came. Followed by, 'Thank you, thank you so much!'

The video Grace had seen half an hour ago was playing again now on the monitor on the wall of the Major Crime Suite conference room, his whole team watching.

'It's my dog!' the woman in the red cagoule yelled. 'It's my dog! I'm the owner!'

They watched as the white van raced off, almost hitting the woman. Then a cyclist appeared, swerving past her and shaking his fist.

Grace froze the video with his remote.

'Looks like she thought the van driver was helping her stop her dog running off,' Glenn Branson commented. 'For a few moments.'

Grace turned to Stanstead. 'Luke, can you get Digital Forensics to see if they can enhance the video and maybe get a clearer image of this man? Perhaps enough to give to a super recognizer as I suggested to you earlier.'

'Brighton CID are already on it, sir – the video came from them. They believe it could well be a current Person of Interest to them involved in dog theft – name of Marion Willingham.'

'A female?' Velvet Wilde quizzed.

'No, male.' Stanstead spelled it. 'It can be a male or female name. M-a-r-i-o-n.'

'John Wayne!' Branson announced. 'That was his real name. Marion Morrison!' Narrowing his eyes, he said in a deep cod American drawl, 'Talk low, talk slow and don't say too much.'

Jack Alexander asked, 'Wasn't he the cowboy?'

Branson gave him a bemused look. 'The cowboy? He was The Duke!'

The young DS shook his head.

'He died in 1979. You guys need to read up on your movie history. This guy was a legend!'

'Does the name Marion Willingham ring a bell with anyone?' Grace asked.

Several of the team shook their heads.

Grace looked at the analyst. 'What intel do we have on this charmer?'

'He's thirty-two,' Luke said. 'Grew up in a single-parent family in Moulsecoomb; his mother was never on our radar – worked, still works, in a nail salon. He's distinctive-looking – pale skin, big bulging wide-set eyes. He was nicked a couple of times in his early teens on suspicion of drug dealing but never convicted. Got six months for joyriding when he was eighteen. Then eighteen months for supplying cannabis when he was twenty-three. His nickname is Gecko.'

Grace looked puzzled. 'Why?'

'Because of his looks, boss. Also he was linked to Clifford Keele for several years.'

Clifford Keele was a name well known to the police. The third generation of a venerable Brighton crime family, with tentacles in protection racketeering, prostitution, cigarette smuggling, and in more recent times drug dealing, before moving to the countryside on his release from prison. Grace remembered Keele only too well. Ten years back, when he had been the Duty Inspector at John Street, Keele had ordered the petrol bombing of a Turkish kebab house, when the proprietor had defaulted on his protection payments. Keele had received a sentence of fifteen years, of which he'd served ten.

'Is Gecko linked to anyone now?' Grace asked.

'We haven't linked him yet,' Luke said.

'Homegrown scum,' Potting added.

'Jack,' Grace turned to DS Alexander. 'Anything from the house-to-house?'

'No, boss. We brought the farmhand in for a cognitive witness interview to see if he could remember more. Mr Denning gave us a slightly clearer description of two of the offenders in terms of height and build, and their accents – both local-sounding – but not much else that's of any help at this stage.'

'That could be useful,' Grace said. 'It tallies with the report from the ANPR cameras that the vehicles didn't leave the Sussex area. It's further indication we could be looking at a local crime family.'

'I've been on to Chief Inspector Steve Biglands,' Alexander said. 'He's sent me a list of all known organized crime gangs operating within this area.'

'Good luck with those,' Potting said.

'I thought you'd like to come with me when I visit them, Norman,' Alexander said with a grin.

'Happily!' Potting smiled. 'To see my old mate Cliff. One of those gangs tucked my ex-mother-in-law up for ten grand for resurfacing her driveway. They might intimidate little old ladies, but not a tough bastard like me.'

'Which one of your ex-mothers-in-law?' asked Velvet Wilde.

'The only one I liked.' He paused. 'Or maybe I should say, the only one who liked me.'

'I've found a report of a farmer in Beddingham, East Sussex – a Mr Tony Monnington, who had his dog stolen near the round-about two months ago, and then ransomed back to him for two hundred quid,' Luke Stanstead said.

'Worth looking into?' Grace asked.

He shook his head. 'They're already under local police surveillance. Just a bunch of messers.'

Grace nodded then said, 'Have we had much response from our press conference?'

'There's an article up on the *Argus* website already, and they're planning to run it on page three tomorrow,' DC Nick Nicholl said. 'There might be a nice photo of you, boss.'

'Page three?' Potting quizzed. 'Did you keep your clothes on, chief?'

Several of the team laughed. 'Sorry to disappoint you, Norman,' Grace replied. 'Have we had any calls?'

'Fifty-two, so far,' Emma-Jane Boutwood replied. 'Mostly time-wasters, and one batty lady who'd lost her hibernating hedgehog, which she thinks was stolen.'

'A prickly case,' Potting commented.

'But there was one that I'm following up,' E-J said. 'It was a woman who saw a man acting strangely in St Ann's Well Gardens yesterday. Her description fits the man we just saw on the video – a short man with a very pale face, in a beanie and anorak.'

'Strangely in what way, E-J?' Grace asked.

'She said he seemed to be watching people with dogs, and on a couple of occasions ducked behind trees, as if not wanting to be spotted. I've got her contact details.'

'Be worth going to see her and having a chat.'

'Will do, sir.'

Grace looked down at his notes then turned to the Family Liaison Officer, DC Gallichan. 'Emma, has Mrs Ruddle given you a list of everyone who visited the farm in the past few days?'

'She has, and they are all being followed up, sir.'

'Has she said anything else at all of possible significance? Any strangers sighted on the property in the days before the murder?

Any unfamiliar vehicles in the area? Did her husband have any concerns about anyone?'

DC Gallichan shook her head. 'Sharon – Mrs Ruddle – just repeated that they, like most people, were worried about money, especially with a young family and the constant need to diversify the farm – which explains why Mr Ruddle was so desperate to stop the offenders.'

'Were the puppies insured for theft?'

'The two adult dogs had pet insurance, but that was all. I have got some more photographs of the parents of the puppies from her,' she said, and circulated several copies around the table.

'Oh my God, they're gorgeous!' said E-J.

Grace thanked her and turned to DC Nicholl. 'Nick, you spent part of yesterday and today trawling through the online sites offering puppies for sale, for any dogs matching any of these. How has that gone?'

'It's a massive task, sir. I've got several hundred possible matches to the puppies being advertised around the country, so I'm focusing on a local radius of thirty miles, to start with.'

'Thanks, Nick,' Grace said, then addressed the whole team. 'You've all viewed the drone footage of the farm and surrounding area. Has anyone spotted anything significant?'

No one had.

He turned to the financial analyst, Emily Denyer. 'Have you found anything of relevance in the Ruddles' finances, Emily?'

She shook her head. 'No, boss – what I've seen so far tallies with what Mrs Ruddle has told me – and what Emma has just said. They've been struggling a bit since they bought the Old Homestead Farm – on a large mortgage. They've just about washed their face, but that's all.'

'Any life insurance policy on Tim Ruddle?'

'None that I've found, so far,' she replied.

Grace clicked on the remote, and a group of seven usable sets of footprints appeared on the monitor. 'I received these this after-noon from Professor Kelly, the Forensic Gait Analyst, via our Exhibits Officer. The first two, marked Exhibit A and B, are iden-tified as belonging to Mr and Mrs Ruddle. The third belongs to the farmhand, Norris Denning. The other four potentially belong to the offenders. The good news is that the UK National Footwear Reference Collection has identified matches. The bad news is two are popular brands of trainers, one is a popular work boot and the other gum boots, widely available. If we tried to identify when and where they were purchased, and by who, it would tie all of you up for the next two years, at least. And no hits in the National Footwear Database for the wear patterns as yet.'

'But if we catch the offenders, these footprints might help put them at the scene, boss,' Glenn Branson said.

'Very definitely,' Grace replied. 'There might be thousands of identical pairs of a brand, but according to Chris Gee, only one pair will be an exact match to each of those prints. The process they use is called feathering. This can be unique which will be very helpful.' He was interrupted by his private phone ringing and saw it was Cleo. He fleetingly thought about sending it to voicemail, then worried just in case it was anything urgent. Raising an apologetic hand, he answered quietly.

'Sorry to disturb you,' Cleo said. 'The puppy people we're seeing tomorrow just rang to confirm we are definitely going – they say they've got a waiting list of four people desperate for that same puppy.'

'We're going,' he said. '3.30 p.m. just outside Bournemouth, right? Glenn's covering for me tomorrow.' He glanced at the DI, who nodded.

Ending the call, he turned back to his team. 'OK,' he said. 'We don't yet know what we're dealing with. The offenders could have been a small bunch of local criminals who hadn't been expecting any resistance and panicked. Or they might be part

PETER JAMES

of an organized crime gang fully prepared to kill anyone who got in their way. My hypothesis is the latter. The number plates on both vehicles clocked by the ANPR cameras matched the vehicles' makes, but actually belonged to a different Range Rover and Ford Ranger pickup, both of which have been eliminated from our enquiries. But both these vehicles live in East Sussex. All the more reason to suspect we are looking for a reasonably local gang. Does anyone have anything to add at this stage?'

No one did.

'I'm extremely concerned by the level of violence these people are prepared to use. Right now every dog owner in the county – and elsewhere – is at risk. And I know several of you are dog owners. The Chief Constable is very disturbed by this horrible crime and has asked me to report to her daily on Operation Brush. Which means each of you is going to be under her eagle eye. We need to find them quickly – and we're going to.'

35

Dr Zoe Dixon-Smith was a small, bubbly woman in her late thirties, with curly brown hair bunched tight on her head and a warm personality that seemed to fill her tiny office. Katy Fairfax had drawn up a complicated will for her some five years ago.

'So, what seems to be the matter, lovely?' she said, addressing a pale-looking Bluebell, seated on her mother's knee.

The seven-year-old, dressed in jeans, a fleece top and sparkly trainers, stared back at her vacantly beneath her tangle of long blonde curls, then turned to her mother.

'She's not eaten anything for over twenty-four hours,' Katy said. 'Her head feels clammy and she's running a temperature of 37.2.'

'What's that mark on your nose from?' Zoe Dixon-Smith leaned forward to peer more closely at it.

'A puppy nipped me when we picked up Moose,' Bluebell replied quietly.

'Moose?'

'Our new puppy,' Chris explained.

The doctor stood up and came around from her desk, peering closer at Bluebell. 'Let's have a look at you, shall we?' Turning to Katy, she asked if she could put her on the examination table. Then, when Bluebell was seated, legs dangling over the side, she pinged a thermometer at her forehead and, a moment later, frowned at the readout. 'Feeling rotten are you, my dear?'

'Yep,' Bluebell replied.

'I love your name, Bluebell. It's a very happy name.'

Bluebell looked at her woozily and managed a smile.

'She's been sick several times,' her father said.

'What's coming up?'

'The last few times, just bile,' her mother replied.

'You're definitely running a fever, aren't you?' Dr Dixon-Smith stared at Bluebell. 'Let's see what's going on, shall we?' She turned to Katy. 'From my records, you've had Covid, three months ago, right?'

Katy nodded.

Then, addressing Chris, she said, 'But you escaped it?'

'So far.'

'OK.' Turning to Bluebell, she asked, 'Have many children at your school had Covid?'

'Quite a few,' Katy answered for her daughter. 'Bluebell does regular lateral flows – we did one this morning and it was negative.'

For the next ten minutes Dr Dixon-Smith carried out a thorough examination of Bluebell, while Chris and Katy watched, occasionally giving their daughter reassurances. Finally, the doctor returned to her chair behind her desk and faced the three of them.

'What do you think it is? Covid?' Katy asked.

Giving a bright smile, but one that was short of a couple of bulbs, Zoe Dixon-Smith said, with a breeziness that didn't quite ring true, 'I'll do a PCR test, but she's not displaying typical Covid symptoms. It's probably just a bug that's going round.' Then she added, with a frown, 'When did that scratch on your nose happen?'

'Yesterday,' Katy said, answering for her again. 'It was a puppy in the same vehicle as Moose. A Staffie bull terrier sort. It was in a separate dog cage on its own and Bluebell was playing with it. But don't panic, she had a tetanus jab last year.'

'Hmm, it looks a nasty scratch – a little bit livid,' the doctor said, pulling out a prescription pad. 'I'll give you some antibiotic cream.' She scribbled a prescription on her pad then looked up. 'This puppy, how exciting! What breed is it?'

'A golden doodle,' Chris Fairfax said.

'Such lovely dogs!' the doctor replied. 'I have two! What fun and what a great choice! You're going to adore her.'

'Yes,' Katy said. 'I'm sure we will. She's just getting used to us at the moment – I think she's a bit shy.'

The doctor cocked her head sideways, focused on Bluebell and did the PCR test. 'They take a while to settle, don't they. Where did you get her, a nice breeder?'

'Yes, we found what we hope was a good one, as much as you can know a stranger,' Chris said. 'Moose is a bit quiet at the moment but maybe that's just her personality.'

'How old is she?'

'Around eight weeks,' Katy replied.

'No doubt she had all the vaccinations?'

'Oh yes,' Chris said. 'We have all the documentation.'

'Good. And you met her parents, presumably?'

Chris and his wife looked at each other. 'Well, no, not exactly. It's pretty hard to find golden doodles at the moment – there's been a lot of demand for them,' Chris said. 'We found this one on the internet but the breeder, who's based in Wales, was very helpful and open.'

The doctor smiled. 'Good, excellent!' She tore off the prescription form and handed it to Katy. 'This is for antibiotic cream to apply to Bluebell's nose three times a day. Give her Calpol and Nurofen and plenty of fluids, but if her temperature goes up further, please call me.'

They thanked the doctor and left.

As they closed the door behind them, Zoe Dixon-Smith sat for some moments in concerned thought. Something about the little girl's temperature, heart rate and blood pressure did not chime, not for a girl of that age. It wasn't Covid-related, it was something else. Hopefully it would all settle down.

36

Roy Grace glanced in the rear-view mirror at Noah, strapped in his child seat, fast asleep – at last. The little chap had been chattering excitedly for much of the past hour about the puppies they were on their way to see. It was a fine, bright afternoon, the dazzling sun shining through the windscreen as he drove west along the M27 motorway, bypassing Southampton. He had his visor down and Cleo was wearing dark sunglasses.

He was in a happy mood, enjoying a rare long drive in his beloved Alfa, and pleased to escape the pressure cooker intensity of Operation Brush for just a few hours. He was genuinely interested by this adventure, seeing the springer spaniel puppies with Noah but making sure to manage his expectations. They still really wanted a rescue dog so were making the journey more out of curiosity, but he knew there was a small chance they'd buy one if they met the right dog.

As ever, during those critical early days of a murder enquiry, he was still churning over the case in his mind as he drove, trying to think of anything he might have missed.

'Dream a Little Dream of Me' was playing on the sound system. Cleo reached across and stroked Grace's left arm. 'Do you?' she asked, smiling.

'Do I – what?'

'Dream a little dream of me?'

'All the time.'

'Fibber!'

'No, it's true, I do!'

'That's how I feel about you,' she said. 'I love this song. Whenever I hear it, I think of you. Us.'

He nodded, smiling fondly, watching the sign coming up ahead for the turn-off. 'I do too. It's our song.'

They had danced to it at their wedding. The opening dance, just them, alone, entwined on the dance floor.

'So, did you think back then that three years later we'd be driving to Bournemouth to look at some puppies, with a three-year-old on the back seat and our baby at home with the nanny?'

'If I had, I'd have bolted for the door!' he said.

She punched him playfully. 'Charming. Why the hell do I love you?'

'My good looks? Genius in the kitchen? My general all-round brilliance? Because I'm a great lover?'

She windmilled her hands. 'Keep going.'

'None of those?' he said, feigning hurt.

'Sorry to disappoint you.'

'So, tell me?'

'I've no idea!' She nuzzled her head against his shoulder. 'But I do, I love you.'

'I love you, too.' And he did. He was in a place that over a decade ago when his first wife, Sandy, had vanished, he'd thought he would never ever be in again.

Cleo leaned across and kissed him on the cheek as he drove in the fast lane, passing a lorry then a car towing a caravan, watching his speed carefully, as always. In his early days on the force, traffic cops were given the moniker Black Rats, because those rats would eat their own progeny. And it was still true today, many of them took a special delight in booking police officers.

For the next thirty minutes after turning off the motorway, Roy Grace followed the directions of the satnav carefully. It took them into a residential area on the outskirts of Bournemouth, and finally into the street Grace had been given. A wide, tree-lined avenue with smart detached houses fronted by well-tended gardens.

'Looks like we're in Bournemouth's Millionaires' Row,' Cleo said.

He nodded, driving slowly now, looking for the house number and name.

'There, on the right!' she called out. 'Number 32, Fernlea.'

He pulled up just beyond two brick pillars, painted white, at the bottom of a steep driveway and switched off the engine. They climbed out, and Cleo unbuckled Noah's seat belt then lifted him out. A tall yew hedge hid the front of the house from view. Each taking one of Noah's hands, they walked up the hard surface of the driveway, towards a dark-coloured Peugeot parked at the top in front of a garage, and saw the front door on the left. Grace pressed the bell. Immediately on the far side he heard a dog barking.

The door was opened by a stocky man, in his mid-fifties Grace guessed, holding a barking spaniel by the collar. He was wearing a thick cardigan over a plaid shirt, baggy blue jeans and carpet slippers, and looked at them suspiciously. 'Yes?'

'We're here to see Mrs Hartley,' Cleo said.

'I'm her husband, Tom,' he said guardedly, in an accent that sounded more Scouse than Bournemouth.

'We made an appointment to see a puppy.'

His demeanour immediately changed to a warm smile. 'Ah, right, Mr and Mrs Grace would it be?'

'Correct.'

'Come on in, come on in! The missus is expecting you – she's the doggie one in our family, her passion!' They now heard the yipping and yapping of puppies.

'You don't sound from around these parts,' Grace said as they followed him through the small hall into a large, bright open-plan living-dining area, with a full-length conservatory at the far end, sunlight shining. It was pleasantly furnished if a little sterile, Grace thought, looking around, taking it all in. The spaniel ran off into another room.

'No, I'm from Liverpool, but the missus was born down here, and we decided to retire down south. And breed dogs, like, for a hobby.'

Noah broke free from his parents, and ran excitedly across to a large basket full of lively brown and white puppies in the middle of the room, where a woman kneeled, teasing them with a ball of paper.

'Madge, love, Mr and Mrs Grace are here!'

She turned and greeted them with a warm smile, then stood up. She was plump, parcelled in a bright smock dress, with a pleasant, dimpled face, her grey-brown hair pulled back into a bun. She reminded Grace of one of those Russian dolls that had endless smaller copies inside them. 'So very nice to meet you both!' she said. Then she kneeled to Noah's height. 'Are you going to help choose the dog?'

'Which is our puppy?' Noah asked, looking very serious.

She ducked into the basket and lifted one up. 'This little monkey with the blue collar – this is the one I saved for you.'

'What's his name?' the boy asked.

'Well, he's Mr Blue, we've nicknamed him Wally, but you can give him any name you like!'

'God, he's adorable, but, Noah, we're just looking, remember. We need to be absolutely sure of the right dog for us!' Cleo said, taking the dog in her arms and stroking one of his big, floppy ears.

'He's very beautiful,' Madge said. 'His grandmother won Best of Breed at Crufts – I have the certificate.'

'Can I hold him?' Noah asked.

Beaming, Cleo handed the dog to him. Noah held him

awkwardly, his hind legs dangling, before releasing him. He dropped onto the pristine cream carpet and ran out of the room. Noah ran after him, his little arms flapping, shouting, 'Wally, Wally!'

They heard barking coming from another room.

'Please have a seat,' Madge said, beckoning them to one of two off-white sofas. 'Let me get you both a drink. Tea or coffee?'

'A cup of tea would be very welcome,' Cleo said. Grace nodded as they both sat down, the Scouser settling opposite them.

'And something for the little one?' The woman winked. 'I'll get him an ice cream – does he have a favourite flavour?'

'He's fine.'

'Chocolate? Vanilla?'

'Honestly, he's fine, thank you,' Cleo said.

The woman raised a finger in the air and grinned mischievously. 'I know what he'd like, a Nobbly Bobbly! I'm a grandmother and I know no child can resist those. I'll see if I can find one in the freezer!' She hurried out of the room.

'Quite a contrast, Tom, Liverpool to Bournemouth,' Grace said, glancing around the room.

The Scouser pursed his lips and nodded. 'We like it here, better climate.'

'So this is your retirement hobby, breeding dogs?' Cleo asked.

'The wife's really,' he replied and shrugged. 'You know, something the missus always wanted to do, like. She's loving it.'

'Can we see the parents?' Cleo asked, remembering from what she had read that it was important to assess the parents before buying a puppy.

'I'm afraid the dad was a pedigree stud we used for the mating, so we don't have him here. Ruby, the mum, you just saw. The wife's locked her away – we don't want her distressed, like, seeing her puppies go – they'll all be gone by this time tomorrow.'

Noah came back into the room, holding the wriggling puppy close to its neck, its legs dangling again and kicking. He kneeled on the floor and put his arms around him. The puppy was calm for some moments. 'Wally,' he said. 'Wally, Wally!' He stroked one of its ears.

'Darling, be gentle!' Cleo admonished.

The barking from another room continued.

The woman came in a few minutes later with a tray with two mugs of tea, a jug of milk, a bowl of sugar, a plate of biscuits and an ice lolly in an opened wrapper. She set the tray down on the coffee table and gave the lolly to Noah. He let go of the puppy, which shot out of the room again.

'You've a beautiful home,' Roy Grace said.

The woman, settling next to her husband, beamed. 'Oh, we love it here!'

He was trying to figure her accent. It was more Scouse infused with Welsh than local Dorset, to his ear. 'How long have you lived down here?'

'Six years now,' her husband said, giving her a pointed look.

'Yes, yes, six years now,' she answered. 'So I'll go and get the papers – Wally's had his second set of vaccinations, so he's good to go. You brought a basket with you for the car?'

Cleo frowned. 'No, actually we didn't – we thought this would be our first visit – we didn't realize he was ready to go. We should have made it clear we just want to have a look at him to see if he's right for us. We have another dog at home, you see, so we need to make sure they will get on together. I hope you understand. Can we see the mother again, please?'

'I'll fetch her.'

Mrs Hartley went out of the room and returned, almost dragging the reluctant spaniel on a lead. It showed no interest in the puppies.

'Hello, Ruby!' Cleo said, leaning down and stroking it. 'You're a clever mum, aren't you!' The dog sat and allowed her to stroke her head.

'You're in the front of a queue of ten people for this puppy,' her husband said. 'No problem if you don't want him. You brought the cash? Two thousand five hundred pounds?'

'We've brought two hundred and fifty, for the deposit, but we just need a moment to think carefully,' Grace said, ignoring Cleo's strange look. 'I thought the deposit was what you wanted at this stage?'

The Scouser shook his head, looking angry suddenly. 'My wife made it very clear to you when she spoke to yours, that we expected you to bring the full purchase price in cash.'

Cleo looked at Roy again. 'I thought you . . .' Then, seeing his raised hand, she fell silent.

'I do have the cash. But it's a big decision – would you give my wife and me five minutes to discuss this?' Grace asked.

'Yes, of course, but as I said, I've got a whole queue of people behind you.'

Grace and Cleo gave each other a knowing look and ushered a puzzled-looking Noah back outside, closing the front door behind them. Roy glanced at the rear of the Peugeot, memorizing the number plate, and they all got back inside the Alfa Romeo.

37

'What about Wally?' Noah said. 'Is Wally coming with us?'

'No, darling.' Cleo looked at him. 'We won't be buying from them. They are not good people and Wally is not the right dog for us.'

'It is a lovely house,' Roy said, tapping the Google app on his phone.

'Yes, very suspicious, I'd say.'

Focused on the phone, still tapping, he said, 'Exactly. Did you have a good look around the living room?'

'Yes,' she said. 'No mess whatsoever.'

He nodded. 'Yes, and the apparent mother who didn't exactly rush over to her puppies. And no photographs. Mrs Hartley said she was a grandmother. But there wasn't a single photograph – no pictures of them, their kids, their grandchildren.'

'Yeah, that is so true, I didn't notice that, but I did see that it was all too spotless.'

'I like Wally!' Noah said.

Cleo looked over her shoulder. 'We like him too, darling. Daddy and I are talking, OK?'

'Cream carpets everywhere and not a stain on them that I could see,' Grace said. 'They're breeding puppies? In my humble experience, puppies pee and poop everywhere constantly, until they're house-trained, right?'

She nodded.

Grace tapped his phone again for some moments, then handed it to her. 'Have a look.'

The page he had open was on the Airbnb website. It showed the house they had just been inside. Fernlea, Bournemouth. Next to it was a calendar showing the availability dates, with the current week and the following one blocked out.

Cleo studied it then looked at him. 'So they rent the house through Airbnb in order to sell the puppies?'

Grace nodded.

'That's awful.'

'Almost certainly rogue dealers, who've rented the house to make themselves appear respectable. Those puppies have very probably been imported illegally from somewhere in the Eastern bloc.'

'But what about the pedigree certificate and all the other paperwork, how do they get that?'

'Fake. All fake.'

Grace pulled his job phone out of his jacket pocket and rang the Control Room. When the operator answered he said, 'This is Detective Superintendent Grace, I need a check on a Peugeot, index Golf X-Ray One Four Golf Papa X-Ray.'

He waited for some moments until the details came back. Its tax and insurance were up to date. Then the name and address of the current owner.

Grace thanked her, ended the call and turned to Cleo. 'That car parked in the driveway is owned by someone called Michael Kendrick. As an educated guess, I'd say that is the name of the person who has rented this house, not Tom Hartley. I can't believe this has happened to us right before our eyes. Lucky we were cautious from the start and had the sense not to take that poor dog. If I'd not been wrapped up in this investigation, I'm not sure I'd have paid much attention to the house. Unbelievable, isn't it? You'd better tell Charlie about the puppy she suggested.'

'Yeah, I'll text her to look out for a nice rescue dog for us instead and stop encouraging us to support criminal activity!' Cleo said jokingly.

Grace called the Operation Brush Incident Room and gave the name and address of the house to Luke Stanstead, asking him to check with Airbnb, as a matter of urgency, the names of the current renters. Then he started the car and drove off.

'What about Wally?' Noah began crying.

Cleo turned and tried to comfort him. 'We'll find another dog, darling. One that will be perfect for us.'

As Roy Grace drove back towards Brighton his brain was churning. Should they have taken the puppy – at the extortionate cost asked for it – and given it a good and happy life? But in doing so lined the pockets of a criminal?

And he knew the answer, however emotionally tough it was.

It was a resounding *no*.

His decision was confirmed to be correct forty minutes later, as they were passing Southampton again, this time heading eastwards. Luke Stanstead called and he took it on hands-free.

'Sir,' Luke said, 'I've just spoken with a manager at Airbnb. The house you gave me, Fernlea, at number 32 Fifth Avenue, is currently rented to a Mr Jonathan Jones, with a home address in Jersey in the Channel Isles.'

'Jonathan Jones?' Grace retorted.

'Yes, correct, sir. Jones as in Juliet Oscar November Echo Sierra.'

Grace said nothing for some moments. Then he said, 'OK, can you ask the manager to give you this Jersey address. If he won't for any reason or cites GDPR data protection let me know and we'll get a warrant.'

'Right away. Is there anything else you need?'

'No, Luke, thanks. That's all I need, for now.'

38

'No!' Gecko shouted, jumping to his feet as the Leicester City striker slotted the ball past the Albion goalkeeper.

Fuelled by the general uproar of the crowd, he stood up at the end of the aisle and began yelling at the visiting supporters' stand to his right.

'Marion!' Elvira, seated beside him, sounded alarmed. 'What's happening?'

'They scored an off-side goal and we've got an idiot of a ref!'

Then he joined in the chant from most of the twenty-seven thousand Albion supporters in the Amex stadium. 'THE REFEREE'S A WANKER!'

He was still shouting out these words long after everyone else had sat down. Elvira was tugging at him to sit too, but he ignored her.

Then he heard a female voice below calling out, 'Sir, sir, SIR!'

He looked down and saw a steward, in a yellow hi-vis jacket, addressing him.

Immediately he sat back down.

'Sir,' she said politely, 'you are in the family stand. Could you please tone down your language and your behaviour – there are young children in here.'

'Sorry,' Gecko said. 'Sorry, sorry. Got carried away.'

Ten minutes later, when Leicester City scored a second goal – a penalty – Gecko was up on his feet again. And this time again,

159

long after everyone else had settled, he was jumping up and down, shouting.

In the glass control room, at the opposite end of the stadium, the head of security, Adrian Morris, was scanning the bank of monitors mounted in front of the wide window that gave everyone in his room an unobstructed view across the pitch and much of the stadium. He spotted the agitated fan in the family enclosure misbehaving again. He zoomed in on him. A weird-looking guy with bulging eyes.

Next to Morris sat Chief Inspector Susan Bliss, a highly trained Public Order officer who was the police Match Commander. Beside her, scanning the monitors intently, zooming in on various sections of the crowds, was DS Matt Nixson from the Divisional Intelligence Unit. Football crowds were always a good place to keep an eye on known criminals, and see who appeared to be associating with whom.

As Morris radioed the steward to have another word with the fan, Nixson studied his face, thinking back to yesterday's briefing at headquarters for Operation Brush. Was this one of the Persons of Interest they'd been alerted to watch for?

'Adie,' Nixson said. 'Is that seat a season ticket holder?'

Morris tapped his keypad, then shook his head. 'No, he's just a punter. I'm sending the steward over again. Final warning. If he doesn't rein it in, next time he's out.'

Both of them watched as the steward spoke to the man, who raised an apologetic hand and sat back down.

'Zoom in on him again, more tightly, could you, please?' Nixson asked.

Moments later Gecko's angry face filled the screen. He was jerking up and down. A young woman, with a white stick and a Seagulls scarf around her neck, sat next to him and seemed to be trying to calm him.

Then Nixson turned to Adrian Morris. 'Could you ask Darren

Balkham to keep an eye on him, I think he might be a person we're looking for. I'll get someone over there.'

'He's doing a great job of being inconspicuous,' joked Morris. He radioed PC Balkham, who was the long-standing Police Liaison Officer with the football club. 'Darren, there's a trouble-maker in Seat 42, Row H, the East Stand.'

'I've got eyes on him, Adie,' Balkham said, positioned in an aisle towards the back of the stand. 'I've got two officers ready if we need to eject him.' There was a sudden roar from the crowd, rapidly building to a crescendo. Brighton had possession, one striker breaking clear of all the defenders. Large numbers of fans rose to their feet and for a moment Balkham's view of the man in Seat 42 was obscured. He glanced at the game for a brief second, just in time to see the ball whistle past the post.

Balkham turned and watched the East Stand as they all grad-ually sat back down. But the man in Seat 42 was no longer there; nor was the woman who had been sitting beside him.

39

Noah, strapped in his seat in the rear of the Alfa as his father followed the satnav directions to take them back home to Henfield, was tearful.

'Darling, we will get a dog, I promise you, we'll get in touch with the rescue centre next week,' Cleo said, trying to pacify him.

'Want Wally.' He banged his fists down either side of the child seat, his voice rising to a scream.

'Darling,' Cleo said, 'there'll be a Wally dog who will choose you and will be perfect for us all, you just have to be patient.'

Roy Grace was feeling sad also. He'd been looking forward to seeing this puppy, even with some reservations, but it had really shocked him to see first-hand how rife this crime was. He tried to concentrate on his driving while thinking about what he had just discovered, but it was impossible with Noah saying the same thing again and again. Finally, he pulled over, stopped the car and switched off the engine. He turned to Noah and reiterated what Cleo had told him about the rescue centre. After a few moments he said to Cleo, 'I need to make an urgent call, be back in a sec.'

She nodded.

Grabbing his job phone from the hands-free cradle, he jumped out of the car and closed the door. Then he strode a few paces along the pavement and called Branson.

The Detective Inspector answered almost immediately. 'How did it go, did you get the puppy?'

Grace told him what had happened.

'Shit,' Branson replied. 'Bummer. You did the right thing, walking away.'

'Try telling that to Noah,' he said grimly. 'Any updates?'

'We've had some more calls from the media coverage of the press conference. Four potential leads – Jack, Velvet, Norman and the team are following them up. And I've just had an interesting call from Susan Bliss – she's at the Amex.'

'She give you the score?'

'Yeah, not great. It's nearly full time and Leicester City are winning 2–1.'

'Terrific,' Grace said sourly. 'And that's why she called you?'

'No, she's the Match Commander today. She has it on her radar that we're interested in Marion Willingham – Gecko. Apparently he was spotted in the crowd, making an idiot of himself.'

'Darren Balkham's there, presumably?'

'He is.'

'We have enough on Willingham to bring him for questioning. Can you get Darren to nick him?'

'I already tried, boss, but they've lost him.'

'They've got extremely sharp CCTV in that stadium – how can they have lost him?'

'They're on it.'

'Good. OK, so what I want you to do is call Dorset CID, and see if you can speak to someone in their Rural Crimes Team. Tell them they should raid that house – I'll give you the address and their false names, and what might be their real ones.' Grace said them clearly, repeating them as Branson noted them down.

'Anything else going on?' Grace asked.

'Nope, otherwise pretty Q. Hey, I'm sorry about the puppy. Life's a bitch, eh?'

'That's a very appropriate word,' Grace retorted.

40

'What is it with you?' Elvira demanded, panting and out of breath as they stood on the platform of Falmer railway station, under half a mile from the Amex Stadium. Marion had dragged her, half-walking, half-running, the whole way. Now they stood on the platform, waiting for the next train to Brighton to arrive. 'I was enjoying myself. You dragged me away, like you dragged me away from that restaurant on the pier on my birthday.'

'What do you mean?' Gecko said stroppily. 'You couldn't see the match, I was having to tell you what was happening.'

'I liked the atmosphere,' she said, hurt.

'The atmosphere? Brighton lost. All those Leicester City fans gloating? What's to like about that?'

'Just being with you,' she said and squeezed his hand. 'I like you telling me what's happening. You're my eyes.'

'Right, yeah,' he said, without squeezing hers back. 'There were too many coppers for my liking.'

'What's your problem with coppers? They're just doing their jobs to keep us all safe, aren't they?'

He gave a little grunt of a laugh. 'You think that's what they do? That's why they were there?'

'I do. My mum always told me if I had a problem to ask a policeman for help.'

He sneered. 'Oh yeah, sure. Excuse me, Mr Plod, I've got a problem. Ha!'

A train was approaching.

'You're in a very funny mood today,' she said.

'I got pressures at work. Targets.'

'Your sales targets?'

'Yeah, sales targets, sort of.'

'But you work for a charity, Marion, rehoming dogs. How do they come up with targets?'

'Well – you know – so many people have bought dogs during Covid, then they find they can't cope with them.' He had to raise his voice against the approaching train, the clatter of its wheels, the screech of its brakes, and the tannoy announcement.

'BRIGHTON TRAIN. THIS IS THE BRIGHTON TRAIN.'

Helping Elvira aboard, holding her stick for her, they entered a busy carriage. He guided her to a seat someone had given up for her and he stood beside her as the train began moving again. 'I've gotta find the right dogs, the right matches.'

'I'm sure you're wonderful at it,' she said. 'Because you *care*.'

Her watch announced, in a quiet, robotic voice, 'Four fifty-eight p.m.'

She found his hand and stroked it with her finger. 'You wanted me to come, I didn't want you to waste money on a seat for me, but you were the one who insisted. I was happy for you to go alone and meet up with your mates for a pie and a pint.'

He put his arm on her shoulder. 'Yeah, I did. I wanted to show you that you can lead a normal life, despite, you know . . .'

'Despite that I'm becoming a little more blind every day?'

'I don't mind about that, I've told you. I love you. I'll always love you, I'll be your eyes. And if you go deaf, I'll be your ears, too.'

She punched him playfully. 'I am not going deaf.'

'Pardon?'

She punched him again. 'Haha!'

The train rolled forward, gathering speed. As it did so Gecko looked out of the window at the platform. No sign of any police officers.

'We're going to change at Brighton then get off at Preston Park and walk five minutes to your house. Then I'm going to take you to bed.'

She shook her head. 'No, Marion my love, that's not going to happen.'

'Oh?'

She shook her head again, grinning. 'I'm going to take YOU to bed.'

41

Normally, having gone into the office in the morning, to catch up while the phones were silent, Saturday afternoons were Chris Fairfax's favourite time of the week. As a season ticket holder, he'd be either at the Amex, supporting his team when they were playing a home game as they were today, or watching sport on television, then maybe collecting Bluebell from a party, and looking forward to going out to dinner with Katy and some friends.

But today, Bluebell was upstairs in bed, feeling too unwell to even play on her iPad, and Katy was fretting about her steadily rising temperature. He'd stayed home, also worried about his daughter, despite Katy having urged him to go to the game and unwind, and telling him it was just a bug as the doctor had said, and it was best if she just took her meds and slept it off.

Moose lay silently in her basket on the floor of the lounge in front of him. Chris watched a rugby match on television and, every five minutes, checked the score on the Albion game against Leicester City, on his iPhone, with an increasing sense of doom. They were now 2–1 down. He had the irrational and frustrating thought, familiar to so many fans, that if he had been there to cheer his team on, maybe the result would be different.

Tomorrow was a whole day off work to look forward to. If Bluebell was feeling better he planned to start with a long bike ride – perhaps along the cycle track into Brighton and then beyond, or instead head west, past Shoreham Harbour and towards Worthing. Followed by a nice lunch at home, or maybe brunch – the three of them – in one of their favourite casual places, and then taking Bluebell out on her roller-skates along the promenade or the undercliff walk at Rottingdean.

Katy had already made the call to cancel the dinner at the Gingerman in Brighton that they had really been looking forward to. She didn't want to leave Bluebell at home, in her current condition, in the hands of a babysitter and he agreed with her. Instead they'd decided they would order a takeaway from the Giggling Squid, their favourite local Thai.

Just as the Welsh forward had possession of the ball and was sprinting towards the touchline, the puppy suddenly stood up and began to retch.

Then she vomited.

Shit. 'Darling!' he called out, rushing to the kitchen to grab some paper towels. 'Darling!'

'What?' Katy shouted from upstairs.

'There's something going on with Moose,' he called out.

She came running down. 'What – what is it?'

He told her what had just happened, as he mopped up the slimy vomit. She went over to the puppy, which looked balefully at her. 'My lovely, what is it, are you not feeling right?'

The puppy vomited again, a small amount of green slime.

'I think we should take her to the vet,' Katy said. 'I'm worried, she's not kept down any food. I was just googling stuff – there's a horrible thing called parvovirus that kills puppies if they don't get immediate treatment.'

'Do you think she has that?' he asked, alarmed.

'I don't know, but we can't chance it. I'll ring the vet before they close.'

Chris winced as Leicester City hit the post and Brighton were still losing 2–1 with less than two minutes, plus injury time, left. The Albion needed a miracle.

'I've managed to get her an appointment, but it's in thirty minutes. Do you want to take care of Bluebell and I'll go with Moose?' Katy said.

'I'll take her if you like?' he offered.

'No, it's fine – just check on Bluebell every half an hour. Her temperature's still high at the moment.'

'Despite the meds Dr Dixon-Smith prescribed?'

Katy nodded, looking very concerned. 'Yes, I've given her all the doses.'

'They probably need more time to kick in.'

'Hopefully,' Katy said, as she scooped up Moose in her arms. 'My poor baby,' she said. 'We'll get you better!'

'Sure you don't want me to come with you?' Chris asked.

'And leave Bluebell alone in the house?' she retorted, more witheringly than she had intended.

'I mean, get the babysitter?'

'You're the babysitter,' she said, and left.

42

It wasn't until they were almost home that Noah fell asleep. As the Alfa bumped and lurched along the potholed cart track towards their cottage he woke again.

'Why can't we have Wally?' Noah whined for the umpteenth time.

'We will find another Wally,' Cleo said.

Roy and Cleo exchanged a glance, then Roy said, firmly, 'We're not having that dog, Noah. As Mummy said, we'll find another.'

For whatever reason, his tone of voice delivered. Noah fell silent again.

As soon as they were back in the house, he rang Glenn Branson for another update.

'Don't ask the Albion score, boss,' he said. 'It'll only put you in a worse mood.'

'I know it,' Grace replied. 'I made the mistake of looking on my phone. Has anything good happened this afternoon? Or does the whole world fall over when I take some down time?'

'Not when you leave your top man in charge, it doesn't.'

Perching on the arm of a sofa, stroking Humphrey, who had jumped up onto it, Grace managed a thin smile. 'Convince me?'

The dog affectionately nuzzled his head against Roy's chest. Humphrey might be bolshy on occasions, but hey, so were humans. And he really loved this creature. Although originally he was Cleo's dog, who she'd got from a rescue centre long before they'd met, he was their dog now and over the past couple of years he had been Roy's constant companion, whether at home or out on his runs across the field.

'The House-to-House Team has identified a farm that might be of interest to us. Good old Clifford Keele, again,' Branson said.

'His place?' Grace asked. 'Clifford must be older than God now.'

'Yeah, I hear he's pretty gaga. Lives in a cottage with a carer – his missus died a couple of years ago.'

'How sad – hope we sent flowers.'

'Haha! So, his daughter, Rula, married to Terry Jim – Big Jim – runs the show now with her charmer of a hubby. They've a big spread out near Hailsham. On the surface, these days they're legit.'

'They wouldn't know the meaning of that word,' Grace said.

'Nope. Emily Denyer's been taking a look at their tax returns – at least what they put in – and she says they don't chime with the kind of money commercially driven agricultural families are making these days – which is very little. British farmers are struggling even more than ever post Brexit. They are all under pressure and apparently it's driving one or two into organized criminality.' He paused again. 'Still with me?'

'I haven't fallen asleep, yet.'

'So,' Branson continued, 'what they have on the surface is a crop-based farm. Potato, sweetcorn, rapeseed, employing locals. They've a vested interest in the local community turning a blind eye to what's going on, so it seems they play the whole feudal lord thing, sponsoring the November 5th village bonfire and the annual fete – all that kind of stuff. Part of their strategy for keeping the community onside and distracted from what they are really up to.'

'Which is what?' Grace asked.

'Intel from East Sussex CID is that they're into illegal waste, tyre dumping, and the usual drugs importation and distribution, as well as growing cannabis – for medical purposes, naturally.

Covid closed down a lot of their drug-dealing opportunities, so it seems they may have been turning to others, muscling in on the traditional crimes of some other groups. Metal theft, catalytic converter theft, copper from new-build houses and boilers. Then they spot the rising prices of dogs. Maybe they've a few themselves, but they realize dogs have become a goldmine. They start nicking the popular breeds and mating them. Bingo! A pair of sprockers could have a couple of litters a year. Fifteen to twenty puppies at two to three grand a pop? Big money.'

'Yep,' Grace said.

'And hey, what do you know? For the same money dealing in drugs, where they could be looking at ten to fifteen years inside if nicked, they can trade in puppies. The sentence for that is six months at the very worst. More likely a fine than a custodial sentence.'

'What's the name of Big Jim's place, Glenn?'

'Appletree Farm.'

'Sounds idyllic.'

'Not if you see the drone footage, boss. It's a tip. There's about four family generations living there, some in cottages, some in caravans. A whole mixture, hens, pigs, mostly scrap metal. It's long been subject of monitoring by East Division Intelligence officers – they suspect it of farming cannabis on a commercial scale and a possible crystal meth factory.'

'Our own home-grown *Breaking Bad*?'

'Could well be. Big Jim's two sons from a former relationship, Dallas and Scott, are both in the business today. Big Jim's wife, Rula, has a daughter, Darcy, who lives and works there too. She seems the only legit member of that family. Dallas Jim has his own farm, Scott lives with his partner in a cottage on Big Jim's spread, he's pretty quiet. Both brothers have recently been granted licences to breed dogs, issued by East Sussex County Council. They're doing everything they can to keep their noses clean, to the outside world at any rate.'

'Good work, Glenn,' Grace said.

'There's something else that might be relevant.'

'Tell me?'

'You mentioned your interest in Marion Willingham? AKA Gecko, who was possibly spotted at the Amex today and then lost?'

'I did.'

'Looks like he may have been picked up again. I'm going to ping you some CCTV footage. Have a look then call me back.'

'I'll do that,' Grace said.

43

Moose sat almost motionless on the vet's examining table, with a sad, lost look in her half-closed brown eyes. Katy stood beside her in the tiny consulting room, stroking her and trying to re-assure her.

The vet, Helen Bradley, a lean, energetic woman in her late thirties, stood beside the table, stroking the puppy's head. She and Katy had a good rapport, especially since Dr Bradley had done so much to make their previous dog, Phoebe, comfortable in her last months.

'You are beautiful, Moose, aren't you, eh? You really are! But you're a bit under the weather, you poor thing.'

She inserted a rectal thermometer and held it with one hand, while continuing to stroke her with the other. 'So you've not been feeling great for a couple of days, have you?' She glanced at Katy, who nodded. 'Might be she's missing her mother or siblings. Have you changed her diet?'

'No, the breeder gave us a small bag of her kibble, and we've bought some more of the same brand.'

After some moments she removed the thermometer and studied it for a moment. 'Mmm,' she said. 'She is running quite a high temperature. Let's see what's going on.'

She put the thermometer into a sterilizing unit, then popped her stethoscope into her ears and listened to the puppy's chest. Moose barely raised her eyelids to look at her. Next, she pulled her mouth open and studied the inside. Then she spent a considerable amount of time feeling all around her body, while the docile creature barely reacted. Finally, she turned and smiled at Katy.

'It's so hard to know how animals are really feeling,' she said. 'Children – and adults – can tell us where something hurts, or how rubbish they're feeling, or how queasy. We can only take an educated guess with these little things.' She shrugged. 'She's a gorgeous puppy.'

'She is,' Katy echoed.

'So, you've only had her two days, you say?'

'Yes, correct.'

'Where did you buy her?'

'Well, she was from a breeder we found online – he said he was based near Carmarthen.'

Immediately she noticed the frown on the vet's face. 'What was his name?'

'John Peat. We were willing to drive to Wales to see her, but he said there was no need, he was in the Sussex area with other puppies, and he would bring this one over for us to take a look at – with no obligation if we didn't like her for any reason.'

Her frown deepened. 'Where did you meet this Mr Peat?'

Sensing the disapproval in her tone, she said, 'In a pub forecourt. Mr Peat gave us her vaccination certificate and paperwork. I've brought it all with me in case you wanted to see – it's in the car.'

'I would like to see it. I'd like to know what vaccinations she has had. Did this breeder say whether she's been chipped?'

'Yes,' Katy said, pleased to be able to give her some positive news.

'Good. I'm going to take a sample of blood and get an analysis from the lab which will test for a range of common diseases. Meanwhile I'll do a faecal antigen test – what we call a SNAP test. It's just a little sample of her poo – she won't feel anything. Hopefully it's just a bug she'll get over – I'll give you some antibiotics.'

'Do you think it might be parvovirus?'

She shook her head. 'Parvovirus is very much around at the moment, and I will know from the SNAP test results, but I don't think she has it – she's not displaying those symptoms. Which is a positive in one way, because parvovirus is a very nasty thing and often fatal for puppies of Moose's age.'

'Oh God,' Katy said anxiously.

'Well, let's not worry too much at this stage. You said she's been running around in your garden?'

'Yes?'

'Is it secure or do any other animals go in there?'

'It's walled. One of our neighbour's cats does come in from time to time to do its business there.'

'She could have picked up some bacteria in your garden, maybe from the cat or a bird dropping – or anything. At her age she has a very weak immune system.' She smiled. 'Don't worry. I'll be back in a sec.'

The vet went out of the room and returned a few moments later with a small black object, the shape and size of a knuckle-duster, with a green LED screen in the middle. She gripped it in her right hand, switched it on, then moved it around the back of Moose's neck. Then she frowned. 'The breeder told you she'd been chipped?'

'Yes, very definitely.'

She held up her hand to show her the instrument. 'This is a microchip scanner. It's not picking anything up. It's possible of course the chip could be faulty, but he should have tested it at the time.'

'Shall I go and get the vaccination certificate?'

She nodded. Katy ran out to the car, and hurried back, holding the certificate and paperwork. She handed it all to the vet.

Dr Bradley studied the documents for some moments then,

frowning again, said, 'Do you mind if I take these to my office for a couple of minutes?'

'No, please do,' she said, suddenly feeling very uncomfortable. As the vet left the room, she again stroked the puppy, talking to her reassuringly, but saw no reaction from her. Panicking, she worried for an instant that the dog was dying. She placed her hands around its tummy and felt a faint, steady beat. Reassured, she nuzzled her face. 'You're going to be OK, Moose,' she murmured. 'You're going to have the best life any dog ever had. We love you so much. The vet's going to give you some stuff and you'll be feeling great in a couple of days. I promise!'

The only response from Moose was a baleful attempt again at raising an eyelid. Then Helen Bradley came back into the room, holding the certificate she'd given her, and looking very serious. She put it down on a shelf. 'This was given to you by the breeder you bought Moose from?'

Her tone of voice made Katy nervous. 'Yes, it was.'

'Mr John Peat?'

'That was him, yes.'

'Mrs Fairfax, did you pay a lot of money for this puppy?'

'We did, yes. Two thousand five hundred pounds.'

'In cash?'

She hesitated, then said, 'Yes, cash.'

Dr Bradley nodded and was silent for some moments. 'I'm sorry to tell you – I'm afraid I've seen this before.' She tapped the documents on the shelf. 'This paperwork – I'm afraid it's all fake. I don't think your puppy has had any vaccinations. I've just run a computer check on Mr John Peat and his name doesn't show up on the list of registered breeders.'

She looked at the vet, increasingly concerned. 'What are you saying?'

'Well, there are a lot of cowboys in the dog-breeding world at the moment, attracted by the high profits they can make. I've seen quite a bit of this recently.' She raised her hands. 'I'm not saying this Mr Peat is one, but I have to be frank with you that I'm concerned I can't find his name anywhere.'

'Couldn't he just be someone whose dog has had a litter of puppies?'

'Well, let's hope that is the case.'

Katy frowned. 'And if it's not?'

Dr Bradley shrugged. 'There have been a number of instances of people illegally importing puppies, from Eastern Europe in particular, providing fake UK backgrounds, and then selling the puppies, which are often carrying diseases, landing their owners with large vet bills.'

'You think this could be the case with Moose?'

'Let's hope not.'

Katy smiled, then – like a handbrake suddenly pulled on, sharply – a thought stopped her in her tracks. 'These diseases they have – can they be transferred to humans?'

Bradley shook her head. 'No, not in my experience.'

'Good,' she replied. 'I've just been a little worried.'

'About what?'

She shrugged. 'Well, it's probably just pure coincidence, but our daughter has been unwell since we brought Moose home.'

'Does she suffer from any allergies?' Bradley asked.

'No – but in the dog breeder's van she was bitten by one of the other puppies; accidentally, I'm sure, but enough to draw blood – and it doesn't seem to be healing. And she had a temperature the next day – she's in bed now, not feeling at all well.'

The vet frowned. 'Has a doctor seen her?'

'Yes, she thinks it's a bug that's going round. She'd been in a public swimming pool – the King Alfred – earlier that day.'

'She very possibly picked something up there. I think it's unlikely to be related to the other puppy: dogs generally have clean mouths – I'd be more worried if it had been a young cat.'

'Good,' she said with a relieved smile.

'As it's the weekend, I won't get the lab results back on the bloods until sometime on Monday,' the vet said. 'I'll let you know as soon as I hear, but hopefully she'll have perked up in the meantime.'

'I'm sure she will,' Katy said. 'Are you able to give her the vaccinations she should have had?'

'Not until she is better.' Then she hesitated. 'Look, I don't want to worry you unduly, but this person you bought her from has clearly lied to you and your husband. He told you she'd been bred in Wales, correct?'

'That was the impression we had. Why?'

'I mentioned about illegally imported puppies. If that was the case here, then by law she would need to be quarantined in government-approved kennels.'

'For how long?'

'Four months.'

'Four months?'

She nodded. 'It sounds extreme, but it's to prevent rabies from coming into the country.'

Katy shook her head. 'I'm certain she was bred in Wales. Our daughter would be devastated if she had to go into quarantine. I'll try to get hold of the documentation from the breeder.'

Dr Bradley looked hard, but sympathetically, at her. 'Mrs Fairfax, I'm sorry, I don't mean to alarm you, but if you can't get the documentation to us by the middle of next week I will have to report Moose to DEFRA – the Department for Environment, Food and Rural Affairs – and it will ultimately be their decision.' She studied the results of the SNAP test for a few moments. 'Well that's come back clear, so no parvovirus. That's jolly good news, and she can go home. I'll write up her notes now and the antibiotics will be ready in a few moments in reception. Please try to avoid her having any contact with other animals as a precaution, just until you get that information from her breeder.'

44

'Darling,' Cleo said. 'I thought you were going to make supper tonight? Early supper and then Netflix you said – that documentary on the extreme climber.'

'I'm on it,' Roy Grace said distractedly, looking at his computer screen.

'It's after eight o'clock.'

'Just give me five more minutes. I've taken the salmon out, I've got everything ready.'

Cleo looked at the kitchen worktops, at her husband's idea of *ready*. A bag of frozen peas, some sliced courgettes on the chopping board, a saucepan with potatoes simmering on the hob, purple sprouting broccoli lying beside the steamer and two salmon fillets still crusted in ice, in front of the microwave.

'So we're going to eat around midnight?' she said, a tad tetchily.

'Please, darling, five minutes, I promise.'

'I'm putting the timer on.'

Molly began bawling, and Cleo hurried upstairs; she was teething and very grizzly.

Grace focused back on the screen.

On the video Glenn Branson had sent him, a man with pale skin and bulging eyes, wearing a blue and white Seagulls beanie and matching scarf, was dragging a stumbling woman, also wearing a Seagulls scarf and holding what looked like a white stick, along a railway station platform with him. They stopped, as if waiting for a train.

Grace froze the video, thinking how much he resembled the blurry image of the man who had made off with the dog in Hove Park, and about something he'd read earlier on the serials. A reported snatch and grab of two watches from a jeweller in Brighton's East Street. He called up the serials again on his computer and after a trawl through found the log of the incident, together with a detailed update. A man, his face largely concealed by a scarf and hat, had taken two watches, one of them a gold Rolex, valued at around £10,000, and the other item, a talking watch for the blind valued at around £70. No question that it was Gecko.

Conscious that his five minutes were up, he replayed the last section of the video of the man in the beanie and woman with the white stick, then made a note for tomorrow morning's briefing meeting.

'Five minutes!' Cleo called out.

He jumped up, hurried into the kitchen, and pulled on the apron Cleo had given him for Christmas. On it was printed in large letters, *ROY GRACE – MASTERCHEF!*

Grabbing bottles of teriyaki sauce, sesame oil and soy sauce from a cupboard, then a bunch of spring onions, a clove of garlic and stem of ginger from the fridge and a sharp knife from the cutting block, he immersed himself in his task, happy for the total distraction from work and to do something different that he also was passionate about.

Fifteen minutes later, with the microwave-defrosted salmon wrapped in foil baking in the oven and the broccoli in the steamer, the timer ticking steadily, and the potatoes soft, Roy felt he had everything under control.

He hurried out of the room, dashed upstairs, returned with a small gift-wrapped box with a ribbon tied in a rather clumsy-looking bow, and presented it, a little sheepishly, to Cleo.

She looked at it with a mixture of surprise and delight, but also a little bemused. 'What's this?' she asked.

'Open it and see,' he said, feeling like an excited child. *She would like it, wouldn't she*, he was wondering, hoping. *Of course she will, she will!*

Sitting down at the kitchen table, she asked, 'Did you wrap this yourself?'

'Does it show?'

'I love it, darling, but your wrapping has a style all of its own!' She untied the bow, then removed the pink paper, revealing a brown box embossed with a name and logo, which she peered at closely. It read, *Swiss Watches Direct*. Then she looked up at Roy quizzically.

He just smiled back.

She opened the box, with some difficulty, then gasped as she saw what was inside. 'Roy!' she said, looking up at him, her eyes shining with delight. 'This is for me?'

'That's the plan!' he said, beaming back.

'I love it, I love the colour. It's exactly the one I've really wanted. You didn't need to do that!'

The silver watch, with a white face and gold and silver link chain, nestled in the white satin cut-out in the box. She put it on her wrist and held it up in awe. 'How does it look, good?'

He nodded vigorously.

She kissed him, her face lit up with joy. 'I can't believe it!' Then she frowned. 'Wait a sec, it's not one of those copies, is it?'

He grinned again. 'Seriously?'

She shook her head. 'No. You wouldn't, I know you wouldn't. I love it, I absolutely love it. But why?' She said it with a huge smile.

He shrugged. 'I wanted to get you something for graduating – something special that you'd always have as a reminder.'

She shook her head, again in awe. 'How did you know I like this particular one so much?'

'You don't remember, do you?' He smiled again. 'When we were in London just before Christmas, you looked in the window of a watch shop, and I saw you staring at this watch, a Longines Conquest, right? I could just see in your face that you liked it – really liked it!'

'Always the detective, even when we're Christmas shopping!' she retorted and kissed him again. 'But these cost a fortune!'

The timer on the broccoli pinged. He hurried over to remove the steamer's lid, careful not to burn his fingers in the process, to stop it cooking any more. 'I managed to get a good deal on it.'

She looked at him quizzically, but smiling. 'How come?'

'Sheer luck. I think I told you I was in Brighton with Glenn last week for a bail hearing at the Crown Court. We went for a coffee afterwards and I bumped into an old friend – a guy called Ashley Beal – with his wife, Yulia. Ashley and I used to play in a snooker league at the old Brighton Police Social Club – it's long gone now – and he reminded me that he always used to beat me – I think he's still playing at quite a high amateur national level. I asked him what he was up to – he was always a bit of an entrepreneur, and he told me he has a very successful online company, Swiss Watches Direct. See where I'm going with this?'

Cleo tilted her head. 'I think I might.'

'So, long story short, I asked him if he could get me one of those Longines at a price I could afford. He said no, he couldn't get it at a price I could afford, but he'd give me his best price.'

'So we can't eat for the next two months, but at least I get to wear an amazing watch!' She was already unstrapping her ancient Apple Watch.

'That's much more important than food, right?'

She strapped it on, then held it up and admired it from a different angle. 'Wow!' she said. 'Wow!'

Ten minutes later, seated opposite Cleo at the wooden table in the kitchen–dining room, he watched anxiously as she cut into the salmon, then added some of his cheat sauce – mayonnaise and English mustard – and took a bite.

'Delicious!' she said, after she had chewed and swallowed. She admired her watch again, then started cutting off another slice.

'So you hate it?'

'It's horrible,' she said. 'The salmon, not the watch.' She looked at it again.

He grinned and ate a mouthful of the soft, pink fish. After some moments he said, 'Yep, I have to agree with you. It's horrible.'

'Horrible – not!' she retorted. 'If you ever decide to quit policing, we could always open a restaurant.'

He grinned again. 'Yep, and I have the perfect name for it.'

'Which is?'

'Mortuary Leftovers.'

45

A few minutes after 9 a.m. on Sunday morning, Roy Grace sat with his team in the conference room, the video, which he'd watched at home last night, playing on the wall-mounted monitor. Glenn Branson had come in, despite Roy's offer of his taking a day off.

The platform was filling up with fans on their way home but they were able to pick up on the couple. The man with a long, pallid face wearing a blue and white Seagulls beanie and matching scarf, was dragging a stumbling woman, also wearing a Seagulls supporters' scarf and holding what looked like a white stick, along a railway station platform with him. They stopped, as if waiting for a train.

'God, he really does deserve his Gecko nickname, doesn't he?' Norman Potting asked.

'Yep, it's uncanny,' Polly Sweeney agreed.

'Yeah,' Potting said drily. 'Sussex Police are looking for a pale lizard accompanied by a blind woman. They'll blend in with the local crowd nicely.'

Several of the team grinned. But, Grace thought, Potting was making a good point – however unintentionally. He turned. 'Polly, these two *would* stand out. I'm giving you – and Jack – the action of liaising with the CCTV camera team for any potential sightings of them.'

It would be a massive ask, Grace knew, to trawl through all the cameras. With over four hundred of them recording areas of the city 24/7, and a team of just three CCTV operators, the words *needle* and *haystack* came to mind. But they could narrow the parameters by focusing on the cameras around the city's parks and other dog-walking areas, such as the seafront, as part of their day-to-day business. Grace would set some very strict guidelines to make it a useful task. He was certain this oddball, *Gecko*, was just a pawn, a hired hand, working for an organized crime group that had muscled in on the new lucrative world of dog crime in all its forms. Maybe if they could establish any kind of a pattern in his behaviour, he could put a surveillance team on him that might lead them to the gang's HQ.

E-J Boutwood raised a hand and he nodded at her.

'Boss,' she said. 'Something that may be of interest. Last night Newhaven Customs opened a container in a lorry inbound from Poland. On its manifest it was carrying plumbing parts. But this container held ten puppies, a mixture of breeds, many in very poor health. The bill of lading was in the name of a Tom Hartley, with an address in Brecon, in South Wales. Turns out to be just an accommodation address.'

Grace looked confused. 'Tom Hartley, E-J?' he quizzed.

'Yes, sir,' the DC replied.

Tom Hartley was the name the man had given to him and Cleo at the house in Bournemouth yesterday. He turned to Branson. 'Glenn, did you get anywhere with Dorset CID yesterday, and their Rural Crimes Team?'

'Well, yes and no, boss. It's the reason I thought I'd better come in this morning. I spoke to a very helpful DI there, Caroline Langridge.'

'Caroline Langridge?' Polly Sweeney exclaimed, interrupting. 'She used to be here in Sussex – we joined together!'

'And she's all over it, she has a real interest in this area of crime,' Branson said. 'She told me they've been keeping close contact with Hampshire CID in Portsmouth and Southampton ports for dog imports over the past year, and they seized a container with two dozen smuggled French bulldog puppies a couple of months ago. No doubt from various litters. She assured me she would send someone to check on the address you gave me – Fernlea, at thirty-two Fifth Avenue, Bournemouth, right?'

Grace nodded. 'Yes, correct.'

'She called me back at nine o'clock last night to say two officers had attended and the property was in darkness. There was no response from their ringing and knocking on the door and there were no vehicles in the driveway. They carried out a visual exterior inspection and could see no sign of anyone, or any animals inside the house, nor any vehicles in the garage. She asked me if I wanted her to apply for a search warrant and, not wanting to bother you, I told her to go ahead.'

'Good,' Grace said. 'Well done.'

'She called me back just before midnight, saying officers had entered the premises, on a warrant, at 11 p.m. and had carried out a search but found no sign of anyone or any animals. No baskets, toys, dog food – nothing.'

Grace shook his head. 'This is not just a coincidence; Cleo and I were there late yesterday afternoon. There were half a dozen puppies and an adult dog but we are not certain she was even the mother of them. Are they all linked together?' He turned to Stanstead. 'Luke, you were going to speak to the Airbnb manager and get the Jersey address of the Mr and Mrs Jonathan Jones who had rented Fernlea – did you have any joy?'

'I did, sir: 47 Bonneville Apartments, Don Street, St Helier.'

Grace wrote it down. 'The current Chief Officer of Jersey Police is Robin Smith – I know him.'

'Robin Smith?' Potting asked. 'The same Robin Smith who was an ACC here in Sussex?'

'That's him,' Grace said.

'He's a good guy,' Glenn Branson said. 'Never heard a bad word about him.'

'He is,' Grace confirmed. 'I'll give him a call and see what he can find out about this couple.' He paused and looked at his notes. 'So, the house, Fernlea, was rented on Airbnb by Mr and Mrs Jonathan Jones. But the man apparently residing there with his wife, a Scouser, gave his name as Tom Hartley,' Grace said. 'But the car on the driveway of this property, a recent-model Peugeot, was registered to a Mr Michael Richard Kendrick. Something is seriously not adding up here.'

'Like dots not joining up, chief?' Potting said.

'Very helpful, Norman,' Grace said.

Potting, either missing or deliberately ignoring Grace's sarcasm, said, 'I was always good at puzzles as a kid.'

'Too bad that talent deserted you when you grew up,' Velvet Wilde chided.

Potting raised a finger in the air. 'That's a debatable question, young lady.'

Grace turned to Luke Stanstead. 'Have you got an out-of-hours contact for this Airbnb manager?'

'He gave me his mobile, sir.'

'Good. I've never rented from this outfit, so I don't know how they operate, but they must have some checks on tenants. See if you can find out from him what information he has on this couple, Mr and Mrs Jonathan Jones. Phone number, email address, bank or credit card details, whatever.'

'Yes, sir.'

Grace turned to Polly Sweeney. 'We have three different names – Michael Kendrick, Jonathan Jones and Tom Hartley. My strong suspicion is that they are all assumed, but I'm giving you the action of seeing if you can come up with any matches of interest to us. We already know that this *Tom Hartley* I met yesterday is likely to be the same fake identity as on the bill of lading on the seized consignment of puppies. See if any of these three names pop up on the internet, or on any police database.'

'I'll start right away,' she said.

Grace looked down at his notes and was quiet for some moments, thinking. Then he asked, 'Does anyone have any further thoughts or questions?'

Velvet Wilde raised her hand, and said, 'Sir, I've been studying the drone footage over the area of East Sussex we think the vehicles may have travelled to after leaving the Ruddles' property, the Old Homestead Farm. There are twenty-seven farms, but I've narrowed those down to an initial nine where there has been known or suspected criminal activity – from cannabis farming, to crystal meth production, to vehicle theft and cut-and-shutting. I've reduced these further to six, where local authority dog-breeding licences have been issued.' She hesitated. 'If I may, I'd like to put these up on the screen.'

'Go ahead,' Grace said, impressed with the DC's work.

For the next fifteen minutes, he and his team watched drone footage, taken with a zoom lens, in the fortunately clear weather yesterday, from too great a height for the drones to have been heard or seen from the ground. The footage was accompanied with a running commentary from Wilde.

The county of East Sussex covered 660 square miles, she told them, with much of it arable or dairy farmland. The six properties she concentrated on were all ones with a sprawl of buildings, some covering a very wide area. Five of them had several residential properties on them where two or more generations of the farming families lived.

And the common denominator was that all had attracted, at some point in the recent past, the interest of the local police. Two were known to be home to farming families with a long history of mostly petty crime, and which Roy Grace decided, for now, he could put to one side. But the other four, including

Appletree Farm, each of which had dog-breeding licences, piqued his interest.

Thanking Velvet, he turned to DS Alexander. 'Jack, I'd like the Outside Enquiry Team to visit all these farms and neighbouring properties as soon as possible – in the next twenty-four hours preferably – and see what you can find out. If any of them refuse to cooperate, tell them you will return with a search warrant.'

Potting raised a hand. 'Chief, a lot of coppers are nervous of these locations. Wusses. I'm not. I'll volunteer to go and talk to them.' He turned to DC Wilde. 'Are you happy to come along with me, Velvet?'

'Sure, I'm not scared.'

'Good,' Grace said. 'They are all yours, Norman and Velvet. But leave Appletree Farm to later so we can build up more intelligence to action a warrant. That farm might be significant.' Then he looked at the researcher, Vanessa Blackmore. 'How's Nick and the team doing with the trawl of websites offering puppies for sale?'

'We've identified sixteen adverts so far, of puppies that could be a match to the ones stolen from the Ruddles, sir. They're all being followed up.'

'Good work.' He looked at the rest of his team. 'Any questions?'

There were none.

'OK, our next briefing will be at 6 p.m. today.'

46

Grace went straight from the briefing to his office and began preparing his notes for his 11 a.m. phone call to update the ACC. As he sat down at his desk he was thinking, *Tom Hartley, who are you? And Jonathan Jones? And Michael Kendrick?*

You are one and the same person, aren't you? And I don't think any of these are your actual names. I'm going to find you. And put you somewhere you really won't like.

He googled the States of Jersey Police, then dialled the main switchboard number which came up. When the operator answered he identified himself and asked if the Chief Officer was available. A moment later he was put through to the Chief's Staff Officer. She told him Robin Smith was off today, but if it was urgent she could message him.

He told her it was urgent.

Less than five minutes later, his phone rang. As he answered he heard the calm, always cheerful voice of his former boss some six years ago.

'Hey, buddy, how are you doing?'

'I'm good, thanks. Married again with a three-year-old boy and a sixteen-month-old daughter.'

'I heard, that's great.'

'How's life in the Channel Isles?'

'Been a testing couple of years,' Robin Smith replied. 'No one told me Covid was about to happen when I took this job.

But hey, it's a beautiful island with different policing chal-
lenges. And you?'

'Same old, same old. And it's been a challenging time here,
too. I guess you heard about my dear son Bruno, who died?'

'I did, yes, Roy. I'm so sorry. Just terrible. Did his mother ever
turn up?'

'Long story,' he said. 'I'll save it for a lunch one day.'

'So, I'm guessing you've not called for a social catch-up, right?'
The Chief sounded genuinely pleased to hear from him, but Grace
got the impression he was in a hurry. He was grateful he'd called
him back so quickly.

'Yep. I've a possible Person of Interest in an enquiry I'm
running, with an address in Jersey. He may be real, but I suspect
not.' He gave Robin Smith the details.

'I'll get this Mr and Mrs Jones checked out right away. What's
the best number to call you on?'

Grace gave it to him.

'I'll get back to you today. I have to tell you I'm already a bit
suspicious – I know this street, it's in the centre of town and I
can't think of any apartment buildings on it – but I've only been
here a short while, so I could be wrong.'

'I have a feeling you're not wrong,' Grace said. He thanked
him and ended the call and sat still for some moments, smiling.
It was good to know in an ever-changing world that some people,
like Robin, remained a constant.

47

'It's itching, it's itching so much.' Bluebell, surrounded by stuffed animals in her pink bed, in her pink room, was frantically scratching the bridge of her nose and crying.

Katy sat on the bed, holding a tube of the prescription ointment. Chris stood beside her.

'Darling,' her mother said. 'Try not to scratch it, you're not giving it a chance to heal.'

'It's tingling so much, Mummy,' she cried. 'Tingling and itching.'

Katy glanced, concerned, at Chris. 'I'll put some more cream on, sweetheart.' She also noticed, to her concern, that one side of Bluebell's face was drooping.

'My tummy's hurting.'

Katy pulled down the duvet, lifted up her daughter's top and put her hand on her stomach. 'Tell Mummy where it hurts.'

Katy touched her forehead, which felt hot, and took her temperature again. It was still rising. She signalled to Chris they should leave the room.

Stepping out onto the landing and closing the door behind them, Katy turned to her husband. 'I'm really worried about her temperature. I looked it up earlier – 38 is considered a fever. Bluebell's is currently 38.5.'

'That's gone up in the past twenty-four hours, right?'

'Right. Dr Dixon-Smith said we should call if it did. And she keeps scratching where that dog bit her.'

'*Nipped* her, darling,' he said.

'Whatever. I'm scared she might have sepsis. I think we should take her to A&E.'

'And wait four hours for anyone to see her? What about calling the emergency out-of-hours doctor? Or we take her to see Dr Dixon-Smith first thing in the morning?'

'I don't want to leave it that long,' Katy said. 'Not with that fever she's running—'

They were interrupted by a terrible scream from their daughter's room and ran in.

Bluebell was sitting up in her bed, looking around bewildered. She had thrown up all down her front and on the duvet.

'My darling!' Katy ran across to her. Then she turned to Chris. 'I'll clean her up, you call the doctor.'

He stood for a moment, rooted to the spot, staring anxiously at their daughter.

'Call the doctor!' Katy yelled at him. 'Now!'

He retreated from the room and did as she said. He called Dr Dixon-Smith's number. After four rings he heard an automated reply. It informed him the Wish Road Medical Centre was closed and gave a number for the emergency out-of-hours doctor. He rang it and left a message.

Then he went back downstairs and, within moments, his phone rang.

It was the after-hours doctor.

He told the woman, who gave her name as Dr Grogan, of Bluebell's symptoms and her high temperature – and relayed Katy's concerns that after the puppy bit her on the nose, their daughter had suffered constant irritation from the wound, and their worry was that it might be sepsis.

Dr Grogan said she would be with them in half an hour.

Ending the call, he poured a glass of water, had a sip, then kneeled down beside Moose's basket. The puppy, at least, seemed to be looking much better since they started her on the antibiotics yesterday.

He drank another sip of his water, thinking back to what Katy had told him after returning from the vet yesterday. And then thinking further back to their meeting with John Peat in the pub car park on Thursday.

Peat had seemed a genuine man, proud that Moose had all the right papers. But Helen Bradley doubted any authenticity and suggested the vaccination certificate was forged. And she had suggested the puppy might even have been imported illegally. They needed to get the correct documentation, or the vet would have to get DEFRA involved.

He and Katy had decided the best way to sort this out would be to call the breeder, tell him what the vet had said and see how he responded. Picking up his phone, he looked in the contacts for John Peat's number and dialled it.

For some moments, nothing happened. Then he got a flat hum. He tried again and got the same tone. He tried a third time and got the same result. Like a number discontinued.

He went up to his office, opened his laptop and clicked on the Gumtree site where he had first found Peat and searched for his name.

He was no longer there.

48

'So, Clees, how are all your dead friends these days?' Charlie asked, unable to mask the faint puzzlement in her voice. Even after all this time, Cleo's younger sister, her constantly up-his-own-backside partner, Lance, and their parents, too, could not understand why with all her academic qualifications, Cleo had chosen the grim task of working in a mortuary for a career.

Charlie was always dressed as if for a photo shoot, Cleo thought, even now when they were out for one of their Sunday afternoon walks in Stanmer Park, their first together this year. Her blonde hair was the same colour as her own, but fashionably razor cut short. She wore a designer duffel coat over flared jeans and huge black boots with soles so thick they added a good couple of inches to her height. A clutch of three tiny Pomeranians on their leads trailed behind her. Further behind, Charlie's five-year-old goddaughter, Jessica, trotted along hand in hand with Noah, who was chatting away to her.

'Never a shortage of them, that's for sure!' Cleo replied, pushing a sleeping Molly in her pushchair. 'And unlike your clients, I don't have to be nice or kowtow to them! But,' she added after a moment, 'I have to say I didn't miss it all that much when I was on maternity leave.'

'Do you think you might do something different one day?'

Cleo nodded. 'I do think about having a career change, from time to time. But . . .' She shrugged. 'I know you and Mum and

Dad find it a bit strange, but I really love what I do, and that I'm sometimes able to comfort people on the worst day of their lives . . .' She shrugged. 'You know, their loved one left home that morning and instead of coming back in the evening ended up in a body bag in the mortuary.'

'Yuck.' Charlie paused. 'So, has Roy found out who those awful rogue breeders are? I'm so sorry it turned out like that. Honestly, the advert looked so genuine; I'm normally super suspicious and it had me completely fooled. The woman sounded so nice on the phone,' she said apologetically.

'No, listen, it's not your fault. As I said in my text, the set-up was clever, it would have fooled most people. It just makes me sick to think of those poor dogs,' Cleo said.

She looked around for Humphrey, who had romped off into the distance in the huge park, happy to be off his lead. 'Humphrey!' she called. 'Humphrey!'

She saw his black shape lumbering at speed towards them, then he swerved around a massive oak tree, stopped and began to sniff something clearly very interesting. She turned to Charlie. 'You know how dogs are always sniffing things when you take them out – it may sound daft, but I sometimes wonder if that's their equivalent of us reading newspapers and magazines.'

Charlie laughed. 'Do they have the doggie equivalent to Agony Aunt pages?'

Cleo grinned. She was in a great mood this Sunday afternoon. Despite the chilly, blustery wind beneath a mostly blue and sunny sky, Cleo loved being out in this weather as long as she was dressed for it. Spring was very definitely here, with clusters of daffodils in bloom in many areas of the park, and she was really happy to be spending time with her sister, who she adored and had not seen since Christmas.

'And you?' she asked. 'How's work?'

Charlie worked long hours for a large PR agency in London

she'd recently joined, and all her clients were household names, most of them very demanding.

'They're worse than children,' Charlie replied. 'So much panic over Covid – I've been trying to encourage all of them – at least those who still don't yet get it – that this is the time to build their online sales.'

Cleo smiled. 'Yep, fish where the fish are. I bet some just don't want to hear it.'

'They are blinkered some of them, they don't want change. It's an uphill struggle but one I'll keep going on with. And you and Roy – how is he coping these days?'

'All very good – except of course he's still hurting over Bruno. We all are, to be honest. Life moves on, people are sympathetic but then they have their own lives to live. But we still miss him so much, the house isn't the same. He taught us things, his quirkiness – the way he saw life a bit differently. Roy bottles it up but I know he's always thinking of him and whether there was anything he could have done to change the outcome.'

'He's bound to. It was just so terrible and it's still raw, Clees, you don't get over that sort of loss in a set time frame. I honestly don't know how any parent gets over the loss of a child.'

'Auntie Charlie! Auntie Charlie!' Jessica shouted. 'Can we get an ice cream? You promised!'

Cleo had noticed, some years back, Charlie always used bribery on her friends' children. And she had determined not to do the same with Noah and now Molly, too.

'Fancy a coffee – or something stronger?' Charlie asked her.

'Coffee sounds a good plan,' Cleo replied. They were just a few hundred yards from the cafe. She turned to call Humphrey. But he had vanished.

'Humphrey!' she shouted. 'Humphrey!'

There was no sign of him.

She called out again, louder, 'Humphrey, HUMPHREY!' She

scanned the hill they'd just walked down. 'COME ON, BOY! SAUSAGES!' She pulled out the plastic tub of sausage slices she used to treat him with. 'SAUSAGES.'

In the distance she saw a woman walking an elderly golden retriever. A man flying a kite with a small boy running beside him. But no sign of Humphrey.

She called out again, then again. She turned to Charlie. 'Bloody dog, he can be so disobedient when he's got the scent of something. You take Jessica and Noah to the cafe – I'll go and find him and join you there.'

'Want me to come with you?'

She shook her head. 'I'll go and find the little bugger. Noah loves chocolate – if you can order him something involving chocolate, he'll be very happy.'

'Want me to take Molly?'

Cleo looked at Charlie's handful of Pomeranians and the two children. 'No, I'll be OK, thanks.' She began pushing Molly back up the hill, through the long grass, calling out again.

The sky clouded over above her, and with it, something clouded over inside her. The case Roy was currently on, the illegal trade in puppies and the epidemic of dog thefts, along with their experience yesterday. Could someone have taken Humphrey?

Impossible, surely. Although he was a rescue mongrel, she knew, to the inexperienced eye, Humphrey could be mistaken for a pedigree Labrador. But only a very inexperienced eye.

'HUMPHREY!' she shouted again, as Molly began crying. 'COME ON, BOY! SAUSAGES!'

She was approaching the woman with the golden retriever, who was repeatedly tossing a tennis ball for it from a ball launcher. Cleo asked her if she'd seen a black Lab. But she hadn't.

None of the other five people she approached, increasingly frantically, over the next ten minutes had either.

Finally, she stopped at the top of the hill and stared around the expanse of park in all directions, ignoring Molly's continued, increasing crying. There was no sign of Humphrey. No sign at all.

49

The dog was a tart, Gecko thought. It sat beside him on the passenger seat of his van, and even though it was anxiously squeaking it was still able to munch the biscuits he drip-fed it as he headed along the A27 dual carriageway towards Brighton. The name on its collar read *Humphrey*, and there was a phone number beneath.

Gecko had decided to do a little private business for himself, spurred on by seeing all the substantial rewards posted online for the return of missing dogs. He had a simple plan – grab the dog and hold it to ransom! Give it a couple of days, during which its owner would become increasingly frantic and willing to pay almost anything to get it back. And then play the white knight, say he'd found the dog wandering around the streets, deliver it back and collect the reward.

Simples!

He reached over and patted the dog on its head. 'Good boy, Humphrey, good boy!' The dog was panting.

He turned off the dual carriageway and wound down through the Hollingbury industrial estate, then made a sharp turn into the car park of the ASDA superstore. Leaving the dog in the van, with his window cracked a little, he dashed in, bought a small sack of cheap dry dog food and several bags of treats, paid and hurried back out, mindful of the police office nearby.

Five minutes later, turning south off the A27, Gecko carefully stuck to the 40 mph then 30 mph speed limits as he headed south into the city limits of Brighton and Hove. Reaching Preston Park, still shovelling treats into the dog's mouth, he made a right turn at the lights and threaded the van up towards the street of Edwardian terraced and semi-detached houses, Kingsley Avenue, and pulled into a space a few yards down from number 18, where Elvira lived and which was now the home they often shared.

After he turned off the engine, he dropped a rope noose over the dog's head and was met with no resistance as he pulled it tight. 'Good boy, good Humphrey!' he said. 'Just one more little thing to do.' He reached around Humphrey's neck, undid his collar and put it in the van's glove locker. 'Good boy!' he said and fed him yet another treat. Then, his shopping in one hand, he encouraged the dog out of the door with the other and locked the van.

As he walked round to the pavement, he saw to his dismay a nosey elderly woman neighbour coming out of her front door with her wheeled shopping cart. She greeted him with a pleasant wave. 'You've got a dog!' she exclaimed.

'It's for Elvira, a guide dog,' he explained, the idea popping into his head from nowhere.

'Oh, good,' she said. 'Such wonderful dogs!'

'They are.'

As she went on her way, he walked up to their front door, Humphrey walking along beside him on the leash, his tail hanging low.

50

Shortly after 11.30 a.m., following leads from the House-to-House Enquiry Team, Velvet Wilde drove the marked police car, with Norman Potting beside her, along a rutted track directly below the South Downs. They passed two large fields of sheep and another of cows, until they came into a farmyard, with a small duck pond and a pretty Georgian-style house on the far side, with a well-tended bed of roses in front. A solitary cocker spaniel ran towards them, barking loudly.

The two detectives climbed out and, accompanied by the dog, which was wearing a collar embossed with the name 'Sophie', walked up to the farmhouse door and rapped hard.

It was opened moments later by a friendly woman with untidy brown hair, dressed in grubby cut-off jeans, a T-shirt and flip-flops. She looked at their warrant cards and said, 'Officers, apologies for my appearance. Are you here about the bloody neighbours down the road?'

There was a tantalizing aroma of fried bacon.

Norman Potting, distracted by the spaniel, was kneeling and stroking his own tummy. 'Got any of that bacon going spare?' he asked.

'Norman!' Velvet Wilde stopped him, and immediately turned to the woman. 'Mrs Yanci Allen?'

'Yes, that's me.'

'Your husband is David?'

'Yes, he is. What's this about, exactly?'

'We are carrying out enquiries at a number of farms in this area regarding puppy farming,' Potting said.

'The Jims? I know they keep dogs,' Yanci Allen said.

'Yes. That's one of the farms we want to talk about.'

They were joined by a tall, burly man, with a bald dome and a long rug of hair either side, wearing dungarees. He was holding a trowel and had muddy knees. Addressing the detectives he said, 'Weeds, the little buggers. This time of year is a nightmare for them.' He waved his trowel in the air. 'No one ever tells the little sods it's Sunday and they should have a day of rest.'

'These are police officers,' his wife said.

'Come to arrest our weeds have you, officers?' He chuckled at his joke.

'Mr David Allen?' Potting asked.

'Well I was when I went to bed last night,' he said amiably.

'We'd just like to ask you a few questions about some of your neighbouring farms – including Appletree as your wife has just mentioned.'

Instantly his expression darkened. 'They might be geographical neighbours,' he said. 'But that's where the word neighbours stops. Are you finally going to do something about them?'

'Would you officers like to come in for a cup of tea?' his wife asked.

'We're fine, thank you,' Wilde replied, glancing at Potting for confirmation. 'It's kind of you but we've a lot of people to see this morning.'

'*Finally* do something about them?' Potting asked, looking at the couple. Then he caught Wilde's eye. 'Have there been any problems with them?'

David Allen gave a sarcastic laugh and his wife nodded. 'Apart from bits constantly being nicked off everyone's tractors and other farm machinery, their dogs chasing and killing sheep, their relatives' kids running wild. And their son, Dallas, up the road is just as bad. All of them drive their 4 x 4s as if the roads around here are a racetrack. They go lamping in the middle of the night all over everyone's property without permission. They've run over cats, dogs and they don't give a toss – they're not farmers, they're villains who live on what used to be farms.'

'So they're not on your Christmas card list?' Potting asked drily.

'I don't think they'd know what a Christmas card is,' Yanci Allen replied.

51

Sunday 28 March

Katy Fairfax gave Dr Victoria Grogan a quick rundown as they headed up the stairs.

Chris followed them up and into Bluebell's room, and the doctor tried to put their drowsy, bewildered daughter at ease. 'Hello, Bluebell,' she said. 'Your mummy and daddy tell me you're not feeling very well. Is that right?'

She nodded weakly.

The doctor beamed at her. 'Well, we don't want you in bed feeling unwell, do we?'

Bluebell shook her head.

Dr Grogan peered at the livid mark on the little girl's nose. 'That's a nasty scratch you have there. How did you get that?'

'A puppy we saw when we picked up Moose,' she murmured.

'Moose? Who is Moose?'

Chris explained.

The doctor nodded, studying the mark even more closely. 'The puppy did that?'

'He didn't mean to,' Bluebell said. 'He was just playing.'

'It wasn't actually our puppy that bit her,' Chris said. 'It was another one we were looking at.'

Grogan frowned. 'When did you start feeling ill?'

'On Friday,' Katy said.

'And you said this happened on Thursday?'

'Yes,' Chris said.

'Your puppy has had all her vaccinations, I presume?'

Chris and Katy looked at each other. 'We're not actually sure she has, but Bluebell is up to date on her tetanus,' Chris said.

Katy qualified this. 'Moose has not been well, but she's really picking up now. The vet thinks she might not have had any vaccinations. That the breeder we bought her from may have lied to us.'

'She was bred in the UK?'

'We're not even sure about that,' Katy admitted, and blushed.

The doctor looked at them both, then smiled. 'My husband and I have dogs and young children. I wouldn't worry too much about that little bite, but we'll all keep an eye on it.' She looked down at Bluebell. 'OK, sweetheart, I'm going to take your temperature and then examine you and see if we can make you better quickly.'

Fifteen minutes later, Chris and Katy went back downstairs with the doctor and through into the kitchen. Out in the garden, Katy watched a thrush drinking in the stone bird bath.

'What do you think is wrong?' Katy asked.

'Well, she's not displaying any Covid symptoms,' the doctor said.

'She's had a negative PCR – the doctor we saw yesterday texted us to say it wasn't Covid,' Katy added.

'I think it's a bug she's picked up – probably from school or it could have been from the swimming pool – there are a couple of nasty ones doing the rounds at the moment. But I'm concerned about her temperature, which is 38.7. I'll give you some pills which should settle her and enable her to sleep tonight, and I'll write you a prescription for tomorrow. I'm sure she'll be fine, but if her temperature doesn't start to come down, or if you get worried during the night, call the emergency number – I'll be around until 7 a.m. tomorrow, or if you get really concerned call 999, but I doubt that will be necessary.' Dr Grogan gave them a brief smile.

'And if she's not better in the morning?' Chris asked.

'Then I think it would be sensible to refer her to the paediatrician at the Royal Alexandra Children's Hospital for blood tests. But hopefully it won't come to that.' She gave them another smile.

They showed Dr Grogan to the door and thanked her again. As they closed it, Bluebell cried out. They both ran back upstairs and into her room.

She was sitting up in bed, tears rolling down her cheeks.

'What is it, darling?' Katy asked. 'What's the matter?'

'Am I going to die?'

52

As Roy Grace drove the Alfa slowly along the cart track towards their cottage, in glorious sunshine, he felt uplifted as he always did at this time of year. The promise of months of long, light evenings ahead. Over to his right he saw sheep dotted across the hill, tufts of fluffy white, like bonsai clouds, he thought.

He passed on his left the open-sided corrugated iron barn belonging to the local farmer, which contained several large pieces of agricultural equipment and a decrepit tractor that had not moved in all the time they'd been here. He was looking forward to a Sunday evening with Cleo, when their happy routine was to enjoy a cheese platter, with a glass or two of red wine – when he wasn't on call – and watch *Antiques Roadshow* and then an ITV drama, or maybe another episode of *Succession*, which they'd got into.

Just as he pulled up behind Cleo's recent acquisition, a second-hand hybrid Kia, his phone rang. It was Robin Smith, calling from Jersey.

'You all right, buddy?' the Chief Officer asked.

'All good.'

'Sorry it's taken a while to get back to you, I just wanted to make double-sure. This Mr and Mrs Jones at the address you gave me, in Don Street – that address, as I suspected, doesn't exist.'

'That's really helpful, Robin, thanks.'

'There are only a few Jonathan Joneses here. One is in his nineties, another only twenty-two. The only one that fits your age description is a Jonathan Jones who's a member of a prominent highly respected Jersey family – they own a number of restaurants and cafes and a pottery business. Jonathan and his partner, Manon, have an interior design business, and he serves as a volunteer on the lifeboats. I can have someone interview him if you'd like, but he doesn't seem like your man and the address doesn't fit. I've just pinged you his photograph from the internet.'

'Thanks, Robin, I'll have a look and get back to you if I need any more on him, if that's OK?'

'Anytime. Come over here with your wife for a holiday sometime – Jersey is the best kept secret of the British Isles – it's gorgeous – and would be good to see you!'

'I might just do that,' Grace replied and thanked him for his help.

As soon as he had ended the call, he opened the attachment in the email Smith had sent. The picture he saw, of a good-looking, silver-haired man with elegant glasses, was nothing like the Tom Hartley he'd met, yesterday, in Bournemouth.

He climbed out of the car and walked up to the front door, smiling at the rows of daffodils in full bloom on either side of the path, and the sound of the hens in the garden on the far side of the cottage. But as he put his key in the lock he frowned, puzzled by the silence from the other side of the door. Normally, Humphrey barked excitedly, greeting him home any time of the day or night.

Nor was there any sign of him as he opened the door. Instead, he saw Cleo standing up from the sofa, phone in hand, her eyes raw with tears.

53

Gecko had told Elvira, all along, that he worked for a dog rescue charity, and she loved that so much, loved that he did such a wonderful and kind thing. So she wasn't surprised when he came into her little house with the docile, friendly dog, and let it come up to her, then removed the rope halter.

Seated on the sofa, in her thick glasses, some mindless programme was on the large-screen television, just a few feet from her. She patted Humphrey's neck with both hands, then stroked his head. 'You are lovely and soft! What's your name?'

'I don't know,' Gecko lied. 'He didn't have a collar or name tag. We'll need to give him a name.'

'Where was he?'

'In Stanmer Park. I was walking a couple of rescue dogs for the charity – you know, as I do – and he was just wandering around, looking very lost. He came up to me, like he figured I might be able to help him.'

Elvira smiled. 'That's because he was drawn to you by your aura of kindness. He knew you could help him.' She stroked Marion's arm, then took his hand and kissed it. 'Animals have instincts that tell them when someone is a kind person. That's why he was drawn to you.'

He kissed her cheek. 'You say the sweetest things. Yeah, maybe.'

She shook her head. 'Not *maybe*. He knew you were the

211

person who could help him.' She hesitated. 'But why didn't you leave him at the rescue centre – at Raystede?'

'Yeah, well, I thought about it. But he seemed pretty distressed. Figured I'd bring him here for the night so we could take care of him, give him some love and attention, and I'll have a look on the internet. There's a Facebook forum where people often post about lost dogs – that's how we return a lot of them to their owners. And they often post on Twitter, too – thought it might speed up the process. He looked at me so soulfully, you know, I hadn't the heart to leave him in kennels overnight.'

She squeezed his hand. 'You are such a kind man. It's one of so many things I love about you.'

'It is five thirty p.m.,' her talking watch announced.

She raised her wrist so he could see the watch. 'And I love this – you are just so thoughtful.'

'Humphrey,' he said.

'Humphrey?'

'The dog,' he said. 'He feels like a Humphrey to me.'

'OK,' she said and smiled. 'Hello, Humphrey!'

The dog nuzzled her.

'Humphrey!' Gecko called.

Immediately the dog looked at him.

'I think he likes that name!' he said. 'Are you hungry, Humphrey? Food?' He shook the carrier bag full of food and treats.

Humphrey cocked his leg and peed on the carpet.

'Jesus!' Gecko shouted at him, startling Elvira. 'Bad boy, bad boy!'

Humphrey barked and ran out of the room.

'What's he done?'

'He's pissed on the floor – on the carpet.'

'Don't be angry with him – he's probably nervous.'

'I'll give him bloody *nervous*.' He hurried out of the room and saw Humphrey again cocking his leg on the bottom step of the staircase.

'Humphrey, what the hell are you doing?'

The dog looked at him balefully and began licking one of his front paws.

'There is no pissing in this house!' he admonished angrily.

Scared of the tone of his voice, Humphrey dashed off and into the kitchen, where he again cocked his leg and peed on the tiles.

'What the hell do you think you're doing?' Gecko opened the rear door and shoved him, roughly, out into the garden, slamming the door behind him.

'My love, don't be angry at him, he's probably confused.'

'Confused? He's pissed again on the stairs and now on the kitchen floor.'

'Don't scare him, I'll help you clean it up. The poor thing's probably terrified.'

'Terrified?'

They could both hear him barking loudly, then whining.

Gecko opened the back door and yelled, 'Quiet!'

'Marion!' Elvira called out. 'This isn't like you, calm down, you're frightening me.'

'Frightening you?'

'What's come over you, my love?'

'What's come over me? I rescue him out of the kindness of my heart and this is how he rewards me?' He went outside and saw Humphrey cowering against the wall on the far side of the tiny garden. The dog was shaking.

Elvira came out and stood beside Gecko. 'Where is he?'

'He's cowering against the wall.'

'Be kind to him, he's probably completely traumatized. Humphrey!' she called gently. 'Humphrey, darling, are you hungry? Would you like some food?'

Gecko again shook the bag of dog treats. Humphrey stayed

where he was by the wall, looking at them both with scared eyes. 'Come on, boy,' he said. 'Dinner!'

The dog did not move.

Gecko filled a cereal bowl with dry food, then placed it on the floor. He filled another cereal bowl with water and laid it on the floor beside it. Then, helped by Elvira, he cleaned up the three indoor places where the dog had peed.

When they had finished, he went upstairs, into the spare room which was Elvira's office and which he now shared, opened his laptop and logged on to the Sussex dog forum. There was no mention of any missing dog called Humphrey.

He checked Twitter and found nothing there either.

Too soon, he decided.

He would check again in an hour.

As he went back downstairs, he smelled a vile stench. It became worse as he walked into the kitchen, and he saw a pile of poo on the floor, just beside the little dining table. There was no sign of the dog.

He stormed into the living room. Elvira was again sat right in front of the television, now watching David Attenborough talking about bird migration. She loved his programmes.

'Can you fucking believe it?'

'Is Humphrey OK? Is he eating his dinner now?'

'Can't you smell it?'

She raised her head and sniffed, then screwed up her face. 'Ewwww.'

'Yep. *Yech*. I put out his dinner and the little bugger came inside, didn't touch his food, shat on the floor and went back out into the garden again.'

'Maybe he's trying to tell you something,' she said with a smile.

'Yeah, what?'

'That you should watch *MasterChef* more and improve your culinary skills.'

'That is so not funny.'

They both heard the dog barking again, loudly, enthusiastically.

'Humphrey thinks it is!' she said.

54

Sunday 28 March

Roy Grace immediately put his arms around Cleo, hugging her tight. 'Vanished?'

She began sobbing uncontrollably. 'It's been awful. I've been trying to call you.'

'I only just saw your messages, what happened?'

They perched on the sofa. He noticed the bottle of red wine, a partially filled glass beside it, as Cleo related what had happened in Stanmer Park earlier. 'Oh God,' she said. 'Do you think he's been stolen?'

He sat still for some moments, thinking it through, staring at the obstacle course of Noah's toys on the floor.

'Darling,' he said, shaking his head. 'Humphrey is not a dog that would be of any interest to the puppy trade – they don't want mongrels.'

She nodded bleakly, looking unconvinced, still sobbing.

'And he's seven years old. He's not remotely in the target zone for the dog thieves.'

'But someone's stolen him, Roy,' she said. 'They've bloody stolen him.'

'Listen,' he said, heavy-hearted and trying to calm her down. 'I love him as much as you do. He can be a monkey. There's a few times when I've been out with him and he's just run off. He gets the scent of a rabbit, or even another dog, and boom – he's gone.'

'So why didn't he come back?' she asked. 'I was there for ages calling him. Over an hour.'

'Maybe someone found him and thought he was lost. That happened to me once, on a run up on the Devil's Dyke, remember? He'd vanished and I found him with a young couple he'd just gone up to as if looking for help. We think dogs are smart, but sometimes they're just like us – like kids who get lost.'

'I hope you're right,' she said. 'He's just such a soppy dog, he loves everyone. He'd go with anyone at all – especially if they offered him treats.'

'Have you reported him missing to the police, or shall I?' he asked.

She nodded. 'I have – and the RSPCA, and the dog warden.'

'What about social media? Facebook, Twitter?'

'I was thinking about that.'

'Tell me exactly where you last saw him and I'll go back and look for him.'

'It's getting dark.'

'I'll take a torch. If he's wandering about, I just want to check all around where you were when you last saw him, he may come back to that area. But first let's find a good picture of him and post it on the Facebook dog forum, and on Twitter and Instagram.'

'Should we offer a reward?' she asked.

He thought for some moments. 'Well, if it gets Humphrey back it's probably worth it. It's not like we are being ransomed. Let's give it some thought.'

'You know all about how many dogs are being stolen at the moment,' she said.

'Yes, but as I said, it's young, pedigree dogs – or popular cross-breeds that people will pay big money for. Bless Humphrey, we adore him, but he doesn't fit the profile of dogs at risk.'

Nodding through her tears, she opened her laptop and began

to look for pictures of Humphrey. There were dozens and dozens. The cutest of all was one she had taken a week ago, in long grass in the field behind their cottage, looking straight at the camera as if he was grinning.

'If someone's found him, why wouldn't they have done something about it already, Roy? That's what's worrying me. He's got his name and my mobile number on his collar and he's chipped.'

That was worrying him, too, but he didn't want to distress Cleo further. The one thing he did know from all his team's research since the start of Operation Brush was that the criminals involved were after high-value dogs and Humphrey just did not fit into that category. So where was he?

He formed two hypotheses in his mind. The first that Humphrey had been taken by someone who genuinely thought he was lost and intended to inform either the police or the RSPCA, but had not yet got around to doing it. The second was that he'd been taken by a similar person to the one who had taken Sara Gurner's dog, mistaking it for a dog of some monetary value. In which case they might release him back onto the street.

As they looked at more photos of Humphrey, Cleo's phone rang. She saw from the display it was her sister, sounding more subdued than usual. 'Hey, Clees. Any news of Humphrey?'

'No,' she replied. 'I'm going to put out some posts on social media. We're just getting some photos ready now and I'll think of some wording. Roy's going back to the park to have another look for him. We're thinking of offering a reward – what do you think?'

'Good idea, but not too much – you don't want to be deluged with people trying to con you. There's a lot of nasty people out there.'

'OK,' Cleo said. 'How much?'

Charlie was quiet for a moment, then she said, 'I'd go for something modest, but a sum that would be useful to many people. One hundred pounds?'

'Thanks, that's helpful.'

'No worries. Listen, I'll meet Roy there and help him.'

'No, please don't worry, I can't imagine Humphrey is still in the park.'

'He might be, Clees. Don't you remember that time you and I left Toby on top of Firle Beacon?'

Cleo frowned, thinking back, distantly remembering something about it. Then it came flooding, so embarrassingly, back. She'd not long passed her driving test, and had borrowed their mother's car to take her adored miniature poodle for a walk on the Downs – it was more an excuse to go for a drive than anything else.

They'd driven up to the famed beauty spot, had a glorious walk, chatting away, then gone back home. An hour after they got home their mother had said it was strange, but she'd called Toby and he hadn't come for his dinner. At which point both Cleo and Charlie realized to their horror they could not remember bringing the dog back – they'd been so absorbed talking. They shot back up there and found a woman – a total saint – who'd seen the very lost little dog and had stayed with it, in the hope its owner would return.

'I'll be there ASAP, Clees. I'll call Roy when I'm there.'

Cleo thought for a moment, then realized that it would be helpful. Stanmer Park was vast and it would be hard to tell him exactly where she had last seen Humphrey. 'Are you really sure? I don't want to ruin your nice cosy Sunday evening with Lance.'

'I'm one hundred per cent sure.' Then Charlie lowered her voice. 'I feel so guilty about the breeder I sent you to. I want to help and make it up to you both. And I'm sure we'll get him back quickly. I know it's hard but try not to worry. In all honesty, it will be a joy to get away from Lance for a couple of hours, he's doing my head in!'

Cleo smiled fleetingly. She didn't think anything could make her smile at this moment. But all her life, Charlie had managed to surprise her.

55

The Exhibits Office was housed in a group of rooms on the ground floor of the Major Crime Suite of Sussex Police Headquarters. Entering it always felt to Glenn Branson like walking into a labyrinth. The walls on both sides were lined floor-to-ceiling with grey shelves stacked with green and blue plastic boxes crammed with items. And some bigger items which would not fit in lay on the shelves wrapped in polythene or brown paper and tagged.

Stuck on one wall of each room was the list of names of all the operations. Glenn glanced at one. *Op Magnesium*; *Op Sunlight*; *Op Maytree*; *Op Clyde*.

Laid out on two plain tables that had been pushed together were all the exhibits recovered so far for Op Brush, each in a clear plastic evidence bag. The DI and the Exhibits Officer, Michelle Boshoff, both wearing latex gloves, were identifying the fast-track items that would be sent initially for forensic examination. So far these consisted of a cigarette butt, part of a number plate and fibres from the outer clothing of the victim, Tim Ruddle.

There was a black baseball cap that had been found on the muddy ground near the farmer. It had been shown to his wife who said she had never seen it before, and nor had their farmhand. Glenn picked up the bag containing it and turned it round, looking at it closely, thinking it could well have been on the head of one of the assailants, and could reveal vital DNA clues. He added that to the fast-track items. Then as he put it down, he wrinkled his nose at an unpleasant smell. Some kind of animal dung, he realized, and then saw the possible culprit. A small plastic water bottle, half-empty, inside an evidence bag. On the bottle itself was a small brown smear – so small he had almost missed it.

He picked the bag up, momentarily holding it away from himself. 'Can you smell anything, Michelle?' he asked.

'Your cologne?' she said.

'Seriously?'

She smiled. 'It's very nice – and a lot better than most of the smells I have to put up with in here!'

He held the bag closer to his nose. Then immediately said, 'Yuk!'

'A rival cologne?' she asked.

He handed it to her. She sniffed and then quickly pushed it well away from her face. 'I definitely prefer yours, Glenn.'

'Thanks a bunch!'

She sniffed again, harder this time. 'You know what this reminds me of? Pigs.'

'You think?'

She nodded. 'About four years ago I had to deal with two skip loads of pig excrement seized from a farm near Guildford and sent to the lab for sieving, looking for body parts, bones, teeth etcetera – it was on a murder enquiry, Op Morgan. I had to live with that smell for days and it's very distinctive. I'd say that's what this is.'

'I'll put the cap and bottle on the fast-track list to be checked for prints or DNA.'

Branson sniffed it again disdainfully. 'Definitely pig shit.'

'Stay with the brand you're wearing, Glenn,' she said. 'It suits you better.'

56

Sunday 28 March

Chris Fairfax had suffered Sunday night blues from right back into his childhood. Unlike many of his friends who had loved their schooldays, he'd had an unhappy time. His father, insisting it would make a man out of him, had made him become a weekly boarder at a school near Brighton from the age of seven.

Sunday nights back in his childhood had been a time of dread, when one of his parents would drop him back at school, to the same Sunday supper in the refectory of cold, cremated beef encircled by a large amount of fat, mashed potato, beetroot and cabbage, followed by a banana custard dessert. Even today, he still could not eat fat or bananas.

Katy, although she'd had a much happier childhood, also shared that Sunday night feeling. So they had agreed to make Sunday nights a time to properly relax and enjoy.

Normally.

A time to chill before the Monday morning onslaught of human misery. Sure, it paid good money, but sure, too, it took a toll on their own life. There were days when they came home laughing at the absurdity of some of the things their clients had told them. But there were other days when they came home close to tears, astonished by the way one human being could treat another – especially a partner they had at one time truly loved.

Normally on a Sunday night they'd be lounging in front of the television, pigging out on a pizza – extra pepperoni for him and extra anchovies for her – and a few glasses of wine, followed by far too many pieces from a selection of whatever chocolates they had in the house, watching a box set, catching up on shows they'd been recommended. Last week it had been *Call My Agent*, and they had loved the previous two episodes and had watched some more during the week. They had planned to watch the final two of the series tonight.

But instead, they were both up in Bluebell's all-pink bedroom, increasingly worried about her. She was hot, perspiring and her temperature was steadily creeping up even more. The last time they'd taken it, an hour ago on Chris's watch, it was a very concerning 38.8. She lay back, her duvet with its princess gown motif pulled up to her neck, her head framed by the princess crown motif on her pillow, moaning that she was so hot.

Chris opened the window, letting a cold wind blow in. Almost straight away, Bluebell screamed. 'No, no, it hurts, close it, Daddy, it hurts!'

Chris and Katy stared at each other, puzzled. He immediately shut it. Katy went out into their bedroom and returned with a face towel which she had soaked under a cold tap. But as she dabbed their daughter's face, Bluebell screamed out in terror. 'No, no, no. NOOOOO!'

Katy jumped back in shock, staring bewildered at her husband. Then she turned to Bluebell. 'Would you like a cooling shower, darling?'

Bluebell writhed in her bed and screamed, 'No, no, no! No shower, please, Mummy.'

Whispering to her husband, Katy said, 'I'll get the thermometer and see if there's been any change.'

He nodded.

She slipped out of the room, closing the door behind her. As she did so, he felt a faint draught of air and, to his shock, Bluebell reacted to it. 'That hurts, Mummy, Daddy, that hurts!'

'The air, darling?' he asked gently. 'The air hurts?'

Her voice a high-pitched squeal, she said, 'So much, so much.' She began sobbing.

He sat on the bed, scared and bewildered, stroking her face, looking around the little room, with the pink dressing table covered in bottles of nail varnish. At Bluebell's dressing-up clothes she loved so much, spilling out of her over-stuffed wardrobe.

Katy came back in, took her temperature, then, alarmed, showed Chris the reading.

38.9.

Gesturing him to follow her out of the room, they went and stood on the landing. As a precaution, Katy shut Bluebell's door as gently as she could to avoid any draught. 'Dr Grogan said if her temperature continued to rise we should call her.'

'Yes.'

Katy dialled the number and got Dr Grogan's voicemail. She left a message asking her to call back urgently. When she ended the call she turned to her husband. 'I'm really worried,' she said, her face pale. 'There's something very wrong with her.'

He nodded, feeling utterly helpless.

'Maybe we should take her to A&E at the hospital?'

'Let's give the doctor a chance to call back. Half an hour?'

'Half an hour, no more. If she doesn't call back, we're taking her to the hospital.'

'I agree.'

'I'll go and sit with her. Shit, we've completely forgotten about Moose—'

'I'll check on her,' he said.

He went downstairs. Moose was up and about. He saw she'd eaten all of her food.

Chris was pleased, at least, to see her getting better, but was increasingly worried about the seeming disappearance of the breeder, John Peat, from whom they had bought the puppy. His and Katy's concerns had been deepened by an article in yesterday's local paper, the *Argus*, about a farmer who had been murdered while, apparently, attempting to stop criminals from stealing a litter of puppies from his farm.

In buying Moose, had they, albeit unintentionally, contributed to this vile trade in puppies? he wondered.

But it wasn't Moose's fault. She was a beautiful, sweet puppy. All his thoughts went back to Bluebell.

Then he heard Katy's voice.

'Darling, it's Doctor Grogan.' She came into the room, holding her phone to her ear. 'One moment, doctor, I'm just putting you on speaker.' She tapped a button on the phone and after a moment he heard the woman's voice.

'Bluebell's temperature has risen to 38.9?' Dr Grogan asked.

'Yes, up from 38.8 in the past hour. And she's very distressed. Could you come over?' Katy asked.

'Is she awake?'

'She is, yes.'

'How is she, generally?'

'She's delirious and very confused. I tried taking her pulse – I did a First Aid course some years ago and I'm trying to remember everything. Her heart's beating fast. She's very hot and sweaty.'

'I think she should be in hospital, I'm afraid. That would be the best place for her with those symptoms, I don't like the sound of that temperature. Jump in the car with her now and get her to the hospital immediately.'

Thanking her, Katy ended the call shakily and looked at Chris. He nodded.

57

Sunday 28 March

Earlier that day Velvet Wilde drove while an unusually subdued Norman Potting sat beside her, frowning studiously at his phone and texting in a plodding way with one finger.

'You all right, Norman?' she asked.

'Sort of.' He gave a sad smile. 'Why?'

'You seem a bit quiet.'

He glanced at the satnav. 'Coming up on the left in a few hundred yards,' he said. Then he added, 'Tell you on the way back – I've a new lady in my life but she's going through some tough treatment for cancer at the moment.'

'I'm sorry. Do you want to—'

'Left here!' he called out sharply, interrupting her, as the farm entrance appeared. It was partially obscured by brambles on either side, with a small, faded wooden sign proclaiming SPRING FARM. Next to it was a larger but equally aged sign, with a skull and crossbones at the top and, in large red capital letters, the words KEEP OUT. TRESPASSERS WILL BE SHOT.

As they lurched onto a potholed and rutted cart track, Wilde said, 'Nothing like a nice welcome to make you feel all warm and fuzzy.'

Potting raised his eyebrows. 'Did you see the Public Footpath sign almost buried in the brambles?'

'No.'

He jerked a finger. 'Just back there. He's probably breaking the law with that sign.'

'You going to tell him?'

He looked at her dubiously. 'Toss you for the privilege.'

The hedgerow lining the drive on both sides was as unkempt as the entrance. Sheep grazed in one large field and cows in another. At least the animals looked healthy, Potting – who had been brought up on a farm – thought. One point in John Roke's favour. He suspected there wouldn't be many more.

There might have been a spring after which Spring Farm was named, but it wasn't in evidence as they passed an open-sided barn containing rusted agricultural equipment that looked like it hadn't been used in years, an old US Army Jeep on blocks, minus its wheels, and a small mountain of vehicle parts that looked modern – Potting recognized a door and tailgate that would have been on a Ford Transit van. Wilde stared at the parts.

'Buys his vehicles from IKEA, does he?' Wilde asked with a smile.

'More likely has someone nick them, dismantle them here and flog the bits as spares around the local pubs. But that's not our problem at the moment.' He nodded ahead as they entered a muddy farmyard, with a ramshackle flint farmhouse, the ivy cladding seemingly the only thing holding it together. All the windows looked rotten, with only flecks of their original white paint visible, and the front door was the same.

Two large black and tan dogs, with pointy ears and mouths that were all teeth, snarled and barked at them. They were tethered by chains restraining them a few feet from a green kennel that was in a lot better shape than the owner's house. Several white geese ran, honking and clucking aggressively, towards their car, and a white and silver cockerel shrieked piercingly nearby. There was a rank cocktail of the smell of animals, stagnant water, straw, rust and timber.

To their right, in a black indent that might once have been a duck pond fed by the eponymous but now absent spring, were a rusted-out 1950s Chevrolet pickup truck, resting on its wheel rims, the skeletal remains of an old motorbike, and a lopsided caravan. There was a row of caravans beyond, all looking in varying states of disrepair, and several barns beyond these from which came a distant cacophony of barking.

'Bit of a restoration project that bike, do you think?' Wilde asked.

'More like a resurrection needed, if you ask me,' he replied. Then he said, 'Oh, hello, we're in luck, looks like Squire Roke is in residence!'

Both of them saw a heavily bearded man with angry hair appear in the front doorway, looking as happy as his dogs, and brandishing an over-and-under shotgun. Tall and very over-weight, dressed in a checked shirt, a grimy puffer torn in several places, brown corduroy trousers and heavy mud-caked boots, he pretty much filled the door frame.

'You call that *luck*?' Wilde murmured dubiously.

'We're on the side of the angels, remember.' Potting threw her a grin, opened his door and climbed out. Immediately a goose ran up and pecked him on the leg. 'Boo!' he retorted and heard his colleague giggle as she got out of the car too.

'Come one foot closer and I'll shoot!' the man shouted out in a voice with a strong Sussex accent. 'Just one foot, I'm telling you!'

Potting held up his warrant card and Wilde did the same. 'We're police officers,' he shouted back. 'Detective Sergeant Norman Potting and Detective Constable Velvet Wilde from Surrey and Sussex Major Crime Team. We're looking for John Roke.' All the time he was speaking he carried on walking towards the man.

'You've found him,' the man replied, lowering his gun, but only a little. 'What do you bastards want to nick me for this time?' Roke had a string of past convictions, and his last prison sentence had been for stealing copper from church roofs.

'We're not here to nick you for anything, Mr Roke,' Potting said. Then could not help himself from adding, 'Well not yet, anyway.'

The farmer studied both of them, fleetingly, with sharp, ice-coloured eyes. Then he nodded at his gun. 'I keep this for the likes of vermin like you.'

'And I'm sure your gun licence is up to date,' Potting said.

'Want me to get it and show you?'

'We're not here to talk about your gun licence, Mr Roke.'

'So you're not here to nick me for anything and you're not here to talk about my gun licence, so this is just a social visit, is it – in which case you can both fuck off.'

'Actually, Mr Roke, we're here because we'd like to take a look around, if you're willing to let us.'

The man's expression suddenly became dangerous, momentarily unnerving both detectives. 'You're having a laugh, right? A look around? What do you think this place is, a stately home that's open to the public? Clear off, the pair of you.' He raised the gun menacingly.

'You're committing a criminal offence pointing a gun at a police officer,' Velvet Wilde said sharply. 'If you continue I will radio for an Armed Response Unit and you will never be allowed to hold a gun permit again. Do you understand me?'

Roke hesitated for a moment, then reluctantly lowered the gun.

'Break the barrels,' Wilde commanded.

Again, Roke hesitated, then complied. As he broke them open, both cartridges ejected and fell to the ground.

'Now we're getting somewhere,' Potting said, kneeling and picking them up. 'I'll give these back to you before we leave.'

'You're leaving right now.'

Potting shook his head. 'No, I'm afraid we've only just arrived. We're looking for some missing dogs and you're down as a licensed breeder. So what we'd like to do is have a good look around your premises.'

'You've got a warrant?'

The DS looked at the farmer, who stood several inches taller than himself. 'Listen to me, sunshine. We don't have a search warrant, but what I do have are these.' He dug his hand into the inside breast pocket of his jacket and produced a wad of papers. 'Six warrants for your arrest for unpaid fines.' He raised a finger, seeing Roke on the verge of exploding.

Roke glared at him.

'Now I'm going to give you two choices. Either you let DC Wilde and myself take a good look around your premises, without any interference, or we'll go and get a warrant. If we have to do that, we'll be back with the biggest army of coppers you've ever seen in your life, and we'll tie you up for the next six months as we go through the provenance of every vehicle and animal you have on this site.' Then he held up the arrest warrants. 'And if you're a good boy I'll stick these back in my pocket and forget about them – for now anyway.'

Roke looked nonplussed. 'Go ahead, do what you have to do, fill your boots, you won't find anything. I don't know why you're bothering with me, it's Terry Jim you should be taking a look at, him and his little shit of a son, Dallas.'

'We're visiting all the farms in this area,' Potting replied.

'Shouldn't you be doing something useful with your time?' Roke asked sarcastically. 'Like nicking motorists for speeding?'

58

Less than twenty minutes after Cleo had put out the posts on social media, offering a reward of one hundred pounds and giving her mobile phone number as the contact, her phone rang.

'I have your dog,' a female voice said.

For an instant, Cleo was elated. 'Oh my God! You've found Humphrey? Thank you for calling, thank God! Where was he?'

'In Stanmer Park. I was walking my own dog and this beautiful black Labrador type came over to us and then just stood there – he barked a couple of times and then whined. He followed us back to my car. I waited there for some while, thinking his owner would turn up, but no one came, and it was starting to get dark. I tried to shoo him away but he wouldn't go – and he was friendly to my own dog.'

'He's friendly to all dogs!' Cleo said. 'Oh God, I'm so relieved. Thank you so much!'

'This reward you are offering, of one hundred pounds. Might you consider making it a little higher?'

The caller had an odd accent, she thought, after her initial moment of elation – it sounded part Brummy – and an odd delivery, as if she was reading from a script. For whatever reason, it made Cleo a tad suspicious. 'How much do you think would be reasonable?' she tested.

'One thousand pounds?'

'One thousand pounds?' Cleo repeated.

'I know I would pay that and more if my little Tilly went missing,' she said.

'OK,' Cleo said, very wary now but not wanting to show it, and thinking fast. 'Can you describe the dog you have, so I can be sure it's him?'

'Of course – hang on, boy!' There was silence for a moment, then the woman said, 'Sorry, the darling wanted a biscuit. He's quite greedy, isn't he?'

'He is.'

'So, describing him, he's a little smaller than most Labs, black hair with a lot of grey in it. I'm not sure how much more description you want?'

'That's fine,' Cleo said. 'So, how would I pay you the money?'

'Cash, dear. I'd need it up front – not that I don't trust you.'

'Of course,' Cleo said.

'You know about What3Words?'

'I do, I have the app.'

'Good. I'll give you a location, you leave the money there and then you give me a What3Words address and I'll bring Humphrey to you.'

'That sounds fine,' Cleo said. 'What is your name?'

'Hazel.'

'Hazel who?'

There was a faint hesitation before she replied. 'Hazel Trussler.'

'OK, Hazel, I'm hugely grateful. We can do this now?'

'Of course.'

'You'll have to give me time to get the money from a cash machine.'

'Yes, absolutely.'

'One quick question – just a final check – what colour collar is Humphrey wearing?'

'It's green.'

'Green? You are sure?'

'Emerald green.'

Cleo hung up on the woman angrily.

The collar Humphrey had been wearing when she'd taken that photograph last week was bright green. But the next day, when Roy had taken him for a long run, somehow the collar had come off and was lost. She'd bought him a new one three days ago, along with a new tag. The new collar was bright red.

59

Roy Grace drove through the entrance to Stanmer Park that Cleo had directed him to, and followed the tree-lined road around the perimeter. After nearly a mile the Alfa's headlights lit up a sign to the cafe, and a short distance on, he saw a silver MX-5 in a parking area at the side of the road. Cleo's sister flashed her headlights twice in recognition.

But just as he pulled up alongside her car, his phone rang. It was Branson. 'Can you talk, boss?'

'Sure if it's quick. I've got a bit of a personal problem.'

'Not your deodorant again?'

'I'm not in the mood for humour. Humphrey's gone missing.'

'Humphrey?'

'Yes.'

'You mean *missing* as in lost, or stolen?'

'I don't know. Cleo was walking him in Stanmer Park and he ran off and disappeared. I've just arrived at the park to see if I can find him.'

'Shit. Tell me where you are and I'll come straight over.'

'No, it's OK, her sister's here to help me, but thank you.'

'If one of those bastards has stolen him, that's too much of a coincidence, right?'

'Exactly. He's probably just run off and got lost – he did it once before. Anyhow, what were you calling about?'

'We may have an interesting development in Operation Brush.

Polly Sweeney just took a call from a woman she said sounded very frightened – wouldn't give her name. This person said she worked in the kennels of a dog breeder – mucking them out and exercising the dogs and that. She'd seen on the news about the farmer who'd been murdered and his French bulldogs stolen. She thinks some of these dogs might be at her kennels.'

Cleo's sister, Charlie, was out of her car and walking towards him. Grace put down his window and signalled to her he would be a moment. 'What made her think that?'

'Five puppies and two adults – a match to the ones from the Ruddles' farm – and the photograph of them that had been in the *Argus* and on television.'

'What else did Polly get from her?'

'That she's scared for her life – like – terrified. She told Polly she's certain there's an illegal operation going on. A co-worker wasn't happy about the condition the dogs were being kept in and said she was going to talk to her boss about it. She's not seen her again and she's really worried what's happened to her.'

'Maybe she just quit?' Grace suggested.

'No, it doesn't sound like it, boss. She'd become friends with this co-worker, and they were going to meet for a drink in a pub, lunchtime today. The woman never turned up. She's called her mobile several times since, and there's no answer.'

'Did she give this co-worker's name?'

'She did, she said it was Rosalind Esche – Romeo Oscar Sierra Alpha Lima India November Delta, Echo Sierra Charlie Hotel Echo. We're going to run some checks on the name.'

'Did Polly get this caller's number?' Grace asked.

'Nope, she said she was too scared to give that either. She withheld the number.'

'Do we know where she was calling from?' Grace said.

'She would only say somewhere in Hailsham.'

'East Sussex,' Grace said. 'In the zone of our suspects.'

'Right in the zone,' Branson confirmed.

'So what happens next with this lady?'

'She's agreed to meet Polly tomorrow evening, after work.'

'She has? Where?'

'She's that angry about the way the puppies are being treated. She's told Polly she'll call her after work and say where to meet.'

'Brilliant,' Grace said. 'I'll be in for the morning briefing, but this sounds as if it could be significant.'

'You sure you don't want me to come over and help look for Humphrey?'

'Thanks, but if he's here, we'll find him. I want you to start developing intelligence on this information. Ring me later with what you find, we need to get on to this straight away.'

Ending the call, Grace climbed out of the car holding his powerful torch and went over to Charlie. He thanked her for coming out.

'Let's go find that rascal, starting with where he was last seen,' she said.

He shone the beam up into the darkness, playing it over several oak and chestnut trees. 'Humphrey!' he called. 'HUMPHREY!'

60

Anish Shah was exhausted and relieved he was just twenty minutes from ending his double shift – covering for a colleague who was unwell – at the hospital. The twenty-seven-year-old paediatric registrar had been on his feet for eighteen hours straight, in the children's department.

Sunday evenings were normally a relatively quiet time, but in the past two hours he'd had to deal with a nine-year-old who'd had his finger severed in a car door, a seven-year-old girl with suspected meningitis, and he'd just sent a four-year-old boy, who'd fallen out of a loft and had a suspected skull fracture, up for an X-ray. He sat down at the nursing station and, feeling low on sugar, began peeling a banana.

Two years ago, he had just qualified as a doctor in his native city of Peshawar, when he'd seen an advertisement for the field of medicine in which he really wanted to specialize – paediatrics – in Brighton, England. It offered much better pay, as well as financial help with accommodation – and the attraction of a beautiful seaside city. He'd applied and been accepted. The advert had not warned about the long hours – and it was no one's fault that sickness had added substantially to these.

Just as he took his first bite, he heard the voice of triage nurse Kelsei Price, right behind him.

'Dr Shah,' she said. 'I've got a seven-year-old girl just admitted who I'm very concerned about.'

He turned round, chewing and swallowing, looking at her with exhausted eyes. The dark-haired woman looked back at him, with equally tired eyes behind black-rimmed glasses. 'What are your concerns?' he asked, scrupulously polite as always and, despite everything, determined to give his all, as ever.

'According to her parents, the little girl began presenting flu-like symptoms on Friday – Covid was quickly eliminated. Since then she has steadily deteriorated, with her temperature rising – it is currently 38.9.'

He frowned. '38.9?'

'Yes.'

'OK, what else can you tell me?'

'She was seen by the family doctor on Saturday who advised the parents to give her the usual stuff – Calpol and Nurofen and plenty of fluids. They don't seem to have had any effect and she has become delirious. She is very clammy and the parents say she's been hot for the past two days.'

'What tests have you done on this girl?'

'I've done her bloods. They've come back with a raised white count. She appears to have a non-specific but serious infection. I've checked her urine for a possible urinary tract infection and I've done nose and throat swabs. I've also sent off for blood cultures, but we won't get those back for twenty-four hours.'

'I think you should send her up for a chest X-ray,' Shah said. 'Is she on a drip?'

'Yes, I've cannulated her, doctor. But there's something very strange going on, which I don't understand.'

'And that's what?' He took another bite of his banana.

'Her mother tells me she tried to sponge her face with cold water earlier, and the girl screamed, rejecting it. She also screamed when they opened a window, saying the wind was hurting her.'

He put the rest of the banana on the work surface and stood up. 'I'll come straight up and see her.'

'Thank you,' she said and briefed him on the names.

A few moments later, Dr Shah and Nurse Price entered the small cubicle and swished the blue curtains closed behind them. Shah saw a small girl with a tangle of blonde curls on the bed, and a very concerned, sensible-looking couple standing beside her, both casually dressed. 'Good evening,' he said. 'Mr and Mrs Fairfax?'

They nodded.

He looked down at the semi-conscious little girl. 'And this is Bluebell?'

'It is,' her mother said, her voice choked.

For some moments the young doctor looked at Bluebell. 'Hello,' he said. 'I'm Dr Shah. You're Bluebell, right?'

Her eyelids opened halfway. She looked bewildered and did not respond for some moments, then, she mumbled, 'Want to see Moose.'

He frowned. 'Moose?' he asked gently.

She did not reply, her eyelids closing again.

'What happened to your nose, Bluebell? Did you scrape it?'

There was no response from her.

'It was a puppy,' Katy replied, after some moments.

'Your puppy?' Dr Shah questioned.

'No, we bought her a puppy,' Chris Fairfax explained. 'And when we picked it up there was another puppy that Bluebell was playing with and it play-bit her on the nose.'

Shah frowned. 'When was this?'

'On Thursday.'

Shah did a mental calculation. The wound still looked livid, and it should have settled down by now and begun scabbing, he thought. 'I understand that although she has a high temperature and is hot, that she doesn't want any water on her body? Or cooling air?'

Katy Fairfax nodded. 'Yes, she – she seems terrified of it. I suppose because she's delirious and she thinks we're trying to harm her.' She shrugged helplessly. And not liking the look on the doctor's face.

'Any other symptoms?'

'Her face drooped a little yesterday when she stood up, and she was unsteady on her legs. It was like . . .' She hesitated.

'Like?' Shah prompted.

'Almost like she'd had a stroke or something,' Katy replied.

Shah checked Bluebell's tummy with his stethoscope, and moved it around her abdomen and chest for some while, before hanging it back around his neck and turning to the Fairfaxes. He gestured for them to follow him outside, into the corridor. Then he said, 'I'm very concerned about your daughter and you've done the right thing by bringing her in. I need to know some more – particularly about this bite on her nose.'

'It's just a scratch!' Katy blurted.

'Darling,' Chris took her arm, trying to calm her.

'Can you tell me a little bit about the puppy who did this?'

'We don't know much about it. It was a Staffie type,' Chris replied. 'We can't get hold of the breeder.'

'The breeder lied to us,' Katy cut in. 'When I took our puppy, Moose, to the vet it turns out her vaccination certificate is false.'

Shah stood still for some moments. 'You bought her from a breeder?'

'Yes,' Chris said. 'We found him on Gumtree, he said the dogs were from Wales. He seemed a nice man – except he's vanished. I've tried to contact him – on the number he gave us, and on his email. The number doesn't ring and his email bounces back. He's disappeared from Gumtree.'

Dr Shah stood, trying to compute all this. 'Are you saying, Mr and Mrs Fairfax, that you can't be sure of the provenance of this puppy that bit your daughter?'

'Yes, I guess we are,' Chris said. 'But what's that got to do with anything – I mean – with Bluebell's condition?'

'Hopefully nothing at all,' the doctor answered. He tried, and only partially succeeded, to give them a reassuring smile. 'Do you think there is any possibility your puppy and the one who nipped Bluebell might have been bred abroad and not in Wales – as you've been told?'

Chris and Katy looked at each other in confused silence. Finally, Chris said, 'I can't answer that, we simply don't know.'

Excusing himself, telling the Fairfaxes he would be back in a couple of minutes, Dr Shah stepped outside and walked along the corridor, back to the nursing station where he was well out of earshot of the couple. Then he called the duty consultant. After two rings he heard the rather bolshy-sounding Welsh accent of George Pallant, who had told him a couple of hours ago that he was going home, but to call if there was an emergency.

'Good evening, Anish, you're still at the hospital?'

The registrar could hear what sounded like a television in the background. 'I am, sir, I've stayed on, covering for Zeenat Hussein – she's off with Covid. I'm very concerned about a seven-year-old girl who has just been admitted. She's currently presenting a temperature of 38.9, and is delirious – three days after being bitten by a dog of dubious provenance. I'm extremely concerned that she could, possibly, be suffering from rabies.'

'Rabies?' he repeated in a tone of utter disbelief.

'Yes, sir.'

'Rabies doesn't exist in England. We've not had a case here since the beginning of the twentieth century. It's been eliminated from the UK, and we've kept it that way with our stringent border controls and quarantine for animals.'

'Exactly, sir. That is exactly my point.'

'Your point? What is *exactly* your point?'

'That we do not have rabies in this country.'

'Anish,' he said, sounding increasingly tetchy. 'I'm very tired, would you mind not talking in riddles?'

'I'm sorry, sir, I'm not trying to talk in riddles, I'm trying to explain.'

'Explain what, exactly?'

'I'm trying to explain to you that, because there has been no incident of rabies in this country for well over a century, it is not something any doctor would be looking for. But we have it in Pakistan, and I've had experience of dealing with patients suffering from this horrible disease.'

'I'm sure you have. Fortunately, it's not something I've ever had to worry about.'

'Maybe not, sir,' Shah replied. 'Not until now.'

61

Roy Grace arrived home dejectedly, shortly after 10.30 p.m., hoping against hope as he climbed out of his car that he would hear the familiar sound of Humphrey's excited barking. But as he slammed the door shut behind him, all he heard was the faint, distant bleating of sheep.

An equally downbeat Cleo greeted him as he entered the house. They hugged.

'God,' she said tearfully, 'I'm so worried about him.'

'He's not in the park – I shouted myself hoarse and so did Charlie.'

'He could have run out into the main road, the A27, and been hit by a car,' she said. 'He could just be lying there at the roadside. Do you think we should go and look there?'

'I already did,' he said. 'I drove up and down it slowly enough, all along the side of the park, looking for just that, and I didn't see anything. I've also called it in, in case any patrols see a stray dog out and about.'

They went into the kitchen and sat down on bar stools. 'Do you want a drink?' she asked.

'I'll have a small whisky. I'll get it.'

'I'll do it,' she said, and told him about the call from the con-woman as she poured him a generous portion of his favourite, Craigellachie. Handing him the glass, she said, 'I've been in contact with a Facebook group. They say if you suspect your dog has been stolen, the best way to get it back is to make it too hot to handle, then they'll release the dog because they can't sell it. Spread the word via local Facebook pages and missing pet pages. I've been doing that all evening.'

'With the reward?'

She nodded. 'One hundred pounds, yes.'

He took a sip, feeling the welcome burn of the neat whisky down his throat and hitting the spot in his stomach, and thinking hard about what else they could do.

'Have you eaten anything?' Cleo asked, concerned.

'I had a cereal bar in the car.'

'You need more than that. Shall I make you a sandwich, or microwave something from the freezer?'

He shook his head. 'I'm fine, really. Look, I'm sure he's going to turn up.'

'Why hasn't anyone called? Apart from that prank bitch?'

He shrugged. 'I guess – you know – it's Sunday night. Maybe whoever's found him hasn't been looking at social media yet. Or perhaps they're planning to take him to the RSPCA or maybe somewhere like Raystede over near Hailsham in the morning.'

'I've rung the RSPCA and Raystede and all the other animal rescue places I could find on the internet – nothing.'

'It's early doors, darling.'

'God, I hope you're right.'

Silently, sipping some more whisky, he hoped, too, he was right. 'I can't imagine anyone has just stolen him. Not a mature dog of his age. And when they do look on the internet and see the reward, they'll be in touch. I'm sure they will.'

Although with what he knew about the current levels of criminality in the dog world, he was less confident than he sounded.

'I just hate to think of him all scared in some stranger's house. Or still out there in the park somewhere.'

'I'll get up at dawn and go back, just in case he is still there.'

She shook her head. 'No, you need your rest and you've got to work. I'll sort something out with work and call Kaitlynn to look after the kids then I'll go back there in the morning. It feels wrong here without him. Shit, I love that damned dog so much.' She squeezed his hand. 'I know you do, too – he's your running buddy!'

He smiled thinly. 'Yep, my running buddy.'

Where are you at this moment, Humphrey, he thought. *Where are you, my running buddy?* Then he turned to Cleo. 'There could well be someone looking online at this moment, and seeing your post, and thinking it's late to call now – and they'll call in the morning. Eh?'

She gave a wan smile back.

62

There was someone looking at the Facebook post at this very moment. And thinking he would call in the morning. But not because it was late.

Gecko sat at his laptop up in the little spare room of Elvira's house. He was staring at the photograph of Humphrey sitting in the midst of a bed of daffodils, looking appealing. A lot more damned appealing than the bloody shit-factory that was walking endlessly round and round the living room, the hallway and the kitchen, pissing on the walls and the carpet, whining and, twice tonight so far, shitting on the floor.

He figured that the longer he held out from calling, the more desperate his owners would be. Which meant he might be able to squeeze more out of them than the £100 reward currently on offer. And any more would be nice, since business had pretty much ground to a halt these past few days. All the publicity about dog theft in the papers and on the television news had meant owners taking extra care. He'd pushed an old lady over last week – which he'd almost felt bad about – and made off with her Westie puppy, for which Mr Jim had paid him just fifty pounds. So this reward on offer for Humphrey would be very sweet.

His nostrils twitched. He could smell the foul stench of dog faeces again. How much damned shit did Humphrey have inside him?

Elvira called out from the bedroom. 'My love, I think the dog has done something again.'

'I'm on it,' he said.

'Any luck finding his owners?'

'Not so far,' he said. 'I'll go down and clear it up.'

'Don't be angry with him, he's probably just very confused.'

'Yeah, well I get confused sometimes, but I don't go and crap in people's houses.'

She giggled.

'It's not funny.'

She mimicked his voice, sounding oh-so-serious. 'It's not funny. It is soooo not funny.'

'Hey!' he said, feigning a hurt voice. 'Out of the goodness of my heart I bring this lost dog home, and all you can do is take the piss.'

'I thought it was the dog that was taking the piss – rather a lot of times.'

'Not funny.'

63

At a few minutes past 11 p.m., the consultant paediatrician, George Pallant, strutted into the room, casually dressed in a waxed jacket over a cardigan and jeans, unlike his usual work attire of either a dark suit and tie or scrubs. A short man with swept-back black hair, who reminded many people of the actor Stephen Graham, he walked very erect to compensate for his lack of stature. He always spoke to people with his head tilted back slightly, giving the impression he was looking down his nose at them, as if to say *I don't give a damn about being shorter than you, I'm still superior, I'm a god here.*

Anish Shah, who was a good six inches taller and had always found Pallant's manner a little unsettling, met him at the front entrance and they walked in silence past all the cubicles to an empty corridor at the rear, before the consultant, who looked as shattered as Shah felt, spoke. 'Rabies? This has to be nonsense, Anish.'

'I hope so, sir,' the registrar replied.

Keeping his voice low, the consultant said, 'For starters, do you have any idea what a diagnosis of rabies would mean?'

'For the patient?'

Pallant shook his head. 'Not just for the patient – but for this country.'

Shah shook his head. 'No, what do you mean? I don't under-stand.'

'Then you'd better start understanding, and fast.'

Shah had never liked this man and he liked him even less than usual at this moment. And he liked him even less still when Pallant jabbed him in the chest with his slender, manicured index finger.

'Like I told you, we don't have rabies in this country. It's been eliminated and has been so for over a hundred years. It's arrant nonsense to suggest we might have a case now. Do you have any idea of the significance of what you are saying – without foundation? That this little girl – Bluebell Fairfax – may have rabies is opening a very dangerous can of worms. You would, effectively, be saying that we have rabies in our animal population. The implication of this would be simply devastating.'

'You want to cover it up?' Shah asked, both confused and astonished.

Pallant shook his head. 'I'm not a fool, man. But you're young and inexperienced. I respect your concerns, but we need to carry out a number of tests and eliminate all other possibilities before we can even begin to contemplate your diagnosis – or rather – assertion.'

'I understand that, sir.'

'Good. Has she been vaccinated against rabies? If not, could you arrange it, as a precaution?'

'We are too late for that, sir – the first jab has to be done within twenty-four hours of the bite and we are several days past that now. Without that crucial first jab the disease is almost always fatal.'

Pallant was quiet for some moments, taking on board the significance of this. 'Let me go and take a look at her.'

They walked through the ward, passing several empty cubicles, and then came to the curtained-off one, a nurse, with a clipboard containing Bluebell's readings, standing outside.

Pallant studied the sheet for a moment then nodded to Shah,

who pulled open the blue curtain. Inside, the consultant saw an anxious-looking man and a tearful woman, the small child with her blonde ringlets on the bed beyond them, eyes shut.

'Mr and Mrs Fairfax, this is Dr Pallant, our paediatric consultant. He's come in specially to see Bluebell,' Shah said.

Briefly acknowledging them then switching on his bedside charm, the consultant took a careful look at Bluebell. 'Hello, how are you feeling?'

'My legs hurt,' she murmured, opening her eyes a fraction, her voice weak. Her eyelids closed again.

'Your legs hurt?'

'I can't move them,' she repeated, her eyes still closed.

Pallant tenderly removed the sheet then touched her right leg below the knee. 'Can you feel that?' he asked.

There was no response.

He pressed hard. 'Can you feel that, Bluebell?'

'I feel, I . . .' she murmured.

'OK,' the consultant said. He tapped her right leg harder with one finger. 'Can you feel that?'

There was no reaction.

He tried the other leg, with the same result. Then he beckoned the parents to follow him and Shah outside into the corridor and along, until they were safely out of Bluebell's earshot. 'My colleague, Dr Shah, has told me the history of the past few days, but I'd be grateful if you would repeat it all again.'

When they had finished, Pallant nodded gravely.

'What do you think it is, doctor?' Katy asked.

'I'm afraid at this stage I don't know, Mrs Fairfax. Your daughter is very sick, but it is likely to be one of the bugs going around that has hit her particularly badly.'

'Could it be an infection she's picked up from the puppy biting her?'

'Well, I think that should have healed better by now – but

everyone's immune system is different, and if your daughter has something else going on, that wouldn't help the healing process.'

'Something else going on?' Chris queried.

Pallant nodded. 'She has an extremely high temperature and a raised white blood count.' He held his hands up. 'As a precaution I would like to admit her overnight for observation.'

The Fairfaxes looked at each other, then Katy turned back to the consultant. 'Admit her?'

'Yes.'

'Could one of us stay with her?'

He smiled. 'Well, yes, we have some beds in the relatives area, but you might be better off going home and trying to get some sleep. The beds are somewhat uncomfortable.' He smiled apologetically. 'I'm going to send her to the ICU.'

'Intensive Care?' Katy asked, close to crying again.

'She'll have a dedicated nurse with her all the time, around the clock,' Pallant said. 'Really there's nothing you can do tonight. We're going to run tests to find out what's going on. I want to eliminate any possibility of sepsis or viral meningitis.'

'That can be fatal, viral meningitis, can't it?' Katy said, her voice trembling.

'I'm not going to lie to you,' Pallant said. 'Your daughter is extremely unwell.'

'Oh God,' Katy said, and began crying. Chris put an arm around her, trying to comfort her, while feeling terrified for Bluebell himself.

'But she is in the best place,' Pallant said. 'You did the right thing bringing her in.'

'Chris, you'll need to call Helen and Vivek – apologize for how late it is and ask them to look after Moose while we're here. They can leave her at ours but visit every few hours,' Katy said desperately, thinking through the knock-on impact of their sudden change in circumstance. Helen and Vivek Malik were the Fairfax's neighbours who were always happy to help out, often at the last minute.

'I'm on it, I'll call them now,' Chris replied.

'Wha-what – what tests are you going to do?' Katy asked.

'Well, Dr Shah has already organized her bloods to be sent for cultures, which will take twenty-four hours for the results to come back. Under local anaesthetic we'll do a lumbar puncture to take fluid from her spine and send that for analysis as well. We'll keep her cannulated and put her on a high dose of antibiotics and antiviral drugs. I've seen the report on her chest X-ray and that's clear, which is a good sign.'

'In what way?' Chris asked.

'There are no shadows or scar tissue so we can eliminate TB and a number of other diseases of the lungs.'

'Yeah, well, she was never a heavy smoker,' Katy said.

The consultant looked at her, as if unsure whether she was joking.

64

Monday 29 March

At 8.30 a.m. Gecko kissed Elvira goodbye, telling her he was taking the dog to the rescue centre, and that he would forage in a supermarket later for something for tonight's dinner. Then, securing the rope around his neck, he struggled to get Humphrey, who was suddenly very reluctant to move, towards the front door of the house.

'Come on, boy, what is it?' he said petulantly.

'He likes it here,' she said. 'Why don't we keep him?'

'We can't,' he said. 'He must belong to someone, it would be stealing to keep him.'

'Goodbye, Humphrey,' she said, putting her arms around his neck and giving him a kiss. 'He's got such a wet nose.'

Earlier, in semi-darkness, Gecko had taken the dog for a short walk around the neighbourhood. He'd stopped as Humphrey stubbornly insisted on pooping on the pathway of a house up the road, then hurried on, leaving the mess there because it hadn't occured to him to bring any plastic bags.

It now took him a good two minutes, with Humphrey resisting every step, to get him to the van, and he'd had to lift him up into it. Humphrey whined constantly as he drove, ignoring all the treats he bunged at him. 'Shut up, will you? Shut up!'

But Humphrey refused to shut up. He sat on the passenger seat whining and whimpering.

After a few minutes, driving up through a residential area

towards Dyke Road Avenue, Gecko pulled over to the kerb and turned to the dog. 'SHUT UP!' he yelled.

The dog looked at him, like he could see right through him. The look unnerved Gecko. 'What's the matter? I rescued you, gave you food and you're just whingeing. Shut it.'

Humphrey was startled into an uneasy silence for a few seconds, while Gecko dialled the number he'd seen on Facebook. It was answered on the third ring. A woman's voice. Posh. Anxious. 'Yes, hello?'

'I saw your post on Facebook about a missing dog,' he said, stroking Humphrey with his free hand.

'Have you found him? You've found him?' She sounded elated. Overjoyed.

'I think possibly. I was in Stanmer Park last night, walking my dogs, and this black dog, looked a little like a Lab, just came up to me and began whimpering. I tried to walk on,' he lied. 'I figured his owner would be calling and he would run off back to them. But he just kept following me all the way to my car. I didn't know what to do. I checked and he didn't have a collar on, so I had no way of contacting the owner. I waited for half an hour, hoping someone would turn up – my own dogs were getting anxious – and hungry.'

'Of course,' she said, taking a breath.

'Then he started whining, like he was hungry also. I called the police to see if anyone had reported a dog of this description missing, but no one had, and they referred me to the council. I just didn't know what to do. I thought of driving him to the RSPCA, but it was getting late. In the end I thought the best thing would be to take him home – my partner and I are real dog lovers – feed him and check on social media – you know – the missing dogs posts. And if I didn't see anything I'd take him to the RSPCA this morning. I just didn't want him spending the night alone and frightened in a strange kennel.'

'That was really kind of you,' she said.

'I didn't see your post until after 11 p.m., and I thought it would be too late to call. So I'm calling now.'

'I'm so grateful,' she said. 'Where are you, I can come over.'

'Well,' he said. 'I need to be sure you really are his owner. I've been reading about all the dog theft going on at the moment, you know? Dogs are fetching big money. How can I be sure you are this dog's owner?'

'Humphrey,' she said with a trace of desperation in her voice. 'His name is Humphrey.'

'Sure,' he replied. 'But the owner posted that on Facebook. How can I be sure you are really the owner?'

'I can email you photos of him – different to the ones I posted.'

'OK,' he replied. 'Text me a couple.'

'Give me two minutes, then call me back when you've got them.'

Gecko ended the call, waving more treats around Humphrey's mouth to keep him silent. His phone warbled and he checked the messages. Two different photographs of the dog, one in which he was sitting, one in which he was running across a field. A bit of a pointless request to send him photos, he knew damn well she was his owner, but at least now she'd have no doubt he was a good person trying to make sure he'd found the right person.

He phoned her back.

'Yes?' she answered anxiously, on the first ring.

'I think it is him,' he replied.

'Thank you, thank God, thank you. Where can I meet you?'

'Well, there is just one more thing,' Gecko said.

'Yes?'

'You see, I've been giving him treats and food. You're offering a reward of one hundred pounds, correct?'

'Yes, correct.'

'Could you up that a bit to cover – like – my expenses?'

'Of course!' she replied. 'How would two hundred pounds sound?'

He blinked in astonishment, thinking that had been easy, too easy. Maybe he should have asked for more? 'In cash?'

'In cash.'

'How about we meet in Stanmer Park, where you lost him?' he replied. Knowing there were no CCTV cameras there.

'By the cafe?'

'What vehicle will you be in?'

'A Kia Sportage – dark blue,' Cleo answered.

'Thirty minutes?'

65

After dozing fitfully, and tossing and turning for hours worrying about Humphrey, at 4.30 a.m., wide awake, Roy Grace had abandoned trying to get any more sleep. He got out of bed, showered and dressed, then drove back to Stanmer Park, and for two and a half hours walked around in vain, looking for Humphrey and calling his name.

Finally, tired and upset, he'd given up and returned to his office, shortly before 8 a.m., to prepare for the morning briefing on Operation Brush. It was now a few minutes to the start, and he was just about to head across to the conference room when his phone rang. It was Cleo and she was excited, telling him about the call she'd received.

'It really does sound like it's Humphrey!' she continued. 'I texted him some pictures and he's confirmed he thinks it is him.'

'You're sure it's not another scammer?' Grace asked, his joy tinged with doubt.

'No, he sounds really nice and caring. But . . .'

'What *but*?'

'Well – I wasn't going to tell you, he was very sweet about it – he asked if we could up the reward just a little to cover his expenses.'

Alarm bells began clanging in his head. 'Up the reward? I don't like the sound of that at all.'

'Maybe he doesn't have much money,' Cleo replied defensively. 'He said he'd had to buy food and treats.'

'But you just told me he has two dogs of his own – he was walking them in the park when Humphrey came up to him.'

She was silent for a moment then she said, 'Does it matter, so long as we get Humphrey back?'

The deep emotion in her voice got to him. 'No, darling, no it doesn't. Let's just hope this is real.'

'I'm meeting him in twenty minutes,' she said.

'Where?'

'By the cafe in Stanmer Park.'

That eased his mind a little. At least they would be meeting in a very public place and there would be other people around. All the same, he was concerned for her safety. 'I could be there in twenty minutes myself and join you.'

'No,' she said. 'Don't worry, I can handle this. I'll be fine.'

'You're sure?' he asked hesitantly, aware of the heavy agenda he had for the meeting.

'I'm sure, I'll swing by a cash machine in Henfield High Street on the way.'

'OK,' he said dubiously. 'I'll try to get a response car to be close by. Call me when you have Humphrey back – or if there are any problems.'

'I will. I love you.'

'Love you – and be careful.'

'I'm a big girl!'

Grace ended the call, his joy that Humphrey might be OK and back tinged with anxiety about what Cleo had said about the reward. Maybe the guy was genuinely short of money. But something didn't feel right. Aware he was slightly abusing his position, he called the Control Room and asked if there was a car in the vicinity in case Cleo needed assistance. The operator said it was a crazy morning, with two big RTCs on the A23 and A27, and he had nothing free at the moment, unless it was an emergency, but he'd do his very best.

Thanking him, Grace grabbed himself a strong coffee, wondering again if he should join Cleo. Equally he didn't want to spook the man. It was daylight, there would be people about. If he was genuine, and really had found Humphrey wandering around, he'd hand the dog over and she'd give him the reward. If he'd kidnapped Humphrey for a ransom payment, then the same would apply, he reasoned. He would do the hand-over, take the cash and bugger off. He couldn't see with either scenario that Cleo would be in any danger, and they would have Humphrey back, which they both desperately wanted.

Even so, he was fretting as he walked along towards the conference room, and suddenly stopped in the corridor. He texted Cleo, asking her to try to get a photo of the man, and to send it to him as soon as she could.

66

Monday 29 March

Cleo sat anxiously in her Kia, pulled over to the side of the wide avenue in the park, a short distance from the agreed rendezvous of the cafe. The cash, in fresh banknotes, was tucked inside a pocket of her coat. She'd written down their numbers, on Roy's advice.

Two people were talking on Radio Sussex, but she was barely listening, as she looked around for any sign of Humphrey.

So far nothing.

It was ten minutes past the rendezvous time she'd set. Was she in the right place? she wondered. But this was the only cafe in the park.

How long should she wait? Was he going to be a no-show? Just a cruel hoaxer?

Two cyclists shot by, pedalling hard. Several people were walking dogs. Another five minutes passed. She was on the verge of calling the man, when the ping of a text startled her and she looked hopefully at her phone. It was from Roy.

All OK? XX

She heard a faint distant bark. Humphrey? She put the window down and listened. Another bark. Still faint, but it did sound like Humphrey. She smiled with joy and texted back.

So far. XX

Then she saw an odd-looking figure walking down from a thicket of trees, in the direction of her car. A man, in a hoodie, baggy jeans and trainers. He had the hood down low over his forehead, and a Seagulls scarf masking the lower half of his face. He stopped fifty yards away and stared at the car.

Cleo raised her phone and tried to discreetly take a photograph.

'Hey!' he shouted angrily. 'No photographs. No photographs!'

Recognizing his reedy voice, she jumped out of the car and shouted back, 'I didn't, I was just holding my phone up. Do you have my dog?'

'I'm going to get him – just had to check it was you.'

She frowned, her suspicions now deepening. Why didn't he have Humphrey with him? 'What do you mean, get him?' she demanded, walking closer towards him. Saw his pale white skin on the part of his face that was visible.

'I had a few more expenses than I realized.' His voice was tinged with arrogance. 'He wasn't well, you see, had to take him to the vet. Had to pay the vet in cash, so I'll need a bit more than I told you.'

'Really? Which vet?' she asked sharply.

He looked thrown, for a moment. 'Um – you know – the one—'

Cleo heard a bark again. Louder. It really did sound like Humphrey's bark. She suddenly yelled, 'HUMPHREY!'

Instantly she heard his bark of recognition, followed by a whine, then more barks. Excited barks. She spotted him tied to a tree not far away, straining against the rope leash.

The man looked nervous. 'I'll swallow the vet bill,' he said.

'Very big of you.' She took a step closer to him. Now she was just a couple of feet away, inside his personal space, staring into his nervous eyes. He smelled a little rank.

'Yeah, I'll just take the – you know – what we agreed.'

'Really?'

'Yeah, really.'

'Are you sure you wouldn't like a kick in the balls instead?'

He gave her an odd look. 'No, no I wouldn't.'

'Good.' She kicked her stiff leather hiking boot with all her force at his crotch, and felt the satisfying crunch of it hitting its target. Saw him gasp instantly, and double up in agony.

She sprinted towards the thicket where she could see Humphrey, calling his name, and hearing him barking and whining increasingly excitedly. 'Humphrey! Humphrey! Good boy, good boy!'

Barely able to see through his tears, his whole insides burning, Gecko was about to go stumbling after her when he saw something moving through the trees some distance away. Blue and yellow. Blue and yellow. Blue and yellow.

A police car.

67

Roy Grace made his way into the conference room, sat down and began by apologizing to his team for their screwed-up weekends. Then he turned to Polly Sweeney. 'Can you tell me more about the call you had yesterday from the woman working in the kennels of a dog breeder?'

'Yes, sir. As I told DI Branson, she sounded frightened and wouldn't give her name or any details of where she worked.'

'And her number was withheld?'

'Yes. She said she thought some of the dogs might have been stolen, and they were all unhappy about the condition the dogs were being kept in at the kennels. One of them said she was going to complain to her boss about it. She's not seen her again, even though they'd agreed to meet up at a pub yesterday lunchtime, and she's really worried what's happened to her.'

'Did she say anything else about this co-worker?'

'She said she was Ukrainian, her name is Rosalind Esche and she's quite a lively person; I got the impression she didn't have a work permit, so she didn't really have much status as an employee – but she's concerned something has happened to her.'

'As in their boss getting rid of her?'

'That was the implication, yes – sir. The woman who called had seen on the news about the murder of Tim Ruddle and the photograph of the dogs that had been taken, which she then also saw on the *Argus* newspaper online. She started to wonder and mentioned it to her colleagues. She tried to contact Rosalind repeatedly over the weekend and became increasingly worried about what might have happened to her if she did in fact confront her boss or if he might have overheard their conversation – which is why she called us yesterday. Apparently, he's not a nice person.'

Grace nodded, making a note. 'Have we run checks on this Rosalind Esche?'

'We have,' Luke Stanstead said. 'Nothing. I've checked immigration records and they've no one of this name. Quite possibly she's here as an illegal, which would fit the kind of job she was doing, working for a dodgy breeder and being paid cash.'

'Pretty brave of her, if she is an illegal, to stand up to her boss.'

'That's what I said to the woman who called me,' Sweeney replied. 'She told me Rosalind cared passionately about dogs and was really upset and angry at their treatment at the kennels. She said the other colleague warned Rosalind that complaining to the boss could get her into trouble, but that Rosalind had probably gone ahead with it anyway. She wanted the conditions improved for the dogs.'

'Good for her,' E-J spoke out. 'I'd have done the same.'

'OK,' Grace said. 'And this informant – this woman who called – is willing to meet you, Polly?'

'This evening, after work, sir.'

He considered this for a moment. There were strict protocols about handling informants, requiring a sterile corridor between them and case officers, but he decided he didn't need to worry about that here, this sounded simply like an unhappy employee willing to blow the whistle on her boss. 'Has she said where she'll meet you?'

'No.'

'Has she given you a time?'

'She's going to call just after five and give me a location.'

'Do you want backup with you when you go to meet her?'

'No, sir, I think I will get more out of seeing her alone. I have arranged to have officers standing by who will monitor me, and I will have my radio also. All she has said is that it will be in East Sussex.'

East Sussex, Grace thought. That once more fitted with the little they knew so far about the offenders. 'Let me know as soon as she makes contact,' he said.

'Absolutely, sir.'

Grace's private phone rang. He glanced at the display and saw it was Cleo. Raising a hand, he answered it quietly, concerned about her news.

She sounded elated. 'The eagle has landed!'

'No kidding?' he said, his voice almost a shout, unable to hide his relief.

'He's in my car, he's fine and we're on our way home!'

68

Monday 29 March

Aware the whole team was looking at him, and not giving a damn at this moment, Roy Grace let out a whoop of joy. Then, telling Cleo he'd call her back as soon as he could, and ending the call, he beamed. 'Sorry, coincidentally our dog, Humphrey, went missing yesterday, but he's turned up safe and sound, picked up by another dog owner, thank God!'

'A shaggy dog story, chief?' Potting said.

Everyone smiled, including Grace. Then, suddenly, he found himself fighting off a wave of emotion. With difficulty, he focused back on his task, again addressing Polly Sweeney. 'I heard back from Robin Smith, last night. The Mr and Mrs Jonathan Jones who had given an address in St Helier, Jersey, appear to have stolen someone else's identity. I think it's likely that Tom Hartley and Michael Richard Kendrick are also assumed or borrowed names. Did you find any connection between them?'

She shook her head. 'No, sir. There are plenty of individuals with each of those names, but I've been working with Vanessa' – she turned to the researcher, Vanessa Blackmore – 'and we've not found any link between three people of those names.'

Blackmore nodded in confirmation.

Grace turned to the Financial Investigator. 'Money would have changed hands for the Airbnb that our mystery Hartley/ Jones/Kendrick rented. We need to know where those payments were made, and find out more about the Peugeot that was in the driveway, Emily.'

'Yes, sir,' Denyer said. 'I have already put in a request to Airbnb for the bank account details where the payment was made from, but I don't think I'll get a quick answer. I'll keep on it. And likewise, the car.'

Thanking her, Grace turned to Velvet Wilde and Norman Potting, seated next to each other. 'How've you got on with your farm visits?'

'We've covered a couple, so far, sir,' Wilde said. 'One of them a large and not particularly salubrious place run by John Roke.'

'A name well known to us,' Grace said.

'I have to say Norman handled him pretty well, sir.' Grace saw she actually gave Potting a look of admiration.

Norman shrugged and blushed.

'And did you find anything of interest?' Grace asked.

'We didn't *find* anything of interest,' the DC said.

Potting nodded confirmation. 'Just a handful of farm dogs – we can eliminate the Roke community from this particular enquiry. We're back on farm visits after this briefing.'

'Lucky you,' E-J said. 'Nothing like a day in the countryside, eh?'

'If walking through pig shit, cow shit and chicken shit floats your boat, absolutely, E-J,' Potting replied. 'As Velvet said, we didn't *find* anything of interest, but Roke seemed keen to dob in Big Jim, who I dealt with years ago, and his piece-of-crap son Dallas.'

'What did he say about them?' Grace asked.

'That that's one of the places where we should be looking.'

'We're building the evidence to get a warrant.' Grace studied his notes for a moment then turned to the Exhibits Officer, Michelle Boshoff. 'Anything to report?'

With her black-rimmed glasses perched on the end of her nose, she had the look of a studious academic. 'Possibly, sir. There was debris recovered from the scene at the Ruddles' farm – broken glass and plastic, which the Collision Investigation Unit believe came from the headlight of one vehicle and the bumper of another – or possibly the same vehicle. They're working on this now and are pretty confident from what they have they'll be able to identify the vehicle makes and types. And we have tyre marks recovered from the scene by the CSI, which will also help in identifying the vehicle types.'

'Good work, Michelle,' he said.

'Thank you, sir. As you know, I also ran Dr Haydn Kelly's plaster of Paris impressions of the footprints, which he took at the scene, by the UK National Reference Collection and they came up with some matches.' She hesitated. 'I'm not sure how helpful these will be at this stage, because the footwear is very widely sold both in retail outlets and online. I have four sets of shoe sizes but we really need Dr Kelly's further analysis. I've sent all the information to him, and he said he will try to have his initial findings in time for our evening briefing.'

Grace thanked her then turned to DS Alexander. 'What updates do you have, Jack?'

The Detective Sergeant stood up and walked over to the association chart on the whiteboard, next to the one on which were photographs of Tim and Sharon Ruddle as well as the seven French bulldogs. 'I now have a list of all close relatives, friends and associates of the Ruddles, which I've given to the Outside Enquiry Team, who are working their way through them.'

Polly nodded in confirmation.

Jack Alexander continued. 'The Intelligence Team, who you'll hear from in a moment, have obtained from the phone companies a list of all calls made and received by Mr and Mrs Ruddle in the past four weeks. They are also having the onboard computers of both their cars analysed, which will give us a plot of all journeys each of them made in this same time period. Luke and Vanessa are now working on these.'

DS Julian Ross from the Intelligence Team was next on Grace's agenda to speak. 'Sir,' he said, 'I've been running a detailed check on the Sussex Police Database for any similar crimes to the one at Old Homestead Farm and have pulled up the files. I have identified seven instances in Sussex where puppies have been stolen in overnight burglaries – three in East Sussex, the other four in West Sussex – but there was no violence involved. In each of these cases the dogs were stolen during the night without the owners being disturbed. There was a farmer murdered in Robertsbridge, East Sussex, in 2012, but in that instance, he was trying to prevent theft of agricultural machinery, and the offenders are currently still in prison – I've checked. There are twenty-seven cases of owners of dogs around the county being attacked in parks and open countryside and their dogs stolen, but nothing matching the severity of what we have here.'

Grace thanked him and moved on down his list. Ten minutes later, anxious to call Cleo, he ended the meeting and suggested the evening briefing would take place at 7 p.m. This would give Polly the chance to have met the informant and reported back, by phone if necessary.

Then he hurried to his office.

69

Monday 29 March

Katy and Chris had spent a mostly sleepless night in the hospital, crashing out fitfully on the hard camp beds that had been set up for them in the Relatives Room, and resisting all the suggestions from the nursing staff that they should go home and get some rest.

But finally, realizing they had a lot of stuff to sort out – in addition to all their appointments with clients, which neither of them could face today – Chris agreed to stay on in the hospital while Katy went home, to freshen up and deal with anything urgent before returning via her office.

After a hot shower, and a bowl of cereal and some very strong coffee, Katy was feeling a little more awake and ready to take on a long and challenging day ahead. She made a series of phone calls, starting with Bluebell's school, explaining the situation to them, and then to her parents and Chris's, as well as to the mum who was doing the school pick-up today.

Then she popped next door to see Helen and Vivek Malik to give them the latest news about Bluebell and to find out how Moose had been while they were looking after her. Vivek said he'd actually slept the night on the sofa in their house so Moose wouldn't be alone. He said that Moose had been good as gold apart from one pee on the carpet.

Then she headed off to the office before going back to the hospital.

At her desk she dialled Chris for an update on Bluebell.

He answered after six rings, sounding out of breath and very flat. 'Sorry, I had to run out of the ward when I saw you calling.'

'How is she?'

There was a brief pause before he replied emotionally. 'Not great. She's had a lumbar puncture and she's wired up to all kinds of apparatus. There's been no improvement in her condition so far – if anything she's deteriorated. She keeps drifting in and out of consciousness. The staff are being lovely, but I've actually had one hell of a morning.'

'In what way?' Katy asked anxiously.

'I've spoken to the consultant, Dr Pallant, and the registrar, Dr Shah. They've had the results back from Bluebell's bloods and they're very concerned – so concerned they've couriered them, along with the fluids from the lumbar puncture, to the Hospital for Tropical Diseases for analysis.'

'What?' Katy said, very alarmed. 'What – what do they think it might be?'

'They – they're not saying but . . .' He fell silent.

She waited patiently. Finally, he continued. 'Dr Shah, the registrar we saw last night, is worried about the dog that bit her. He says it's vital we speak to the breeder, because Bluebell's symptoms aren't consistent with any normal disease she might have picked up from a dog bite.'

'What does he mean by *normal*?'

'I don't know, I just don't know.'

'I'm coming straight over,' she said.

'I've got to find that breeder, Peat, John Peat. I have a feeling that's going to be really important.'

'In what way?'

'Because,' he said and paused again. She could hear him breathing hard, fighting his emotions. 'Because I don't think they believe me – us.'

'What do you mean, darling? What do you mean they don't believe us? Who doesn't believe us?'

'Dr Pallant and Dr Shah.'

'I don't understand – they don't *believe* us? Don't believe what?'

'They don't believe our story that it was another puppy that bit Bluebell. I'm getting the feeling they think we've invented the other puppy to cover up for Moose.'

'That's ridiculous!'

'It's not ridiculous,' he said, sounding calmer now. 'Dr Shah has asked me for the name and contact number for our vet.'

'Why does he want to speak to her?'

'I don't know,' he said. 'I think he has an agenda.'

'Agenda? What kind of agenda?'

'Stop firing questions at me, we need to find that breeder.'

'I'm not firing questions, Chris, I just need to know what the hell is going on.'

'OK,' he said. 'Dr Shah took me aside. He told me he began his medical studies in Pakistan. He's seen this stuff over there. He is really concerned that the symptoms Bluebell is presenting look similar to early-stage rabies.'

Katy felt a hollow chill deep inside her. 'Rabies?'

'He – he says it's extremely unlikely and he wants to eliminate it as a possibility – and that's very urgent because of . . .' He went quiet again.

'Because of what?' Katy prompted gently.

'Because of the speed at which rabies develops,' he blurted.

'But there is no rabies in England.'

'Correct. Dr Shah said that. He told me the disease was eradicated here in 1922. But—' He broke off again, his voice choked. 'Oh God, Katy.'

'Darling,' she said, trying to mask her alarm and deep concern. 'Could she not be vaccinated, as a precaution?'

'The first vaccination has to be given within twenty-four hours. It doesn't work after that.'

'God.' She was silent for a moment. Then, nervously pushing for the answer she wanted to hear, she said, 'But, it's pretty unlikely Bluebell has it, right?'

'Yes – unlikely if she had been bitten by a British dog. But the vet told us Moose's vaccination certificate was false, right?'

'Yes.'

'Which means Moose and the other puppies might have come from anywhere – possibly from abroad – and the one that bit her might have been illegally imported. We were really stupid buying her from a van in a car park. I've been reading about it online – that you should never buy a puppy without seeing its mother.'

'But the breeder was convincing,' she said desperately.

'I've been googling it, and a dog with rabies can present as fine for some time,' Chris said.

Katy replied, 'But the vet phoned me earlier. Moose's bloods are all fine. It was just a nasty bug she must have had. She's already better.' Then, increasingly worried, she asked, 'Surely we can get Bluebell tested for rabies? I mean it's so unlikely she would have that, isn't it? There must be a test that would definitively show it, or clear her?'

'They need to test the dog that bit Bluebell. And if that dog has rabies and Moose came from the same breeder she might have it too. Moose isn't showing any signs and seems OK now, thank God, but only a brain-stem test would tell us, with one hundred per cent accuracy. That is the only way.'

'Couldn't we get that done?'

'We have to find that breeder to test that Staffie. If we can't, they might have to do the test on Moose.'

'Couldn't they do that anyway, as a precaution?'

'They could, Katy. But to do a brain-stem test,' he said

bleakly, 'they first have to euthanize the dog. They'd have to destroy Moose.' He paused. 'And God knows where that leaves Bluebell.'

70

Katy Fairfax ended the call with Chris in shock. She thought hard, desperately, what she could do to help him find John Peat. She again googled the name and the first hit that came up was an American sea captain who had died in 1794. There were many more, none remotely fitting the man who had sold them Moose.

Her intercom buzzed. Their assistant, Khalid, told her the 2 p.m. appointment, Mrs Dunwoody, was in reception. Katy told him to apologize and explain that due to an emergency she needed to rearrange the appointment, to move it to next week. Then she returned to her searches, checking out again all the sites she and Chris had originally gone to when they'd been looking for a puppy for Bluebell, hoping that John Peat's absence might just have been a temporary glitch.

But there was still no sign of him.

Then she sat for some moments deep in thought. They had to find this breeder, had to find the dog that had injured Bluebell, critically to know she was OK and, also, to safeguard Moose. How? Where else could she look?

She stood up and paced around her office. Then she realized exactly who might be able to help them.

She opened the address book on her computer and tapped out the name Ken Grundy.

Moments later his contact details appeared.

She dialled the number, preparing to leave a voicemail message, but to her relief she heard the voice of a receptionist.

'Ken Grundy Associates, how can I help you?' she answered formally but warmly.

The private detective agency was one which she and Chris had recommended to several clients over the years. Some who suspected their partners of cheating on them, and some who they suspected had been less than honest in their declarations of assets to their partners or family. The proprietor, a tough Yorkshireman and former police CID officer, with a great sense of humour, had proved reliable and diligent and had achieved results for his clients, many times, beyond their expectations.

Introducing herself, she asked if Ken was around.

'One moment, Mrs Fairfax.'

And just a few seconds later she heard Grundy's jokey-sounding voice. 'Hello there, how are you doing?' He over-emphasized the '*you*'.

'I've been better,' Katy said, and told him the situation.

'I'm hearing about rogue breeders all over the place at the moment,' Grundy said. 'I'd be happy to help you – and seeing how much business you've put my way, how about I give you the first ten hours free of charge – just cover our out-of-pocket expenses?'

'Really? That's incredibly generous of you.'

'John Peat. So, what can you tell me about him?'

71

On Friday last week, disgusted by the Jims' couldn't-care-less attitude, which amounted to neglect, Rosalind had told Lyndsey and Darcy that she was thinking of confronting Mr Jim.

Lyndsey had had to leave early that day for a dental appointment and they'd agreed to meet at a pub in Hastings on Sunday lunchtime. Rosalind had never turned up and she'd not answered her phone all weekend or responded to any messages.

In addition, two adult and five puppy French bulldogs had come into the kennels overnight on Thursday morning.

Lyndsey had been fretting about her decision to call the police yesterday, before she finally, very nervously, had done so. Fortunately, Mr and Mrs Jim were out all day today – they were visiting family in Essex. To her surprise they had taken Darcy with them so she couldn't speak to her about the lack of communication from Rosalind and plan what they were going to do. She would have to see her tomorrow. And when Rosalind had not turned up for work, and she still hadn't heard from her, she was glad that she had called the police – and was becoming increasingly worried about what might have happened to her friend. Rosalind was a fearless driver and had a rickety old car and it was possible she'd had an accident. But she'd not found any reports of any accident online that fitted. Maybe the Jims had sacked her?

All day, as she mucked out the kennels and tried to comfort

the hungry dogs, she contemplated speaking to someone at the farm herself. But they were a rough lot, and they scared her.

For the past hour, she had been looking repeatedly at her watch as she went from cage to smelly cage, with all the dirty straw, topping up the water and partially filling the bowls with the paltry rations she had to distribute, and watching, heart-broken, as the little creatures, many caked in mud and faeces which she tried her hardest to clean, fell on their food and gobbled it down in seconds.

It was 4.45 p.m. and pelting with rain, some of which leaked through the inadequate roof in Kennel 2, soaking the already filthy straw beds of some of the puppies. In fifteen minutes, she could leave without arousing suspicion, but not before, and she was nervous and scared about meeting up with the police lady she'd spoken to yesterday. But hopefully, when she told her what was really going on in this farm, the police would act and bring in an RSPCA inspector.

In the constant din of barking and yapping, she kneeled and stroked some of the French bulldog puppies. 'Hello, you lovely things. You're hungry, aren't you?' She dug some treats from her anorak pocket and doled them out to each of them. Then she moved onto the next cage and did her best to console them, too.

Finally it was 5 p.m. 'Goodbye, my sweeties, see you all tomorrow!' she called out, then left the damp building, and hurried across the farmyard, in the drenching rain, to the little Nissan Leaf her mother had handed down to her, when she'd upgraded to a new model a few months ago. Her nerves were jelly. She was scared as hell of what she was about to do. But she had to do it.

In the shelter of the car, with the rain drumming on the roof, she checked the range, as she always did: 98 miles. Plenty to get her to the rendezvous with the police officer and then home.

She headed the silent car back down the farm track and waited, nervously, for the automatic gates to open. To her relief they did.

Suddenly, her phone pinged. She looked at the display, wondering if it was at last a message from Rosalind. But it wasn't, it was a match on Tinder. And although she and Rosalind had had a friendly bet on who would be first to meet someone that they actually liked, she wasn't in the mood for this today.

She pulled over into a passing area, a short distance along the single country lane, opened the app and swiped right to look at the sender. Shit, it was a really nice-looking, fair-haired guy, called Jason, although – big negative for her – he had a man-bun. **U free 4 a drink tonight – Hastings area?** was the message.

Busy tonight, later in the week? she replied.

Instantly he messaged her back. **Tomo? Weds?**

Driving @ moment. Reply laters, she tapped back.

A thumbs-up followed by an X appeared on the display.

She opened her purse and pulled out the note on which she'd written the name and number of the police officer she'd spoken to yesterday. Then hesitated. She tapped it in, then hesitated again. Something loomed in her rear-view mirrors. A massive 4 x 4. As the vehicle shot past at an almost reckless speed, millimetres from wiping out her door mirror, she stared at the phone in her left hand. Was she about to waste the police officer's time? Had Rosalind simply quit and not bothered to tell her? Was there some other explanation for her disappearance that was perfectly innocent and which she hadn't considered?

No. Something had happened to her, she was certain. She hit the dial button.

Moments later the phone was answered by a male voice with a rural burr. 'Sussex Police – Operation Brush Incident Room.'

'May I speak to Polly Sweeney, please?' she asked nervously.

Almost immediately, she heard a reassuring, pleasant voice. 'Hello, Major Crime Team, Polly speaking.'

'I rang you yesterday about my work colleague, Rosalind Esche, who has gone missing.'

'You did, yes, has she turned up?'

'No.'

'OK, are you still up for meeting?'

'Yes,' Lyndsey Cheetham said.

'Can you let me have your name?'

'No, I'm sorry, no.'

'OK, no problem,' the woman said. 'Where would you like to meet?'

'On the seafront in Eastbourne. There's a slope that goes up towards Beachy Head. There are several benches on the lower level of the promenade just to the east of the slope. I could meet you at 5.45 p.m. on the one nearest the hill.'

'OK, how will I recognize you?'

'I'm twenty-one, brown hair in a ponytail, and I'll be wearing a purple puffer and jeans.'

'Right. I'm in my late forties, fair hair, and I'll be wearing a short black coat.'

'I'll see you in half an hour,' Lyndsey said.

'Don't be nervous,' Polly Sweeney said. 'I'll protect your confidentiality. You are doing the right thing.'

Lyndsey tried to reply, but she was shaking so much that only the faintest croak came out. She tried again and managed a whispered, 'Thank you.'

72

Roy Grace sat in his office at 5.30 p.m., studying on his computer screen the photograph Cleo had sent him of the man who had, seemingly, kidnapped Humphrey. Who had then run off – presumably spooked by the presence of a police car, after she had kicked him. Really, really hard in the nuts, he hoped.

The man clearly wasn't the sharpest tack in the box, leaving Humphrey tied to a tree a few hundred yards from where they met, and he sure did not look it. But something was bothering him about the whole incident. Was it pure random chance, in this current epidemic of dog-related criminality, that Humphrey had been kidnapped?

Despite his face being only partially visible, what he could see matched the digital tape Norman Potting had been given a few days ago from the video recording of the man driving away from Hove Park after stealing a dog from a woman there. He was convinced it was Gecko.

He first called the Forensic Digital Media Unit of the Surrey and Sussex Major Crime Team, which was now based in Guildford, not sure if anyone would still be there at this hour. He wanted to get the photo of Gecko, his suspect, to them; they told him to send by email.

Next, he called his Intelligence Manager, DS Julian Ross, gave him the number of the man, which Cleo had noted down, and gave him the time and location where Cleo had met him for the handover. He asked Ross if he could get a full analysis of the phone's movements for the past two weeks and further back, if possible, and the history of all calls it had made and received.

Then Grace stared down at the problem-solving triangle he had drawn in his notebook – something he sometimes turned to when he was working on a case where other similar offences had occurred.

Inside the smallest triangle he had written *Theft of dogs*. In the next, enveloping it, was the name *Tim Ruddle*. Then a larger triangle in which he had written *Guardian – Norris Denning/ Sharon Ruddle*, meaning there had been the lack of a suitable guardian to prevent Ruddle's murder and the theft of the dogs from happening. Then a larger triangle still in which he had written *4 motivated offenders present*.

Researchers had identified several nocturnal break-ins and thefts of puppies from breeders in East Sussex in the past month and more cases in West Sussex and the surrounding counties of Kent, Hampshire and Surrey, but only two other instances where the owners had put up resistance and just one where there had been violence, resulting in minor injuries. Tim Ruddle, it seemed to him, had been unlucky – or had defended his dogs more spiritedly than the others. Grace asked Jack Alexander to have those owners interviewed to find out if they had any further information.

Norman Potting and Velvet Wilde had now visited four of the identified farms in their target area of East Sussex, two of them known to be controlled by individuals with extensive criminal links, but as of yet hadn't come up with anything conclusive enough to warrant a raid. PCs Mike Shaw and Eldhos Matthew would also continue with other house-to-house enquiries tomorrow.

He looked back down at the triangle. At the name of the farm-hand, Norris Denning, one possible guardian who could have prevented Ruddle's murder and the theft. From the reports of the interviews with Denning, Grace was confident he could be eliminated as a suspect. As he was also about Ruddle's wife, Sharon. Which left four men, according to Forensic Gait analysis by Professor Haydn Kelly. And from the professor's analysis he had their approximate size and build. But no idea where they might be. Still, he had the feeling this information from Kelly could prove valuable.

He was distracted by a knock on his door, and called, pointlessly, 'Come in!' Because Norman Potting, as usual, had already entered without waiting for a response.

'Chief, got some possible good news from the Collision Investigation Unit at Shoreham. Think they must all be wizards at jigsaw puzzles, because they've come up with matches from the broken glass recovered at the Ruddles' farm, and the plastic fragments, also recovered there.'

'Tell me?'

'The glass is from the headlight of a 2014 model Ford Ranger pickup truck, and the plastic fragments are from the front bumper of a 2011 model Range Rover.'

'They're certain?'

'Pretty certain.'

'Did you notice either of these vehicles on the farms you and Velvet have visited so far, Norman?'

'No, chief. But we'll be keeping an extra lookout tomorrow, although these vehicles might be concealed in a garage or outbuilding. I've also asked Vanessa to check all auto repair centres and parts depots in the area to see if anyone has bought a replacement headlight or bumper.'

'Good work – so, we need to identify all vehicles matching these two in the East Sussex area, right?'

'I'm already on it, chief.'

Grace made a note in the *Offenders* triangle, then smiled fondly at him. 'Of course you are.'

73

Lyndsey Cheetham sat in her car in the passing area of the narrow lane for several minutes after ending her call with the officer, Polly Sweeney. She stared ahead at the sheeting rain, blurry through the windscreen, wondering if she was doing the right thing. If Mr and Mrs Jim heard about this, it would be the end of her job at Appletree Farm. Polly Sweeney had assured her of absolute confidentiality but what if it got back to her employers? She was frightened of how angry they might be.

Maybe if Rosalind had gone to confront Mr Jim he had fired her on the spot and forbidden her to speak to her, perhaps threatened her if she did. Maybe he had tortured her like Darcy had warned? Darcy would have known if that had happened, surely. She would have said. But Darcy had been out all day in Essex and Lyndsey hadn't spoken to her. Why didn't Rosalind answer her phone? Maybe she was too scared. Could they trust Darcy?

Should she forget meeting the police?

Or was she jumping to all the wrong conclusions about Rosalind? She had mentioned she'd been in contact with a nice-looking guy from another of the dating apps they'd both registered with, a rich guy. Maybe she was just loved-up with him and whisked away by him to somewhere exotic, and wasn't taking her calls because she didn't want the distraction. Rosalind had told her it was her dream, to marry a rich man.

Maybe that was the explanation.

But maybe not.

A farmer had been murdered trying to prevent his dogs from being stolen, from a farm just thirty miles away. Five French bulldog puppies and the parent dogs had been stolen from his farm in the early hours of last Thursday. When she'd arrived for work that morning, there were five new French bulldog puppies and two adult ones.

Beyond coincidence, despite what Darcy thought.

She twisted the ignition key and the wipers arced across the screen, clearing the rain briefly. Then she glided the car forward, carrying on down the lane that, with the bushes on either side, was barely wide enough for her little car to go through without touching the sides. After a mile or so she took the back road and headed down towards Eastbourne.

She would be there in half an hour, she had told the police officer, and was regretting that now. In this shit weather, she was going to have to step on it. A nervous driver at the best of times, she was particularly wary of wet roads, and even more so when the visibility was lousy as it was now and there were several deep puddles across the road. Despite that, anxious not to be late – concerned the officer, Polly Sweeney, might not wait – she drove faster than she was comfortable with.

A red double-bend warning triangle appeared ahead, and she slowed, feeling the car skittish beneath her over the slippery surface. Then to her relief the road straightened and she cautiously increased her speed. Then another warning triangle loomed up.

But, to her relief, it just depicted a deer.

All the same, she slowed from 50 mph to 40 mph.

Ahead, she could now see another red triangle. As she closed on it she could see it warned of a sharp right-hand bend. And it looked like a very sharp bend, with trees to the left and dense shrubbery to the right.

Approaching it, and braking gently, she glanced in her mirror.

The rear window was filled with a dark shape, looming rapidly closer.

A truck, she realized. A massive 4 x 4. The same one as before?

She glanced at the speedometer: she'd crept up to 45 mph. She dabbed the brakes and the speed dropped to 40 mph. Then 35 mph.

And suddenly she was jolted forward as the 4 x 4 bumped into the rear of her car.

'Hey!' she shouted out angrily. 'What the—'

It bumped her again, slamming her whole upper body forward against her seat belt.

Then again.

In panic, she pressed the accelerator, but it nudged her again, harder still. Until it was actually pushing her.

'No, no, stop!' she cried out in terror. 'Stop, stop!' In desperation she pressed the brake pedal hard. But the car carried on forward. The steering wheel became light in her hands. They were at the start of the bend now, a massive tree ahead, right on its apex. In her terror she saw a wreath of mostly dead flowers that was attached to it.

As it zoomed closer.

Closer.

She screamed. Stamped as hard as she could on the brake pedal. Spun the useless steering wheel.

For an instant, she had the illusion she had stopped and the gnarled elm tree was hurtling towards her like an express train.

Moments later, there was a massive explosion of shards of metal and glass. The airbag ballooned in front of her face, the seat belt stretched but held, searing into her flesh. Unrestrained, all her internal organs continued their forward momentum at 50 mph.

74

Ordinarily, PC Ralph Cornish-Sheasby might not have bothered to stop the lorry for having just a single tail light out. On his night shifts, single-crewed more often than not, the young Roads Policing Unit officer would be run ragged. As one of only three patrol cars covering East Sussex, he would have been rushing on blue lights from incident to incident – everything from major RTCs to stray animals on the roads, to assisting in pursuits of joyriders or more serious criminals, to the myriad of other shouts, from removing an object from a lane of the motorway to helping a motorist in a dangerous place.

But tonight was Q – quiet. Two people stopped on suspicion of drink-driving, both of whom had blown negative. One ticket issued for lapsed insurance. He'd just driven west, from Polegate to Brighton, the boundary where the West Sussex RPU took primacy, and was now heading east on the A27, when he saw the rigid-sided articulated lorry ahead of him negotiate the Beddingham roundabout and turn east towards Polegate.

Just one rear light on.

He accelerated, moving the BMW estate close to the lorry's tail. It had a foreign registration, with a PL for Poland plate. Fresh off the Dieppe–Newhaven night ferry, he assumed. Stopping it would relieve the monotony. He flashed his headlights several times, then switched on his blues, overtook the lorry and tucked

287

back in a safe distance ahead of it. Then he tapped the matrix board for the sign to display in the rear window: FOLLOW ME.

He slowed, and the lorry slowed. There was a safe lay-by a quarter of a mile ahead, and he pulled over into it, glad to see the lorry follow him and halt behind him.

He pulled his white cap on, picked up his torch, climbed out into the glare of the lorry's headlights and walked up to the cab. A man in his thirties, thin-faced, with short hair, smiled nervously down at him, blinking in the glare of the torch.

'Good morning, sir,' Cornish-Sheasby said. 'You speak English?'

'A leetle,' the man said pleasantly, in a heavy accent.

'I've stopped you because you have a tail light out. Switch off your engine and I'll take you round the back and show you.'

The driver complied and jumped down. He looked willing enough and no threat, Cornish-Sheasby assessed. Headlights loomed out of darkness, then a car, travelling way too fast, roared past then braked hard, clearly clocking the police car. As it disappeared, the officer heard a different sound. Like a cry. Coming from inside the rear of the lorry.

He frowned and asked, 'What do you have on board?'

'On board?' The driver looked like he did not understand.

Cornish-Sheasby pointed at the cargo section of the lorry. 'What is in there?'

The driver smiled. But nervously this time. 'Hay. Farming. For farming.'

There was another cry, and the traffic officer clocked the anxious look on the driver's face. 'Hay? Just hay? Are you sure?'

He saw the driver shaking now. 'Hay,' he responded.

'Hay from where?'

'Poland.'

'OK, what is your name?'

'Mikolaj.'

'Mikolaj what?'

'Dragon. Mikolaj Dragon.'

'OK, Mikolaj, do you have keys to open the rear of your lorry?'

'Kees?'

Cornish-Sheasby mimed keys turning in a lock and pointed to the rear. The driver looked hesitant and for an instant the officer braced himself for an attack. But instead he nodded and climbed back into the cab. As he did so, the officer radioed the Control Room. 'Got this lorry stopped, need backup. We might have a people-smuggling job here.'

He was told a unit would be with him in approximately ten minutes. He then led the driver around to the rear of the lorry and, again through sign language, indicated for him to unlock the tailgate. As the driver pushed the tailgate up, Cornish-Sheasby saw a wall of hay bales. Beyond were sounds, more distinct now. Whines, yip-yips. Then a weak bark.

He looked at the driver, who was standing beside him. 'Dogs?' he asked.

He got a *maybe* shrug in response.

Climbing up onto the tailgate and breathing in the sour, dry smell of the hay, he tugged at a bale, pulling it loose, and handed it to the driver, who took it with only slight reluctance. He indicated for the driver to put it down on the ground then removed another. After only a couple of minutes, he had a gap big enough to squeeze through. And as he did so, he stood still in astonishment, his torch beam lighting up row after row of cages, stacked five high, each one containing tiny, mostly sleeping puppies.

The driver stood behind him, wide-eyed, as if he too was surprised, although Cornish-Sheasby was pretty sure he wasn't. 'I'd like to see your documentation. Paperwork?'

The driver nodded and he followed him back round to the cab, but climbed in ahead of him and took possession of the ignition key. Then he glanced at the documentation. The bill of lading indicated the cargo was hay, bound for two farms in

East Sussex. There was nothing about dogs that Cornish-Sheasby could see anywhere in the paperwork. Then he saw a glint of light in the rear-view mirror. White light, then blue light. Strobing blue light. The cavalry arriving.

He turned to the driver. 'Mikolaj Dragon, I'm arresting you on suspicion of illegally importing dogs into the United Kingdom.' Then, after reading out the caution, he explained he would be provided with a solicitor and a translator and asked him if he understood.

Dragon nodded, and Cornish-Sheasby had the feeling he understood it all a lot more than he was giving away.

75

'Mummy?' Bluebell murmured deliriously. 'Mummy?' She was cannulated and taped with electrodes on her chest, arms and head.

'Mummy's here, darling,' Chris said. 'We're both here with you.'

Chris and Katy glanced at each other, exchanging thin smiles of even thinner comfort, as they kept their vigil beside her screened-off bed in the Children's Intensive Care Unit. It was coming up to 7.30 a.m. but it felt like twilight in here, Chris thought.

Twilight on some other planet, an alien world of constant beeps with a landscape that was a forest of wires and drips and digital numbers and zigzagging graphs on display screens. Occasionally there was the sound of an alarm somewhere else on the ward, and a rush of footsteps, reminding him there were other desperately sick children in here, each fighting their own battle for life. And no doubt other equally worried parents.

His eyes roamed the graphs and the readouts in a constant sequence. He was gripped by them. Mesmerized by each of their new readings. And scared as hell for Bluebell. Good she was being so thoroughly monitored, but at the same time he felt completely alienated.

They had both ignored the advice of Dr Shah and the staff sister last night to go home and get some rest, that there was nothing they could do, that it would be better if they and Bluebell were able to get a night's sleep. They'd insisted on remaining at the hospital, wanting to be there to comfort her, to reassure her and wanting to believe that just knowing they were near her might speed up her recovery. Despite their exhaustion, neither was able to get much sleep. Their neighbours, Helen and Vivek, had called to ask how Bluebell was. They said they were enjoying looking after Moose at the Fairfaxes' and she was adorable. She'd been making them laugh while watching the rugby with them, looking behind the TV for the rugby ball.

During the seemingly eternal night, Chris and Katy alternated visits to Bluebell's screened-off bedside. Each time a nurse or doctor – most often Dr Shah – came in through the curtains to take a reading or adjust the meds, when Chris was there, he would trail them back out. When safely out of earshot of the bed, like a child in the back of a car repeatedly demanding, *Are we nearly there yet?* he would nervously ask if there were any indications of improvement in Bluebell's heart rate, ECG, blood pressure, blood-oxygen level and all the other vital signs in which he'd become a self-taught expert during these past hours. Each time he was given the platitude that she was stable – when she patently wasn't. He could see the changes, small admittedly, but none of them in the right direction.

At some point during the night, Bluebell, increasingly clammy, had begun complaining that she couldn't feel her legs and he could see Dr Shah was very concerned about this development although he kept telling both of them not to worry. Dr Shah, looking more and more drained, had been the one constant throughout the long night.

'You'll be coming home in a day or so, darling,' Katy said. 'Moose can't wait to see you!'

'I want to go home!' she yelled, suddenly, so loudly it startled them.

'Darling,' Katy said, quietly and more calmly than she felt. 'We'll take you home just as soon as you feel better.'

'I'm not ill,' Bluebell said, grumpily and suddenly very lucid. 'I want to go home now.'

'Are you really feeling better, Bluebell?' Chris asked hopefully.

'I'm thirsty.'

Katy picked up the paper cup of water on the bedside table and held it out to her. But as the cup neared her mouth, Bluebell suddenly and terrifyingly screamed, 'NO, NO, NO!' She flung out her arms, sending the cup flying onto the floor, the remaining water spilling out onto the tiles. Then she screamed again, 'NO WATER NO WATER NO WATER.'

Chris and Katy looked at each other, bewildered.

'Darling,' Katy said. 'What—'

At that moment Dr Shah came in, followed by the nurse who had been assigned to Bluebell throughout the night. He went straight to the little girl and looked down at her tenderly. 'Do you want water, Bluebell?'

She screamed, 'NO NO NO!'

He turned and spoke quietly to the nurse.

'I'm just going to give your daughter some sedation to help her sleep,' she told Chris and Katy. Then she hooked another drip up and switched lines to it.

The effect was almost instant, calming Bluebell right down. In less than a minute, it seemed, she was asleep.

Shah beckoned Chris and Katy to follow him. They went out of the unit and into the small, bare Relatives Room next door. 'Please sit down, you must be exhausted.'

'And you,' Chris said. 'You've been up all night too.'

He gave a wan smile as the three of them squeezed past the camp beds and sat on the hard plastic chairs. 'It's OK, I'm used to it, goes with the territory,' Shah said, and frowned. 'This reaction to water – has Bluebell done this before?'

'No,' Chris replied. He looked at a Covid hygiene poster above Shah's head.

'Never, I mean – she didn't want a wet flannel on her, but this is crazy,' Katy added. 'It – it was – when I offered her a cup of water – it was like there was some demon inside her.' She dropped her face into her hands, crying. 'Oh Jesus, what's happened to our darling?'

Chris, feeling useless, draped an arm around her shoulder, but immediately felt her pull away. He looked at the registrar. 'Bluebell's not improving, is she?'

Shah looked directly back at him for some moments, then at Katy. He wrung his hands together. 'As I told your husband yesterday, Mrs Fairfax, your daughter is displaying early signs of the disease rabies. Most medics in this hospital – indeed, in this country – would be unaware of these signs, because no one has caught the disease here for over a hundred years. But I worked as an intern in Pakistan before I came here, and I saw too many cases there.'

'Right,' Katy said forlornly.

Chris looked at him, both terrified for their child and bewildered. 'I'm sorry to ask – but how are you so sure that it's not something like sepsis?'

Remaining very calm, Shah said, 'Bluebell was bitten on the nose by a puppy, drawing blood, and soon after became seriously ill. She is not responding to antibiotics and all other medications we would expect to clear up an infection from a wound in a healthy young person.' He paused and looked at them both, gently and with caring eyes. 'We've taken bloods and, as you know, a lumbar puncture, to try to eliminate any underlying problems, and we've sent samples to the London Hospital for Tropical Diseases for their analysis. It is possible that an unvaccinated puppy from somewhere in Europe could have given Bluebell some other form of infection we are not familiar with.' Then he hesitated.

'And?' Chris prompted.

'I had deep concerns yesterday that Bluebell was possibly displaying symptoms of a rabies victim. Her rejection and seeming fear of ingesting water – *hydrophobia* – is further evidence of that. I won't know for sure either way until we get the results back from London. But I think you need to prepare yourselves for the worst.'

'The worst?' Katy's voice sounded like a high-pitched tremble.

Calmly, his eyes moving from one of them to the other, he said, 'I don't want to deceive you. Her condition has been steadily worsening during the night. If she does indeed have rabies, the prognosis is not good.'

'What – what does that mean?' Chris asked. 'Is there a different vaccination or antidote that can be given at this stage?'

It seemed an eternity before the registrar replied. 'There is a two-stage vaccination that a human bitten or scratched by a rabid animal can be given. But the first vaccination needs to be given within twenty-four hours of the wound occurring. It is not just ineffective after that, it is counter-productive and will aggravate the symptoms.'

'I know, yes,' Katy said a little impatiently. 'That's what you said to my husband before. But the doctor saw her on Saturday as soon as she was feeling unwell – why didn't she see this then?' Katy demanded.

'Because,' Shah said calmly, 'this is just not a condition most medics in this country know about. Only around twenty people in the world have ever survived the disease without a vaccination. There is very little chance of a cure.'

'Oh God,' Katy said sadly.

'Darling,' Chris said and pressed his arm around her, but she pulled away.

'If you are right, Dr Shah,' Chris asked, 'and Bluebell does have rabies, and you don't think the vaccine is going to work, what – what then – what do we do? I mean, like what are our options? Where do we take Bluebell to get treated?'

The registrar raised his hands. 'Let's deal with this one step at a time.'

Katy shook her head in terror. 'Oh God, I just want her cured.'

There was a long silence, during which the air in the little room felt heavy, oppressive, hostile.

76

Tuesday 30 March

Roy Grace liked to be at his desk even earlier than normal in the crucial first days and weeks of a major crime investigation, getting a jump on the world. He would check for important emails, reading the online report of all incidents and criminal activity in the county, before the day became hectic with meetings, calls and even more emails poured in.

And there was one that particularly interested him. A Polish lorry driver, arrested at 4 a.m. today, after arriving on the Dieppe–Newhaven ferry, with twenty-seven puppies concealed in the rear of his lorry. The arresting officer had been from the Roads Policing Unit, but Tom Cartwright, from the Rural Crimes Unit, was being brought in, along with the RSPCA, to organize temporary homes for the dogs. He made a note to find out where the lorry's journey had originated from, its destination, and who was the UK contact. Then he looked at his watch.

It was 7.15 a.m. He checked his calendar on his screen: 9 a.m. briefing on Operation Brush, followed by a 10.30 a.m. meeting with the ACC to update her. And a raft of further meetings on Operation Brush throughout the day, including a 3 p.m. with the Chief Constable, Lesley Manning, who wanted not only an update on the current operation but to discuss the wider issue of the dog crime epidemic both in the county and also nationwide.

But most of all at this moment, he was anxious to get an update on how Polly Sweeney had got on with the informant she had been due to meet last night. She had told him yesterday evening when he last spoke to her that the girl had not yet shown up. He was about to call her when there was a rap on his door.

'Come in!' he called.

To his surprise, it was the officer herself. She came in, dressed elegantly, as always, in a smart black blouson top, black and white checked trousers and black shoes, her fair hair pinned up, but her normal smiling face was crinkled into a frown.

'I was about to call you,' he said. 'To see if your contact did turn up?' He indicated a chair in front of his desk, and she sat with a smile that was possibly incubating another frown.

'I'm afraid she didn't.'

'Chickened out?' he asked, disappointed.

'She sounded very nervous on the phone, but equally very determined.'

'Shame – it sounded like she might have been helpful.'

'I thought so too – and I'm very surprised. I was due to meet her in Eastbourne at 5.45 p.m. I waited until 8 p.m.'

'She didn't call or text or anything?'

'Not after the call I mentioned to you last night where she sounded anxious at around 5.15 p.m. and suggested a place to meet – a sheltered bench on the promenade in Eastbourne. It was a filthy night, so I imagine she thought there wouldn't be anyone around.'

'So we know nothing about her? Other than she's working at a kennels where she suspects the dogs stolen from the Ruddles might have landed, and the name of her absent co-worker, Rosalind Esche? No phone number?'

'It was withheld, boss, we're following it up, but she did give me a description of herself for when we met – it's not much but it might be helpful.'

'Tell me?'

'She said she was twenty-one, with brown hair in a ponytail and that she'd be wearing a purple puffer and jeans.'

Grace felt a sudden, wintry chill. 'You've no idea where exactly she worked, Polly?'

'No.'

'Bear with me.' He called up the overnight serials again on his screen and scrolled through to one he'd noticed on his scan through them earlier, but it hadn't stuck out. Now it did, like a red flag.

He found it. A fatal road traffic accident on the B2014, at approximately 5.30 p.m. yesterday. A single vehicle colliding with a tree. He followed the update trail. The driver was identified as a twenty-one-year-old female. He memorized the names of the two traffic officers who had arrived on the scene. PCs Richard Trundle and Pip Edwards.

They would have remained at the scene for many hours, while the Collision Investigation Unit carried out their laser measurements and other investigations, and were now probably home and sound asleep. He knew both officers and that they were diligent, and he had PC Trundle's number on his address book. He dialled it, expecting it to go straight to voicemail. But it was answered after four rings by a predictably sleepy voice.

'Hello?'

'Richard? It's Roy Grace.'

'Sir, sorry, *Detective Superintendent*, sir.'

'I'm sorry to wake you.'

'No problem. Good to hear from you. How – how are you, sir?'

'You attended a fatal yesterday evening?'

'The one near Hailsham? Yes.'

'Can you tell me anything about it? It may be relevant to a murder investigation I'm running.'

Sounding more awake, Trundle said, 'It was a DODI – at least that's what it seemed at first.'

A DODI, Grace knew, was cynical traffic police language for a single vehicle accident. *Dead One Done It.*

'At first?' Grace pressed.

'A wet road, water pooling, a nasty bend, a young girl possibly an inexperienced driver – a textbook accident. We had a fatal there just four weeks ago in similar conditions. But . . .' he hesitated.

'But?'

'The Collision Investigation Team found dents on the rear of the car – a Nissan Leaf. They might have been historic, but they reckoned they were evidence of a rear-end shunt. And there were skid marks on the road that they weren't happy with.'

'Not happy in what way?'

'It's early doors, sir, but they didn't feel the marks on the road were consistent with the driver of the Leaf losing control on the bend. They'll be examining the car today and they've closed the road to study the skid markings in daylight.'

'This is really helpful,' Grace said. 'Do you know the victim's name?'

'I do. I had to break the news to her parents at two o'clock this morning. One of my least favourite tasks.'

'I can imagine. Not a nice part of the job.'

'Yes, just hope and pray you never have a copper in a white cap turn up on your doorstep in the middle of the night, because it's never going to be good news. Her name is Lyndsey Cheetham.'

Grace wrote down the name and address. 'Can you describe her and what she was wearing?'

'She was English rose-looking, twenty-one, brown hair in a ponytail, wearing a purple jacket and jeans.'

'Thanks, that's helpful. I'll let you go back to sleep.'

'Kind of you to say that, sir. But I've been awake all night thinking about her. Thinking that might have been my daughter. That one day it could be.'

77

'No cure?' Chris Fairfax said, looking straight back at Dr Shah.

The registrar looked at them both with genuine sadness in his eyes.

'I want to speak to the consultant,' Katy demanded. 'And, as I said, why didn't our doctor suggest it when she first saw our daughter?' she asked desperately.

'Darling,' Chris said, trying to calm her. 'Dr Shah has already explained – because no one knew.'

Katy heard footsteps behind her and ignored them. 'Why didn't anyone know?'

'Because as Dr Shah says, England has been rabies-free for so long. It's been eliminated.'

'Well obviously it bloody well hasn't been, has it?' She rounded on the registrar. 'All you medics have just sodding assumed it, right? That's some crazy assumption.' Tears were rolling down her face. 'Isn't that just irresponsible of all of you?'

Shah shot an anxious glance over her shoulder, as a voice behind her, calm but with a Welsh accent laced with thinly veiled disdain, said, 'Mrs Fairfax, the people who are irresponsible are the ones illegally importing unvaccinated dogs into this country, and, I'm afraid, people like you and your husband who unintentionally support their criminal activity by buying these dogs and supporting this illegal trade.'

Chris and Katy spun round to face the diminutive figure of

301

the consultant, George Pallant, standing erect in a chalk-striped suit, who was positively glaring at them. 'What?' Katy said. 'This is our fault?'

Pallant stared up at both of them, his face stern beneath his neat, slicked-back hair. 'Criminals only prosper when the public buy what they have to offer.'

His tone was so imperious that for an instant both Chris and Katy were silenced. They stood, staring back at him as if in some kind of a Mexican stand-off. After a few moments, Pallant continued, his tone softer, more conciliatory and understanding. 'I appreciate the enormity of what you have both been told, but losing tempers is not going to help your daughter.'

Chris, his voice tight with anxiety and an icy vortex of terror swirling in his guts, said, almost pleading, 'Dr Pallant – Dr Shah said that only twenty or so people in the world are known to have survived rabies. Can we not do any research on these survivors – on the treatment they were given?'

'Dr Shah is on that now,' the consultant said. 'We are short of staff but I've asked a couple of retired doctors to come and locum while he works on doing whatever he can to save your little girl.' He looked at Shah, who nodded. 'There is one other thing, Mr and Mrs Fairfax,' Pallant said, suddenly formal and stiff again now. 'Rabies is a reportable disease.'

'Meaning?' Chris asked, although he had a pretty good idea.

'It will be this hospital's duty to report that we have a possible rabies case to Public Health England.'

'And the implications are – are what, exactly?' Katy questioned, her voice trembling.'

'Well, that will be for them to decide,' Pallant replied.

'Decide?' Chris asked. 'Decide what?'

'I honestly don't know. Those are the regulations, that's all I can tell you at this stage.'

Katy, calmer, turned to the registrar. 'I'm sorry' – she shrugged

– 'for shouting at you. I-I-I'm just desperate with worry – Chris and I both are.'

He nodded with sympathy. 'I have a young daughter. I know how scared I get for her whenever she's unwell. Just be assured she is in the best place and we'll be doing everything we can for her. You both look utterly exhausted – I suggest you go home, have a little rest, freshen up and come back later in the day, and we'll see if we have any more news then.'

'Is there anything else we can do?' Chris asked. 'Anything else at all?'

Shah looked at each of them in turn, his gentle brown eyes bloodshot, and gave them a smile. 'Pray.'

78

Roy Grace knew just what the Roads Policing Officer Richard Trundle had meant when he'd said, a short while earlier, that sometimes the job made you think about your own circumstances and how it could have been one of your loved ones. Delivering a death message was a part of the job that many officers hated the most.

He could vouch for that from when he'd started in the force as a uniform beat copper. He'd been sent to deliver such messages on three different occasions and could still remember them too clearly. His first was when a young male student at Sussex University had hung himself in his lodgings. His second was a twenty-seven-year-old young woman who had died of a drugs overdose. And the third when an eighteen-year-old girl had gone under the wheels of a lorry on her bicycle.

On each occasion the reaction had been different. One mother had collapsed on the floor. Another had attacked him, pummelling him with her fists. And the father of the girl who'd been killed on her bike simply stood there with a blank smile, as if Grace had delivered the news that the day to put the bins out had changed.

He'd decided to send Polly Sweeney and Emma-Jane Boutwood to interview Lyndsey Cheetham's parents, thinking they were the two members of his team who might come across as the most empathetic and elicit the best information. They were also both trained as Family Liaison Officers.

He explained the reason for their absence to the rest of his assembled team at the start of the 9 a.m. briefing meeting on Operation Brush, then pointed at the video screen on which were images of an older-model Range Rover and a Ford Ranger pickup truck.

'We now believe, thanks to the work of the Collision Investigation Unit, that the offenders who we suspect murdered Tim Ruddle, in the process of stealing the dogs from Old Homestead Farm, used two vehicles similar to these. We don't know the actual registration plates of either vehicle, but it is likely they were on the two cloned plates picked up on the ANPR cameras.' He paused and saw all his team nod in concurrence.

He held up several pages of printout. 'I have a report here of the ANPR records of all matching vehicles in the East and West Sussex area, as well as our three neighbouring counties. Just two vehicles, a Ford Ranger and a Range Rover, stand out as both on cloned plates, both heading towards the Ruddles' farm, the Old Homestead, in the early hours of Thursday, March 25th, and later heading away from it. After being clocked by a camera four miles outside of Hailsham, in East Sussex, neither vehicle was picked up again. Which means they ended their journey somewhere within this rural area. I believe these are our suspect vehicles.'

He stood up and walked over to a fifth whiteboard, alongside the association charts, which had been brought in, on which there was a section of a large-scale map encircled in red. 'Norman and Velvet are in the process of visiting all farms in this target area where we have intel of previous criminal activity.' He looked at them both and they nodded in confirmation.

Grace moved on, pressing his clicker. On the screen now appeared the low-res CCTV footage of the man who had stolen the dog in Hove Park last Thursday.

'Hello, hello,' Potting said. 'It's our friend the gecko!'

Grace found himself smiling. 'This handsome fellow appears to be in the business of stealing dogs in the Brighton and Hove area. Including Humphrey, the dog Cleo and I own, which he tried to ransom back to us. Whether out of the kindness of his heart, or sheer dim-wittedness, he has allowed Cleo to capture his phone number.'

'Must be the kindness of his heart, chief,' Potting interrupted. 'With a face like that you wouldn't even get on radio, would you?'

Suppressing another grin, Grace continued. 'We are now onto plotting its movements, but it might be a burner. It is my hypothesis, from all the reports of dogs that have been stolen in the city and environs during the past four weeks, and the descriptions of the offender, that this fellow with the moniker Gecko may be working for an organized crime gang – and perhaps, on occasions, as we suspect he did with our dog, creaming off a few quid for himself.'

'Thought it was only the cat that got the cream, boss,' Jack Alexander quipped and met a half-smile from Grace.

'He is also linked to the theft of two watches from a jeweller in East Street Brighton last Thursday – one a high-value Rolex, the other, in contrast, an inexpensive talking watch. The kind used by blind or partially sighted people.' Grace turned to DS Jo Dillon, the office manager, a serious, studious woman who, in another life, could have been a brilliant librarian. 'Jo, you have some updated intel on this Gecko character that a lot of this team won't have heard yet.'

'I do, boss. I was contacted late yesterday by DS Matt Nixson from Brighton who was at the Albion match on Saturday, doing routine observation of people in the crowd for known villains.'

'Hope he didn't have to drown his sorrows after the result,' Potting commented.

'Fortunately not, Norman,' she replied, unsmiling, and asked Grace to pass her the clicker. 'There was an over-excited character in the family stand whom Adrian Morris noticed – he had to send a steward over twice, to ask him to calm down and stop swearing. As you know, the CCTV coverage in the Amex stadium is such that they can zoom in on any individual.'

'They boast the quality's so good they can tell time on anyone's watch in the whole stadium,' Potting said.

'Quite right, Norman,' Dillon said, almost condescendingly, before continuing. 'When they focused on this individual, DS Nixson radioed the Football Liaison Officer, PC Balkham, to keep an eye on him, recognizing him as a potential POI to Brighton Police in relation to dog crime. But it seems this gentleman and the lady he was with took flight. I've a video of them heading out of the stadium and to the railway platform.'

On the monitor there appeared a series of images of a short, stubby man in his late thirties, in a blue and white Seagulls beanie, puffer and jeans, hurrying across the stadium concourse. He was accompanied by a plain-looking woman, similarly dressed with a Seagulls scarf around her neck, and clutching a white stick. The final image of them before she paused the tape was of the two of them on the platform of Falmer station.

'They're on the southbound platform,' Dillon said.

'Next stop would be Brighton,' Jack Alexander said. 'Then they either left the station or changed trains, right?'

'They changed trains, Jack,' Dillon replied. 'But I only got as far as checking the CCTV at Preston Park – which is where they got off.'

'Did you get on the Preston Park CCTV what they did next?' Grace asked.

'They left the station, sir. I checked with the local taxi company and they didn't pick up anyone of that description.'

'Could have got an Uber,' Potting said.

'Possibly,' Jack Alexander murmured. 'Or that's where they'd parked their vehicle. Or perhaps that's the area where they live?'

'The white stick,' Grace said suddenly. 'The way he's holding her arm in all the footage indicates he's guiding her. Wind the tape back, Jo. Go back to the first image of him at the Amex, the one with him jumping up in the air and waving his arms.'

The tape reversed, fast, overshot, then returned to the image Roy Grace had requested. 'OK,' he said. 'Zoom in on his right hand. Show me his wrist – his watch.'

Moments later an image of a wristwatch, in slightly soft focus now, almost filled the screen. 'Anyone here an expert on watches?' Grace asked.

'That looks like a Rolex, sir,' Jack Alexander said. 'The crown above the name. I know because I really wanted one – until I found out how much they cost! Think I'm going to have to wait until I collect my pension before I can afford one.'

'You could always buy a fake,' Potting said. 'Nicked a bloke about ten years ago who had two thousand of 'em.'

'Kept a few did you, Norman? Give me a good price, will you?'

'We had a steamroller drive over them,' Potting harrumphed. 'Although I have to admit it was a bit of a shame, some of them looked damned good.'

Ignoring the chatter, and focused on the image on the screen, Grace said, 'Jack, you're one hundred per cent sure that's a Rolex?'

'Yes, sir.'

'OK,' Grace said. 'So, confirming what we know and what we've just heard, we have a robbery at a jeweller in East Street last Thursday, in which a Rolex watch is stolen along with a talking watch for the blind. I think we are all now up to speed with the connection, right?'

79

Tuesday 30 March

Chris Fairfax left the hospital to go back home, shower, and spend some time with Moose. He made a phone call to their assistant, Khalid, to reschedule both his and Katy's clients for the next week at the least. While finishing the phone call he saw the Maliks at the window, waving to get his attention. He invited them in to update them on the news from the hospital. The chatter made him more and more weary. Noticing his tiredness, they left, saying to contact them at any time to take on puppy care duties. That it was the least they could do to help.

He managed to pull himself together in order to spend a little time trawling more of the internet for everything he could find out about rabies.

As he sat down at his laptop his phone rang, with *number withheld* displayed on the screen. 'Chris Fairfax,' he answered and immediately heard a chirpy voice he recognized as the private detective, Ken Grundy.

'All right, Chris, how's it going?'

'I've been better.'

'Just tried calling your missus but she's not picking up.'

'Do you have news, Ken?'

'I think I may have. Your John Peat seems like a pretty busy character. I've had my team on to him, and it seems that whoever he really is, he goes under a number of aliases, including so far Tom Hartley, Jonathan Jones and Michael

Kendrick, advertising puppies for sale pretty widely across numerous sites. We've not yet been able to establish his true identity, but we've found a link to an organized crime gang headed by a very unsavoury character called Terry Jim, with past form for theft, threatening behaviour and ABH. He now owns a large rural property near Hailsham in East Sussex, called Appletree Farm. It looks possible this elusive Peat-Hartley-Jones-Kendrick character is fronting for Jim – selling his puppies for him.'

'Do you have the address?'

'I do.' He gave it to Chris, who entered it on his phone. Then he added, 'But I'd advise against paying him a visit on your own.'

'I'm a big boy, Ken.'

'I'm bigger than you and uglier, mate. If you want to go and see him, I'll come with you and bring a few even bigger and uglier blokes as a posse. But I can't get to you for three days because of a job we're all on.'

Chris thanked him, saying he would let him know, then ended the call. Immediately, he entered the address the PI had given him for Appletree Farm into his phone. It showed a journey time of 47 minutes. Moments later, his phone rang. It was Katy and she sounded completely exhausted.

'Hi, darling, what news? How is she?' he asked.

'They keep telling me she's stable,' she replied.

'OK,' he said. 'Well that's good.'

'Is it?'

He felt the fear in his voice. The fear for his daughter that coiled cold and relentlessly through him. 'Darling, listen. I may have tracked down where Moose actually came from. I'm going to drive over there now and see what I can find out. You need to come home and get some rest, a shower, freshen up. If Bluebell is stable, then there's nothing you can do by exhausting yourself. Come home. I'll go and talk to the breeder and see what I can find out about the dog that bit Bluebell, then go straight to the hospital and stay there until you've had a rest.'

'I don't want to leave her alone for long,' Katy said adamantly. 'I'll come home quickly while she's sleeping, see you back at the hospital later.'

'I'll be as quick as I can.' He glanced at his watch. 'It's 12.45 – I'll be there 3 p.m. latest. Love you.'

'Love you,' she replied bleakly.

80

Roy Grace had just come out of his meeting with the Chief Constable, updating her on Operation Brush and discussing with her possible ways to tackle the wave of dog crime in the county on a broader scale. This included asking the Police and Crime Commissioner to provide extra funding for policing the county's ports. He was about to take a break and stroll into Lewes, now the rain had stopped, and grab a sandwich for his very late lunch, when his phone rang.

It was DS Ross from Intelligence. 'Boss, is this a good moment?'

'Sure.'

'The phone number you gave me, from the chap who found your dog – the one your wife had logged on her phone, right?'

'Yes?' he said hesitantly.

'We've got a plot on its movements back from the phone company.'

'Brilliant – what does it show, Julian?'

'The team's working on a full mapping of its movements of the past four weeks. But it looks like he might be based in the Preston Park area of Brighton.'

'Preston Park, interesting.'

'It's always hard to get an accurate plot in a dense residential area, but there is a section of one street that he seems to gravitate towards and then remain static there for many hours. Kingsley Avenue.'

'I know it,' Grace said. 'Sandy had an aunt who used to live there.'

'From what we can work out he stays constant – usually from early evening until early morning – somewhere between number 8 and 22 – we can't tell you which side of the street, and I don't know how densely populated it is.'

'It's a nice street, pretty houses – mostly terraced. Quite small properties – what estate agents might term "bijou", so I would think most are intact and not divided up into flats – single person or family occupants.' He felt a beat of excitement at Julian's news.

'I guess that will help narrow your search. I'll try to get the wider map back to you later today – we're a bit under the cosh with two other urgent jobs today, but I'll do my best.'

'You're a star, Julian!'

'Yeah, I know!'

Grinning, Grace ended the call, all thoughts of lunch gone from his mind. He hurried back across the campus towards the Major Crime Suite and went straight to Luke Stanstead in the Detectives Room. 'Luke, I need you urgently to do some research on Kingsley Avenue, Brighton. Check the electoral register for the names of all householders between numbers 8 and 22.'

'I'll get on it right away, sir.'

Grace walked back to his office, thinking of the best way he could use this intel from Julian Ross. The electoral register would give him the house owners – or current occupants' names if they were renting – and maybe one of those would raise a flag when run through the PNC. He could instigate a house-to-house with officers equipped with Gecko's photo and of the woman with him, but that could warn Gecko they were on his trail and drive him into hiding. It would be smarter, he thought, to put surveillance on the street.

Grace returned to his office and, as he reached it, he heard Polly Sweeney's voice call out to him. 'Sir!'

He turned and saw her. 'How did it go at Lyndsey Cheetham's parents – any joy, Polly?'

After he had ushered her into his office, Sweeney said, 'Joy's not the word I'd use to describe it, sir. Lyndsey's parents are on the floor – as you'd expect. Lyndsey's an only child and they had her relatively late in life – and utterly doted on her. They told us she was studying to become a veterinary nurse and was doing some work in the kennels of a dog breeder to gain experience.'

His excitement increasing, Grace said, 'So it sounds like she was the informant you were due to meet – the timing and location fit, right?'

'They do, sir,' Sweeney replied hesitantly. 'The location where she had her accident puts her between the Hailsham area and our planned RV at approximately the right time. The clothing she said she'd be wearing confirms it also.'

'You got the name of these kennels from the Cheethams?'

She shook her head. 'No, sir – unbelievably they don't know.'

'She never told them or are they covering up something?'

'They're not in any state to cover up anything. Seems like they never actually asked her the name of the farm. Lyndsey was very happy it was so close to their home – just a half-hour drive.'

From his knowledge of the county, Grace was aware that a thirty-minute drive created a pretty big radius – albeit one inside the red circle drawn on the map in the conference room. 'OK, we should be able to get a plot of her phone from the phone provider that should take us to her place of work.'

Sweeney shook her head. 'I've already spoken to the Road Policing Unit SIO who's running the investigation. She said none of the officers or any of the Collision Investigation members who attended could find a mobile phone. Lorraine Bute, who was part of the team mapping the collision scene, said she'd spoken to PC Trundle, who was the first officer at the scene. He said he'd meant to tell you earlier, when you called him, but given his sleepiness he didn't have his brain fully in gear. He and his colleagues did a thorough search around the area of the collision, in case the phone had been ejected from the vehicle, but they couldn't find one anywhere. He thought that strange – particularly as it was a young person driving, who almost certainly would have had a phone with her – she must have done because she called me from her car. I have obtained her mobile number from her parents, and we can use that for our enquiries.'

'Thanks, did the car roll?' Grace asked. 'It might have been flung out of a window into undergrowth.'

'Lorraine said the car didn't roll – it went straight off the road and into a tree. They're certain they didn't miss anywhere it could have landed if ejected from the car – and the windows were all up, which makes that very unlikely, in any case.'

Grace was pensive for some moments. 'There were marks at the rear of the car indicating a possible rear-end shunt from a larger vehicle. There is some possible red-paint transfer from that vehicle, but more lab analysis is needed to confirm. Tyre marks on the road inconsistent with a skid from entering the bend too fast. Could it be she was deliberately shunted off the road and into the tree? And whoever did that, then took her phone?'

'It's a very credible hypothesis, sir.'

'The vehicle Lyndsey was driving was an older-model Nissan Leaf, from 2011,' Grace said. 'All electric. It must either have an onboard satnav or some other recording device that would have logged its journeys. See what the Collision Investigation team can interrogate from it – or else get them to take the vehicle to a Nissan dealer if that will be quicker.'

'I'll get on it right away, sir.'

As Polly Sweeney left his office, Roy Grace sat, thinking hard, reflecting. Lyndsey Cheetham's accident might not be connected in any way to Operation Brush. He could be sending Polly Sweeney down a rabbit hole. And yet, all his instincts were telling him there was a link here. Polly was due to meet an informant who worked in a dog breeder's kennels. The informant never turned up. Lyndsey Cheetham worked in a breeder's kennels. She died in a car accident somewhere between her place of work and the planned rendezvous with Sweeney. There was evidence another vehicle had been involved in her fatal accident – which had disappeared from the scene. As had her mobile phone. The clothes matched.

As he entered the details into his policy book, he was certain that the informant and Lyndsey Cheetham were one and the same person, particularly as this was confirmed by the phone research that Polly had carried out.

He turned his thoughts back to Gecko, and called the ACC, Hannah Robinson. He was relieved when her Staff Officer put her through immediately. After he had given her his reasons, the ACC agreed without hesitation with his decision to deploy surveillance on Kingsley Avenue, which had been approved by the Force Authorizing Officer.

81

PCs Eldhos Matthew and Mike Shaw sat in their marked car, in a lay-by a few hundred yards from the scene of Lyndsey Cheetham's fatal collision with a tree. Folded open in front of them was a small-scale Ordnance Survey map of the area. They had been given the action of calling at houses and business premises in the vicinity of the scene. Eldhos was a lot more excited than his colleague about the task they were now carrying out.

Mike Shaw, who was twenty-four and had been in the force for five years, had just applied, for the second time, to join the Roads Policing Unit. Ever since his early teens he had wanted to be a traffic cop, and now they were recruiting again, he had an interview coming up in two weeks. He considered this current task, of endless knocking on doors, boring. In complete contrast to his younger colleague who seemed to love it.

Eldhos Matthew knew they were both very small cogs in the investigation into the collision. But equally, from all the information he had acquired on roles in policing that could help him with his ambition to become a detective, he had learned that normally in a fatal road traffic collision, an inspector from the Roads Policing Unit would have been appointed as the Senior Investigating Officer. The SIO!

Those three letters held a kind of magic for him. One day, he would be an SIO. In charge of a murder investigation. Then he would be able to tell his father, who had been so against him joining the police, that he had truly made a good decision.

And this current task, which his handsome but rather laid-back colleague, Mike Shaw, found so tedious, he found very exciting. Because although the SIO was Roads Policing Inspector James Biggs, there was a bigger picture to this whole investigation, and at the top of it was a possible link to Operation Brush, the investigation that they were working on into the murder of a farmer called Timothy Ruddle, being run by Detective Superintendent Roy Grace. It was a long shot, but there was a possibility, nonetheless, to impress the detective he would so much like to work under.

He pointed his finger at a road leading to a village they'd not yet covered. 'Here next?' he said to Shaw. 'Two miles away.'

Shaw looked at his watch. 'We've done four hours. How about we go to the RPU at Polegate for a coffee – they're only about fifteen minutes from here?' he suggested hopefully. He liked the idea of having the chance to talk to some Roads Policing officers at Polegate police station.

'Let's do the village and then we'll take a break,' Eldhos suggested.

Shaw agreed reluctantly.

A few minutes later they passed a 30 mph sign and immediately saw a row of pretty terraced thatched cottages on their right. Several vehicles were parked on the street in front of them, but they found a gap and Eldhos reversed into it. They walked up a short, steep flight of steps and Shaw rapped on the door of the first one, the end-of-terrace house.

After several more raps on the door, and pressing a bell button that made no sound, they moved on to the next cottage.

Within moments of knocking, the door, which had a spyhole, opened a crack on a safety chain, which Eldhos immediately thought was odd in such a relatively remote village community. A gruff male voice called out, 'I'm sorry, I don't talk to police.'

'Sir,' Eldhos Matthew replied, 'we are investigating a serious car crash two miles from here yesterday evening. We would just like to talk to you about any vehicles you might have seen around that time.'

The door closed on them, and both officers looked at each other, wondering if that was it. Then there was a metallic clank, and the door opened, to reveal a silver-haired man – in his seventies, Eldhos guessed – wearing a baggy Iron Maiden T-shirt, shorts and Crocs. 'That was the young lady who died?'

They held up their warrant cards. 'Yes, sir,' Eldhos said.

'A dangerous bend, I don't understand why the council done nothing about it. There was a fatal there about ten years ago and another last month – a teenage boy – hit that same tree.'

'Maybe they will do something about it now, sir,' Mike Shaw said.

'Bunch of wankers, the council, no chance. Come in, I did see something, since you're here.'

He limped ahead of them, through a hallway hung with framed Formula One motor racing pictures into a tiny kitchen, with a view onto a large well-tended garden. He ushered them to sit at a pine table and offered them tea or coffee, which they declined – Mike Shaw reluctantly.

Pulling out his electronic pad, Eldhos asked the man his name. Looking around, he saw some framed family photographs on a Welsh dresser, the man in front of them with a woman, and several of young children beside them.

'What's your name, sir?' Shaw asked.

'Simon Cronin,' he replied. 'I'm sorry but I'm pretty pissed off with you lot. You're always stopping people outside our local. Don't you have anything better to do?'

Ignoring the comment, Eldhos asked him, 'You said you'd seen something, sir?'

'That piece of shit from up the road driving his ridiculous red

Yank 4 x 4 like he owns the road, yet again.' Cronin's round, amiable face had turned a little red. 'He doesn't give a monkey's about anyone else. Nearly took me out last week.'

A large red 4 x 4, being driven recklessly – Eldhos knew it was worth checking out. 'Do you know the driver, sir?'

'I do, just about everyone in the village has had a run-in with him at some time or another. He lives just up the road. His name's Dallas Jim. Oh, and I can tell you, I saw it earlier and there was some damage to the front of the vehicle.'

The two PCs thanked him and left, after it was evident he had little further to add. Eldhos was excited, and as soon as they were back in his car sent a report to Inspector Biggs.

82

Following the directions of his satnav, which now showed 14 minutes to Appletree Farm, Chris Fairfax rounded a series of bends in the fast, sweeping two-lane road, bordered by hedges to the left and woods to the right, then as the road straightened, he saw ahead a blue and white POLICE – ACCIDENT sign. A short distance behind it a marked police car was parked diagonally across the road, with two officers standing beside it, and tape across the road behind them.

He halted and lowered his window and told one of the officers where he was heading. She directed him to turn round and take the first left, about a half-mile away, which would bring him back on his route on the far side of the road closure.

Following her directions for a short distance before the satnav re-routed, he wound along a network of narrow, twisting country lanes, having to stop twice to let oncoming vehicles pass, and finally the satnav read, *Your destination is ahead to your right.*

A barely visible, crooked and badly weathered wooden sign, partially concealed by brambles, at the entrance to what was little more than a cart track, read APPLETREE FARM.

He turned onto the potholed track and drove slowly along it for some distance, with fields of crops on either side, until he reached a five-barred gate with a sign on it saying KINDLY CLOSE THE GATE. As he got out to open it, he noticed a CCTV camera on a tall pole pointed down towards the gate. Uncannily, as he looked up at it, the camera swivelled towards him.

He drove through and closed the gate behind him. After bouncing along the track for another half-mile, now with barren fields on either side, and the green hills of the South Downs in the distance to the right, and driving slowly to avoid risking a puncture, he reached a tall, spiked steel security gate that could have been the entrance to a fortress. On his right was a pod with an entryphone panel and the round lens of another camera.

Chris lowered his window and pressed the button that was unmarked, but which he presumed was the bell. After a few moments there was a crackle followed by a harsh male voice. 'Yeah?'

Well aware of Ken Grundy's warning to him, Chris said politely, 'I'd like to talk to someone about buying a puppy.'

'We don't sell puppies,' came the bland reply.

'I'm looking for John Peat?' he said.

After a long silence, in which he began to wonder if he'd had a wasted journey, the crackle came again, followed by the same man's voice. 'What the fuck do you want?'

'My name's Christopher Fairfax. I bought a puppy from a Mr John Peat and—'

'Wait there,' the voice said aggressively. Chris waited for some minutes, with a building apprehension about what he was doing here and if he had made the right decision.

The steel gate suddenly slid sideways and he saw a man far in the distance with a big dog next to him.

Chris got out of his car but did not dare step any further and instead stood subtly scanning the area, taking it all in. The cluster of farm buildings ahead. The stench that he thought at first was manure, but then realized, from visiting a pig-farmer client a couple of years ago, was the unmistakable smell of pigs.

To his right was a decrepit open-sided barn, in which was

parked a massive tractor, and alongside it a trailer, a plough and several other large pieces of farm machinery, all looking dirty but in working condition. He heard the barking of other dogs. It was loud and frantic. A hideous concrete walled building to his left, with open slits for windows high up and a corrugated iron roof. It reminded him, unpleasantly, of images of Nazi concentration camps he'd seen in documentaries.

Next to it was an almost identical building. Much further in the distance he could see a sizeable, but sad and neglected-looking house at the far end, outside which stood a grimy Land Rover, a horsebox and a Toyota pickup truck on jacked-up suspension with a row of roof-lights. For rabbiting, Chris guessed. There was a row of stables to the right, with one chestnut horse peering out somewhat mournfully.

The dog and the big oaf of a man marched towards him menacingly. A big, muscular, shaven-headed ugly bastard, wearing tracksuit bottoms and trainers, bare-chested, much of his flabby upper torso covered in tattoos, he strode towards Chris's Audi, looking about as welcoming as a nuclear warhead on a guided missile.

Making a split-second decision whether to get back in his car and make a dash for it or stay and try to engage, he chose the latter. He had just put his car keys in his pocket to free up his hand to give the man a handshake, when the charmer reached him, coming too close for comfort, into his personal space, almost eyeball to eyeball. So close that when he spoke, Chris could smell recent cigarette smoke on his body and stale garlic on his breath. 'What do you want here?' he asked by way of introduction.

'My name's Christopher Fairfax – and you are?'

'Yeah, you said. What's it to you who I am?'

'I'm looking for Terry Jim. I was given this address for him.'

The man gave him a smile that contained anything but humour.

'Were you now? Well, you've found him, this must be your lucky day. I'd go and buy a lottery ticket if I was you.'

Unsure quite how to respond, Chris composed his thoughts for a few seconds, as Terry Jim moved his face even closer. 'My wife and I bought a puppy a few days ago from a man who gave his name as John Peat – do you know him?'

Jim shook his head guilelessly.

'I understand he also goes under the names of Tom Hartley, Jonathan Jones and Michael Kendrick.'

'Must be a busy guy,' Jim retorted.

'You need to hear me out,' Chris said, determined not to be cowed or intimidated, despite feeling very nervous.

'Do I?'

'My daughter went into a van with some puppies in cages that this John Peat had. One of these puppies bit my daughter, and she is now displaying symptoms of rabies.'

'My condolences.'

Chris glared at him. 'I've come here for two reasons, Mr Jim. The first is to try to establish if the puppy that bit my daughter, and might have given her rabies, was one of yours. And secondly to warn you that rabies is a notifiable disease, which means we have to inform both the police and Public Health England where we bought our puppy and where we suspect the source of the disease is. I hope you'll cooperate?'

'Am I understanding you're accusing me of something, Mr Fairfax? You think I would sell a rabid dog? Really? Let me tell you, all our dogs are well cared for, as you can see by looking at Caesar here. All dogs we sell are seen by vets and signed off by them before we pass them on to any third party. That OK with you?'

'Yes, and I don't doubt it,' Chris said, emboldened by his anger. 'But do you know the provenance of all the dogs you trade in?'

Jim raised a massive fist in front of Chris's face. 'Do you see this?'

'I do.'

'What do you see?'

'Your right hand.'

'Do you doubt its provenance?'

'If you mean does it belong to you, no.'

'Good.'

Jim's fist smashed into Chris's face, slamming him back against his Audi.

83

Roy Grace was seated in his office, with Glenn Branson standing over his shoulder. They were studying a map spread out on the desk, showing a twenty-mile radius around the town of Hailsham in East Sussex.

It was marked with a series of red crosses, each of them a plot of cell phone masts that Lyndsey Cheetham's phone had 'talked to' on the journeys she had made during the past four weeks. Two of them were additionally circled in yellow, indicating the start and finishing points of each journey and the times spent at each destination. Grace was still waiting for the analysis of the onboards of the dead girl's car, but he was pretty confident the plot from her phone was giving all the mapping information he needed. But it would be good to get the onboard, in due course, for belt and braces.

'Chiddingly,' Branson said. 'That's her home, right?'

'Where she lives – lived – with her parents.'

'Nice pub there,' he said. 'Been there with Siobhan a few times, they have local bands playing at weekends.'

'What will they be playing this weekend, the Funeral March?' Grace said grimly.

'You're a sick puppy sometimes, aren't you?'

Grace looked up and gave him a thin smile. 'Yeah, that's about the right expression. Good choice of words, mate. I'm sorry, I've had a long day. I'm tired. Tired of this fucking shit. Tired of these people who think they can do what they want, kill who they want, to line their filthy pockets. Sometimes I think the only progress we've made since the scumbags Dickens wrote about is that now they have technology.'

Branson looked at him sympathetically. 'You need to take a break – chill for a couple of days, I'll run the team.'

Grace smiled again, even more thinly. 'Thanks, mate, but I'm OK, I'm good. I'll take a break, a good long one, when we've locked up the people who murdered Tim Ruddle and Lyndsey Cheetham. I think we're getting close.' He pointed at the map. 'So, six days a week for the past month, Lyndsey drove from her parents' place to here.' He stabbed the second yellow circle. 'Appletree Farm.' He paused.

'Now one of the things we know about Appletree Farm is that a Polish-registered lorry was stopped in the early hours of this morning, a few miles from Newhaven, with twenty-seven puppies concealed behind hay bales. This cargo of "hay"' – he made air-quotation marks with his fingers – 'was destined for two farms: Appletree, owned by the lovely Terry Jim, and Long Acre, a few miles away, owned by his equally lovely son Dallas. Their names seem to be popping up a bit too regularly. From Norman and Velvet on Monday and this keen young PC, Eldhos Matthew, today. Lyndsey spent from approximately 9 a.m. to 5 p.m. at Appletree Farm every day before driving back to Chiddingly. And on each of these four Saturday evenings she drove into Eastbourne, where she remained until well after midnight. For the nightlife?'

'Nightlife in Eastbourne?' Branson grinned.

'Exactly, it's full of old folk,' Grace said.

'Not any longer, mate,' Branson said. 'Same as Worthing – now Worthing's cool. Well it's got to be – me and Siobhan are looking at buying a place there!'

Worthing was a seaside town of around 100,000 people, a few miles west of Brighton, with a reputation as a retirement place.

'Worthing's cool? Seriously? When I was a kid, Worthing was known as God's Waiting Room – all the shop windows were in bi-focal.'

'Yeah? Well, the Almighty's going to have to wait a long time these days – like, if we're buying there.'

'I hope so,' Grace retorted. Then, focusing back on the map, he said, 'Lyndsey's last journey was somewhat off-piste. Monday night, she left Appletree Farm and instead of driving home to Chiddingly, she appeared to be heading towards Eastbourne. A bit early for the bars, wouldn't you think?'

'In her work clothes? She'd been spending all day looking after dogs in kennels. That's not how you go partying.'

'Which makes it all the more likely she was heading to RV with Polly?'

Branson nodded. 'Then she gets run off the road. Hits a tree. And ends up brown bread. No chance to tell Polly about the disappearance of Rosalind Esche. Another brown bread?'

Grace looked at him again, for some moments. '"Brown bread"? I never took you for a Cockney.' He glanced at the time on Branson's flashy watch, the size of a not particularly small planet: 4.35. The next briefing was in twenty-five minutes.

Branson beamed and made a circle with his forefinger and thumb. 'Me and Cockney rhyming slang – love it. Just like I like your whistle.'

'Yeah, yeah, whistle and flute – suit, I know that one.' The slang was used by criminals, historically, so they could talk in pubs without risk of arrest by any coppers who might be in there having a drink.

'Uncle Bert? Know that one?' Branson said eagerly.

'No, you got me, go on.'

'It's obvious, matey . . . *shirt*!'

'I learn something new every day,' Grace said. 'Thanks for the education.'

'Be grateful. A day in which I don't learn something new is a day wasted.'

After a few moments, Roy Grace nodded. 'There's something in that. So, if we can cut through your philosophical pearls for a moment – no disrespect – and focus on the map in front of us, we have a pattern with Lyndsey Cheetham, driving to and from work six days a week, until Monday. She diverts from the route she would ordinarily have taken home to her parents, on a weekday, taking a road that could have taken her to Eastbourne. To a meeting with Polly. To tell her something in person she was too scared to tell her over the phone.'

As Grace was about to continue, his job phone rang. It was Detective Sergeant Mark Taylor, who was running the surveillance team Grace had requested. He put him on loudspeaker so Branson could hear.

'Boss, we're set up on the location you gave us, Kingsley Avenue, with eyes on the target street numbers, 8 to 22. We're parked up in a van and I've just emailed you a live video link.'

Grace thanked him, opened his inbox, found the email and opened the link. Moments later they saw a clear image of Kingsley Avenue, which was on a steep incline. From the camera angle, the surveillance team were looking up from near the bottom of the hill.

To the immediate left, a car underneath a cover was stationed off-road outside a double garage. All the other vehicles were parked pretty much nose-to-tail on both sides of the pleasant-looking street. The houses were terraced, in a mix of architectural styles dating back to the 1930s, some exteriors painted white, some tiled and some red brick. Roy Grace's attention was drawn to a house to the right, on which he could read the number 18. A white Ford Transit panel van was parked outside, the same make and model as the one he had seen Gecko in on Goldstone Crescent, on Friday, after taking Sara Gurner's labradoodle.

But that van was marked, he remembered, with the name of a drainage company emblazoned along the side in orange and black. A company that had turned out not to exist. This one had the name K. GATTON TV SOLUTIONS on it. Nonetheless, it held his interest. The signage on the van in Goldstone Crescent had turned out to have been fake and could have been simply magnetic panels. He called the analyst and asked for a PNC check on it.

The information came back within seconds. The van was registered to a Keith Gatton and was taxed and fully insured. A short distance along the street he saw a man up a ladder, making adjustments to a Sky aerial. Keith Gatton or one of his employees, he thought, and probably just coincidence it was parked outside a house that interested them.

There were steep steps up to the front door of number 18, and mounted on the wall by the door was a long black grab-handle.

He looked up at Branson. 'Who has a handle like that installed by their front door?'

'Someone elderly? Someone unsteady on their pins?' the DI suggested.

'How about a blind or partially sighted person who needs something to hold onto while they put their key in the lock, like you after a night out?' He winked at Branson.

Squinting at the image, Branson said, 'Haha! There's something by the doorbell – can you see it?'

Grace called Taylor back and asked him to zoom in on number 18 and give them a close-up of the note.

Moments later, he and Glenn could see it clearly. It was a handwritten yellow note, taped just above the doorbell. It read, *I'M DISABLED, IT TAKES ME A WHILE TO GET TO THE DOOR. DON'T GO AWAY!*

They looked at each other. 'Could be a blind person,' Grace said.

Branson nodded. 'Or just someone with mobility issues.'

'One way to find out,' Grace replied. 'Mark, how many are you in the van?'

'Three of us on this shift, boss. Two of us in the van and DC Erin Brown is parked up a couple of streets away.'

'I need her to go and knock on the door on a pretext. I don't want to spook them – we need to think of a story.'

'Lost her cat?' Branson suggested.

'I'm already there, sir. Erin has a framed photograph of a cat in her vehicle with her.'

'Seriously?'

'We have all kinds of props, boss – and disguises.'

'Brilliant!' Grace replied. He thought for a moment, trying to remember the surrounding streets. One, he knew, was Matlock Road. 'Mark, get her to knock on the door and say she lives in Matlock Road and her cat's gone missing, she's going around the neighbourhood in case anyone's seen it – and keep the camera tight on the front door. Then she'll have to go on doing all the other houses afterwards to make it look real.'

'Right away, boss. Erin's already bored out of her skull, she'll be happy to stretch her legs. And she's a cat lover.'

'Is that relevant?'

'What do they say, boss? If you can fake sincerity, the rest is easy.'

The two detectives watched as, a few minutes later, the tall, young PC, dressed in jeans and a leather jacket, and with a mane of red hair which would have very effectively concealed her earpiece, walked purposefully up the street, with a photograph frame under her arm. She went first up to number 26 and knocked on the door. A young man answered, they appeared to exchange a few words, then she moved on to number 24. It was opened by an elderly lady who shook her head.

Grace smiled. Erin deserved an Oscar! He watched her walk

up to number 22, climb the steps and press the bell. She waited some while, then rang again. Then again.

Mark Taylor rang Grace. 'Do you want her to keep trying, boss?'

'Give it another minute then tell her to move on. Just keep it natural, Mark,' Grace said, trying not to sound frustrated.

As Erin moved on to the next house, number 20, there was a knock on Grace's office door and Norman Potting barged in, clutching a sheaf of printouts, then hovered in the doorway for some moments seeing they were preoccupied.

Grace looked up at him. 'Yes, Norman?'

Nodding respectfully at Glenn Branson, he addressed Grace. 'Chief, I thought you'd like to see this ahead of our evening briefing. I've got another plot from the phone company of Gecko's – Marion Willingham's – mobile phone, thanks to the smart work of your wife capturing his number.'

'Good work,' Grace said and waved him over.

Potting approached his desk and laid the sheaf down beside the computer monitor. 'It shows us two things, chief. I've been liaising with John Street CID on the recent spate of dog thefts from the city's parks, and this would appear to put Gecko at the scene of each of them, including the one on Thursday in Goldstone Crescent – a Mrs Sara Gurner, I believe.'

He spread the papers out excitedly, almost knocking over Grace's framed photos of Cleo, Bruno, Noah and Molly in the process. 'Possibly even more of interest is the plot of the journey he made after each reported dog theft. It was over towards Hailsham, to a location I've identified as a farm owned by a suspected crime gang boss.'

'Don't tell us it's Terry Jim?' Grace quizzed.

Looking deflated, as if the wind had suddenly gone from his sails, Potting said, 'Move to the top of the class, chief.'

'He's already there, Norman,' Branson retorted with a grin.

84

Chris Fairfax leaned back against his car, so dazed he was unable to move for some moments. His brain felt like it had been inside a blender, and his eyes were streaming tears. His nose was hurting like hell.

As he looked down, he saw his white shirt and pale blue tie were splattered with red stains. He put his hand to his nose. It felt like jelly, and was painful to touch. Pulling out his handkerchief, he dabbed his nostrils gingerly, and it came away covered in fresh, bright red blood.

Busted, he thought. *You bastard. You absolute—*

He remembered Ken Grundy's warning and wished now he had heeded it and turned up with a posse of heavies. And it was now likely that any evidence that might be here would be long gone before the police got near this place.

The farm was deserted. Terry Jim and the dog had disappeared, and the security gate was now shut. There was no sign of anyone around. Just the faint stench of pigs and the squealing and yapping of puppies, the distant crowing of a rooster, and the muted drone of a tractor way off in the distance. He felt very disoriented. Looked at the fields all around, with a fuse of anger burning down somewhere deep inside him.

In his growing rage, he wanted to walk over to the gate and kick it in but he knew who would come off worse.

A thought, emerging somewhere deeper in his mind, told him

he needed to get out of here. And – the lawyer inside him – report the assault.

Still very dazed, he somehow got the car door open, climbed into the driver's seat, but then sat there, gripping the wheel and staring down along the bonnet at the rutted track in front of him.

'Bastard,' he murmured, then checked his mouth in the mirror to make sure no teeth were missing. To his relief, they were intact.

He started the engine, not confident about driving with his fuzzy brain state, but wanting to get away as quickly as he could before the thug came back. Despite his vision being blurry, he drove as fast as he dared away from the tall steel gate, stopping only to get out and dutifully shut the wooden five-barred gate. As he clicked it closed, he gave a suppressed, almost soundless laugh at the absurdity of him bothering to shut the gate for this vile ape who had just punched him in the face.

Need to go to hospital, he thought. *Get the bleeding stopped, my nose fixed.* But he could be there hours, he knew, all the horror stories in the *Argus* about waiting times in A&E. He didn't have time, right now, he was needed at Bluebell's bedside.

Balling his handkerchief and pressing it as gently but firmly as he could against his nose, he held it there with his left hand, gladder than ever at this moment that the car was an automatic, and steered with his right. There was a small town a few miles ahead where he would find a chemist and get a proper dressing for his nose.

There was so much fury boiling inside him.

Bastard.

You don't do that and get away with it. Not in my world you don't, Mr Shirtless Jim. In my world you will play by my rules. You vile tosser.

Then his phone began ringing, and he saw on the display it was Katy.

Letting go of the wheel and reaching his right arm across, perilously, for a few seconds, he stabbed the hands-free answer button.

'Hi, baby,' he answered, suddenly back in the real world.

Katy was sobbing hysterically down the phone. 'Oh God,' she said. 'Oh God, no. Chris, you have to stop them, you have to stop them.'

'Stop who, darling?' he asked as calmly as he could, his nerves tight as razor wire at the stark terror in her voice.

'Where are you?'

'I'm just east of Hailsham.'

'Why – why are you there? Oh Jesus, I need you here.'

'I'll explain later – stop who, darling? Who do I have to stop?'

'Your voice sounds strange, are you all right?'

'What's going on?'

'They've come to take Moose.'

'Katy, I'm driving, I'm going to pull over, just bear with me a second. They've come to take Moose? Who has come, why?'

'They're going to euthanize her.'

'Euthanize her? You mean *kill* her?'

'Yes!' she yelled back hysterically. 'KILL HER.'

85

Tuesday 30 March

There was no answer at number 20. Erin waited at the kerb for two cars to pass before she approached number 18. This was the house that most interested Grace – because of the big grab-handle at the top of the steep flight of steps to the front door.

He knew some elderly people had balance issues. But he also reckoned that, for someone with impaired vision, the top of these steps would be a scary place.

He saw Erin press the doorbell. Wait. Knock. Wait. Press the bell then knock again.

After some moments, the door began to open, slowly, cautiously. Then a woman's face appeared.

'Go in tight, Mark,' Grace asked.

As the camera zoomed in, Grace could see without any doubt this was the woman who had been with Gecko at the Amex Stadium. Her glasses had lenses as thick as bottle-glass. Her voice, plain, a flat Brighton twang like an Estuary accent toned down, but pleasant and eager to please, came through the speaker. 'No, sorry, I've not seen any cat.'

'Does anyone else live here who might have seen her?'

'My boyfriend. He loves animals, too, I'm sure he'd have said. Although he's more of a dog person.'

'Any chance of a word with him?'

'He's out, working.'

'What time will he be home?'

'It varies – he works for a dog charity and it all depends what situations they have. Could be any time between 6 and 8 p.m. I'm sure he'd have said if he'd seen a cat in the garden.'

'What's the name of the charity?' Erin pressed.

'Umm – I – actually – it may sound daft, I don't know the actual name. Something like the East Sussex Dog Rescue Association at Raystede, I think.'

As Erin thanked her and moved on to the next house, Grace phoned Luke Stanstead, asking him if he could find any charity of a similar name.

'I'll check right away. I've just got the electoral register information back on the Kingsley Avenue houses, sir,' Stanstead said.

'Immaculate timing, Luke,' Grace replied. 'I'm looking at number 18 as we speak. What do you have on it?'

After a brief moment, the researcher replied, 'The current owner/occupier is a Ms Elvira Joan Polkinhorne. There's no one else on the register recorded as living there. She has owned the house since 2016.'

'Ask Emily Denyer to take a look at her finances – does this woman have a mortgage and does she earn enough to cover the monthly charges?'

'I just googled her name while we were talking, sir. She has a bit of a profile on LinkedIn – she's registered blind and works on a helpline for a tech company.'

'OK, speak to the company and see what they can tell you about her.'

Ending the call, Grace watched Erin crossing the road once more. He called Mark Taylor and told him she could end the charade after a couple more houses – he doubted Elvira Polkinhorne could see much beyond the end of her nose. Then he asked him to let him know the moment Gecko returned to the house, and when he did, to be fully prepared to keep him under surveillance when he left again.

Taylor assured him he was ready, with a team of three surveillance cars and a motorcycle standing by. Once they had eyes on Gecko, they would be keeping them on him, 24/7.

Thanking him, Grace looked down at the section of the map showing Appletree Farm and the yellow line around its approximate borders. Another yellow line enclosed Long Acre Farm.

'Planning a raid, chief?' Potting asked.

Grace nodded. 'I am, but not yet. We know the Jim family by reputation. They're vile but not stupid. When we strike, we need to stop them dead. We need to know exactly what we're doing and who and what we're looking for. From the intelligence we've gathered, this farm is now our number one target. I want to make an arrest for Tim Ruddle's murder, and for what looks increasingly like Lyndsey Cheetham's murder, too. And I'm very concerned about her co-worker, Rosalind Esche. Terry Jim's a confident bastard, always reckoned he's untouchable. He's spent too many years playing the *You can't put a finger on me, I'm an innocent member of the community and I know my rights* card. We have time on our side. I don't think he's going anywhere, anytime soon.'

'The lorry from Poland that got busted last night with the consignment of puppies for him – that didn't ruffle any feathers?' Branson asked.

Grace shook his head. 'Apparently not. The bill of lading had them consigned to him, but like pretty much all the rest of the documentation, that was forged. We got the Polish lorry driver to send a text to Terry Jim to say the consignment of hay was delayed.'

Potting gave him a sideways look. 'This Terry Jim and his son are starting to sound like the proverbial bad pennies.'

Grace looked up at both detectives. 'I spoke to the Forensic Gait Analyst, Haydn Kelly, earlier and asked him if we put a drone up above Appletree Farm, could we get any useful information from anyone we spotted moving around. He said, from the foot-print casts and photographs he took at the Ruddles' farm on the morning after the murder, he'd have a good chance of picking anyone out from the aerial footage, if directly overhead.'

'A drone's a smart idea, boss,' Branson said. 'Could give us an aerial map of the farm without the Jims being aware, if it's high enough.'

'Exactly.'

'Friend of one of my exes got photographed skinny dipping by a drone,' Norman Potting said.

'Unfortunate for them,' Branson replied.

'It was,' Potting replied. 'She was with her new husband's best friend, in his pool.'

86

Normally a cautious driver, and as a Brighton solicitor, Chris Fairfax always kept strictly within the speed limits, ever mindful of the *Argus*. In a city that increasingly prided itself on its Green culture, its principal newspaper liked few things better, on a quiet news day, than to name and shame prominent citizens who flouted its traffic laws.

But at this moment, Chris didn't care. He drove like the wind, ignoring the burning pain in his nose and forgetting his plan to stop at a chemist. He just had to get home, to Katy, to help in any way he could.

Euthanize Moose?

Bluebell would be devastated.

No way.

He was heading downhill, in slow traffic, towards the roundabout near the end of the Cuilfail Tunnel in Lewes. Cursing the queue of traffic ahead. 'Come on, come on, come on, Jesus!'

So slow.

He was so desperate to get back, he contemplated for a second recklessly overtaking the whole damned lot, in the oncoming lane, and even began moving out, until a lorry thundering up the hill deterred him and he swerved back in.

He followed the single-line traffic through the tunnel and as he emerged on the far side his phone rang again. It was Katy.

'Are you far?' she asked. 'I've told them you're on your way but – I – oh Jesus.' Her voice exploded into tears.

'Ten minutes,' he lied.

On the A27 dual carriageway he hogged the fast lane. In his mirror he saw a flash. Maybe it was a camera, but he didn't care. Nothing mattered any more but getting home.

Trying to calculate the fastest, most traffic-free route, he arrived in Hove, and turned into their road. And for the first time slowed down, right down.

Ahead, down to the right, he saw a whole cluster of vehicles. All parked outside their house.

What???

As he drew closer, he saw a marked police car which was double-parked, a white van with blue and white RSPCA markings, a dark grey van and several unfamiliar cars all lined up in front of the house. Several neighbours were out in the street, gawping.

Then, and his heart felt like it had been wrenched around in his chest, he saw Katy, standing, almost defiantly, in the porch, arms crossed, her back to the front door. Several people, including two uniformed police officers, stood on the pavement in front of the garden gate.

Chris pulled into the kerb, several houses back, switched off the engine and ran towards Katy, weaving through everyone in his path, still holding his handkerchief to his nose. 'Darling!' he said, throwing his arms around her.

'We can't let them do this,' she said, hugging him tightly back. 'Oh my God, what's happened to you?'

'I'm fine, it's nothing. I'll tell you later,' he said dismissively. 'What the hell's going on?' he asked. 'What's this damned circus?'

'Mr Fairfax?'

A woman's voice, serious, polite but not friendly.

He turned and saw a police officer, brown hair clipped up, slim figure bulked out by all her equipment. 'Yes?'

'I'm PC Traynor. My colleague, PC Norton, and I are here at the request of Public Health England, DEFRA, the RSPCA and

Trading Standards to ensure the safe handover of your golden doodle puppy to the RSPCA.' She turned and indicated a man in his early forties, dressed in a dark jacket, white shirt and black tie. He had a kind but no-nonsense face, framed by dark hair combed slick and flat. 'This is Inspector Hopkins from the RSPCA. Your wife, understandably, did not want to hand your dog over until you were here to approve it.'

'That's not what I said,' Katy insisted.

Chris looked at the PC. 'What is all this about handing our puppy over? And what are you all doing here?'

The RSPCA inspector moved towards him. 'Sir, I can appreciate you are feeling a bit overwhelmed.'

'You're not joking.'

Hopkins gave him a hesitant smile. 'Our understanding is that your daughter is in the Royal Alexandra Hospital, after being bitten by a puppy last week?'

'Correct,' he said sharply, aware that all eyes were on him.

'Very unfortunately your daughter is presenting symptoms of rabies, which is a notifiable disease. The hospital has – as they are obliged by law – notified the authorities of this. The protocol in this situation is for any animal that may have been in contact with your daughter to be examined, quarantined and, if necessary, destroyed.'

'Destroyed? Why the hell do you have to destroy our dog?' he asked.

'The only certain test for rabies in an animal is to take fluids from the brain stem and that can only be done postmortem.'

A scraggy-haired, cadaverous-looking man in his fifties suddenly stepped forward. He was dressed in an ill-fitting grey suit that hung from his shoulders as if he'd put it on without removing the coat-hanger and wore scuffed grey shoes. He held up a sheet of paper. 'Mr Fairfax, I'm Dominic Fortnam from Trading Standards. We have a court seizure order for your dog, Moose.'

Chris stared back at him levelly. 'Mr Fortnam, you would be quite within your rights to enter our home and remove our dog, Moose, and subsequently euthanize her, if she had bitten our daughter, resulting in the subsequent possible rabies diagnosis. But Moose did not harm our daughter, it was another puppy in the breeder's van that nipped her nose. And as I understand it, our daughter may be presenting symptoms, but the diagnosis has not been confirmed.'

'And you can prove that your puppy, Moose, did not bite your daughter, can you, Mr Fairfax?' the Trading Standards Officer said pedantically.

'Can you prove she did?' Chris retorted.

87

The Trading Standards Officer reacted uncomfortably to Chris Fairfax's reply. 'Sir,' he said, addressing him as if he were talking down to a child. 'It is the duty of every responsible citizen to ensure we keep England free of rabies – you as a lawyer must understand that more than most.'

'I do, Mr Fortnam, and I know the law better than most, too. There's something called innocent until proved guilty – maybe you've not heard of that? You can't just turn up at our home, mob-handed, brandishing a bit of paper and claim it gives you the right to seize and destroy our dog. Shall we get that straight?'

Dominic Fortnam looked at him hesitantly. 'I—'

Chris interrupted. 'The puppy that bit our daughter's nose was one of two she looked at in a van belonging to someone we now know to have been a rogue breeder, who gave us the false name of John Peat. The dogs were in separate cages. The law states that if our puppy was in close contact with the one who bit Bluebell, which she likely was, then she doesn't need to be destroyed, but can be kept in isolation in kennels for a quarantine period. Correct?'

The officer looked at him and nodded. 'That is the case, yes. We can take your puppy, Moose, to quarantine kennels at Heathrow Airport, if you are prepared to meet the costs.'

'Which are?'

'About two thousand pounds for the quarantine period.'

'How – how long in quarantine?' Katy asked.

'Four months,' the Trading Standards Officer said.

'Jesus – what are we going to tell Bluebell – she's desperate to see her?' Katy said.

'We'll think of something, darling,' Chris said, knowing that was the least of their problems at this moment. Then, looking back at the officer, he said, 'That's fine.'

'But there's another consideration, Mr Fairfax. And this is one you and your wife need to discuss very carefully.' Fortnam sounded more sympathetic than officious now. 'If we did euthanize your puppy we'd be able to establish if she is infected with this disease very quickly, which might speed up the diagnosis of your daughter.'

Chris looked at him, as he put his arm around Katy. 'Moose did not bite our daughter. You're not going to achieve anything by killing the dog – don't you understand? If you're seriously worried about stopping rabies coming in, you need to find this breeder – and fast. You're dealing with someone who cares about one thing only and that's money.'

Fortnam turned and looked at the posse behind him, then turned back to Chris. 'Mr Fairfax, you are correct. If you and your wife are prepared to pay the quarantine fee, then you can hand the dog over to us, and one or both of you follow us to the Heathrow kennels, where you can sign the relevant documentation. Are you willing to do that?'

Chris looked at Katy and she nodded fervently.

They went into the house, closing the front door behind them. 'Well done, darling,' she said.

'No, well done, you, you're the one who stopped them taking Moose. If you hadn't done that, by the time I got here they'd have gone. I should have mentioned my visit to Appletree Farm but I was too focused on losing Moose. I'll report it to the police. How was Bluebell when you left her?'

'Asleep. Dr Shah was saying that maybe she needs to be moved to London, to the Hospital for Tropical Diseases. But . . .' She fell silent.

'But what?'

'He doesn't think they have any more knowledge of rabies than he does. He's trying to get hold of a doctor in America who saved the life of a girl with it a few years ago.' She blinked, her face bleak. Then she grabbed a carrier bag from under the sink and began to throw Moose's toys and chews into it.

'It's all we can do,' Chris said. 'I'll go with them to Heathrow; you go to the hospital. Once Bluebell is better, we can take her up to see Moose in quarantine.'

'Four months is a long time for a puppy,' Katy said. 'Bluebell won't be able to bond with her, not properly.'

'So are you saying there's no point in spending two thousand pounds and waiting four months – that we should let her be euthanized and we find another puppy for Bluebell?'

'If Bluebell survives, Chris.'

'What? Why did you say that?'

'Are you in denial?'

'I'm not in anything.'

She dropped the sack of goodies for Moose on the floor and glared at him.

'She has rabies and she's dying, Chris. Our darling daughter is dying of a disease there's no cure for.'

'Twenty people have survived it, Katy. If that number have survived then there is a cure. There must be.'

She looked back at him. There was trust in her eyes, a desperate, needy trust. She said nothing.

88

Roy Grace and Glenn Branson, along with several other members of Operation Brush, gathered around the oval table, watching the video screen intently.

High-resolution footage from a drone showed a spread of farmland, some of the fields ploughed, some with sheep or cattle grazing. In the centre was a farmhouse with several vehicles outside, stables to the right and a row of long, ugly, concrete outbuildings beyond. And slightly further away what looked like an area of pigsties, with porkers wandering or wallowing. There were other buildings of varying sizes dotted around, as well as a messy assortment of caravans, mobile homes, cars and vans, some obviously roadworthy, others in various states of repair.

The drone was high enough to be invisible in the hazy sky to anyone on the ground and pretty much out of earshot.

'OK,' Grace said. 'It would appear that the series of outbuildings to the west of the farmhouse are the kennels.'

'Stalag Luft Seven,' Norman Potting said. 'That's what they look like – Nazi concentration camp buildings.'

'Probably what it feels like for the poor dogs inside,' E-J Boutwood said.

Acknowledging this with a nod, Grace said, 'We believe, from the fragments recovered at the scene, that a Range Rover and a Ford Ranger pickup were the vehicles the offenders used in their raid on Old Homestead Farm, in which Tim Ruddle died. So far, from our trawl of spare parts suppliers, nothing has been ordered for either of these two particular models. I don't think the offenders would be stupid enough to drive around in damaged vehicles – although we have got lucky in the past.'

'Never underestimate the power of human stupidity,' Potting said.

'Quite,' Grace replied.

'You think the vehicles might be hidden, sir?' Jack Alexander asked.

'I think it's a strong possibility, Jack, yes.' Then he said, 'Hello, who are you?'

All eyes focused on a male figure emerging from the front door of the farmhouse.

Grace issued an instruction over his radio and instantly the drone zoomed in tight on a muscular but pot-bellied, shaven-headed man, shirtless, in tracksuit bottoms, striding across the yard to one of the concrete outbuildings. There was something angry about the way he walked. There were some people, Grace knew, who were just born angry and never changed. Their anger got them what they wanted in life, but it also, eventually, did for them.

'Well, well, that definitely looks like my old buddy, Terry Jim,' Potting said.

'Tell me about your past dealings with him,' Grace said.

The DS nodded. 'Yeah, evicted him from a travellers' site at Beddingham, must be twenty years ago. He was small time, back then, stealing Ford Transits, dismantling them and selling the parts as spares in pubs around Sussex. Then one of his sons, Dallas, got into drugs – proper into the drugs trade – and bingo.' He raised a hand in the air and rubbed his forefinger and thumb together. 'Payola, big time. Terry had the rule of the roost for some years, until the Albanians started queering his pitch. Ended up owning farms as a way of laundering the cash. Looks like the lifestyle suits him judging by his size! I'd enjoy having a cosy reunion with him.'

'Maybe we can arrange it,' Grace smiled. On his instruction, the camera zoomed back out.

'I'm sure Terry Jim talks highly of you, too, Norman,' Polly Sweeney said.

Several of the team laughed. Then they almost instantly focused on a man who emerged from an outlying building and began walking over to the farmyard. He was followed by two more, and then a fourth.

One, the first to appear, walking with a slight limp, looked solidly overweight. The others were slighter built.

'What have they all been doing in that building?' Grace asked.

'Having a crafty fag?' Potting replied.

'It was four people who carried out the attack on the Ruddles' farm,' Jack Alexander said. 'These four?'

'Twenty guesses for what might be in that building,' Polly Sweeney said. 'Two vehicles? A Range Rover and a Ford Ranger?'

'Terry's smart,' Potting said. 'He wouldn't have the vehicles on his premises. They'll be somewhere else.'

Focused on the screen, Grace radioed the drone operator, asking her to zoom in tight on each of the men in turn. As she complied, he captured and saved the videos on his computer terminal.

The men walked for several minutes across the farmland and headed over to the front door of the farmhouse. Grace could see the door was opened by Terry Jim, who must have returned there in the past few minutes, he thought. Jim ushered all four of them inside.

He would have given anything, at this moment, to have been a fly on the wall inside that house. Then, focusing on the computer screen, he sent each of the videos via WhatsApp to the Forensic Gait Analyst, Haydn Kelly, asking him to take a look at them and call him as soon as he had. Moments later his phone rang. It was Tom Cartwright.

'Sir,' the Rural Crimes Sergeant said. 'I have some significant news to report – it looks very likely we have a case of rabies here in Sussex, a family called Fairfax in Hove.'

89

Chris Fairfax walked away from the modern, single-storey complex of buildings housing the Airpets quarantine centre, near Heathrow Airport, with a heavy heart despite knowing it was the right decision. All he could see was Moose's baleful look, her eyes such deep wells of sadness. Eyes that said, 'I trusted you, I gave you unconditional love and now you've put me in this concrete and steel prison for four months. That's two years in dog time. Thanks a lot, pal.' But at least the lady who was taking charge of her, Charlotte Seaman, seemed genuinely caring.

Climbing into his car, he pulled the door shut and called Katy.

'I'm just leaving the quarantine centre now. Moose is fine, honestly, and four months will whizz by.'

'OK, sure,' she replied sadly.

'How is Bluebell?'

Her voice was bleak. 'No change.'

'I guess that's a positive,' he said, trying to sound upbeat. 'Any more news on her diagnosis?'

'Dr Shah said he's still waiting for the results from London. They should be back sometime this evening or tomorrow morning. He – he said – that will tell us one way or the other – for sure. Shit, Chris. I keep googling rabies on my phone. It's – it's – just – the most horrible—'

'Katy, darling, we've got to hope that it's not. There's other things it could be.'

There was a long silence before Katy replied, with a catch in her voice. 'I had a long talk with Dr Shah and – and . . .' She fell silent. Then he could hear her sobbing. And what sounded like her hyperventilating.

'What – what, Katy, darling?'

He heard the catch in her voice as she tried to get the words out. But all he could hear again for some moments was sobbing. He waited, patiently and with anxiety, an icy chill of mounting terror spiralling through him. 'What did he say, Katy?' he prompted gently.

'He – he – he – oh God.' She sobbed again. 'You know he said they might consider transferring her to the Hospital for Tropical Diseases in London – well they now say she may be too weak for that.'

'What? Too weak to *survive the journey*?'

'He said we need to prepare for the worst,' she blurted. Then, sounding calm, she continued. 'That Bluebell is going to die.'

'No way,' he replied. 'That is not going to happen, don't go there.'

'If she has full-on developed rabies, Chris, she is going to die. It's not survivable.'

'Darling, hang on. That's not completely true.'

'Bluebell is going to die. She's going to die. Don't be in denial. Our daughter is going to die, and all because she wanted a puppy and we were stupid enough to agree to buy her one.'

'Look, my love, we know what's happened is nobody's fault. But she is not going to die. She won't die.'

'Dr Shah knows all about rabies, he's seen it in his home country. He's seen many patients infected by rabid dogs and other animals and tried to treat them. Oh God, Chris, I can't – I can't—' she sobbed again. It sounded to him as if she was crying her heart out.

Trying to keep composed, he reassured her. 'I'm on my way.

I'm heading off now, and I'll be there as soon as I can, but it's going to take me a while with the rush-hour traffic. I love you.'

He waited for a reply but all he could hear was the continued and increasingly hysterical sobbing.

Ending the call, he sat still for some moments. Twenty unvaccinated people in all of recorded medical history had apparently survived rabies. OK, so how had they done that?'

He opened Google and typed in *Rabies survivors*. And seconds later found a documentary on YouTube that transfixed him.

Fifteen minutes later he was still watching it, riveted to his phone screen, when Katy rang.

'Where are you?'

'Literally just about to leave,' he said. 'I'll be with you as soon as I can.'

'Please come soon, I need you.'

Ending the call, his heart torn to shreds, he focused back on the documentary. As soon as it had ended, he started the engine and drove as fast as the traffic would allow back towards Brighton, a spark of hope ignited inside him. A tiny spark.

90

After what felt like an even longer day than usual, Roy Grace decided, for once, to heed the advice Glenn Branson had given him when Noah had been born. Which was to make sure, as much as was possible, that he didn't let work make him miss the magic of his kids growing up.

He left the office soon after the evening briefing had ended and now, at just 6.45 p.m., drove his Alfa slowly up the cart track towards home. Thanks to the clocks having gone forward it was still daylight, but there was a swirl of darkness inside him.

Rabies.

A seven-year-old girl. He didn't have all the details yet but he'd left a message for the family to contact him. He did, however, already have enough to be worried about, to look around the countryside with different eyes, as he drove between the hedgerow on his left and the rail-and-post fence on his right. A rabbit darted urgently across in front of him. Despite having always been a townie prior to moving here, he'd never regretted it for a single moment, and he knew Cleo didn't either. It always felt like an oasis away from the grimness of both their jobs. Was it now going to be sullied by the threat of rabies lurking anywhere and everywhere?

He'd called her before he left work, telling her he hoped Noah and Molly might still be up, and she had teased him saying they might have a surprise for him. Despite his concerns about the disease, he smiled in anticipation as he rounded the final bend, wondering just what that surprise might be, as the gorgeous, ramshackle exterior of the remote cottage he loved so much came into view and he could see the intense pink and crimson colours of the tulips that Cleo had recently planted in the front garden glowing in the falling dusk. Then his job phone rang.

Answering on the hands-free, he said, 'Roy Grace.' And heard DS Taylor's voice.

'The Gecko has landed.'

'Number 18?'

'Number 18, sir,' the surveillance officer said. 'Touching reunion with his missus on the doorstep – proper lovebirds.'

'Brilliant, Mark. What vehicle did he arrive in?'

'A white Ford Transit panel van, marked up with AP Builders insignia. I've run the registration through the PNC – it's taxed and insured and owned by a company called Yelbourne Holdings.'

'Yelbourne Holdings?' Grace said, thinking for a moment. 'That's the same company the van Gecko was seen driving in Goldstone Crescent was registered to – but then it was liveried as Jason Plunkett Pumps and Drains, which also did not exist.' He was suddenly feeling the excitement he always got when they were closing in on a suspect. The thrill of the chase, the adrenaline rush that was one of the parts of his job he loved so much. 'Do you have anything on AP Builders, Mark?'

'From a quick Google search, there are only two companies with that name in the British Isles, sir,' Taylor said. 'One in Newcastle and one in the Channel Isles.'

'Ask Vanessa Blackmore to contact them both and check they don't have a van currently in Brighton,' Grace said. Although he was pretty certain of the answer. 'I need you to keep eyes on the house all night, and then follow Gecko when he leaves.'

'I have a full team ready around the clock, sir. I'll update you when the target is next on the move.'

Thanking him, Roy Grace pulled up behind Cleo's Kia Sportage. As he climbed out of his Alfa, he heard a strange sound and stopped to listen for a moment. A cacophony of vaguely musical noise was coming from the cottage. Reaching the front door, the sound was momentarily drowned out by Humphrey's barking.

Then, going inside, fending off Humphrey jumping up at him, and stroking him at the same time, his heart gave a flip of joy as he saw the source of the din.

Noah, in his dinosaur pyjamas, squatting on the carpeted floor, was strumming his peppermint-coloured ukulele which he held flat across his knees, while singing a song about a little, little cow. He was accompanied by sixteen-month-old Molly, in her Peter Rabbit Babygro, crouched intently over a xylophone, running a plastic spatula back and forth across the coloured keys as if it was the most important task in the world.

Cleo, on the edge of the sofa, was watching them proudly.

'Whey-heyyyyy!' Grace clapped loudly.

Noah looked up at him. 'Would you like another song, Daddy?'

'I would! What are you going to play?'

'Ummm.'

'I think it's bath time, then maybe Daddy will read you a story!' Cleo interrupted, seeing how shattered Roy looked.

He winked at her gratefully.

'Awwww!' Noah said. 'One more song?'

'Tomorrow, darling,' she said, scooping him in her arms and carrying him upstairs. Grace kneeled and looked quizzically at Molly. 'Going to play for Daddy?'

'Addy! she said and ran the spatula along the keys. 'Addy!'

And as he watched her, his heart almost bursting with love for this tiny, gorgeous creature, all his worries about work just fell away. He and his former wife, Sandy, had never been able to have children – at least so they'd thought for many years. During all that time he'd never been able to fully comprehend the gooey-eyed adoration friends and colleagues had for their offspring. The same adoration he had now, the knowledge that he would do anything for Noah and Molly. Absolutely anything. He would take a bullet for either of them without a second's hesitation. He often felt sad when he reflected that he never had this time with Bruno.

He reached out a hand and ran his fingernail along the xylophone keys, and Molly giggled. He did it again and she giggled even louder.

Then his job phone rang again.

Part of him was tempted to ignore it, he was loving this moment too much to want it to end. He glanced at the display. Caller unknown. He answered it, thinking it was probably Taylor again. And heard the voice of the Forensic Gait Analyst, Haydn Kelly, sounding even more tired than Grace was feeling.

'Hi, Roy, sorry to be so long getting back to you, I'm in South Korea.'

'What time is it with you?' Grace asked.

'2.50 a.m.' Then Kelly momentarily put on a cod East End accent. 'But don't worry, me old China – good old jet lag eh! Has its benefits – as I can't sleep, I've been taking a look at the drone videos you sent and running them through my software. You got some good hi-res images, sixty frames per second as I asked. And some directly from above, of four men, without parallax distortion. I've gone for the low-hanging fruit first – the large guy with the limp. There's a match with one of the impressions I took at the Old Homestead Farm crime scene, no question.'

'You're certain, Haydn? You'd say this in court?'

'One hundred per cent.'

Back in 1993, Haydn Kelly had secured the world's first ever conviction based on forensic gait analysis. Since then his technology, viewed with suspicion by many criminal justice systems around the world which eschewed modern technology, had played a significant part in putting a number of offenders behind bars. Two of the recent murders Grace had investigated had resulted in successful prosecution and conviction of the offenders, in no small part thanks to Kelly. Which was why he took him so seriously.

Kelly's forensic gait evidence, linking the man with the limp to Tim Ruddle's murder and to Appletree Farm, would be sufficient to get him the crucial search warrants he needed for raids on both Appletree and Long Acre farms.

'You're brilliant!' Grace said.

'Yeah, I know,' Haydn Kelly replied, and after a second added, 'Me old China.'

91

It felt to Chris Fairfax, alone in his car in the falling darkness, smarting with anger at Terry Jim, his nose hurting like hell, and desperately worried about Bluebell, that everything was against them. The stop–go of the M25 had not eased after he had turned south onto the M23 Merstham interchange, thanks to a broken-down lorry, and then a five-vehicle accident a few miles on.

It was approaching 7.15 p.m. when he finally reached the car park at the rear of the hospital, and climbed, stiffly, out of the Audi. Then he broke into a run along the labyrinth of corridors, dutifully tugging on a face mask, ignored the lift and negotiated the staircase. Confused by the array of signs, he asked an orderly, wheeling an elderly, white-haired woman on a trolley, for directions. He followed them along another maze of corridors, until he finally reached the locked door of the Intensive Care Unit and rang the bell.

A few moments later he was led through to the curtained-off bay by a friendly but harassed-looking nurse. Bluebell, eyes shut, looked more like she was in a spaceship than a hospital bed. She was surrounded by technology – dials, gauges, LED graphs, electrodes taped on her head, chest, arms and legs, and cannulated. She looked terrifyingly pale beneath a forest of drip lines and stands. The colour of death, he thought, with a sudden shiver. The only signs that she was still alive came from the occasional twitch or shudder from her body, or moan from her dry lips, and the jigging, spiking, flickering readouts on the dials and gauges on the racks of monitoring equipment on the wall beside her. She barely looked like his daughter. It was as if she was a shell, an empty vessel, and the real Bluebell was somewhere else. Only the pale plastic tag around her wrist confirmed it was her.

He turned away in shock, as Katy, pale and distraught, jumped up from her chair beside the bed, then stared at his face. 'So, what did happen to your face? Who hit you?'

He shrugged it off – 'It's a long story, but it's fine, honestly.'

'You need to get it cleaned up and dressed.'

'Guess I'm in the right place for that,' he joked grimly.

Katy hugged him tearfully. 'Thank God you're here.'

'Sorry it took so long. Where's Dr Shah? I need to speak to him urgently.'

'He wants to speak to us,' she said ominously. 'He said he'd be back around now.'

'What – what does he want to – to speak about?'

Before she could answer, the curtains parted and a very solemn Anish Shah, in scrubs, stethoscope hanging from his neck, looking exhausted as usual, came in and closed the curtains behind him. Chris clocked the nervous twitch in his right eye.

'Mr and Mrs Fairfax, we need to have a conversation. I'd rather do it in private and not in front of your daughter. Shall we go into the Relatives Room, we can be private in there.'

They followed him out and into the small, brightly coloured room where last night they'd slept, intermittently, on the camp beds. These were now folded up and leaning against a wall, beneath a sign taped to the wall requesting masks be worn, and another sign, with coloured balloons, offering counselling services. There were four plastic chairs around a tiny table. Dr Shah gestured for them to sit and did so himself.

Then he leaned across towards them, his hands clasped

suppliantly together, his expression grim. 'We have the result back from the Hospital for Tropical Diseases. It's not good news, I'm afraid. It's not good news at all.' He looked at them both with eyes that were, for a moment, like those of a frightened animal. 'There's no easy way to tell you this – I'm afraid your daughter does have rabies.'

Even though it was the news Chris and Katy had been primed for, she let out a wail of shock. 'No,' she said. 'No. She – she can't have, it's not possible.'

'It *is* survivable, Dr Shah,' Chris said. 'I've seen the video on YouTube. Becky Adams from Milwaukee, Wisconsin. When she was fifteen she was bitten by a rabid bat she'd tried to free from inside a church. Her brilliant doctor, Rodney Willoughby, came up with an experimental treatment that no one had ever tried before and saved her life.' He looked challengingly at Dr Shah. 'Do you know anything about that?'

'I do, Mr Fairfax, I found that same video,' Shah replied calmly. 'What he did is known as the Milwaukee Protocol. I came off an hour-long phone call with Dr Willoughby a few minutes ago. There's good news and bad news.'

92

'There's good news and bad news,' Norman Potting said to the assembled company at the morning briefing.

'Good news is you've won the lottery – bad news it's only ten quid,' Jack Alexander said.

The DS looked at him for a moment. 'You've more chance of being killed by a goat falling on you than winning the lottery, Jack. I prefer to spend my money wisely – on quality beer.' He paused for a moment. 'As a result of Long Acre Farm featuring on the Polish lorry driver's documentation, visiting that farm has been put on ice until we are ready to hit both at the same time. Me and Velvet spoke to a local PC who had happened to call on them a couple of weeks ago because of complaints and disturbances with vehicles. He told us they were both run by very rough people, wouldn't you say?' He looked at Wilde questioningly.

She grimaced and looked around the team. 'I'd say so, yes. Unless you're a fan of either Terry Jim or his son, Dallas. They have the same tailor that a lot of bullies seem to favour – baggy tracksuit bottoms, trainers and bare chests with tattooed arms. And both of them seem to have learned only one phrase from all their English lessons at school. *Fuck off.*'

There were several chuckles.

'Is that the good or the bad news, Norman?' Polly Sweeney asked.

Potting gave a sly smile. 'Actually, Polly, that's the bad news.

The good news is I had a phone call, just ten minutes ago, from a young lady. Gave her name as Darcy Jim – said she's Terry Jim's daughter – stepdaughter actually – and I think she might be quite interesting to us.'

'In what way, Norman?' Grace asked. He was still fretting and distracted by the news Tom Cartwright had given him yesterday, on rabies, and was waiting a further update from him.

'She told me she was never happy about her mum taking up with Jim – that was about a decade or so ago. They're always arguing, even turning into physical fights. And he treats the staff and the animals even worse. She's seen him kick and beat them and she's sick of it. Now here's the interesting bit.' He paused and gave a knowing smile. 'Darcy says she became friends with two young women who worked in the kennels at Appletree Farm, and enjoyed helping them out – mucking out the kennels, feeding the dogs, that sort of thing – but like her, they were both unhappy at the condition the dogs were kept in, as well as being concerned where many of them came from.'

Potting turned and gave a nod at one of the whiteboards behind him, on which were the association charts for Terry Jim, Appletree and Long Acre farms. 'One of the employees at Appletree Farm is Rosalind Esche. We know from Polly's informant and our subsequent enquiries that she has disappeared – apparently after going to complain to Jim about the state of the kennels and the treatment of the dogs. Another name, Lyndsey Cheetham, who Darcy Jim just confirmed to me was her and Rosalind's friend and colleague, died in a mysterious car crash – as we now understand, possibly on her way to meet Polly. I'm only a humble detective, but can't say it looks good to me.'

'Do we have any intel on Darcy Jim, Norman?' Grace asked.

'We do. Her passion is riding those things that jump over fences and fart.'

'Horses, Norman?' Polly Sweeney interjected. 'Ponies?'

'Yeah, that kind of stuff.'

Grace said, frowning, 'So why did she call?'

'Turns out she hasn't seen Lyndsey or Rosalind and is extremely worried,' Potting said.

'Are you sure she is who she says she is, Norman?' Branson quizzed. 'I've been reading up the intel on Terry Jim, and he's a pretty manipulative guy. He wouldn't hesitate to use members of his family to send us off down blind alleys.'

'I'm not sure, Glenn, no. But . . .' Potting tapped his nose. 'Know what I'm saying?'

'Is she willing to come in and give a statement?' Grace asked.

'I don't know, chief. She sounded nervous when I spoke to her. I think I would too if Terry Jim was my stepfather.'

'Doesn't exactly speak volumes about her mother either. So why did she call at all? What did she tell you that we don't already know?' Grace asked.

Potting gave him a look, one Grace knew well from all the years of his regular Thursday night poker games with colleagues. That supremely confident expression of someone who was certain he held an unbeatable hand – four aces or even higher. Someone who was about to scoop the very large pot but didn't want to look smug about it.

'Ms Jim – Darcy – said that when she went into the kennels last Thursday, which would be March 25th, seven French bulldogs – five puppies and two adult dogs, a male and a bitch – which had a potential collective value of tens of thousands of pounds had appeared there, without any explanation.'

For an instant, everyone in the room was silent.

'And then,' Grace said. 'Let me guess. She saw the news later about the murder of Tim Ruddle and the theft of the dogs and put two and two together and came up with seven? Am I close to the mark?'

Potting curled his hand into the shape of a gun and pointed

it at his boss. Squinting, he pulled an imaginary trigger with his forefinger. 'Bang on, chief. She'd been chatting about it with the two girls and now they have disappeared she's worried her stepdad overheard, and she's concerned something terrible has happened, knowing what he might be capable of. But she also said that Rosalind did have the habit of going off comms when she was in a new relationship so maybe that's it. She really doesn't know what to think.'

Moments later, Roy Grace's phone rang. It was Mark Taylor. 'Target is on the move, sir.'

'Keep eyes on him, Mark. Report to me wherever he goes and especially if he leaves his vehicle and goes into one of the parks. But no intervention unless, obviously, one of your officers feels a life is in danger – but I don't think that's his MO.'

'Understood, boss, yes-yes.'

93

Chris Fairfax was woken by excruciating cramp in his right hamstring. He stared, disoriented for some moments, around the brightly coloured room. At the bunch of toys in a pen in the corner. His watch showed 8.40 a.m.

Slowly, wincing and massaging his leg, he remembered, at some point during the long night, Katy coming in to join him on one of the camp beds in the Relatives Room. He'd been too exhausted to undress or brush his teeth or anything else. Now, the conversation last night with Dr Shah was coming back to him. The young doctor staring at them both solemnly. He had a kind face but there was a sadness in his eyes, as if he'd suffered a personal tragedy at some point in his life.

'This good news I'm going to give you from my conversation with Dr Willoughby in Wisconsin is that, through his pioneering work, a number of unvaccinated people around the globe who had contracted rabies, a virus previously thought to be incurable, have survived.' But despite the positive message he was conveying, Chris had seen nothing in his demeanour to signal any real optimism.

'The first unvaccinated person in the world to survive rabies was this fifteen-year-old girl, in Milwaukee, Becky Adams. Her life was saved at her local hospital, by Dr Willoughby, a paediatrician who had never dealt with a rabies patient before. This was because there had never been a rabies patient in his area of the US before. He devised an experiment which has been named, as you know, as the Milwaukee Protocol. It worked, Becky survived and is the mother of two children today, living a completely normal life.'

Katy had said, 'So, we have a way forward, right, with this protocol, Dr Shah?'

The registrar had looked back at her nervously. 'I wish I could say with confidence that we do, Mrs Fairfax. But I'm not going to lie to you or get your hopes up falsely. Becky Adams did survive rabies. If you believe in miracles, you could put it down to an act of God. But if, like me, you prefer to believe in the power of medicine, then I would suggest it was Dr Willoughby who saved Becky's life. That's the good news.'

'And the bad?' Chris remembered Katy asking.

'I'm afraid there are a lot of risks with this procedure. Since Becky Adams's diagnosis in 2004, there have been over one hundred rabies cases confirmed in the United States. The Milwaukee Protocol treatment has been used on them all, but the survival rate is approximately twenty per cent. By survival rate I mean the patients who were completely cured and returned to a normal life. The virus is savage in the way it attacks the brain and the central nervous system, and some victims who survive are left with severe brain damage – in pretty much a vegetative state with no quality of life as we know it. The ones who die during the treatment do so either from cardiac arrest or multiple organ failure – part of the havoc the virus wreaks with general functioning of human bodies. I need you both to understand the risks.'

As he reflected on Shah's words last night, Chris's hamstring cramped up again. He bent and rubbed it vigorously, then hobbled around the room, feeling the pain slowly subsiding. There was a warbling sound from his phone; he looked at it and saw a ton of texts, messages and emails, which he didn't bother to look at. They didn't matter. Only one thing mattered right now, Bluebell.

Then the cramp took another savage bite into his muscle and he doubled up, rubbing it vigorously again. Maybe take a walk down the corridor, he figured. But as he reached the door, it opened.

It was Dr Shah, looking, Chris thought, battle weary. For a moment, panic spiralled through him as he feared the worst.

'Good morning, Mr Fairfax, I'm sorry to disturb you.'

'It's OK – what – what news – how is Bluebell?'

The registrar hesitated for a moment. 'Dr Pallant and I have been here all night, having online discussions with Dr Willoughby and two of his colleagues, and making sure if we are going to go with the Milwaukee Protocol on Bluebell, we fully understand all we need to do.'

'*If* you are going to go with it?' Chris asked. 'There's no alternative is there, right?'

'That is correct,' Shah said meekly, his eyes looking sadder than ever.

Moments later, Katy came into the room, her face tight and pasty, her hair a tangled mess. Chris, standing unsteadily, hugged her.

She said nothing but pressed her tearful face against his neck.

Then Dr Pallant, solemn-faced, came in. His cream shirt was rumpled, the top button undone and his tie at half-mast. His eyes looked tired and there was a day's growth of stubble on his chin. All his self-importance seemed to have gone, too.

Ushering them to sit, he joined them, and sat, hunched on his chair, his eyes darting from Katy to Chris and back repeatedly, fingers interlocked tightly. 'Mr and Mrs Fairfax, Dr Shah has put you in the picture. We are in a very difficult situation as, I know you understand, this disease is not something any of the staff have experience with.'

'I read that someone died of it in Scotland in 2002 after being bitten by a bat?' Chris said.

'That's correct,' the consultant said. 'That appears to have been the only case contracted in the British Isles in the last hundred years. So, now Bluebell has had her diagnosis confirmed, it's a question of what options are open to us. Dr Shah and I have been on calls pretty much all night to Dr Willoughby and his team in Wisconsin, and also to Professor Solomon in Liverpool here, and two other British experts who've made studies on rabies, and we feel there is just one way forward but it carries a big risk.'

'Dr Pallant, if Bluebell was your daughter, what would you do?' Katy asked pointedly. 'Wouldn't you try anything?'

'I would, yes, no question.'

'I've been googling rabies victims, during the night,' Katy said. 'Some of the videos on YouTube. It's horrific. In their final stages they're restrained with cords around their wrists and legs, thrashing about in their beds, frothing at the mouth. They look in agony.'

Pallant nodded bleakly. 'I don't want to put you through more distress than you are already suffering, but—'

'But?' Katy prompted.

'There's no easy way to say this and I want to be honest with you. The terminal stage of rabies is very distressing, both to the patients and their loved ones.'

'Why?' Chris said. 'Can you explain what's going on when the disease progresses?'

Pallant and Shah exchanged a look. The registrar responded. 'Like other viruses, the rabies one has what I can only describe as some kind of intelligence. It's smart, cunning, which is what makes it so difficult to contain. By the time symptoms appear, it's too late for vaccination, and the virus is already at work destroying its host and programming the host's brain to pass it on to other victims.'

Katy asked, 'How – how does it know to do this?'

'It's like – it's *evil*,' Chris said.

Pallant nodded. 'Those were the words Dr Willoughby used when we last spoke to him, an hour ago. He said, in reference to the virus, that the older he gets, the more he believes in the concept of pure evil, a malign intelligence.'

'In what sense?' Chris asked.

'Well,' he shrugged. 'In addition to secretly planting itself in the brain, the next thing it does is attack the parts of the nervous system that allow humans to swallow, and the respiratory system, making it harder for them to breathe and impossible to drink. It makes its victims febrile, dehydrated and thirsty, so that although they crave water, they become too scared to drink because they know they cannot swallow. They become fearful that the water – or whatever fluid – will choke them. Then, in the final stages, it urges the victim to bite anyone it can, to pass the virus on.'

Chris and Katy stared at him for some moments in stunned silence. Finally, Katy said, 'And what stage is Bluebell at?'

'From Dr Willoughby's assessment on what we've told him, she has two to four days left to live, if we do nothing.'

'But we're not going to do nothing, are we?' Katy said.

'With your consent,' Pallant said, looking at each of them in turn, 'we would like to try the Milwaukee Protocol on Bluebell. But you do need to understand the risks. That it could kill her.'

Chris looked at Pallant, then at his wife, then Shah, before looking back at the consultant. 'She is going to die if we do nothing, right?'

'Yes,' Pallant said heavily. 'I'm afraid she is.'

'Within a few days?' Chris asked as if for confirmation.

'And your proposed treatment might kill her, perhaps more quickly than letting nature take its course, but it could save her life?' Katy asked, squeezing Chris's hand so tightly she was crushing it.

'Correct, Mrs Fairfax. I know it's not a great choice.'

'It's not a choice at all,' Chris said. He looked at Katy and she nodded. 'Do it, just please do it.'

94

Straight after the morning briefing ended, Roy Grace hurried out of the conference room. As he strode down the corridor towards his office, Mark Taylor phoned him.

'Boss,' the surveillance DS said. 'Target has just confronted a young woman with a baby in Wild Park, and made off with her dog while she was lifting the baby out of the pushchair. A small, black dog, with a curly coat – one of my team thinks it is a shih-poo.'

'A shih-tzu crossed with a poodle, right?' Grace queried.

'Correct.'

'They're on the list of highly desirables – worth several thousand.'

'Shall we nick him now, boss?'

Grace hesitated. 'How's the woman?'

'She's fine, not injured. She had the dog on a lead because it was on heat and not spayed. He just shoved her and pulled the lead out of her hand.'

The correct thing would be to have Gecko arrested on the spot, and immediately return the dog to the young woman, Grace knew. But, if his hunch was right, this was too good an opportunity. He decided to take the gamble, trusting Taylor's team not to lose him. 'No, stay with him and keep out of sight, I need to know where he's going. This could be a significant development for us if he's going where I think. If he starts getting close to Appletree Farm, call me.'

'Roger that, boss.'

As he ended the call, he heard Potting right behind him. 'Chief, that sounds like the fellow who went to a zoo which had only one animal.'

Grace turned and frowned. 'A zoo with only one animal?'

Potting nodded, his expression inscrutable. 'He said it was a shih-tzu. A shit zoo, geddit?'

Grace gave him a thin smile. 'Very good. But a bit of advice, Norman, don't give up the day job just yet, OK?'

Back in his office, he sat behind his desk, wanting to get his ducks in a row as fast as he could. He started by lining up the files of evidence he was going to present to his boss, ACC Hannah Robinson. He was hoping to get her sanction to carry out what might well be the biggest raid of his career so far, in terms of manpower, and one of the most dangerous for his team.

Although every police officer who signed up for the job knew the risks, was aware that one day his or her life might be on the line, few officers ever thought about that when they swung the bosher at the door of a suspect, or stopped a vehicle on an unlit road in the middle of the night. But after a previous operation some while back, which had resulted in E-J Boutwood being crushed by a van and Glenn Branson being shot in the leg, his first priority ever since had been the safety of his team. A big part of that safety was to have sufficient numbers of trained firearms and public order officers to neutralize any threat.

Terry Jim – and his revolting son Dallas – posed a very real and dangerous threat. A decade ago, a severed hand in a Tesco carrier bag had been left on the counter of a pub in East Sussex shortly after Terry, Dallas and a bunch of their associates had invaded the place for a heavy drinking session. The hand had been later identified as belonging to Erroll Donleavy, scion of a rival former crime gang to Jim's, who had vanished and the rest of his body was never found, but the police had never been able to establish a link to Terry Jim or any of his associates. Fifty people had been in the pub that night and not one of them, including the landlord and bar staff – clearly scared witless – would admit to having seen anything.

The first file Grace had in place was the work around the phones, an hour either side of Tim Ruddle's murder. The plots showed four phone numbers, all belonging to burner phones, travelling towards the area where the Ruddles' farm was, from somewhere in the area of Hailsham in East Sussex and returning there. Next was the investigation into the disappearance of Rosalind Esche. Then the phone work around Lyndsey Cheetham, who had died in a suspicious car accident – en route to rendezvous with Polly Sweeney. That was significant because, from the time-lines, it put her as almost certainly working at Appletree Farm.

Next was the Polish-registered lorry, stopped in the early hours of yesterday morning by a traffic officer. It was carrying a concealed cargo of puppies, all high-value breeds with fake vaccination certificates. Subsequent interrogation of the vehicle's satnav showed its destination to be Long Acre Farm – run by Terry Jim's son Dallas.

He took a swig of coffee, then added a further file, the evidence from the Forensic Gait Analyst Haydn Kelly, linking the footprint at the Ruddles' farm to the man with a limp filmed by the drone at Appletree Farm. And, finally, was the damning evidence from Darcy Jim. If – and it might be a big if – they could get her to come in and give a statement under caution.

In the absence of that, he reviewed everything he had in front of him, aware of what he needed to convince the Crown Prosecution Service that he had a case against the suspects. The holes they'd pick in all of this, even if, as he expected, Hannah Robinson did sanction his raid, would be the same holes a smart defence barrister would find. He needed to get rock solid evidence from the raids on Appletree and Long Acre farms to be sure of convicting Terry Jim and, hopefully, Dallas, on either murder or conspiracy to murder charges – on top of conspiracy charges to traffic, illegally import, breed and sell dogs.

The crucial evidence he needed was something that would link Terry and Dallas Jim incontrovertibly to the murder of Tim Ruddle. Something that put them or their employees at the crime scene. Evidence strong enough to convince a jury. It needn't be anything big – sometimes, where evidence was concerned, small could be beautiful. A single fingerprint. DNA from a droplet of blood. Or just a footprint. If they arrested any of the suspects and then could find their shoes, from the footprint moulds Kelly had taken, these could either put them at the crime scene – or eliminate them.

He was distracted from his thoughts by DS Taylor ringing with an update.

'Target is heading east on the A27 in the direction of Hailsham, boss.'

Grace thought quickly, with growing excitement. He turned to the aerial-view map showing both Appletree and Long Acre farms – a printout of Google Earth – he'd put up on the wall. A mile west of Appletree Farm there was a roundabout with four turn-offs. The one leading to Appletree was a minor, almost single-track road. If Gecko took that, there would be little doubt about his intended destination. And the turn-off left, a couple of miles further on, was again a narrow lane leading to Long Acre Farm. His hunch was looking good. Hopefully Gecko was on his way to one of these. But he needed to be stopped before entering either.

'Mark, we need a couple of Traffic cars on standby to intercept if he approaches either Appletree or Long Acre – I don't want you to blow your cover – we may need you for further surveillance on these two farms.'

'I've got it covered, boss. Two cars from the Road Policing Unit at Polegate are in position, ready for your instructions.'

Grace smiled. He loved nothing better than to work with smart professionals, who were capable of thinking ahead and anticipating. 'Nice work. Update me as soon as we see which direction Gecko chooses – and let's hope I haven't got this wrong.'

Moments after he ended the call, his phone rang again. It was DS Alexander. 'Sir, we've just taken a call in the incident room from someone I think you might want to speak to. He says he's a solicitor – and he doesn't sound a flake. I've got him on hold. He says you left him a message yesterday to contact you ASAP.'

One of the problems with any enquiry in which appeals were put out to the public, Grace knew, was that a significant number of them were simply bored people who figured that a marked police car turning up outside their residence would be exciting. But just occasionally, there was a nugget. And a big part of his role was to identify and mine that nugget. And maybe, just maybe, this caller, Chris Fairfax, might be that nugget.

'This is Detective Superintendent Grace, the Senior Investigating Officer of Operation Brush. Hello, Mr Fairfax?'

The voice was hesitant, nervous, someone clearly under stress. 'Detective Superintendent, I'm a family law solicitor in Brighton. I read in the *Argus* about your investigation and I was just going to call you when I received the message that you wanted to speak to me – I may have some information that could be helpful. Perhaps I should have contacted you earlier, but I wasn't thinking straight, as you'll understand.'

'Thank you, Mr Fairfax,' he replied. 'Please, tell me?'

Chris Fairfax related the events leading up to their buying the puppy from a van in a pub forecourt north-east of Horsham, and how their daughter was bitten on the nose by another puppy in the van. And subsequently how she came to be diagnosed with rabies. His hiring of the private detective, Ken Grundy, and how it led to him driving to Appletree Farm yesterday in search of John Peat, and then being assaulted.

As Roy Grace listened to this seemingly decent man's story, concluding with the terrible diagnosis of his daughter's illness, anger rose inside him. But excitement too, when the solicitor told him of the other names connected to John Peat – Tom Hartley, Jonathan Jones and Michael Kendrick.

Ending the call, he stared down at the notes he had been writing on his pad. And at the name of the so-called breeder Chris Fairfax and his wife, Katy, had bought their puppy from.

And he thought back to Bournemouth. Tom Hartley. Jonathan Jones. Michael Kendrick. All but the last duck was now lined up.

He picked up his phone and called the ACC. Her Staff Officer answered, and Grace asked him to set up a meeting urgently.

She was free at 2 p.m., he told Grace.

The moment he ended the call, Mark Taylor rang again. 'Boss, Gecko has turned off the roundabout onto the lane leading to Appletree Farm, three miles ahead. I've informed the RPU vehicle a mile up the lane. I think it's pretty clear where he is heading.'

Roy Grace, phone cradled between his shoulder and his ear, punched his right hand into his left fist. *Yesss!* 'Instruct them to stop and arrest him initially on suspicion of stealing a dog.'

'Copy that, boss, yes-yes.'

Turning back to his row of files, Grace flipped open Gecko's. Thanks to his stealing Humphrey and then trying to extort reward money from Cleo, they had his phone number. They had established, through its plots, the regular journeys from the Brighton and Hove area to Appletree Farm that Gecko had made over the past month or so.

Good evidence, but not the cigar. He decided that, as soon as Mark Taylor called to confirm Gecko had been arrested, he would tell him to have Gecko taken to Brighton Custody Centre and booked in there. Then he would pay him a visit and have a cosy chat.

95

Chris and Katy stood by Bluebell's bed, hands linked tightly, staring at her through tearful, fearful eyes. They'd been left alone with her. Dr Shah had suggested they might like to spend a few minutes before the procedure to put her into an induced coma started.

They knew the subtext. The words that Dr Shah did not say but which they heard anyway.

You might like to spend a few minutes with your daughter, to say your goodbye in case she doesn't come round from the coma.

Because eighty per cent don't.

Katy felt so utterly helpless, staring down at Bluebell, who was tossing, moaning, perspiring and sounding at times as if she was struggling to breathe. Chris dabbed her forehead with his handkerchief, but she shook her head wildly, crying, 'No – no – no . . .'

In a few minutes she would be wheeled into theatre, where, under Dr Pallant's observation, along with Dr Shah and the consultant neurologist, the anaesthetist would steadily, over the next twenty-four hours, sedate her through drip lines with ketamine, propofol and benzodiazepine, until she was completely paralysed and the virus paralysed too, in the hope of enabling her own immune system to begin to destroy it.

Broken-hearted, they watched their child, this beautiful girl with her angelic face and golden curls, murmuring in her delirium. Eyes closed one moment, then open, staring up at them, almost accusatorily, the next. There were beads of spittle in the corner of her mouth. 'Thirsty,' she murmured. 'So thirsty. So thirsty. Please. Please. So thirsty. Drink, please drink, a drink.'

Chris and Katy looked around for water, and Katy hurried out towards the nursing station, then returned with a tiny paper cone of water. But as she reached the bed, Bluebell suddenly screamed. Eyes wide open, she was flailing her arms. 'Nooooooo! Noooooo! Noooooooooo!' She struck Katy, sending the cone flying, some of it spilling on Chris.

The pitiful terror in her voice felt to him that it was ripping the very lining of his heart. He looked at Katy in bewilderment. All around them in the Intensive Care Unit, children lay in beds, suspended between life and death, their desperate parents, like themselves, at their sides.

Bleakly, Chris thought that if you believed in Hell, despite the calm, despite the genuinely caring and kind attitude of everyone working here, this place, right now, with what Bluebell was enduring, was as close to Hell as he could imagine. *Evil.* Maybe Dr Willoughby was right. The rabies virus that was trying to destroy their beautiful daughter was pure and utter evil.

He gripped Katy's hand even more tightly, as tears rolled down his cheeks. Bluebell had to live. She had to pull through this. A little scratch on the nose wasn't going to kill her, it wasn't, it damned well wasn't.

He turned away and pressed his sodden handkerchief against his eyes. Then he turned sharply back as Bluebell screamed again, even more loudly.

Dr Shah came into the room, looking more nervous than either of them had seen him before.

'What can we do?' Chris asked. 'Anything?'

Shah hesitated then said quietly, 'We need to take her into theatre soon. We're doing all we can, then we all just have to wait.'

96

'Come up and see me, make me smile!' Gecko sang along to the Steve Harley and Cockney Rebel song playing on the van's radio, feeling so happy. Yessss sir!

The shih-poo, tied to the passenger seat belt by her leash, barked at him, but he didn't care, he was singing louder than the dumb dog could bark. He fed it another treat. It was like shoving coins into a fruit machine, just a few seconds of respite while the wheels spun. Yet another bloody dog that barked constantly, not that he cared. He was used to it. All his life dogs had barked at him, and people had laughed at him, but now he had Elvira. Beautiful, sweet, kind Elvira who didn't have a nasty bone in her body, who loved him for what he was, for everything he was – that she knew about – and for what she didn't know about, too.

Elvira never laughed at him. Last night she'd held his face in her hands, and as she kissed him repeatedly whispered that she wished she could see him properly, because she was sure he was even more handsome than she imagined him.

He loved her. He loved her so much. Insanely! Glancing at his Rolex, he saw it was coming up to 10.45. Maybe, he thought with a big smile, he'd truly make this a special day. She would be working at home as normal. A plan was forming in his mind as the small, familiar roundabout loomed up ahead. Feeling so happy, as he sang along for a few more lines, he was thinking . . .

I'm in love, truly, properly, head-over-heels in love!

Then the bloody dog distracted him by barking again. But he didn't mind, because he knew Mr Jim would be pleased with this one. The name on her collar tag said 'Rose'. A bitch, she appeared. Hopefully an un-spayed bitch – they were generally what Mr Jim paid him the most for, and he was expecting a decent wad of cash when he arrived at Appletree Farm in just a few minutes. A couple of hundred for a bitch, at least.

Enough to buy an engagement ring from one of the shops in the Brighton Lanes on his way home to Elvira, he thought. Or maybe steal an expensive one! Save the money for the wedding, and then the honeymoon!

His heart filled with joy, he took the first turn-off onto the single-track, hedge-bordered lane. Just two miles to go to the farm entrance. The song ended and he heard the voice of Danny Pike, the BBC Radio Sussex presenter. 'Steve Harley – what a great song, love it! Right now, I have a regular listener, Margaret Duncton, on the line talking about the parking in Blunts Way. Margaret, tell me the latest.'

At that moment, as he crested a small rise, Gecko saw what looked like a shard of broken glass glinting through the greenery ahead. Seconds later, as he began rounding a long bend, he saw a police car heading towards him, headlights on full, blue lights flashing on the roof.

And he felt a deep, cold flush of fear in his stomach.

There wasn't room for the two vehicles to pass.

A red LED display between the blue lights on the roof-light rack read, STOP.

Panicked, he crunched the gears into reverse and shot back, trying to steer with his mirrors, swerving right, then left, then right again.

He looked at the police car through the windscreen. The officer in the passenger seat was signalling to him. STOP.

Frantic now, he accelerated hard, thinking if he could just make it in reverse to the roundabout he—

The rear of the van swerved hard to the right, towards the edge, towards the ditch. He over-corrected and the rear of the van fishtailed left, then right, then left, making larger and larger arcs as the wheel spun in his hands. And moments later he was just a passenger as the rear of the van plunged off the side of the road and tilted up in the air, both he and the dog thrown flat against their seat backs.

The bloody dog started barking again. Totally disoriented, lying on his back, Gecko groped for his seat-belt buckle. He found it and pressed the release. Instantly he slid further back and was stopped by the headrest.

Got to get out. Get out and run.

He reached out a hand and found the driver's door handle. Pulled on it. Nothing happened. He was lying against the door, he realized. The greenery of the hedgerow was pressing against the window.

Shit.

The passenger door? Or get in the back and out the rear doors?

Then the passenger door opened and a police officer's face appeared. The officer ignored the barking dog. 'Marion Willingham, I'm arresting you on suspicion of stealing this dog. You do not have to say anything, but it may harm your defence if you do not mention, when questioned, something which you later rely on in court. Anything you do say may be given in evidence.'

Gecko looked up at him. 'You've got the wrong guy, officer. I found this dog wandering on the street. I'm taking it to Raystede, the animal charity rescue centre.'

'You are?'

'Yeah!'

The officer tapped his stab vest. 'Know who I am?'

Gecko shook his head.

'I'm the Pope.'

97

Wednesday 31 March

'Maybe we should pray,' Chris said, seated beside Katy in the Relatives Room, head in his hands. His words sounded like they were dropping into a void.

There was no response from Katy.

After a few moments he shrugged. 'You know, ask God to help us – to make this work and save Bluebell.'

There was a long silence before she responded. 'When did you last pray? I don't mean kneeling in church at a wedding or funeral, mumbling into your hands – when did you last *really* pray – *properly* pray – to a God you believed in?'

He was silent for a moment. 'Honestly? I don't remember. Maybe when I was ten. Perhaps a little older.'

'Why did you stop?'

He remained with his head in his hands. 'It probably sounds really shallow. I was a good sprinter, always used to win the 100 metres at every school sports day. But there was this guy, David Browne, who used to win all the other distances and the hurdles and the long jump. Every year. I asked God to let me beat him just once, just for this sports day when my grandparents were coming, and I wanted them to be super proud of me. You know what happened?'

'I can guess.'

'He beat me at the 100 metres, which he'd never done before, and as usual, everything else.' He shrugged. 'I thought about

383

it afterwards. Maybe David Browne had prayed too, and God had to decide between us – and went with him. It's like the farmer and the organizer of an outdoor charity concert, isn't it? The farmer's praying for rain for his crops, the concert guy is praying for it to be fine. Who does God choose – He can't answer both requests, can He? So, what the hell was the point in prayer, I thought. I've never prayed again.'

'But you're suggesting doing it now?' Katy said bleakly.

Chris looked at his watch. An hour since Bluebell had gone into theatre. 'What about you – when did you last pray?'

She shook her head. 'You know my dad. His whole view on religion is about whose imaginary friend is better than the other. My mother had faith. All the way through the breast cancer that killed her at forty-two, she held her faith.'

They sat in charged silence for some moments.

Then Chris stood up and paced around the tiny room. 'Oh shit, I'm sorry, Katy, I'm so sorry. This is all my bloody fault.'

'What do you mean?'

'You weren't keen when Bluebell wanted a puppy. I was the one who thought it would be great for her to have another pet to look after, and wonderful to have another dog, because we missed our dear Phoebe. You were hesitant, because you thought she'd probably get bored of it, and we'd be the ones ending up looking after it.'

Katy reached out a hand and gently touched his leg. 'It's not your fault at all. I went along with it, I agreed, I wanted us to have another dog, too. If anyone's to blame it's me, for ignoring all the RSPCA guidelines and thinking it was a good idea to look online for a puppy.'

He sat back down and put his arm around his wife. 'It's going to work, Katy, what they're doing. I trust Dr Pallant and Dr Shah. It *is* going to work, it is.'

'It works for very few.'

'Yep, well it's going to work for Bluebell because she's one in a million!'

She stared ahead. 'I wish I could share your optimism, but we need to get real, darling, manage our expectations – God, I hate that phrase.'

'It's not about *managing expectations*,' he said. 'It's about being positive. We need to think positively for her. We need to *believe*.'

'I just keep thinking about all the stuff Dr Shah and Dr Pallant told us. That if she doesn't die, she might have so much brain damage she'd just be a—' She hesitated, unable to say the word. 'One moment I think, yes, she's going to be one of that twenty per cent, then next I think we're grasping at sodding straws and need to get real.'

He turned to her, put his hands either side of her face and held it tightly. 'My darling, I hear you. This protocol may have saved the lives of only a few victims, but it saved them! It wasn't a miracle. I don't think you believe in miracles and I sure as hell don't. But I do believe in science and medicine. This is going to work. It is. It bloody well is.'

Katy looked back at him. 'I wish I could believe you. I wish it more than anything, ever.'

'I do, too,' he said.

'She's going to be in a coma for days or even weeks. And then, if she survives that it will be at least another week to two weeks before we know if—' Katy said.

'If it's worked?' Chris finished the sentence for her.

She nodded. 'If she's going to have any quality of life.'

They were both silent for a short while. Chris looked at his watch again: 10.30 a.m. This little room, with its bright colours and posters on the wall and hard furniture, was feeling right now like the loneliest place on earth.

98

Roy Grace felt strangely nostalgic passing his old stomping ground, as he turned into the approach to the Brighton Custody Centre, on the Hollingbury industrial estate. He pulled up in front of the tall green gate with spikes that meant business along the top.

To his left was the three-storey rectangular building, Sussex House, the former CID headquarters, where he had spent over ten years of his service in the police. A few years back, budget cuts had forced the sale of the building, and the Major Crime Team had been shoehorned into the old dormitory buildings of the Sussex Police HQ at Lewes, where there was not enough parking, and no convenient ASDA superstore two minutes across the road.

Glenn Branson, beside him, said, 'I miss this building. Funny, isn't it. We all hated it at the time with its crap air-con and heating, but I'd move back in a heartbeat if we had the option.'

Grace smiled. 'And me.'

The gate slid open and he drove the Alfa up the steep ramp into the custody block enclosure, parking well clear of the doors of the receiving bays for newly arrested suspects.

Inside, in the large reception area, all was typically calm for an afternoon, mid-week. A world-weary custody sergeant was seated in an elevated position at the futuristic custody desk, from which he could look down at all suspects being booked in. The height made it near-on impossible for anyone to vault it and assault a custody officer, and, Grace knew, it had the dual effect of intimidating any suspect being processed here.

There was just one at the moment, a thin man, with crew-cut hair and heavily tattooed, in a baggy tracksuit and filthy trainers. He looked like he had come ready-dressed for prison, Grace thought wryly. The suspect's uniformed arresting officer stood behind him.

It had been a long while since he had last been in here, normally leaving interviews of newly arrested suspects to members of his team. But Grace was on a fact-finding mission and wanted to see what – if anything – he could get from Gecko about John Peat and Appletree and Long Acre farms.

The detectives were led by a custody officer to one of the small, windowless interview rooms on the far side of the reception area. Entering, they saw two men, Gecko and his solicitor, Paul Donnelley, seated side by side at the metal table, facing them.

'Good afternoon, gentlemen,' Grace said. They sat down opposite them, Grace facing Gecko, who was wearing an olive sweatshirt beneath a padded puffer.

He viewed Donnelly's presence with mixed feelings. In his experience, on-call solicitors fell into two brackets. The Government's Legal Aid payment tariff was so low that the majority of these lawyers ended up, despite all their experience, earning less than the minimum wage on the cases they were obliged to take on. For some, in Grace's view, it was all they deserved, because they were too rubbish at their job to ever make a higher grade.

But others, like Donnelley, were different. These were intelligent people who could have made vast salaries practising a different kind of legal work – such as corporate law in London – but chose instead to dedicate their entire careers to helping some of life's underdogs.

Smartly suited, with receding grey hair and a poker face, Paul Donnelley was one of the latter. The solicitor, in his late forties, had a confident, authoritative and calm, but almost avuncular presence. He would have looked equally at home as a bank manager or even a school headmaster. Much though Grace viewed lawyers as the enemy, he had a sneaking admiration for the dedication of ones like Donnelley.

Dispensing with any introduction, he leaned forward and pressed the record button. 'The time is 2.45 p.m. Detective Superintendent Grace and Detective Inspector Branson interviewing Marion Willingham in the presence of his solicitor, Paul Donnelley.' Looking at each of them, he asked, 'Would you please state your names for the recording?'

'Paul Donnelley,' the solicitor said.

The Detective Superintendent indicated for Gecko to speak. In response, he opened his mouth and stuck his tongue partially out. Grace momentarily recoiled in disgust as he saw a large fly stuck to it. An instant later, Gecko closed his mouth and made a swallowing motion.

'On a high-protein diet, are you?' Branson quipped.

Grace watched Gecko's eyes carefully. 'Marion Willingham, are you sometimes known as Gecko?' Grace asked.

The man stared insolently back at him and said nothing.

Sensibly, Donnelley interjected. 'I can confirm my client is referred to by that name.'

'When you were booked in, a Rolex watch you were wearing was taken from you. I have it here.' Grace showed him a plastic exhibit bag containing the watch. 'Where did you get that from?'

'Is this relevant, Detective Superintendent?' Donnelly interjected.

'It is.'

Gecko said, with an insolent smile, 'Family heirloom – was me dad's.'

His body language indicated what Grace already knew, that he was lying. 'Are you sure you didn't steal it from Brighton Antique and Modern Watch Co, last Thursday?'

'What does this have to do with why my client has been arrested?' Donnelley demanded.

'Quite a lot,' Grace answered. 'If you'd like to see the CCTV footage from inside the jeweller's I can show it to you now?'

The solicitor shook his head.

Grace then arrested and cautioned Gecko on suspicion of robbery. 'I'll rephrase my question,' Grace said to Gecko. 'Did you steal that watch, along with a Verbalise talking watch, from Brighton Antique and Modern Watch Co in East Street, Brighton, last Thursday at approximately 5 p.m.?'

Donnelly leaned across and whispered to his client.

'No comment,' Gecko answered.

It was the response Grace always hated in suspect interviews. But today he was ready for it. 'I really think you and your client should take a look at the CCTV from inside the shop,' he said and turned to Branson, who leaned down, pulled his laptop out of his bag, and set it on the table. Turning the screen so that both Donnelley and Gecko could see it, the DI hit the keys and a video began to play.

The resolution wasn't perfect but was good enough. It showed a man, dressed almost identically to how Gecko was now, wearing a black beanie pulled low down his forehead and a scarf, enter the shop.

It was clearly Gecko.

They then watched the rest of the sequence, as the assistant appeared and passed him a watch. There was some conversation. The assistant and proprietor bent down behind the counter, then they popped back up and Gecko appeared to have put something in his mouth. He opened his mouth and the two men backed away. The assistant jumped over the counter, Gecko punched him in the face and then ran off with two watches.

Glenn Branson froze the recording.

Grace looked quizzically at Gecko. 'Has that jogged your mind at all? Was that you in the Antique and Modern Watch Co in East Street, Brighton, last Thursday at approximately 5 p.m.?'

'Fake news,' Gecko said.

'That's what you really think, Marion?' Grace asked.

'Just cos I look different. Fake news,' he replied again.

Grace tried another tack. 'Marion, because you are under arrest – on suspicion of the theft of dogs and of two watches – we are entitled to search your residence.'

'Elvira won't like that,' he blurted.

'Is Elvira your girlfriend, Marion?' Grace went on.

Gecko did not reply.

'You often stay over at her house, right?'

'No comment,' he said.

'Elvira's partially sighted, isn't she? Is she wearing the watch you stole for her, Marion?' Grace pressed, and glanced at Donnelley, half expecting him to say something, but he was impassive.

'Didn't steal it, bought it on eBay,' he replied.

'So, you'll have the transaction history on your computer, will you?'

Gecko stared back at him defiantly.

'I'm very flattered,' Donnelley said laconically, 'as I'm sure my client is, that he is being interviewed for relatively minor offences by the head of the Surrey and Sussex Major Crime Team and his deputy, when ordinarily we might expect a lower-ranking pair of interviewers. Is there a negotiation to be had here, possibly?'

Grace smiled at him. 'You know I can't influence a judge.'

'But you can put in a good word for my client,' Donnelley came back at him.

'Indeed. Personally, and off the record, I'm not just interested in your client's theft of the watches. I'm also at this moment not just interested in the multiple thefts of dogs from around the Brighton and Hove area, including my own family pet, in which he is the prime suspect. I would like to know his involvement – if any – with Terry Jim at Appletree Farm in East Sussex, and with his son, Dallas, at Long Acre Farm. If he's willing to cooperate with information, I would be very happy to talk to the Crown Prosecution Service to let them know that your client has cooperated and this can be brought to the attention of the judge who will deal with him, but obviously we can give no guarantees.'

'Understood. Give me five minutes with my client.'

Grace and Branson left the room.

99

Despite Dr Shah's attempts to assure them that Bluebell would be aware of nothing for the next few days, Katy was feeling torn between staying at the hospital, to be close to her, and dealing with a couple of her very vulnerable clients to whom she felt a duty of care. Khalid had managed to get adjournments on both their court hearings, but both were at risk from abuse by their spouses, which was playing on her mind. She asked Khalid to check up on them with a call and see if they were OK.

Throughout the rest of today, and through the night, the anaesthetist, Kyle Dougherty, would steadily be introducing doses of ketamine and other paralysing agents, suppressing Bluebell's brain until it was almost completely shut down – effectively switched off. The medical team were following the strict protocol, attempting to stop the rabies virus which had installed itself in her brain from being able to send any instructions to other parts of her body, where it was also installed. And then let Bluebell's natural immune system set to work and destroy the virus. And hope against hope that during this highly dangerous procedure Bluebell did not go into cardiac arrest.

As she drove, in slow traffic, past the Peace statue she tried to focus back on her clients. But it was impossible. She kept being drawn back to Bluebell. To Doctors Shah and Pallant.

And the statistics.

Thirty per cent of rabies victims went into cardiac arrest and died during the process of inducing the coma. Another thirty per cent died from cardiac arrest during the following days when their immune systems were battling the virus. And another twenty per cent came out of the coma with severe brain damage.

Suddenly, a quote she had heard years ago and which she had always loved, popped into her mind. It was from Martin Luther, a German priest who had died in the sixteenth century. *Even if I knew the world would end tomorrow, I would still plant my apple tree.*

Hope.

Always keep that hope.

Bluebell was the apple tree that she and Chris had planted in this ever-uncertain world.

100

Roy Grace, digital clicker in one hand, laser pen in the other, stood below a large, wall-mounted screen in the HQ staff canteen, which could hold 200 people. There were thirty-five police officers currently seated on the rows of fold-up chairs put out for this briefing. It was being held here because the conference room in the Major Crime Suite was not big enough to accommodate the teams he had assembled for raids on Appletree and Long Acre farms, the following morning.

He was flanked on one side by Glenn Branson and on the other by the ACC, Hannah Robinson, who was there to show her support for Roy and demonstrate by her presence the magnitude and importance of tomorrow's operation. She was also there to apprise the Police and Crime Commissioner so that she wouldn't be caught unawares in the morning.

Maps on whiteboards either side of the screen showed aerial images of the two farms. On a third whiteboard were large photographs of a Ford Ranger pickup truck and an older-model Range Rover. On the fourth were photographs of Terry and Dallas Jim.

Grace glanced at his watch. A few minutes past two. He waited for the last few stragglers to come in and sit down. In addition to his Major Crime Team members, a sea of mostly uniformed officers, of all shapes and sizes, faced him. There were the elite Public Order officers, highly trained for riots, for putting in doors and carrying out arrests, all of them there because they were tough as nails and loved few things more than getting into a good bundle. The rest included Armed Response Unit supervisors, drone operators, dog handlers and search officers. There was also a member of the police media team, taking notes for briefings to the press and media which would be given after the raids. The RSPCA also had officers present to deal with any animals that might be found at the premises.

'Good afternoon, everyone,' Grace said. 'Tomorrow morning we will be executing warrants to enter and search Appletree and Long Acre farms, both in the proximity of Hailsham, East Sussex. At the end of this briefing, you will be allocated to either Team A, led by myself, accompanied by DS Potting and DC Nicholl, which will carry out the raid on Appletree Farm.' He pointed to the white-board to the right. 'Or to Team B, led by DI Branson, DS Alexander and DC Wilde, which will carry out the raid on Long Acre Farm.'

He paused for a moment before continuing. 'Our command structure will be as follows. ACC Robinson will act as Gold, setting the strategy, and although she will not be directly involved, she will have overall authority throughout the raids. DCI Andy Wolstenholme will be the Tactical Firearms Commander. Chief Superintendent Justin Burtenshaw will be Strategic Firearms Commander and I will be Investigations Bronze Commander, responsible for managing the arrest teams, securing evidence and with overall responsibility for the raids.'

He pressed the digital clicker and a woman in her late teens or early twenties, wearing dungarees, appeared on the screen. She had a round face, framed with two short plaits, and was smiling at the camera. Behind her was a cage containing what looked like several puppies.

'To summarize our objectives in this operation: We have a missing person, this young lady, Rosalind Esche from Ukraine. She has not been heard from since Friday evening of last week and was last seen at Appletree Farm. We are concerned as to her whereabouts and finding her takes precedence over everything. She may be being held against her will, or something has happened to her.'

He pressed the clicker to bring up the next image. 'In the raid on Appletree Farm we will be looking to arrest this hunky Chippendale, Terry Jim, behind me.'

There were several laughs and sniggers. Someone called out, 'Never saw a Chippendale with a pot belly, boss!'

Grace clicked again. 'And his chip-off-the-old-block son, Dallas Jim at Long Acre Farm. They will be charged at this stage with conspiracy to import, breed and traffic dogs. We have good reason to believe Terry Jim has an associate who goes under the name of John Peat and possibly several other pseudonyms.'

He let this sink in before continuing. 'We will also be looking for evidence that could link these two suspects to the murder of Timothy Ruddle on the night of Thursday, March 25th at the Old Homestead Farm, and in particular we are looking for two vehicles with minor damage on them, a 2014 Ford Ranger and a 2011 Range Rover.' He indicated the whiteboard with each. Then he clicked again and a Collision Investigation Unit photograph of Lyndsey Cheetham's Nissan Leaf, embedded in a tree and surrounded by debris, appeared on the screen above him.

'This is the vehicle in which a twenty-one-year-old, Lyndsey Cheetham, died last Monday. She was working at Appletree Farm and was, we understand, good friends with Rosalind Esche. We believe this was not an accident but that she was pushed off the road on this bend. We don't have absolute proof of this, at this stage, but red paint particles were found at the scene, and we believe a 4 x 4 or other large vehicle of that colour may have been involved. We have strong suspicions she was on her way to meet Polly Sweeney to give her information about Rosalind's disappearance.' He caught Polly's eye and she nodded in confirmation.

'From enquiries in the area we have a witness who believes he saw Dallas Jim driving a red Dodge RAM recklessly. We believe this may be the vehicle that shunted Lyndsey Cheetham. We may find it at one of the farms. In terms of safeguarding,' he continued, 'we have potential firearms issues. On the night Tim Ruddle was murdered, the offenders seized a loaded shotgun from his farmhand, Norris Denning. We also know that most farmers have guns – mostly shotguns and small-bore rifles. We have established from the firearms licence records that both Terry and Dallas have in the past applied for licences for shotguns and a .22 rifle. These licences were not granted, but from what we know about these characters, they are likely to have these weapons, regardless. That means all of you are in potential danger from firearms. The first two points on Gold's strategy is to maximize the safety of the public and to minimize the risk to you. Is that understood?'

There was a show of nods, but a lot of them half-hearted. The Public Order team were veterans of these kinds of briefing and safety warnings. Not many of them looked too worried. The message on most of their faces seemed to read, *Mess with me and you'll live to regret it.*

'So,' he continued, 'when I give the signal for the raids to start, only the Firearms team go in, and no one else follows until I hear from them that they've neutralized any firearms threat. Is that absolutely clear?' He looked pointedly at Glenn Branson, who had been shot, but fortunately not critically injured, after rushing in too soon in a previous raid some while back.

The DI grimaced and nodded.

Roy Grace pressed the clicker, and a drone video began to play on the screen behind him. 'OK, this is location A, Terry Jim's place, Appletree Farm.' He turned and aimed the red laser dot at the screen. 'This is the driveway off Beeches Lane, which winds up for a quarter of a mile until it comes to these steel gates, which are covered by CCTV. Under earlier cover of darkness, the Public Order team will have taped over the cameras. So far as our intel informs us, there is no one in the farm monitoring these 24/7 – there is just Terry and his wife, Rula, and her daughter, Darcy, in the main house, and a few other members of their family living in some of the campers and caravans dotted around.'

The camera panned over the dog sheds, the Jims' house, and various farm buildings behind, including a row of pigsties, and then over an assortment of derelict cars and vans, outbuildings, caravans, trailers and mobile homes.

'It would make a lovely holiday camp!' one of the Public Order supervisors called out. 'Just imagine the reviews on TripAdvisor – *charming rural location with authentic rustic dwellings . . .'*

Grace smiled, then focused on the next drone video which was of Dallas Jim's farm. There was open access to it, which indicated to him that Dallas had less, if anything, to hide. But the team weren't to assume anything, and he told them the same safeguarding applied, with the Firearms Unit going in first to ensure it was safe before anyone else entered.

He then spoke. 'The interview team who spent several hours with our friend Gecko have ascertained a detailed description of what we may find at the farms. He has cooperated with us hoping to reduce his sentence. At this stage we don't believe he was one of the four men involved in the killing of Tim Ruddle.'

The RSPCA inspector, Kirsty Withnall, then briefed those present with details of how her teams would deal with any animals found on the farms to ensure everybody's safety.

'Thank you, Kirsty. The weather forecast is good, clear skies,' Grace said. 'Drones will be up, giving overhead coverage on both farms. I want all of you with radios to have the channel set to 8, and I'll be issuing instructions on this airwave. We will be assembling at Polegate police station at 4.30 a.m., approximately fifteen minutes' drive from each of our targets. Any questions at this stage, before I go into the details of each of the raids?'

There were none.

101

As she left home Katy was filled with cold, dark dread about Bluebell. Her fear deepened the closer she came to the hospital.

When she'd parked, and made her way to the ICU ward, a nurse told her Bluebell was in recovery, and had diverted her to the Relatives Room, where she'd found Chris, hunched over his laptop, dealing with emails. He had no further news other than that Dr Shah had popped in to tell him that everything was going to plan. They both knew it was going to be many long days before Bluebell started to come out of the induced coma and more long days before they would know, assuming she survived that long, whether all her faculties were intact and she would be able to live a normal life.

Long days of utter hell for both of them – during which at any moment Dr Shah or Dr Pallant might come and tell them that they were sorry, Bluebell had not made it.

At 7 p.m. Dr Shah, looking weary, came into the room. 'You know,' he said, 'this may sound harsh, but you really should go home and get on with your lives and your business – for your own health and sanity. For the next week or so, Bluebell won't have any brain activity at all. Even if you believe in telepathy, her brain functions will be so low I doubt that would be possible. You can come and visit all you want, and if there are any developments, I'll call you. But all you can achieve right now by being here is to torment yourselves.'

'I just want to be near her, I can't help going over and over how low the odds are. I just want her alive and healthy,' Katy said dolefully.

Shah shook his head. 'She's young and strong. I think her chances could be very much better than the statistics.'

'How much better?' Katy asked, desperate for a straw she could cling to.

'I can't put a number on it,' Shah said. 'It would be wrong to do that. But I would take comfort, if I were you, that we are treating your daughter step by step on the instructions of Dr Rodney Willoughby, to whom we are speaking every few hours.'

'Thank you,' Chris said. 'That's comforting to know.'

'Good. So, go home, then come back in tomorrow to see your daughter. For the next week, honestly, there is nothing you can do.'

'Can we see her, at least, before we go?' Katy asked.

Shah shook his head. 'She is still in the recovery room, under the care of the team of anaesthetists who put her into the induced coma. Once she is back in the ICU, then you can be with her as much as you want.'

'When will that be?' Chris asked.

Shah glanced at his watch. 'Two more hours, at least. Honestly, please take my advice. Go home, try to get a night's sleep. Let's see what tomorrow brings.'

Chris turned to Katy. She looked every bit as exhausted as he felt.

Katy nodded. *Yes. Let's do that. Let's see what tomorrow brings.*

102

The stars and the full moon were invisible behind the blackout curtain of cloud. A light drizzle was falling, despite the forecast last night that the clouds would have dispersed by now. The weather was a mixed blessing, Roy Grace thought, cradling a thermos of coffee and checking his watch: 4.16 a.m.

The cover of complete darkness gave the members of his team equipped with night vision binoculars an advantage, but the dark also made it easier for anyone on the property to escape unnoticed. Farmers rose early, he knew, but well before any of the Jim community woke – doubtless having dreamed of charitable works and kindness to their fellow human beings and all animals, he thought cynically – there would be cordons around both properties that no one was going to get through in a vehicle. But both properties had large perimeters and someone could flee on foot, which was why he'd decided, with Silver's agreement, it would be better to wait for dawn, where the drones would provide clearer images than through their night lenses.

His interview with Gecko on Wednesday had been helpful. The oddball was clearly just a minion and an outsider minion at that. He stole dogs to order for Terry Jim and got paid in cash when he delivered. He told Grace about Humphrey, and the opportunity he saw to make a bit of cash on the side. Grace had already learned that Humphrey's collar and tag had been found in the glove locker of Gecko's seized van.

But Gecko did tell him about two other connected families who lived on Appletree Farm, one in a cottage some distance from the main house and the other in a mobile home, again some distance away. He was unable to say what specific role they performed but he thought they were relatives.

The other thing Gecko gave him, which interested him, was that Terry Jim regularly frightened people by threatening to feed them to his pigs. Grace knew that crime gangs feeding victims to pigs was not a myth, these creatures ate and digested just about everything. His detective friend in New York, Pat Lanigan, had told him some years back that pigs were a favoured tool of the Mafia for disposing of bodies, and he knew that there were some seriously nasty crime families here in England who had developed an interest in breeding porkers.

Roy Grace gingerly sipped some more scalding coffee, wary of frizzing his tongue. He had butterflies in his stomach, as he always did before the start of a raid, adrenaline coursing through him along with his thoughts. He was mindful of the old saying that the darkest hour is the hour before dawn, and his darkest fears always came an hour before an operation started. The fear of something going badly wrong and an officer being injured, or the fear of finding nothing at all and arresting no one, and the resulting egg on his face. Especially right now, with seventy officers who would be receiving handsome overtime payments that he would have to answer for.

He sat in the front passenger seat of the unmarked Mondeo, in the car park of Polegate police station, as a steady stream of vehicles parked up around him, before extinguishing their lights. Next to him, behind the wheel, Norman Potting suggested drily, 'You could always say it was a late April Fool's joke, if it all went tits up, couldn't you, chief?'

Grace took another tiny sip of the coffee, then screwed the top back on the flask. His Kevlar vest beneath his jacket was on too tight, making him feel constricted. About to get out and adjust it, his radio came to life, and he heard the voice of the Tactical Firearms Commander, DCI Wolstenholme. 'Charlie Tango One?'

'Charlie Tango One,' Grace responded.

'Good morning, Roy, everything good?' Wolstenholme's voice was friendly but precise. And he sounded almost ridiculously perky for this dead hour. As if he was fresh out of the gym.

'We're in assembly position A, Andy. I'll be doing a roll call in ten minutes, then a final briefing before we head off and move into positions B and C.' He glanced down at his lap, at the chart of names, vehicles and call signs attached to the clipboard, stifling a yawn. He'd barely had any sleep last night and doubted Wolstenholme had either – they'd been in the command room with Gold and the firearms Bronze until after 9 p.m., going through and fine-tuning the plans. One of their last decisions was to include two hostage negotiators, in case the missing Rosalind Esche was seized as a pawn by either the Jims or their associates, on either premises.

'Good, let me know when you're in position at B and C.'

Polegate police station, located in the middle of a housing estate, wasn't the ideal place for such a mass assembly of vehicles, but it was perfectly located for the two farms. It principally served as the hub for the Roads Policing Unit for the entire east of the county, and a large contingent of its traffic officers were being deployed as part of this morning's operation. They would set roadblocks on all possible escape routes from the two farms. Grace had already worked out from maps, and the previous drone footage, all roads and lanes that could be accessed by someone desperate in an off-road vehicle, or even a tractor, from either farm.

Moments after Andy Wolstenholme signed off, Roy Grace heard Glenn Branson's voice, 'Charlie Tango One?'

'Charlie Tango One,' he responded. 'What do you have for me, Charlie Tango Two?'

'Me and DC Wilde and all our team are here, boss.'

'Good man.' Grace looked at his watch again: 4.25 a.m.

At 5 a.m. both teams would move into prearranged positions, approximately half a mile from the two target farms. They had roughly half an hour before the sky began to lighten, and the level of that would depend on whether the cloud cover was still there or had begun to disperse. As soon as the drone operator informed him there was sufficient light to see everything on the ground, he would give the signal for both Firearms teams, backed up by Public Order officers, to go in.

'I was reading this book, chief,' Norman Potting said. 'About the great military battles of history. It said that most of them weren't won by the generals leading the charge, they were lost by the other side's mistakes.'

'Is that right?' Grace asked absently, focused on his task ahead.

'Uh huh. Take Agincourt. Our history lessons in school tell us we defeated the Frogs – I mean French – because the firepower of our longbows was better than their crossbows. Not true. We won the battle of Agincourt because the French won the toss. Their leader, Charles d'Albret, got to choose the battle site and he chose a ploughed field. It rained heavily the night before, and all the French horses and archers got bogged down in the mud – and were easy pickings.'

'Is this relevant to now, Norman?' Grace asked. 'Other than it's raining?'

'Just saying, chief. It was the same at Dunkirk. The Germans could have wiped us out, if Hitler hadn't decided to divert his army to go after Russia.'

'Very helpful, Norman, thanks. I'll make sure if I win the toss, to take the Jims on terra firma. And I'll avoid attacking Russia.'

Potting raised a finger in the air. 'Wise decision, chief.'

103

Chris and Katy Fairfax had done their best to comply with Dr Shah's suggestion to go home and try to get some sleep. They'd dug a moussaka out of the freezer – the only thing in there that could be cooked from frozen.

Try to have a normal evening, Dr Shah had said. Would either of them ever have another *normal* evening in their lives? Chris wondered. He'd quit smoking over five years ago, but if there had been any cigarettes in the house he would have had one. Probably more than one. Probably the entire damned packet.

For several hours he'd lain in bed in some twilight world, neither asleep nor awake. As he sensed Katy had too. He kept thumping and moving his pillows around, too hard one moment, too soft the next. And, it seemed, he kept needing to get up to pee.

Finally, as the alarm clock showed 4.30 a.m., Katy had said starkly, 'Want to do this any longer, or shall we go back to the hospital?'

Now, at a few minutes to 6 a.m., they stood alongside Dr Shah, looking down at what looked more like a NASA space capsule than a hospital bed. Only parts of Bluebell were visible inside it, her eyes closed, dead to the world. All of her nose except the tip, her forehead and cheeks were covered in the opaque plastic of the oxygen mask and the white tapes holding it in place. A breathing tube lay between her lips. Electrodes were taped to her head, the hair shaven off around each of them. Several bands and tags were around her left wrist, and her left foot protruded from the bottom of the bedclothes. Katy, instinctively, stepped forward, wanted to cover it, then stopped, scared to do anything that might jeopardize Bluebell's treatment. Maybe the left foot was out for a reason.

She looked so peaceful, Katy thought. And for some moments she found it hard to believe that hideous virus was lurking insidiously inside her darling baby's body. That it was wanting to control her body and kill her.

She felt Chris gripping her hand as she looked at the oscillating gauges, the red LED displays, the zigzagging red and green lines, the graphs, the numerical displays, trying to read optimism into each of them, the only signs that their daughter was still actually alive.

In the room the women come and go, talking of Michelangelo. The words of T. S. Eliot popped into her head. She'd loved his poem 'The Love Song of J. Alfred Prufrock' the very first time she'd read it, although she'd not understood it; any more than she understood it now. But that one line repeated itself. Over and over, somehow giving her comfort. Like a piece of driftwood she was clinging to after being shipwrecked.

'She doesn't look as pale as yesterday,' Chris said. 'Like, she has more colour in her cheeks, don't you think, darling?'

Like a patient etherized upon a table, Katy thought. Another line of the poem coming into her mind. Another image.

Bluebell etherized in front of them.

'Don't you think?' Chris asked again.

She stared at him blankly. 'Think? About what?'

'That she's got more colour in her face now?'

'She's still alive,' she replied, her voice shaky. 'That's all I can think. She's still alive, she's still with us.'

'She's a fighter,' Dr Shah said. 'That I can tell you. In my experience the first rule in beating any illness is that you have to *want* to beat it. And Bluebell does, I can tell. She's doing OK, as well as we could expect at this early stage.'

'When will you know any more about how she's doing?' Chris asked.

The registrar pointed at the battery of instruments providing constant readouts. With a gentle smile he said, 'For the next few days, only through these. Right now, her heart is looking strong, her blood oxygen levels are good, and her brain activity is as I would have hoped, as close to shut down as is possible.'

'As is possible without her actually being dead?' Katy quizzed.

Shah nodded, then surprised them both by biting his thumb-nail. It was one of only a few times he'd shown any hint of nervousness. 'What we are doing is the best chance to save your daughter's life. It is what worked for Becky Adams, and it is what has worked for some other rabies victims around the world in the past seventeen years. Hold onto that for your daughter.'

'I am holding onto it,' she said. 'I'm holding on so hard it hurts.'

'Then hold even harder,' Shah replied. 'That's what we all need to do right now.' He looked down at the inert Bluebell. 'You most of all, you very special person, you.'

104

Dallas Jim woke, with a pounding head, to the sound of his Rottweilers barking, as well as the puppies in the kennels kicking off. His head was properly thumping – after another night on the lash with the lads, his farmhands. He couldn't remember what time they'd staggered out of the Cross Keys – around midnight maybe. As usual he'd driven them home in the Land Rover, mostly across fields to avoid the cops, headlights and roof spotlights blaring, lamping rabbits. Niall riding shotgun up front with him, gun poking out the window, blasting away and mostly missing, useless drunken fucker.

Shit, his head was bad, he needed some paracetamol. What were the dogs barking at in the middle of the sodding night? Suddenly they stopped and his thoughts went to that girl, Rosalind. He knew he had to go back to his dad's farm and sort out what to do with her body today. She should be dead by the morning because no one could survive the gases from the slurry for long. He'd probably feed her to the pigs. They had started her disposal by putting her in the slurry pit late last night, making very sure that Darcy didn't see any of it. They needed her to think Rosalind had just gone off. They'd read her the riot act about family loyalty and what would happen if she snitched when she confronted them about Lyndsey's car accident. They said they had nothing to do with it but she didn't believe them. She was told family loyalty is everything, talk to the police and she would regret it. Then, slowly, he realized it wasn't the middle of the night, and it took him some moments to notice pre-dawn light was bleaching the thin curtains.

It took him some moments, also, to realize his bed was empty. Where was his partner, Deryn?

The dogs were barking again, even louder and more urgently now.

'SHUT THE FUCK UP!' he yelled. 'BRUTUS, NERO!'

He badly needed to pee. And he badly needed something for his headache. He swung his legs out of the bed, placing his feet on the carpet, then stood unsteadily, his brain doing the round-abouts. He wobbled and nearly fell over, grabbing hold of the bedside table to steady himself. He felt himself swaying from side to side, as if he was in a boat in a rough sea.

Shit, I'm still pissed.

Vague memories of a row with Deryn were coming back to him. As he walked through into the bathroom and began to pee, they were coming back even more clearly. She'd been angry at him for driving home from the pub, yet again. He told her he hadn't hit anything, so what was the problem? And he knew the answer – it was starting to become a pattern, that was the problem. Deryn was the problem. He'd go out having a good time with the lads, come home horny, have a row and she'd go off to the spare room. Followed by two or even three days when she wouldn't speak to him. Stupid bitch. They'd been together three years, time for a replacement?

The dogs were barking even more loudly now.

He walked over to the bathroom window. 'SHUT UPPPPP—'

Then he saw them.

Shadowy in the weak half-light, but distinct. Like something out of a fucking movie. Figures crouched low, creeping forward, two of them leading, wearing dark beanies like the ones right behind them. He grabbed a pair of binoculars, raised them, peered through them and focused on the figures. On the first two. On the white printed word on each of their black beanies.

POLICE.

105

For an instant, Terry Jim, emerging muzzily from a deep sleep, thought it was his alarm ringing. Before Rula, beside him, stirred, and none too happily mumbled, 'Phone.'

He grabbed it off the bedside table. Who the hell was calling him at this hour, whatever this hour was? He stared at the display.

DALLAS.

The phone said it was 5.27 a.m.

'Do you have any idea what time it is, son?' he answered quietly.

'I do, Dad. We have a problem. There's a posse of cops crawling up my drive and I don't think they've come to deliver the morning papers.'

Terry Jim was instantly awake, his brain a blur of thoughts. He'd been expecting this, but not so soon, not yet. He'd thought it would take weeks before those dim-witted cops connected all the dots and rocked up. By which time all the evidence would have been long gone.

Shit. Shit. Shit.

'The barn, boy!' he shouted. 'The barn with the motors. Torch it!'

'Torch it?'

'You fucking deaf? Torch it – go torch it – got your DNA and the others all over it. Don't let them get to it, not unless you want to spend the next twenty years having a crap in front of

411

your cell buddy. You hear me? I knew killing the girl would bring it all crashing down. I told you just to frighten her in her car, not kill her.'

'They're getting closer.' There was panic in Dallas's voice. There were times Terry Jim had believed his elder son could be a worthy successor; his brother, Scott, didn't have the balls. There were other times when he thought Dallas was an idiot. Like now.

'You know what, Dallas? They're going to keep on getting closer. GO! While you still can. GO! TORCH IT!'

Dallas's reply was drowned out by the sound of banging downstairs, simultaneously with several loud rings of the door-bell and voices shouting, 'ARMED POLICE! THIS IS THE POLICE! ARMED POLICE! OPEN THE DOOR AND COME OUT OF THE BUILDING.'

'Don't let them in, Terry,' his wife, now sitting up in bed, hair looking like she'd been electrocuted, said. 'Tell 'em to go to hell.'

'You tell 'em,' Terry Jim said, jerking on a pair of trousers. 'You bloody tell 'em.' He shoved his bare feet into slip-on trainers then hurried down the stairs into the hallway.

He knew that very soon they would be trying to break down the front door. Two minutes, he'd been assured by the locksmith who'd done the reinforcing. It would take two minutes, minimum, to bust it open.

Eyeing the straining edges warily, he grabbed the loaded twelve-bore shotgun he kept propped by the door, ran for the kitchen, then stopped at the equally strong, reinforced back door. Someone moved stealthily past the window. Dark clothes and a beanie.

Holding his breath and crouched low, he crabbed back over towards the pantry, then kneeled, put the gun down and unbolted and lifted the heavy trapdoor. Grabbing the gun, he descended a few steps into the darkness, and pulled the trapdoor back down, sliding the bolts on the underside he'd installed long ago for a situation like this.

Snapping on the light switch, he reached the bottom step then hurried across the vast, brick-floored cellar. The house had been built by a Victorian farmer, long before fridges had been invented. The cellar provided a summer cold store on a commercial scale, for dairy, fruit and vegetable produce as well as animal feed, and was accessed from a barn located a short distance behind the house. He raced towards the steps up to it now, his mind focused on one thing. He had to reach it.

He clambered up the wooden staircase until he reached the ceiling and the second trapdoor. Praying nobody had slid the bolts home on the top. This had always been his emergency escape route, but he'd never really seriously thought he would have to use it.

The trapdoor would not budge.

He put the gun down and pushed up with all his considerable strength. Nothing.

The police would be inside the house now, for sure. It wouldn't take them long to find the trapdoor when they couldn't find him.

He pushed up again. Then again. Then, in desperation, he grabbed the shotgun. Normal cartridges contained small lead pellets, varying in size depending on the size of prey to be shot. The two cartridges loaded in this gun contained the heaviest shot made. Suitable for bringing down a large animal – or a human. Fired from a point-blank range at a person's midriff there would be enough force to literally cut that person in half.

He flicked off the safety catch, then, holding the twin barrels just a couple of feet from the trapdoor, closed both eyes to protect them and pulled both triggers almost simultaneously.

The explosions numbed his ears and his face felt like it had been burned by searing fat spat from a pan. It was accompanied a millisecond later by a stench of cordite. He opened his eyes, his ears ringing, and saw faint light above him. The trapdoor had mostly gone.

He dropped the gun, useless now its chambers were empty, squeezed through the ragged hole in the trapdoor, ignoring jagged pieces of wood tearing at his clothes and flesh, kneeled briefly on the open-sided barn floor, and tried to gather his thoughts. To plan his route. Out of the rear of the barn – hopefully the cops wouldn't have got this far, yet.

Stupid stubborn bitch. She should have been dead by now, but she had kept going.

He had to get to her before the police did. Dead, it would just look like an accident. There would be no proof. Just a stupid woman going where he'd told her strictly to avoid. Alive, and with what she would tell the police, he'd be facing attempted murder. And the rest.

Topless, feeling the cold morning air against his chest, the tall, muscular, but flabby-bellied fifty-five-year-old ran as hard as he had ever run in his life. Desperate and scared for one of the few times in his life. And Terry Jim didn't scare easily.

106

All Dallas Jim's life, he'd been confident his dad had known what to do in any situation. He particularly admired how his dad dealt with anyone who crossed the family – the torture he'd devised for them. Terry Jim believed anyone who crossed him – and therefore the family – deserved to die slowly.

'No point in giving them a quick death, son. They need time to think about what they done, right? And we need time to savour the moment, right? Someone tries to screw us over, we need to set an example to anyone else what might be thinking about it.'

Which was why they had the CCTV cameras above Sty 9, the extreme left hand of the nine pigsties. Sty 9 was deeper than the rest. It was four feet deep. Filled to that depth with pig slurry. Its surrounding walls were higher than the other eight sties, also. Nine feet high, smooth concrete, with nothing to grip if you wanted to try to climb out. And everyone they had put in there did want to climb out. So very desperately.

And no one ever had succeeded.

It was a very effective torture chamber and disposal mechanism, all combined in one. They simply dropped their victim over the wall into the slurry. So long as he or she was able to stand, they would be fine – not great, obviously – but fine. But there was nowhere to sit. So when they became too exhausted to stand or were overcome by the fumes, the only option was to sink down into the slurry, where they would drown.

It was a method that his dad had learned from the American Mafia. And once the victims had succumbed and drowned, they would then be served to and devoured by the pigs, which ate and digested everything – pacemakers, titanium implants and false teeth excluded. And few things tasted better to a porker than a human being marinated in their own slurry.

Over the years, Dallas had enjoyed watching with his dad the live video feed of several of their enemies being threatened in this way, sometimes tortured, and he believed that at least one person had been killed. Most of the time the torture was enough to shut these people up for good. His dad had always been supremely confident. Untouchable. The boss of bosses.

Which was why the panic in his voice a few minutes ago had freaked him out.

The barn, boy, the barn with the motors. Torch it.

The barn where they'd been concealing the two cars, the Range Rover and the Ford Ranger that had gone to the Old Homestead Farm when Tim Ruddle was killed, was a few hundred yards behind the house. They'd been waiting for it all to die down before quietly disposing of the vehicles.

How the hell was he going to torch the barn?

Then he remembered the twenty-litre jerrycan of diesel that was kept for emergencies in the adjoining barn which housed some vehicles. Diesel was harder to ignite than petrol, but it would have to do. He grabbed the gas igniter from the shelf beside the oven, jammed it into the pocket of his puffer, let himself out of the rear door of the kitchen and sprinted towards the barn. To his relief, it was still barely light.

Reaching the adjoining barn, he grabbed the heavy jerrycan and began lugging it towards the one housing the two vehicles, looking worriedly around every few seconds as the daylight steadily increased.

He reached the barn, put down the can and pulled open the

door. The two vehicles sat in front of him, shrouded by dust sheets. He tugged open the wire cap of the can, and it released with a hiss of air. Then he hurried around the vehicles, pouring diesel oil on the straw-covered floor, and splashing it liberally over the vehicle covers.

Then, when the jerrycan was nearly empty, he tugged the gas oven igniter from the rear pocket of his cargo trousers and was about to fire it at the Ranger's cover when he heard a shout behind him.

'ARMED POLICE! STAY WHERE YOU ARE! PUT YOUR HANDS ON YOUR HEAD!'

Ignoring the instruction, he attempted to press the trigger button on the canister.

But as he did so, he heard a series of quick-fire clicking sounds and simultaneously it felt like every muscle in his body had suddenly gone into agonizing spasm.

He cried out, unable to take a step forward or move a limb. The canister fell from his hand, and he collapsed onto the ground.

107

'All clear!' shouted the lead Firearms officer, exiting through the breached front door of the Jims' house.

There was a dawn chorus in the early morning air, but one of barking dogs, not songbirds. It sounded like hundreds of them, but not the kind of *happy-to-see-you* barks that Humphrey always gave him, Roy Grace thought. These were mournful. Deep, throaty barks from the adult dogs and yipping and yapping from the puppies he guessed were in the ugly, prison-camp kennels behind them.

As he and Norman Potting were about to follow the Public Order squad through into the house, he heard the voice of the drone operator in his earpiece. Potting would have heard it too, they were synched.

'Boss, this is Eagle One.'

'Eagle One,' he responded.

'There's something going on in one of the pigsties. It's difficult to tell exactly what from this overhead view, from the gap in the roof, but there is a female who looks trapped in one of the sties, and up to her chest in dark stuff – it looks like liquid shit. She is quite obviously very distressed. There's a man running towards her – he's come out of a barn behind the house where we've heard shots – he's topless and not carrying anything but he doesn't look like a lifeguard,' he added wryly.

Grace thought for an instant. He knew from the map of the farm

418

that he'd pretty much memorized where the pigsties were located. His agreed strategy with the Gold and Silver commanders had been, from the instant the firearms risk was neutralized, to have officers cover all the likely places where someone might make a dash for it on foot or on a quad bike. There were several points of escape over the lanes bordering Appletree Farm with access into neighbouring fields. He had discounted the area beyond the pigsties because of dense hedgerows behind and around them, effectively boxing them in – as well as concealing them from anyone on the ground.

A male running from a barn behind the farmhouse? From the intel, and confirmed by Gecko, the only people living in the farmhouse were Terry Jim, his wife and her daughter, Darcy. Could this be Terry running towards the pigsties where he'd been keeping the girl prisoner?

He looked around for someone to send over to intercept the man, but all the frontline Public Order officers and dog handlers were pouring into and around the house. 'Norman,' he said urgently. 'Follow me!'

Grace sprinted across the farmyard, around the back of the house, and then following the map from memory, around the rear of a large, open-sided wooden barn. A good two hundred yards or so ahead of him, in the rapidly increasing daylight, he now clearly saw a hunk of a man in tracksuit bottoms and no shirt, running like hell.

Grace ran like hell, too, after him. For several seconds he heard the rasping of Potting's heavy breathing right behind him, then, at some point, it fell away, but he didn't notice. He was focused on one thing only. Shirtless man. Heading towards the pigsties. Towards a distressed woman trapped in one of them.

A dark thought was forming, but he pushed it away, focusing all his energy on reaching the man. Whatever he was doing, this man was not, in the middle of a raid, on a chivalrous mission.

The low buildings of the sties were now just a short distance ahead, framed by the tall hedges. Shirtless man was making for the left hand one. Grace, sprinting over the uneven and muddy ground, was narrowing the gap between them but it was still a good hundred yards.

Then, right in front of his eyes, the man disappeared.

Vanished, seemingly into thin air.

Fifteen seconds later, Roy Grace, his lungs bursting from the exertion, approached the spot where the man had been. And as he reached it, oblivious to the foul stench, he saw a five-foot-tall concrete wall to his left, and rows of sties, all occupied, to his right.

Then he heard a pitiful, rasping cry, from behind the wall. A woman's voice in a foreign accent. 'Help me, help me, please help me! Oh God, please help me!'

Then a scream.

Then silence.

Grace jumped at the wall, grabbing the rough top of it with both hands, and hauled himself up, then peered over the other side in utter shock.

108

His eyes stinging from some invisible, acrid, rising gas, Roy Grace was looking at a deep pit, enclosed by walls, in which the shirtless man now confirmed as Terry Jim was standing a good eight feet below him, waist high in brown slurry. He was bent over and holding something – or, Grace realized with horror, *someone* – below the surface.

He put his phone down on the rim of the wall, and without hesitating or thinking to call for backup, he launched himself off the wall, down at the man, hitting his bare, flabby skin with such impact the man fell sideways, momentarily disappearing beneath the slurry. As he did so a young woman's head, covered in stinking brown slime, broke the surface; she was choking and gasping for air, looking barely alive.

Grace took a stride towards her. Almost instantly, something with the force of a sledgehammer struck Grace's face, hurling him sideways. Somehow, despite the pain and shock, he had the presence of mind to close his eyes and mouth before he hit the surface and plunged beneath it, the heavy weight of his stab vest dragging him to the bottom.

Then an instant later he felt his shoulders being pressed down, pinning him, beneath the surface, to the floor of this vile pit. He tried desperately to move, to throw himself sideways, but he could not break the grip. Fighting panic, his chest tightening from lack of air, he knew had to get to the surface, had to get his head above this and he only had seconds, only a small amount of air in his lungs. He was shaking, his ears popping, every last drop of air sucked into the vacuum inside his collapsing lungs. His body was contorting. He was starting to lose consciousness. Could not hold on much longer, only seconds, seconds.

His chest tightened more. More. He was starting to convulse and his ears began to ring, which he knew from experience was a sign that he was losing consciousness. Any moment he would not be able to hold it any longer, his mouth would burst open and he'd start gulping in whatever was there.

Fighting. Fighting. Fighting. He thought of Cleo, Noah, Molly, Humphrey as if they were all standing above him, smiling at him. Saying goodbye.

He was shaking, near delirious; had to let go now.

No. No.

In one final desperate movement he jerked his right knee up hard, going for his assailant's groin, and felt a reaction above him, the grip loosened a fraction. Then he forced his right arm up, hard, and felt the bony contours of the man's face. Somehow found his nose, formed two fingers into a V and pushed them up the bridge of the nose as far as he could and into the soft tissue of his eyeballs, ramming his fingers as hard as he could, knuckle deep, as if he was trying to push through the eyes and into the skull.

The weight was instantly gone from his shoulders. He rolled over, pushed himself up with his arms, staggered to his feet, feeling air on his face. He spat, then gulped the rank air in, gratefully, simultaneously opening his eyes which were stinging and fogged with the slurry. He fleetingly saw the terrified girl, then Jim, fists raised, roaring like a crazed bull, lunged at him. Grace sidestepped. Bogged down by the density of the liquid, both of them seemed to be moving in slow motion. Jim turned, grabbing Grace by his shoulders again, his face bursting with rage.

Grace knew what was coming. Typical of the dumb brutality of a man like Jim. And he pre-empted it by head-butting him first. His neck jarred but, albeit fleetingly, he felt a sense of satisfaction at hearing the crunch of broken nose and the yelp of pain. He could feel the grip on his shoulders tighten but this was more for Jim to stay upright, as his knees buckled, than it was to attack further. Grace was also sure that with what he knew was a now broken nose, Jim wouldn't be able to see properly through his tears and was likely choking on blood as well as slurry. But it was only a brief respite and he needed to take advantage of it while the man was momentarily incapacitated; he'd seen enough broken noses to know that loss of sight and balance would be only temporarily compromised.

He stepped sideways and threw an elbow at Jim's forehead but the quagmire of slurry didn't allow the momentum that a move like this would usually deliver, and his attacker was able to hold onto his vest at the shoulders, which partially blocked the blow. Then Jim's hands, like steel vices, clamped around his neck. Starting to crush it. 'You meddling pig, you're in the shit now, you're in it proper. But you should be happy, this is your natural environ—'

Before he could finish, there was a massive explosion of slurry right beside them, showering them both in the muck, then Norman Potting had leaped onto Terry Jim's back, arms around his bull neck, grunting with exertion, trying to choke him. Jim released his hold on Grace, turned and tried to rid himself of the officer clamped to his back, but Potting was holding on for all he was worth. Jim flailed and grunted as he desperately fought to shake the officer loose, bucking like a rodeo bull, with blood still streaming from his nostrils and the gash on the bridge of his mangled nose. Potting was trying to tighten his grip, but the resistance of the slurry on his legs, coupled with how slippery it was on his arms, meant his grip failed and he fell off Jim's back to one side. Almost before he realized he was met with a massive winging punch that sent him stumbling, then tumbling sideways into the mire.

Grace knew he was no match for this former bare-knuckle fighter in strength, his only chance was to outwit or out-manoeuvre him. Jim was already lunging at his neck again with his massive, tattooed arms. He shot his arm out, in between Jim's, and struck his palm hard against his mess of a nose, instantly hearing the moan of pain. He held his palm firmly in place, knowing if Jim pushed forward it would only hurt him more. But he also knew that aggression often overrides logic. As he did so, he kicked out as hard and fast as his leg would move through the liquid, at where he thought Jim's left knee was. And struck something. Jim stumbled, momentarily, back. Towards the terrified girl, who stood, frozen, as Norman Potting threw himself again at Jim's back, giving him a hard punch in the nape of his neck.

Jim jerked his head half-round. Then, startling both Grace and Potting, the girl sprang at Jim, bit his left ear and hung on with her teeth.

Jim screamed in pain, trying to break her free. But she kept on gripping with her teeth, as he tossed and shook her wildly, but her teeth were clenched shut and she was making a deep, almost inhuman growling sound. Terry Jim then suddenly seemed to calm, and grabbed her head, holding her in place while eerily laughing at Grace and yelling, 'You think this is the first time I've been bitten?'

Grace knew that bare-knuckle fighters often resorted to biting if they were in trouble in fights, he'd seen enough half-eared criminals in his time to realize they weren't barbershop injuries.

'Let's see how hard she can bite with a crushed skull,' Jim yelled, and lurched sideways towards the sheer concrete wall, as if he was trying to slam into it – the only thing between his head and the wall was hers, which he was gripping in place.

Potting, realizing what was happening, hurled himself be tween them and the wall, grabbing Jim's wrists. Grace, seizing his chance, again struck Jim in the nose as hard as he could. He screamed again as blood spurted from his face. Jim's hands released Rosalind as he reached to cradle what remained of his nose, but Grace struck him again in the same place, knowing the boxer was pained, bewildered and unable to see.

Moments later, once out of his reach, the girl spat the chunk she had taken of the man's ear into the mire. Jim, looking bewildered and unsteady, roaring in pain and anger, put a hand to the bloodied pulp that was the front of his face, then to his ear which was gouting blood, as if not knowing which to tend to first.

Almost simultaneously there were shouts above them. Grace and Potting glanced up. As did Terry Jim. Four Public Order officers in full riot gear were perched on the rim. One jumped down, secured the girl with a rope and they hauled her up to two colleagues.

Jim looked at them. He had stopped screaming. He just stood, wobbly, dumb with pain and defeat.

Grace shouted at the girl. 'What is your name? Are you Rosalind Esche?'

She nodded at him, bewildered and crying.

He turned back to Jim. The man was looking around, as if sizing up his chances for making a break. He balled his fists menacingly.

'You all right, boss? And sarge?' the officer asked Grace and Potting.

'Do I look all right? Covered in pig shit?' Grace replied.

'Very fitting,' Terry Jim snarled. 'Go fuck yourselves.'

'Nice to see you again too, Terry,' Norman Potting replied, slurry dripping from his clothes and down his face. 'But tell you what, I'm really not impressed with your swimming pool.'

109

Although Dr Shah, as well as Dr Pallant, had urged Chris and Katy to try to get on with their lives as much as possible over the coming days that Bluebell would be in a coma, they both wanted to stay as close as possible to their daughter.

They'd arrived at the hospital prepared, bringing a rucksack containing their laptops and chargers, as well as water, sandwiches and a stash of energy bars. They both had some urgent work they needed to do and planned to hunker down in the Relatives Room so they could be close by if needed. They hoped no one else would be coming in this room today, but Shah had offered to find them an empty office if that happened.

Shortly after 10 a.m. Shah, in scrubs, stethoscope around his neck, entered with a pale face. 'I'm going off shift to get some sleep,' he said. 'Dr Bob Hurst will be taking over for me until I come back this evening – he will come and see you shortly.'

'Any change in Bluebell since earlier this morning?' Chris asked.

Shah, with the air of someone under siege, looked almost too exhausted to manage a smile. His voice, attempting to sound breezy, came out as if someone had forgotten to turn the speaker volume more than a few notches up from mute. 'There is no change, but as I said earlier, the good news is that Bluebell is still with us, that she has made it through the night.'

'That's good news?' Katy said, her voice weak.

The registrar raised his hands apologetically and Chris, momentarily, felt defensive for him.

'Darling,' he said. 'Dr Shah is doing all he can for Bluebell.'

'I know, I know!' she said, looking beaten. 'She made it through the night. What are we supposed to do, Dr Shah?'

Shah looked directly back into her eyes. 'I was speaking via Zoom throughout the night, with Dr Willoughby. Of the one hundred advanced rabies patients he has treated in the past eighteen years, across America, thirty-two per cent made it through to this point. So, we should regard this as extremely positive. Your daughter is a fighter.'

'And a survivor?' Chris asked.

'We can only hope,' Shah said, and clasped his hands together. Not in a gesture of prayer but in an act of friendship.

They walked along the ICU ward, passing beds with young children who Katy tried to avoid looking at. But out of the corner of her eye she saw one little girl, no older than Bluebell, looking very sick and completely bald. She shuddered, thinking, *God, life deals some people shitty hands.*

Dr Shah held open the curtains surrounding Bluebell's bed and, as Katy followed her husband through, she was wondering why it was just Bluebell who was curtained off. Did they only curtain off the ones who were dying, to avoid distressing everyone else on the ward?

Then the shock of seeing her daughter, again, eyes closed, completely encased in apparatus and motionless, was too much and she turned away, letting out a long, agonized moan.

Chris folded his arms around her, holding her tight but at the same time looking over her shoulder at their daughter. Thinking about all they had been through to create her. All the failed IVF treatments, all the heartbreaks.

And, finally, they had made Bluebell.

And now she was trapped somewhere, in some narrow corridor between life and death.

Dr Shah was pointing at a battery of electronic graphs on the wall behind Bluebell. Her brain scans and all the other monitoring equipment. Chris studied in particular the faint peaks and troughs which, Dr Shah had said, were the most important signs of Bluebell's brain activity.

Shah pointed at one continuous, steady electronic graph. 'This is a good sign,' he said.

'In what way?' Katy asked, optimism rising in her heart.

'It means your daughter isn't aware you are here.'

Katy looked at him incredulously. 'And that's good?'

'It means that what we are trying to do, to save Bluebell's life, is possibly working. If we have managed to shut her brain activity down to the point where she doesn't even recognize her mother or father, then maybe we have stopped the rabies virus's ability to effectively mastermind its destruction of your daughter's internal organs.'

Shah pointed at the green line on an oscilloscope. It was almost flat, but not quite. 'This is what we want. If there were big spikes, peaks and troughs, it would be bad, because it would indicate normal brain activity. If it was a completely flat line, that would not be good, either.'

'*In the room the women come and go, talking of Michelangelo*,' Katy murmured.

Shah frowned.

'It's a poem,' Chris explained.

'OK,' the registrar said, looking none the wiser. 'Michelangelo spent years on his back painting the ceiling of the Sistine Chapel.' He looked at Katy for confirmation. For some explanation. For some relevance. But, he knew, he was gone. He would soon be out of here, all he could think of at this moment was his bed, fifteen minutes' walk away.

He smiled with tired eyes at Chris and Katy and said, 'Poetry. Nice.'

He looked like he was about to fall asleep on his feet.

110

Friday 2 April

'Well, get you two lovebirds, all cosied up, eh!'

Roy Grace, wearing a hospital gown, looked up from his chair in the Emergency Department of Eastbourne District General Hospital at a breezy Glenn Branson.

The DI stood in the doorway, immaculately dressed, directing his big, impish grin from Roy Grace to Norman Potting, also in a gown, their chairs a short distance apart in the small, otherwise empty examination area. 'I won't get too close, gather you're both a bit wiffy!' He sniffed and feigned wrinkling his nose.

'Actually, we've been hosed down, showered in disinfectant, and we are now smelling deliciously fragrant!' Roy said, his voice rasping, his throat feeling like it had been stripped raw from the acid fumes.

'Just think of us as a pair of roses,' Potting said.

Branson looked at each of them and frowned. 'I'm trying hard, Norman, but you're not making the cut, either of you. You're just not doing it for me, not as roses. A nice pair of porkers, maybe – oink-oink!'

'Have you just come to gloat?' Grace asked.

Branson shook his head. 'No, I wanted to see how my commanding officer was after his early morning dip.'

'We've had the swimming jokes, Glenn, and the ones about telling the pigs from the police, so unless you've any other business, Norman and I will try to get on with the business of not dying from all the stuff we've breathed in and ingested.'

Branson walked over, stood between their chairs and punched the air with a clenched fist. 'Seriously, guys, well done. Respect for what you did, and' – he had to stifle another grin – 'sorry if it was a bit shit for you.'

Grace raised his right hand and pointed a warning finger at him. 'One more joke and I'm putting you up for a transfer.'

Looking serious now, the DI peered more closely at Grace. At the large bandage on his right cheek; at the blood oxygen meter clipped to his left index finger and pads taped to his chest with monitoring apparatus behind him. All of it, except the bandage, was mirrored with Norman Potting.

'How's the girl, Rosalind Esche?' Grace asked.

'She's in Intensive Care, but she'll be fine. You guys saved her life, for sure. I spoke to the A&E consultant. She'd apparently been standing in that slurry for several hours and was literally at the point of collapse when you guys arrived. She was so exhausted and sick from all the fumes she knew she couldn't stand any longer – she would have just drowned in that stuff.'

Potting shook his head. 'I can think of better ways to go.'

'And no doubt her body would have been fed to the pigs afterwards,' Grace said.

'While I was waiting for you guys to be fumigated, I had an interesting chat with the hospital's resident toxicologist. I'd no idea pig slurry was so poisonous – methane, ammonia and hydrogen sulphide – that's the stuff you make stink bombs with.'

'Thanks for the chemistry lesson, pal,' Grace said.

'Not to mention the bugs,' Potting added. 'They're pumping us full of antibiotics and all kinds of other stuff – but no beer.'

'I can go and get you a couple of six-packs,' Branson volunteered.

'Not actually feeling up to it but thanks all the same,'

Potting said. 'Anything I drink squirts straight out my arse without touching the sides.'

Branson frowned. 'A bit too much information, Norman.'

'Just thought you'd like to know.'

Branson nodded. 'You know, you guys could have been killed by that stuff. The doc said you might get ringworm – that gives you an itchy rash, diarrhoea, nausea, weight loss and cough – or some other infection called Campy something, which gives you the shits for a week.'

'Mate,' Grace said. 'Have you just come here as a harbinger of doom, or do you actually have any news for us about how both the raids have gone?'

Branson smiled again. 'I was just coming to that, boss!' He made a circle with his forefinger and thumb. 'Total A, boss, total A! We nailed it, both Appletree and Long Acre farms. Nine in custody.'

'Nine!' Grace exclaimed.

Branson raised his hands in the air. 'They've been taken to different centres around the county, for processing. Relax, I'm dealing with it all. Everything's under control.'

'Really? Under whose control?'

'Mine, boss.'

'Knowing that is going to make me relax?' Grace retorted. 'Have you arranged a Tier 5 Interview Coordinator? Alec Butler's your man.'

'Yeah, Alec Butler. Yeah – I was – I was going to bring him in.'

'Of course you were.'

Branson looked at him. 'I was.'

Grace nodded. 'Set up a debrief with the team for midday tomorrow. I'll meet you at 11 a.m.'

'You'll be out of here?'

'They're only keeping us in for a few hours, to give us anti-biotics and make sure we poor delicate creatures don't need trauma counselling.' He waved a hand at him. 'Go sort it. I'll see you in the morning.'

'You sure I can't get you guys anything?'

'A bacon sarnie and a butt plug?' Potting said. 'I'd murder one of those if I could keep it down.'

'Maybe tomorrow,' Branson said.

Potting winked at him. 'Good plan.'

After the DI left, Grace said to Potting, 'You grew up on a farm, didn't you, Norman?'

'I did. My old man kept pigs. Love them, but you've got to be careful. It's no myth that mobsters keep them to eat their murder victims. They gobble up the lot, hair and all. The old man gave me a piece of advice when I was a young lad – his version of "health and safety". He said when you go into the pigsty one of the pigs will come up and give you a nudge on the leg, and you need to give it a tap back. If you don't, it'll give you another nudge, and if you still do nothing, next time it'll take a bite out of you. Nothing personal, it just sees you as lunch.'

'I'll remember that next time I'm in a pigsty, Norman, thanks.'

'He gave me another piece of advice also, chief. I should have listened to him – well we both should have, really. He said, *Never wrestle with a pig. You'll both end up covered in shit, and the pig likes it.*'

111

At midday the following morning, as Roy Grace, followed by Glenn Branson, walked into the conference room of the Major Crime Suite, he was greeted by the sight of his entire team seated around the oval table, holding their noses.

'Very funny!' he said, his voice still a long way from being back to normal. He still had a large dressing on his face. His right cheekbone had been badly bruised and two of his teeth had been cracked by Terry Jim's punch and would need extensive dentistry. It angered him, but not as much as what he had learned, since the raid, about the squalor in which Terry and Dallas Jim kept their dogs, and their complete disregard for the rabies regulations that had kept the UK safe from the menace of that disease for almost a century.

It made him all the more determined to charge the Jims with everything they could throw at them. And they had a lot. Enough to see Terry Jim behind bars until well into his old age.

'A bit crap was it, boss?' Nick Nicholl asked.

'Anyone else makes a joke about pigs and shit and they'll spend the next six months in hazmat suits inspecting Sussex pigsties for human remains,' Grace retorted. As he took his seat, he looked around his team, and from his expression they could tell he was not in a joking mood today.

'OK,' he said and turned to the Interview Coordinator, DS Butler. 'Alec, how have the interviews been going?'

'So far, quite well, boss. Terry, Rula and Dallas Jim have gone *no comment* – as I'd expect. But the others are all singing like canaries. Our best result has been with a character – who has plenty of past form with Sussex Police – name of Geoff Taylor. He's the one with the limp – Haydn Kelly has confirmed the match. Taylor was part of the four who raided the Old Homestead Farm and was in the car – the Range Rover – that rammed and killed Timothy Ruddle. He said it was Dallas Jim who was driving. Forensics are on that now. We're waiting for word from Eastbourne Hospital that we can talk to the young woman you rescued, Rosalind Esche. It looks like she could be a very significant witness.'

'Indeed,' Grace said.

Butler continued. 'Another very significant witness is Terry Jim's stepdaughter, Darcy. She's been a little guarded in what she's said so far, but she has made it clear she very much does not support her stepfather's activities of trading in dogs.'

'But, as Emily said previously, she was happy enough for the proceeds to finance her horsey hobbies, right?' Potting said.

'She's genuinely angry at her stepfather, she hates him. He told her that he had sacked the two girls, but she didn't believe him,' Butler said. 'I think she's going to talk to us and expand on the information she gave us in the phone call. Apparently, the family have been trying to keep her quiet with threats so she's obviously nervous, but I believe her loyalty is now out of the window. In any event, she will be a significant witness. From what she's told us so far, it doesn't seem she had any involvement in the puppy business other than peripheral. She wants her stepdad to get done for this. She's even in the process of changing her surname so she has nothing to do with him.'

'OK,' Grace said. 'See how she plays out.' He turned to the DI. 'Glenn, when your team went into Long Acre Farm, the first thing Dallas did was to try to torch the barn where both the

Range Rover and the Ford Ranger involved in the killing of Mr Ruddle were stored. Presumably to get rid of evidence. Good work with the taser, stopping him.'

'Thanks, boss – it was Quick-Draw McGraw here who should get the credit.' He nodded at Nick Nicholl.

Nick Nicholl shrugged and grinned. 'I'd love to have tasered him myself – probably watched too many Westerns as a kid, sir,' he retorted modestly. 'But it was my uniformed colleague who did the business.'

Addressing Grace, the Crime Scene Manager, Chris Gee, said, 'Sir, my team has seized all of Dallas Jim's clothing as well as Geoff Taylor's and the other two suspects. We'll be working with the Collision Investigation Unit's forensic team and the scientists to match clothing fibres to any on the driver's seat of the Range Rover, to see if they can put one of them behind the wheel. There's also something of significance from the CIU regarding the young woman, Lyndsey Cheetham, who was killed last week when her Nissan Leaf ran off the road a few miles from Appletree Farm.'

Chris Gee continued. 'The Collision team found particles of red paint embedded in the rear of the Leaf. It's taken them a while to identify the vehicle type, but they've established it as a Dodge RAM 1500 with huge wheels. We've seized a 4 x 4 vehicle of this make and colour at Appletree Farm – curiously in a barn, concealed behind hay bales. The CIU are examining it now.'

'Good work, Chris,' Grace said. 'How are your team getting on with the general search of the properties?'

'We've so far recovered a number of fake identities.' Gee glanced at his pad. 'One in the name of John Peat, one in the name of Tom Hartley, one in the name of Jonathan Jones and another in the name of Michael Kendrick. Driving licences, passports, national insurance numbers. We have an intel report that a person named John Peat flew, unaccompanied, on a BA flight to Malaga on Friday afternoon – a few hours after the raid.

Interestingly, Spanish immigration have no record of him having arrived in Malaga, but do have details of one Jonathan Jones. We've now given all four aliases to the Spanish police. Additionally, we seized a number of suspected fake Kennel Club registration forms and vaccination certificates, including, very worryingly, ones for rabies vaccinations for dogs imported from Poland, Romania and Spain.'

Grace frowned. 'You know about the little girl, Bluebell Fairfax, who was bitten by a puppy in this John Peat's van and has become very ill with rabies?'

'Do we know how she's doing, boss?' Jack Alexander asked.

'The last update I have is that she is stable,' he replied.

'Sir,' Gee continued. 'DEFRA are extremely concerned about a carcass of a young dog found in the incinerator chamber at Appletree Farm. The incinerator hadn't been lit, but it looks like the Jims were intending to destroy it. They're carrying out a post-mortem on it – and testing for rabies.'

'Could it be the same dog that bit this little girl, Chris?' Polly Sweeney asked.

'I don't have that information, Polly. But we think it's possible. The RSPCA, DEFRA and Public Health England are all involved. Both Appletree and Long Acre farms are in lockdown on DEFRA's orders, with all animals on both premises going to be quarantined and monitored. They are also looking to track down the other puppy in the van with Moose, the dachshund. All these poor creatures have the Jim family to thank.' Grace shook his head.

'Couldn't we put the whole Jim family in a cage with a rabid dog?' DC Nicholl suggested.

'Why, Nick?' Potting asked. 'What have you got against the dog?'

Several of the team smiled.

'Because of our strict quarantine laws, England has been rabies-free for one hundred years,' Grace said. 'Thanks to bastards like the Jims we now have one case. We just have to hope it is only one, and that this dog that's sadly been found dead is the infected one that bit Bluebell Fairfax. And we have to hope that if it is, they destroyed it straight away before it passed the disease on to any wildlife. If an outbreak is confirmed, then in lining their pockets with their illegal activities, the Jims will have left a legacy of putting every man, woman, child and animal in the nation at risk of one of the worst diseases and worst deaths it is possible to have.'

Everyone around the table was silent and solemn, absorbing this. Grace gave a thin smile. 'OK, that's the grim reality. Let's take some positives from this whole sorry saga. We have recovered all the Ruddles' dogs, and they look OK. Thanks to all your brilliant work, we've successfully raided two farms in East Sussex where we believe criminal activity was taking place. Nine suspects are in custody, and we've recovered a misper whose life was in immediate danger. We've cracked an international dog smuggling and illegal breeding gang, and we have significant evidence that at least some of the people we have arrested are linked to the murder of Timothy Ruddle. As well as the attempted murder of Rosalind Esche. And perhaps, from the new evidence from Chris Gee, we may have a second murder charge with Lyndsey Cheetham. At present, many of the people arrested at both farms will be charged with murder, robbery and conspiracy to traffic dogs, in consultation with the CPS. That's not such a shit result, is it?'

'Not when you come up smelling like roses, chief,' Norman Potting said – and ducked.

112

Cafe Marmalade, with its wooden floorboards, shabby chic furniture and the day's newspapers neatly laid out, had the comfortable atmosphere of a country house drawing room. Just a few minutes' walk from the hospital, it had a more welcoming feel than both the garish claustrophobia of the Relatives Room and the grim starkness of the hospital canteen. It had been a kind of sanctuary for Chris and Katy for much of the longest few days of their lives.

Permanently exhausted from worry and lack of sleep, fuelled by endless coffees and a diet of mostly microwaved paninis, they had managed at least to deal with any urgent matters regarding their clients. They had also tried to get permission to visit Moose in her quarantine at the kennels at Heathrow, but had decided to wait and go with Bluebell when she was stronger.

Now, at 9 a.m. on this Sunday morning, they were back in the cafe again, after a few hours' sleep at home, followed by a quick visit to the ward – where there was still no change in Bluebell.

Chris, perched on a battered leather sofa and sipping a double espresso, stared at the front page of the *Sunday Times*, unable to concentrate on any of the stories. He flicked urgently through a few pages then stopped, as he found the headline he had been expecting on the fifth page. Now it really sank in.

RABIES CONFIRMED IN SMUGGLED DOG

He read the article. It was about a police raid on a farm in East Sussex, suspected of illegal puppy importing and farming.

The carcass of a Staffordshire bull terrier found on the premises had been biopsied, and tested positive for rabies. The dog was believed to have been kept caged since its importation, but DEFRA officials had requested all farms to be vigilant, as a precaution. They had also put out a request for anyone who had bought a dog in the past two months from breeders under the names Tom Hartley, Jonathan Jones, Michael Kendrick or John Peat to call the RSPCA national hotline number. Then he saw a name he recognized, the detective to whom he had spoken last night, who had provided him with an update of the investigation and the raid on the farms and told him to expect it to hit the news today.

The Senior Investigating Officer of Operation Brush, Detective Superintendent Roy Grace said, 'A young girl confirmed to be suffering from rabies – the first to contract this hideous disease in England since 1922 – is currently fighting for her life. Evil criminals profiteering for the demand in lockdown dogs have been flouting our puppy importation laws, and this is a tragic example of the consequences. I urge anyone who has recently bought a dog from any breeder they are concerned about to contact the RSPCA urgently.'

He was about to show the piece to Katy, when his phone rang. It was Dr Shah, his voice as guarded as ever, but, Chris wondered, was he imagining it or was the doctor sounding just a little brighter?

'Your daughter is awake,' Shah said. 'We've removed the endotracheal intubation and she's breathing on her own.'

They dropped everything, telling the proprietor – with whom they'd long been on first name terms – they'd be back, and hurried to the hospital. Less than ten minutes after the call, they were standing at Bluebell's bedside, alongside Dr Shah.

Bluebell, eyes open, was looking hazily up at them, through the mass of monitoring wires and tubes, blinking slowly.

'Darling!' Katy said, tears rolling down her cheeks. 'Bluebell, darling.' She kneeled and kissed her daughter's forehead. 'How are you? How are you feeling?'

Chris, through blurry eyes, blinked away his tears but more came. He saw the left side of his daughter's mouth open and her lips move, but no sound came out.

Katy held her right hand. 'My darling, you are back with us!'

'Moose. Where Moose?'

Her speech was slurred, coming just from the left side of her mouth. But at least she was speaking, Chris thought. He exchanged a glance with Katy, then looked at Shah, who was studying their daughter intently.

'Moose is fine, darling,' Katy said.

'Moose.'

Katy smiled at her. 'You'll be able to see her really soon!'

Bluebell's eyes closed, as if the effort of speaking had exhausted her. 'OK.' It came out as a faint whisper.

Chris looked at the array of digital graphs and numbers, trying to remember how some of them had been reading the last time he looked, a few hours ago. In particular, the ones monitoring her brain activity. Was it his imagination, he wondered, or were there deeper spikes and troughs than before?

Bluebell looked asleep again now. But she was seemingly breathing fine, unaided.

Dr Shah nodded for them to follow him. They walked a short distance along the ward, past all the other occupied beds, and stopped by the nurses' station.

'She's doing great, don't you think?' Katy asked excitedly.

The registrar hesitated. 'It is a very positive sign that she is breathing unaided, Katy, but . . .' He fell silent.

'But *what*?' Chris prompted.

Shah looked at each of them solemnly. 'I told you at the very start I would always be truthful to you.' He hesitated, as if uncertain how to go on. 'Yes, it is good that Bluebell is breathing unaided. But we have concerns about her brain activity. I did tell you that an induced coma carries risks of brain damage. The brain patterns you can see, with some of the uneven spikes, indicates her brain is not functioning as well as we could hope, and her speech confirms this—'

'Please don't tell us she is brain-damaged,' Katy blurted.

Shah looked back at her evenly. 'I cannot tell you one way or the other at the moment. But on the positive side, what Bluebell has going for her is that she is so young that her brain is still developing. The consultant neurologist, Dr Nightingale, was here a short while ago, and he thinks there is a reasonable chance her neural pathways will re-route.'

'How reasonable?' Katy asked. 'What percentage chance?'

'On a scale of one to ten?' Chris pressed.

Shah shook his head. 'I really can't give you that figure, because I just don't know.'

'But you've had past experience handling rabies cases in Pakistan, right?' Chris went on.

'I have, Chris. But not a single one of those who weren't vaccinated survived. This is different.'

'Fine, so, give us a percentage chance – of Bluebell returning to one hundred per cent normal?' he pressed again.

He looked at both of them, in turn. 'I can't do that, I just don't know.'

'Try, give us a figure,' Katy said. 'Eighty per cent? Seventy per cent?'

Shah shook his head. 'I'd have to say fifty per cent, at best.'

113

'Wake up, sleepyhead!'

Roy Grace, emerging confused from deep sleep, opened his eyes to see bright daylight, the curtains wide open giving him a view of the downland hill beyond their garden, dotted with sheep looking like dozens of miniature clouds stuck to the steep incline with magnets. He felt a deadweight on his legs.

Cleo was standing over him, in jeans and a baggy jumper, a big smile on her face.

'Wake up, Daddy!' Noah, lying beside him, said.

The deadweight was Humphrey.

'What – what's the time?' Grace murmured.

'Midday,' Cleo said.

'No way.' He glanced at his wristwatch in shock. 'I don't sleep to midday, ever.'

'Exactly!' she retorted. 'Clearly the boss inside your head decided you needed to.'

He tried to move his legs, but Humphrey would not budge.

'Can we go to zoo, Daddy, want to see penguins! You said we could go!'

Grace cuddled his son. 'You want to go to Drusillas?'

Noah nodded vigorously.

'OK. Daddy's going to shower and have some breakfast and then we'll go, yes?'

'Yayyyyyyyyyyy! Penguins!'

Grace smiled happily. Happy for the normality, for the grounding his family gave him in the dark and often skewed world in which he worked. The raids on the two farms had produced even more results than he or any of his team had hoped. But, as he well knew from long and frustrating experience, arrests were only the beginning – the base camp at the bottom of a steep and treacherous slope.

The Crown Prosecution Service demanded a realistic prospect of conviction at court, combined with a bullet-proof chain of evidence before sanctioning a major criminal charge. Convincing them was often harder than catching the villains.

With nine suspects arrested, and only a limited time to keep them in custody, the evidence required to charge them had been challenging but there was enough to charge seven of them and have three remanded in custody. They had been working around the clock for the past two weeks since the raid to develop the case. And with the RSPCA, Public Health England and DEFRA all involved, Operation Brush had become a story of national media interest – and that had added to his workload.

So far, the experts had been able, through forensic examination of Dallas Jim's clothing, the vehicle seats, his mobile phone and the onboard computers of both vehicles, to put him behind the wheel of both the Range Rover that fatally injured Tim Ruddle and the Dodge RAM that forced Lyndsey Cheetham's Nissan off the road and into a tree. That and other evidence had been enough to formally charge him with two counts of murder. Terry Jim had been charged with the attempted murder of Rosalind Esche and conspiracy to murder Lyndsey Cheetham, and his wife, Rula, also charged in connection with these offences. Terry, Rula and Dallas Jim had also been charged with conspiracy to traffic dogs, the illegal importation of dogs, and unlicensed breeding and sale of dogs, cruelty to animals, as well as forgery. All three of them had had bail applications rejected and were remanded in custody.

Others, including Geoff Taylor and two farmhands, Jason Keele and Aaron Keele, believed to have been in the two vehicles that fatally injured Tim Ruddle, as well as Rula Jim's daughter, Darcy, were released pending further investigation. Two other farm-hands were also released for further enquiries to be made. The supposed 'Mrs Hartley' Roy and Cleo had met had thus far eluded them. Monitoring all the charges as well as hours and hours with the Exhibits Officer and his own team, holding a press conference and giving updates to the Chief Officer team, had pushed him to the limits during these past two weeks.

But there was one thing that had made him smile. It was when he'd told Cleo the full story behind Humphrey's kidnapping, and that in a bizarre kind of way, Gecko had been doing them a favour. She'd replied, *I'm still glad I kicked him in the nuts. It felt good!*

A short while later, showered and still feeling dazed from having slept so long, Grace sat at the kitchen table nursing a double espresso, then sliced the top off one of his two boiled eggs, shook some salt onto the bulk of the egg, and glanced back at the front page of the *Sunday Times*.

'So, superhero cop is a Big Endian!'

He frowned at Cleo. 'A what?'

'You never read *Gulliver's Travels*?'

'Another gap in my education?'

She gave him a sad nod. 'Afraid so. The Big Endians were one of two tribes engaged in a long war over whether you should cut the top off the small or the big end of a boiled egg.'

'And who won?'

'Neither side. Like most wars.' She gestured with her hand. 'See, you've cut off the big end of one of your eggs. Is there a subliminal message in that?'

He smiled. 'That it depends on the size of the egg – and the spoon?'

Cleo shook her head. 'Glenn was right, wasn't he? Something he said a long time ago.'

'Which is?'

'That you always answer a question with a question.'

'Do I?'

She gave him a playful punch.

On the floor beside the table, Molly crawled around on her playmat, hitting musical notes on the coloured keyboards. Noah sat opposite his father, messily spooning something that looked like porridge into his mouth.

'Not going for a run today?' Cleo asked.

Grace shook his head. He felt like a drain plug had been pulled inside him. 'I'm done. Today is penguin day. Today is celebration day. Today is cherish Cleo, Noah and Molly day.'

Alongside the stack of Sunday papers they both loved to read was a copy of yesterday's *Argus*. The front page headline was that Rosalind Esche had been nominated for an RSPCA bravery award. Grace had nominated her for it, and he was glad she was getting something for the almost unimaginable suffering she'd been through. The young woman was still in hospital. Hours of standing up, without respite, had caused problems with her kidneys and liver, and she was extremely lucky to be alive. He was planning to visit her tomorrow.

'Is there any update on that poor little girl – Bluebell?' Cleo asked. 'I can't imagine how her parents must be feeling.'

He smiled. 'There is some seriously good news. I checked with the hospital last night and spoke to a doctor there – Anish Shah. He was guarded, but said she has turned a huge corner, and he is confident she will, in good time, make a full recovery.'

'That's incredible, beating all the odds?'

'It is. She's one of the few people to have survived it, it's going to be massive news. The doctor said she was a fighter and she clearly is – a real fighter.'

She looked at him knowingly. 'Like my brave soldier is, right?'

He grinned. 'You think?'

'There you go, another question answered with a question!'

'And here's another – OK? Which end do I cut off my second egg? The big or the little?'

Cleo hesitated. 'Before you make that momentous decision, there's something I want to ask you.'

'OK, tell me?'

She looked coy. 'You know we want another dog?'

Roy Grace said a very slow and steady, 'Uh huh.'

'I've had the RSPCA contact me after our interest with a possible match for us – a really sweet rescue boy.'

'Oh yeah?'

She nodded vigorously. 'Want to see the picture?'

Grinning, Grace replied, 'You know the answer already, don't you? That if I see the photo, I'll say yes.'

She put her hands on her hips. 'I'm not trying to coerce you.'

'I totally understand that.'

'Remember when we went to Rome, to the Colosseum, where the gladiators fought?'

Grace frowned. 'Yes – does this have something to do with this dog?'

'It does. The audience were asked to vote on whether the defeated gladiator lived or died, by putting their thumbs up or down. So, I'm giving you the opportunity to say yay or nay, by choosing which end of your second egg you cut off. The big or the little. Big is yes, small is no. OK?'

Grinning again, he shook his head, then picked the hot egg up from its cup and studied it thoughtfully. 'So long as you can tell me the answer to the eternal question of which came first – the chicken or the egg?'

Cleo looked at him with mock exasperation. 'There you go again. Answering a question with a question.'

He reached across to the knife rack, drew out a small, heavy machete and cleanly sliced off one end of the egg.

GLOSSARY

ANPR – Automatic Number Plate Recognition. Roadside or mobile cameras that automatically capture the registration number of all cars that pass. It can be used to historically track which cars went past a certain camera, and can also create a signal for cars which are stolen, have no insurance or have an alert attached to them.

CID – Criminal Investigation Department. Usually refers to the divisional detectives rather than the specialist squads.

CPS – Crown Prosecution Service.

CSI – Crime Scene Investigators. Formerly SOCO (Scenes of Crime Officers). They are the people who attend crime scenes to search for fingerprints, DNA samples etc.

DIGITAL FORENSICS – The unit which examines and investigates computers and other digital devices.

FLO – Family Liaison Officer.

MO – Modus Operandi (method of operation). The manner by which the offender has committed the offence. Often this can reveal unique features which allow crimes to be linked or suspects to be identified.

SIO – Senior Investigating Officer. Usually a Detective Chief Inspector who is in overall charge of the investigation of a major crime such as murder, kidnap or rape.

CHART OF POLICE RANKS

Police ranks are consistent across all disciplines and the addition of prefixes such as 'detective' (e.g. detective constable) does not affect seniority relative to others of the same rank (e.g. police constable).

Police Constable · Police Sergeant · Inspector · Chief Inspector

Superintendent · Chief Superintendent · Assistant Chief Constable · Deputy Chief Constable · Chief Constable

ACKNOWLEDGEMENTS

I'm often asked whether any of my research into the very dark side of life keeps me awake at night. The answer is yes, but I can honestly say that few things have shocked me more than what I learned during the research for this novel, and above all else, the sheer horror of the disease called rabies.

I seem to be blessed, every time I research a new novel, to meet one person who somehow, almost magically, unlocks the key for me, and with this book I owe enormous thanks to Dr Rodney Willoughby of Milwaukee, Wisconsin, specialist in Paediatric Infectious Diseases. I can honestly say it would have been a lesser story without his incredible help.

Another person who went over and above everything I could have hoped for is Detective Chief Inspector Andy Wolstenholme of the Surrey and Sussex Major Crime Team. Chapeau, Andy!

I want to also give a very special mention to the RSPCA, who have been immensely and enthusiastically helpful in all aspects of my research for this book. In particular, Patrick Bulley, Sarah Howlett, Emily Prideaux, Chloe Wallace and Inspector Kirsty Withnall.

A special shout-out to Ashley and Yulia Beal of Swiss Watches Direct for their help and for their generous donation to the RSB Charitable Foundation.

As ever, so many in Sussex Police have given me invaluable research help. A very big thank you to Police and Crime Commissioner Katy Bourne, OBE, to Chief Constable Jo Shiner, who shares my passion for dogs, and to so many officers and support staff actively serving under them, as well as retirees, from Sussex and other forces. I've listed them in alphabetical order and beg forgiveness for any omissions.

Police Dog Handler Simon Ashton; Inspector James Biggs; PC Jon Bennion-Jones; Chief Inspector Steve Biglands; PC Olli Brooks; Chief Superintendent Justin Burtenshaw; Financial Investigator Emily Denyer; Rural Crime Coordinator Sergeant Tom Carter; CSI James Gartrell; CSI Chris Gee; Aiden Gilbert, Digital Forensics; PC Robbie Groom; Meagan Robinson; Chief Officer, States of Jersey Police, Robin Smith; James Stather, Forensic Services; Major Crime Team Investigator Pauline Sweeney; PC Richard Trundle; Beth Durham, Suzanne Heard, Jill Pedersen and Katie Perkins of Sussex Police Corporate Communications; Chief Inspector Andrew Westwood.

Retired Officers: Chief Superintendent Graham Bartlett; Chief Constable of Kent, Alan Pughlsey QPM; Sergeant Russell Phillips; Detective Superintendent Nick Sloan; DS Mark Taylor.

Heartfelt thanks also to Marc Abraham OBE, Niamh Bartlett, Pete Bryant, Sean Didcott, Dominic Fortnam, Andrew Le Gallais OBE, Anna-Lisa Hancock, Andy Harding, John Hartnett, Andrew Henwood, Dr Bob Hurst, Danielle Kaelin, Haydn Kelly, Joseph Langford, Richard Le Quesne, Dr James Mair, David Martin, Dr Adrian Noon, Dr Graham Ramsden, Kit Robinson, Charlotte Seaman and the team at Airpets, Alan Setterington, Helen Shenston, John Stewart, Amanda Stretton, Orlando Trujillo.

A massive thank you as always to Wayne Brookes, my superstar editor (!), and the team at Pan Macmillan – to name just a few: Jonathan Atkins, Kinza Azira, Lara Borlenghi, Emily Bromfield, Laura Carr, Siân Chilvers, Alex Coward, Stuart Dwyer, Claire Evans, Lucy Hale, Hollie Howe, Daniel Jenkins, Christine Jones, Rebecca Kellaway, Neil Lang, Rebecca Lloyd, Sara Lloyd, James Long, Holly Martin, Ellah Mwale, Rory O'Brien, Joanna Prior, Guy Raphael, Jeremy Trevathan, Charlotte Williams, Leanne Williams. And my brilliant freelance editors: Susan Opie, Nicole Foster, Karen Whitlock, Liz Hatherell and Fraser Crichton.

And, prior to leaving, Sam Fletcher.

A huge thank you to my amazing literary agent Isobel Dixon and to everyone at my UK Literary Agency, Blake Friedmann. Lizzy Attree, Sian Ellis-Martin, Julian Friedmann, Hana Murrell, James Pusey, Conrad Williams, Daisy Way. And a big three cheers to my fabulously gifted UK PR team at Riot Communications: Caitlin Allen, Emily Souders, Niamh Houston and Hedvig Lindstrom.

Although the act of writing itself is a solitary job, I'm blessed with a brilliant support team to help with so much behind the scenes. Dani Brown, Erin Brown, Eagle-eyed Margaret Duncton, Sarah Middle, Emma Gallichan, Mark Tuckwell, Chris Diplock and Chris Webb, along with the wider early reading team of Martin Diplock, Jane Diplock and Lyn Gaylor have all been invaluable to me and I appreciate all they do. And sadly, in memoriam, Sue Ansell, who was a wonderful early reader of every single book I have written.

I'm blessed with two incredibly talented and hardworking people: my wife, Lara, and former Detective Chief Superintendent David Gaylor, who head up Team James.

David Gaylor brings a brilliant range of skills, many of which are from his police background, and contributes so much to my novels, most importantly of all, the authenticity of every aspect of policing I depict. He does the same with the stage plays as well as being retained police advisor to the GRACE TV series, also.

My wife, Lara, deserves a whole row of gold stars, for being so brilliant at analysing my characters, the storylines, and always being incredibly in tune with the mood and ways of our times. And for just being such a brilliant and patient person. And she too has helped shape each of the stage plays as well as the television series, GRACE.

In a troubled world that often feels so dark, all our animals in our ever-growing menagerie bring a touch of lightness. Their antics, whether it's our pygmy goats prancing around, or our gorgeous but rather aggressive rooster, Billy-Big Balls, attacking our wellies, or our guinea fowl rapping on our kitchen window in the morning, demanding sweetcorn, always bring a smile to our faces. Thank you to all our amazing creatures who enrich our lives – Spooky our labradoodle, Wally our goldendoodle, our two Burmese cats, our comical ducks, forty hens, rabbits, quail, guinea fowl, Kakariki parrots, budgies, canaries and finches.

Something else that always makes me happy is to hear from you, my readers – I owe you so much for your support. Do keep your messages coming through any of the channels listed on the About the Author page.

Above all, keep well and keep reading!

Peter James

www.peterjames.com

 @peterjamesuk

 @peterjames.roygrace

 @peterjamesuk

 @thejerseyhomestead

 @mickeymagicandfriends

You Tube Peter James TV

Read the opening chapters of the new novel from Peter James

THEY THOUGHT I WAS DEAD: SANDY'S STORY

COMING MAY 2024

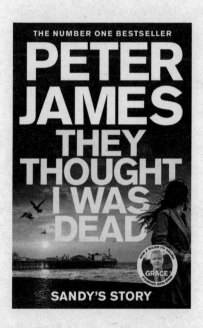

For years Roy Grace searched for his missing wife.
Why did she disappear without a trace?
Who and what was she running from?

This is Sandy's story . . .

PROLOGUE

A lot of us screw up in life, some more than others, and some of us screw up pretty much most of the time. I'm there, right up among the big screw-ups. To paraphrase my favourite comedian, the late Peter Cook: 'I've made loads of mistakes in life and I could repeat them all exactly.'

That's pretty much how I feel.

I read a poem once that I think was called 'The Dash'. It talked about that mark, that hyphen you see on gravestones, linking the date of birth and date of death. It's always struck me as curious that the important thing on those headstones is the two dates. The dash in between is inconsequential. Maybe that's because human lives are generally inconsequential. Is all that matters that we were born and that we died?

But surely everyone has a story to tell? They may not have invented the wheel, or split the atom, or solved the Riemann hypothesis . . . But surely a lot of people deserve more than that tiny dash, don't they?

This is my story. I'm just fleshing out the dash a bit on my odd little life.

1

26 July 2007 – The day I leave

My name is Sandy. I'm driving from Brighton towards Gatwick Airport and I'm nervous as all hell. You would be too if you were me, right now, I promise you. I keep looking in my rear-view mirrors for someone following me. Silly, because no one can possibly know – yet – what I've done.

I've just left my husband, Roy, but he certainly won't have a clue at this moment – he's immersed in his work as ever, on a murder case. It's his thirtieth birthday today and we're supposed to be going out to dinner tonight – we have a reservation at our favourite restaurant – us and another couple – our closest friends. It's a big deal your thirtieth, a milestone. I'd even asked the restaurant to make him a cake with a marzipan goldfish just like his pet, Marlon, on top.

Bad timing, I know. If I'd had a choice, I'd have picked any day but this one. But I don't have that luxury.

I'm not just running from my husband, although that's part of this story – he's a decent guy who doesn't deserve what I'm going to be putting him through. A decent guy but not an ideal husband for me. No, I'm running from a mess I've got myself into – a real, proper mess. A death threat from someone the police have in their sights as a highly dangerous Person of Interest. My husband knows the man, he's talked about him, believes he is behind several killings, but the fact is that the Major Crime Team don't have enough evidence to arrest him. Yet.

Roy doesn't know I have an involvement with this man. He has no idea that I'm the next person he is intending to kill. He doesn't know how terrified I am.

He doesn't know I am taking someone with me, either, but that's another story, for later.

And I've no idea what Roy will do when he can't find me or call or text me. I've not left a note or anything corny like that. But I have left pretty much all my personal stuff, other than just a couple of small photographs he won't miss. He's a smart detective, so I guess he'll start by using all those great skills he has at tracking down murder suspects, both current and long past.

But he is going to find it hard to track me down, for one very simple reason.

I no longer exist.

2

Roel Albazi was forty-seven years old, stocky and squat, and dressed in mismatched Versace. He was Albanian and had lived in England for many years. He had a shaven head, tattooed neck and a pencil-thin moustache that ran down either side of his mouth to his chin. Adorned with a gold necklace, big rocks on his fingers and a bling watch, he sat outside the pizza restaurant in Shoreham High Street that was one of his legitimate business fronts, sipping a macchiato and smoking his short cigar, which was nearly down to the stub.

He had the physique of the kind of non-negotiable muscle you'd find outside any nightclub door on the planet. From a distance he looked a thug and not a man with a degree in international law. A hard man, you'd think. Not someone who would be afraid of anyone.

Until you looked closer and saw his frightened eyes.

He was very afraid right now of one person. Her name was Song Wu. She was a lot richer than him, a lot more ruthless and a lot more powerful. And she owned him – pretty much – since making his company, Albazi Debt Recovery International, an offer he should have refused but could not, three years ago. The offer had been a vastly lucrative contract to work for her company exclusively.

It had been an invitation to sup at the Devil's table, he was well aware of that, but he thought he could handle it. The money on that table just too good to turn down.

463

And the deal had been too good to last.

And at this moment he was in deep trouble with Song Wu.

There was a rumour that she liked to have people who crossed her – or defaulted on her – cut up alive, and then she watched the videos. But Roel Albazi knew it wasn't just a rumour.

Before his rise from mere debt collector to Fu Shan Chu in the triad run by Song Wu – effectively, in Mafia terms, her under-boss – she'd made him watch the video of his predecessor. It was an hour long and involved kitchen knives, a rotary bandsaw and a chainsaw. The man was still conscious fifty-five minutes into the procedure. His mistake had been trying to broker a deal with another employee to siphon off some money. He didn't understand about loyalty. This employee was Chinese, and Albazi's predecessor fatally did not get the way the triad connections worked, and how a Chinese person would always be loyal to another Chinese person over a westerner.

Song Wu was third-generation English, but she was still as pure Chinese as the day her family had left Hong Kong back in 1954. Her father had amassed an empire of thirty-five restaurants and takeaways across the south of England, twenty Chinese grocery stores and a wholesale business supplying Chinese restaurants around the UK.

Privately educated at one of the nation's poshest girls' schools, she had reacted to racist bullying with a ferocity that soon made other pupils steer well clear of her, and she found she enjoyed both the power and inflicting pain. Within five years of her father's death, she had added a dozen more restaurants, a string of launderettes, two fully legal casinos in England and another five around Europe, as well as seven stone of body weight to her existing twelve. She liked an excess of food, but she liked an excess of money even more. She was a glutton for cash. Profits made her eyes light up; losses made her face flame. Nothing melted the ice that was her heart.

She had two brothers who were directly beneath her in the family hierarchy but dealt with other areas of her business. Silent figures in the shadows who executed their sister's instructions with precision. Albazi wasn't aware of anyone who admitted to knowing them, or even having seen them, but everyone in the Song Wu organization feared them.

It was from the Casino d'Azur group that she hauled in the biggest gains – but only in part from the actual gaming tables. The highest margins came from her business model of loaning cash to gamblers who had run out of luck. They were given big loans, always short term, with interest rates of fifty per cent per month. Defaulters were sent a video of someone being tortured, which self-erased after one viewing. Most paid up pretty fast, finding the money somehow. And that was partly because Albazi vetted the people the Casino d'Azur lent to very carefully in advance. He made sure they had assets they could turn to, in desperation. Assets such as the unmortgaged portion of their homes.

But at this moment, Albazi was a worried man. Two people he'd approved big loans to in the past three months had, separately, done a runner, and Song Wu had not been happy. Albazi knew she suspected he was lying to her and had cut some kind of a deal with these people behind her back. Now this third person wasn't showing up either, and he was feeling physically sick at the thought of having to tell Song Wu. She was going to be even more certain he was double-crossing her.

Every five minutes Albazi methodically checked his watch and each of the three phones lined up on the metal table. Traffic streamed past. Pedestrians streamed past. But there was no sign of her. And no message.

She had given him her word. Assured him. They had an appointment. An assignation. At 12 p.m. today she was going to turn up with the £150K she owed him.

It was now 12.20 p.m. Then it was 12.25 p.m. Then 12.30 p.m.

Yet again he checked the middle phone, the one she had the number for, the one they always spoke or texted on. No message.

Bitch.

He stubbed out the cigar in the ashtray. She might think she was clever, but it wasn't clever not to pay him. Sure, the interest rates were high, but so they should be as he never took security for the loans. All of them were on trust and he made sure he collected what he was owed. Always. However long it took. His customers paid either with cash or with their homes or with their lives. He preferred the cash but killing a debtor – and very publicly – served as a great warning to others. Call it a marketing cost.

He picked up the phone on the left and dialled. It was answered almost instantly.

'Sandy Grace,' Albazi said. 'Find her. Now.'

3

I'm on the M23, heading north, and the slip road to Gatwick Airport is coming up a mile ahead. If I take it, I guess that will be the point of no return. How does a relationship get to the point of no return? I have often asked myself if there is a way back to our once blissful marriage. But it is like a broken glass: however brilliantly it gets repaired, there will always be cracks. Roy might call them tiny fractures, but for me they are significant.

Of course, the heat of that first passion can't last, however much we fantasize it will. We go through stages with any 'significant other'. First, we fall in lust, then we fall in love, then we hitch our wagons together and steadily rumble and bounce along Reality Road. Whether we have kids or not, some are destined to end up in some form of compromised state of contentment. Acceptance of our lot. And that is fine for many people. But I want more. I've always wanted more. I *need* more. I just feel the compromises I have to make are too many.

That may seem selfish, given my husband is not a bad person, but it's the only way out I can see. I think it will damage Roy less if I disappear than if I have to tell him what I have become and what I have done. It would ruin his career having a wife who has got into this situation and I can't help feeling that I would, forever after, be an embarrassment to him. The proverbial albatross around his neck.

All I can say is that it isn't easy for me. I dislike myself entirely. I hate what I have become. I wish, desperately, it hadn't got to this.

I like Antoine de Saint-Exupéry's description of love as not gazing into each other's eyes, but looking in the same direction together. I think he got that from Dickens, who was always mentioning people sitting in 'companionable silences'. But wasn't that because they had nothing else to do in his day? No internet, no computer games, no Amazon to browse, no Sky Sports.

So when does that oh so subtle change in your relationship start? The first night that you share a bed and don't make love? The first morning you leave home forgetting to say *I love you*? The first time you don't notice your significant other's new hairstyle? The day you forget the anniversary of when you met? The day you realize, for whatever reason, you no longer come first in your significant other's life?

Tick that last box for me.

The reality of being married to an ambitious Major Crime detective is that you will often come second – sometimes to a corpse.

The more I go over and over this in my head, the more I realize that whatever I now do, even if I somehow sort out this mess, too much has happened for our relationship to continue. I'd always carry the lies and live in fear of Roy finding out about my sordid other life. I have to leave.

Selfishly, it is easier for me if I pass on some blame to him, so I consume myself with thoughts of what he could've done to prevent me getting into this mess: maybe he did prioritize his job over me, maybe he didn't love me enough. That I'm just an appendage, the person who makes the bed, who does the shopping, who cooks, that he doesn't care for my career or any of my ambitions to use my interior design skills, so long as I turn up to functions on his arm. But deep down, if I let myself go there, I'm just trying to ease my guilt.

He's actually a bloody good guy. I should find his dedication to his job a positive thing, but I use it against him. I'm a disgrace. He's better off without me.

THEY THOUGHT I WAS DEAD

Just over a year ago. Our wedding anniversary. He never forgets any significant dates and he'd booked a restaurant as a surprise – our favourite seafood restaurant in the Brighton Lanes – where we had gone on one of our very first dates. He'd sorted a taxi so we could both have a drink, and he'd given me a beautiful present, a white gold eternity ring. I felt bad because I hadn't given him anything special.

This was the evening when I made a terrible decision.

4

2006 – One year earlier

We are in the back of the taxi. Roy has his arm around me and we are all loved up. All these years of marriage and still in love. I feel hugely grateful despite so long trying, fruitlessly, for a baby, which has been arduous and draining for us both.

We are heading east along Church Road, Hove, one road north of the seafront. A wide, buzzy street, lined with shops, cafes, bars and restaurants. The driver is a young, friendly guy. His plate says *Mark Tuckwell*. Roy and I are chatting to him, like we always do to taxi drivers, waiters, shop assistants, pretty much anyone, really. We both share an insatiable curiosity about people. I'm sure Roy banks it all, though, somewhere up in that ten-gazillion gigaflop processor inside his skull, whereas I just remember faces. But I know my husband too well. I can see that all the time he's chatting to this driver he's looking through the windows, taking in both sides of the street, and suddenly he yells, 'Stop! Stop! STOPPPP!'

And my heart stops.

I know what's about to happen because it's happened before. Roy, with his damned near photographic memory, has spotted a villain he's been after for a year, or maybe longer, walking along the street.

As the driver pulls hard over to the kerb, Roy already has his door open. 'Darling, order a bottle of bubbly – I'll see you at the restaurant as soon as I can.'

Then he's gone.

The time is 7.30 p.m.

At 8 p.m. I'm sitting in the restaurant, English's, with a bottle of Champagne, reading the menu over and over. And over. Roy calls with an update. He has chased this suspect down Western Road for over half a mile, finally rugby-tackling and pinning him to the floor at the Clock Tower.

He's now on his way to the custody centre at Hollingbury. He can't hand this charmer over to anyone else yet, because of something to do with *chain of evidence* – after finding Class A drugs on him. But it shouldn't be a problem, he assures me. It's early evening, so he will be able to process him through custody quickly, and then join me.

It's now 10 p.m. I've spent much of the past two hours reading the menu until I've learned it by heart, and texting my best friend, about my progress on this increasingly boring and increasingly non-romantic date. A combination of the booze and the boredom and I'm really pissed off. It's escalating in my head, and I can't stop it even though the evening started so well.

On the plus side I've eaten an entire basket of delicious breads with a fish paste and a very yummy butter, and I've almost finished the bottle of Veuve Clicquot. And now, Roy has just called with yet another update.

For some reason I don't fully understand, he's still stuck in the custody centre but will be with me, he promises, faithfully, in twenty minutes.

I read out the menu to him and he chooses scallops for his starter and monkfish for his main. I select a bottle of Chablis from the wine list, hang the cost. Although I'm feeling a bit smashed and know I shouldn't drink much more.

It is now 10.15 p.m. and Roy has texted to say he is still delayed. I'm so ravenous I've had my starter and half of the bottle of Chablis. Not sure if I'm feeling more pissed or just plain pissed off. Through my haze of alcohol the restaurant appears to be emptying. Actually, it is *empty*.

Am I really the only person still here? I look around and see tables all tidied and laid for lunch tomorrow. Around the corner a couple of waiters are chatting by the bar. One of them has just asked, with a slightly desperate look on his face, if I would like my main course or would I still prefer to wait. I can't remember what I said to him, but I seem to recall ordering some chips. Or French fries, as I'm in a posh place.

Then I hear footsteps clumping down the stairs, and I see a tall man I vaguely recognize, and he appears to vaguely recognize me, too. Everything is vague at this moment. I'm definitely drunk. Last time I went to the bathroom – some while ago – and peered into the mirror, even my hair looked drunk.

This guy is tall, good-looking in a kind of supercilious way, as if everything around him is beneath him, and sharply dressed in a dark jacket, crisp white shirt and tailored jeans. His loafers are so polished they are like black mirrors. I've seen him before somewhere, but I can't think who the hell he is. But he's walking over to me with a knowing look. When he speaks his voice is posh and measured. 'Sandy Grace, right?'

I give him a guarded, 'Yes.'

I'm finding him a bit intimidating. And I'm still trying to think who the hell he is. He smells nice, a cologne I don't recognize.

'Charming little restaurant this, isn't it? Are you and Roy having a pleasant evening?' He looked down, and I could see he was clocking the untouched other side of the table, the glasses and plates and cutlery.

'Well, I can't speak for Roy, but mine's been a bit rubbish, actually.'

He frowned. Or rather, looked pained. Or bewildered. 'Right,' he said, awkwardly. 'Yes, OK. Right – well . . .'

He looked around him, as if expecting Roy to materialize – perhaps from the loo – at any moment.

'He's not here,' I said to put him out of his misery.

'Not here? You've been stood up?'

I shook my head. 'Not *stood up* – not exactly.' I explained the events. When I finished I picked up the bottle of Chablis from the ice bucket and showed him there was still some left and offered him a glass. He hesitated, saying he was driving, then he said, 'Why not, I've not drunk anything all evening,' and accepted, sitting down and clinking his glass against mine. 'I've also been stood up,' he said.

'Seriously?'

'My date never showed.' He shrugged a *What-the-hell*. 'You're wondering who I am and where we've met before, aren't you?'

It threw me, because he was right. 'I'm trying to place you,' I replied diplomatically and took a stab. 'Sussex Police, right?'

'I'm a DI, we met at the Sussex Detectives' Ball, at the Grand Hotel in Brighton, last October. I was on the next table to you and your husband – we chatted briefly about how terrible the comedian was. I'm down on secondment to Sussex Police from the Met – briefing the force on counterterrorism.' He held out his hand and gave a very clammy, limp handshake for much longer than I was comfortable with, all the time staring into my eyes. 'My name is Cassian Pewe. Maybe I can give you a lift home?'

Have you ever come across someone who you found both attractive and repulsive at the same time? If not, you've never met Cassian Pewe. Snake charmers work by hypnotizing venomous reptiles. Cassian Pewe is the reverse. He's the supercilious reptile with the silver tongue and the golden looks. I knew he was dangerous, but as we talked, there was something about him – I can't explain what exactly – I found mesmerizing. Hypnotic?

When it got to 11.15 p.m., and the remaining staff in the restaurant were clearly dying to go home but too polite to say so, Roy rang, his voice full of apology. He was still at work, he said, and he would make up for this evening but best I get a taxi to go home.

I hung up on him. Then I accepted Cassian's gallant offer to give me a lift home in his white convertible Jaguar. He told me it was a classic, although I don't know much about cars, but it was rather gorgeous, with its soft leather seats and mahogany dashboard, and he was clearly proud of it. It was snug and warm inside, with the roof down and the night air blowing in our hair and on our faces. In my woozy state I imagined for a moment we were in the South of France, Cannes maybe, instead of Brighton.

When we pulled up outside our house ten minutes later, I saw Roy's car wasn't on the driveway. He was still at work, still playing with his prisoner. Cassian Pewe suddenly switched off the engine, and before I knew it, had slipped one arm around my neck, pulled me towards him and kissed me passionately on the lips.

Shocked, I was again both attracted and repulsed. Then he stared into my eyes, in the faint glow of a streetlight above us, and said, 'I really like Roy. I like him a lot.'

'Well, I hope you don't kiss him like that,' I replied.

5

I'm faced with a choice as I approach Gatwick Airport. The North or South Terminal? If I had a coin, I'd toss it. I decide South. So many decisions I'm completely free to make.

It's 1.45 p.m. Horrible Roel Albazi can only just about now be figuring I'm a no-show. My mirrors are still clear. But just for belt and braces, to be certain no one is following, I do a full 360-degree loop around the South Terminal before driving up the ramp of the short-term car park. Roy is not going to be happy if he gets stuck with the bill, the size of which will depend on how long it takes them to find my car. But the car is in my name, so it really shouldn't be a problem for him.

I take my ticket and the barrier rises in front of me. Symbolic in a way, as I drive through and into my new life, which begins with an empty space between a white Porsche Cayman and a purple Nissan Micra on the fourth floor of the short-term car park. I lock my little Golf – I've no idea why, habit I guess – toss the keys into a convenient bin, then walk across the bridge into the terminal building.

One bonus, in the situation I find myself in, of being married to a detective is the stuff I've learned from Roy that most people would never, ever, even think about. Like how to disappear in our online, digital world.

How to vanish without trace.

475

Like I'm about to. I am so nervous. Then I remind myself I have no choice.

It's weird when I look at my left hand and don't see my wedding ring or my engagement ring, which have been part of my fourth finger for so long. There's just a faint white band of skin that isn't suntanned. I may have to pawn them, hopefully not, but not too close to home, in case pawnbrokers become a line of enquiry. I dig my hand into the pocket of my lightweight denim jacket as I stroll around the Departures concourse because I'm oddly self-conscious about that white band, my naked finger.

After stopping at WHSmith to buy a newspaper, I head over to the British Airways check-in area, join a short queue and then check in to flight BA 2771 to Malaga. No luggage, I tell the polite young man behind the desk who is looking at my passport.

After a few moments of tapping on his terminal, he hands my passport back to me. 'Have a nice flight, Mrs Gordon.'

Instead of heading for security, I head for the loos. Once securely locked inside the ladies', I open the small holdall slung over my shoulder, pull out a dark brown wig and tug it on. Along with a large pair of dark glasses. Then I reverse my denim jacket, so it is now white. Tug off my jeans and replace them with a sensible skirt. Next, I make my way across to the EasyJet check-in area.

Fifteen minutes later, thanks to my second false passport, Sandra Smith is allocated seat 14C on EZY 243 to Amsterdam. When she arrives, with just hand baggage, she will check in to a London City Airport flight under the name of Sandra Jones. On entering the arrivals lounge there, she will see a limousine driver holding up the name Alison Shipley.

Alison Shipley will be whisked away from the airport in the back of a black Mercedes S Class driven by a courteous man called Meehat El Hadidy, following directions on his satnav to East Grinstead.

Taking her towards her new beginning.

6

They called him Tall Joe, although he was actually very short. Two inches shy of five feet, with a shaved head, snooker-ball shiny, and the body of a Sumo wrestler, he looked even shorter than his height. He had a problem with walking, due to knackered hips from too many fights, so that he strode along in a kind of pendulum motion that had something of the drunken sailor about it, swinging each leg past him and then sort of throwing his body forward. It looked pretty clumsy, but that was deceptive. Nothing about Tall Joe was clumsy. Joe Karter was a man of precision.

He was also a man of light and dark. On the light side, he was scrupulously polite, funny and charming – charming so long as you paid what you owed, when you owed it. On the dark, he was an aikido eighth dan black belt who had killed two men with his bare hands – and five in more painful ways – permanently disabled another eight, and had become a legend in prison, when serving lengthy time for GBH, by throwing a fridge down two flights of stairs, during a tantrum.

Not many people ever messed with Tall Joe Karter, which was why Roel Albazi employed him. If you owed money to Albazi's boss, Song Wu, when Joe Karter, always dressed in a suit and tie, looking like an overgrown schoolboy, knocked on your door, you paid it, or you made arrangements, fast. Albazi, and his associate, Skender Sharka, always ensured that any of their debtors who had fallen behind were made aware of Tall Joe Karter's CV.

Albazi was stressed before he picked up the phone to call Joe, and the fact that his bagman was sounding so calm was making him even more stressed. Not just one but *two* people he'd given substantial loans to, to cover their gambling debts, had gone missing – done runners. And Joe was in the middle of sodding nowhere, in his car, cheerfully telling him that he didn't know where they were.

The wife of one, Alan Mitten, who owed £30,000, plus £15,000 of interest, had just told Joe that she hadn't seen her husband in three weeks and even if she never saw him again it would be too soon. She'd been served a foreclosure notice from the mortgage company, her car had been repossessed and the bailiffs were coming this afternoon to take their furniture. So far, Skender Sharka was making some headway but not quickly enough. Although he was confident of finding him within the next twenty-four hours.

Tall Joe was even more hopeful about the other, Robert Rhys, a lawyer who owed £25,000 plus £15,000 interest. He was close to getting an address. And as soon as Rhys was located, Karter said he would meet him to arrange a payment plan.

'What payment plan do you have in mind?' Albazi quizzed.

'I'll ask him which bone of his body he would least like me to break, boss,' Tall Joe replied in his deep, cheeky-chappie voice. 'So I'll break another one – a toe or a finger – and tell him I'll break another one every twenty-four hours, saving the one he really doesn't want me to break to last, until he's paid. He'll pay tomorrow, boss, I'm confident.'

'He's a card player, isn't he, Joe?'

'Poker.'

'So he won't want you to break his fingers, will he?'

'He won't, boss.'

Albazi thanked him and hung up, fretting about Alan Mitten. He was a double-glazing salesman and his employers hadn't heard from him for over two weeks. At least Robert Rhys had decent employment, a partner in a small firm of solicitors. He would have equity in the firm, although the fact that he was in his late forties and living in a flat gave a clue to his gambling habit, that maybe he'd never amassed enough to afford a house. Gambled it all away. Hopefully Tall Joe would work his magic. Poker with your fingers in splints would not be a good prospect.

He leaned back in his swivel chair in his sixth-floor, white-carpeted penthouse office above his restaurant. It had a magnificent picture window view to the south across the river Adur to the houseboats on the far side and the English Channel beyond, and another across Shoreham High Street to the north. He pulled up a map on his screen. His loyal right hand, Skender Sharka, towered over him, looking down at it, too.

Sharka, a freak of nature, was six foot six tall and totally hairless. He'd been nicknamed 'Deve' at school, which translated into English as 'Camel', because he had two lumps on his skull. He was a gentle person, gentle in all he did, gentle even when he killed.

They'd worked as a team for the past decade, he, Sharka and Tall Joe, collecting debts that weren't legally enforceable – mostly drug debts – and then Albazi had been approached by a representative of Song Wu with the proverbial offer he could not refuse. Although subsequently he had realized the offer was too good to be true.

The tracking system of locating his debtors, devised by Sharka, was highly effective. People in hiding generally did not travel far. Those who needed to hide in a hurry rarely went out of their comfort zone. Albazi had had enough debtors go bad over the years to warrant his investment in the latest technology, with algorithms created by Sharka, whose principal method of tracking people was through payments to a source on the internet who had access to all the different phone companies' records. By cross-referencing numbers, he'd been able to see the burner phones each had bought in the mistaken belief these would make them invisible and impossible to track. It worked so brilliantly Albazi had only ever lost one completely. But he had dealt with that swiftly, by having the man's parents and then grandparents, back in Albania, tortured and murdered.

Now, Song Wu was not happy with him, and he cursed himself for getting reckless. In truth, he hadn't done the full due diligence he would normally do on a customer before lending them the money, he had come to rely too much on his debt-collecting abilities. On top of Mitten and Rhys, and with Sandy Grace playing games, the situation was a whole lot worse.

He sometimes felt his relationship with the Song Wu organization was like being a man trapped in a watery cul-de-sac with a crocodile. So long as he kept throwing it chickens, the crocodile would keep smiling. And all the time growing bigger and needing more chickens . . .

'So where is she right now, Skender?' he asked.

From the moment, a month ago, when Sandy Grace had first defaulted on a repayment instalment to his boss, Tall Joe had placed a tracking device on her car. It was a magnetic transponder, attached beneath the boot, so small she would only have found it if she had been searching for it specifically. Its current location showed as a small blue dot on a map on the computer.

'Brighton, boss. Looks like she's in Churchill Square car park.'

Albazi studied the screen carefully as he drilled a hole in the tip of a Cohiba Robusto, then put the stubby cigar in his mouth without lighting it. 'So she might be trying to get the cash together, as she promised. One hundred and fifty thousand pounds in cash – in fifty-pound notes. Her time is running out. Let's hope she's taking the threats seriously.'

Albazi lit his cigar carefully with his gold Dunhill, turning the end over and over in the flame until it was burning evenly.

His face disappeared in a cloud of blue smoke. His disembodied voice said, 'So wait. Watch the blue dot. Tell me when it moves again.'

Skender assured him he would.

'Know what's going to happen to you and me if she fails to deliver?'

'No, boss.'

'You don't want to know.'

'OK.'

'Which is why I'm going to tell you.'

7

Early July 2007 – Looking back

Where does anything really start, in life? For me, Sandy Grace, or for any of us? The lightbulb moment some people talk about, that sudden flash of inspiration that pops seemingly from nowhere. Or maybe nothing so dramatic, just a simple spark of excitement when we suddenly find ourselves more alive than we ever did before – because we've found our mojo – or whatever.

Or the polar opposite. The feeling one morning, when you wake up, that today is the first day of the rest of your life and you don't want the rest of your life to be this same old, same old, any longer. That was how it was for me. A very short while after I first met Tamzin.

I've heard that a bad back is one of the symptoms of un-happiness – when life is not panning out how you want it to be. Maybe that's true – or maybe people with bad backs say that because misery likes company. Whatever, I'd ricked my back trying to move a sofa into a different place in the living room. I wanted good feng shui in our new home – all that ancient Chinese stuff about bringing balance and good vibes into our living spaces.

So I got great feng shui and a messed-up back. Or, in medical terminology, prolapsed discs L4 and L5. I had sciatica for a year – if you've never had it, you are lucky. You have no idea how painful it is. Think of sliding a red-hot wire all the way down inside the skin of your leg, from your bum to your foot, and then twisting it a few times before plugging it into a live socket for several seconds. I'm not exaggerating.

My best friend, Becky Jackson, had joined a Pilates class. Like Roy and me, she and her husband had been struggling to conceive, and she'd read in a magazine about two women with infertility problems who had been helped by Pilates. Becky gets most of her information from magazines. She was raving about how Pilates made her feel, and her instructor had told her it could help my back. So I gave it a go. And one of the girls in the group was Tamzin Heywood.

And within a few weeks, two things happened. The first was that my back improved dramatically. The second, that I wanted to be Tamzin Heywood.

Badly.

So badly I lay awake at night thinking about her with pure, undiluted envy. It was her lifestyle. I thought about everything she had that I didn't. Someone once told me that the secret of life is to know when it's good. And she was making me feel the exact opposite of that about my life.

My rather grey little life. In our grey house. Just a couple of years ago it was my dream home. Detached, four-bedroom – well, three and a half really – with a good-sized rear garden, and so close to the sea you can hear it. I put my imprint on it, the inside is light and airy, all minimalist, and I created a Zen garden in the rear. I really thought it was fine, lovely, far grander than the bungalow in Seaford where I grew up. Our *forever* home.

I'd planned the children's rooms; the eventual loft conversion, when we could afford it, where we could wake in the morning with a sea view – well, a partial sea view anyway. Then I went to Tamzin's house.

Shit.

She and I are the same age. I'd always liked nice clothes but I'd never been fussed about brands – before now. She wears the coolest – and of course most expensive – gym kit brands, as well as insanely bling and covetable Prada trainers (£550), she has gorgeous hair and, naturally, perfectly manicured nails. Perfect everything.

Her husband, Ferris, owns a string of estate agents, but Tamzin's no idle kept woman, no vacuous airhead *Housewife of Brighton*. Of course she isn't. She's a passionate animal lover who spent two years recently studying to qualify in canine myotherapy – that's dog massage to you and me. It's her passion – as well as her own source of income – helping dogs with their mobility and muscle health. Being a fellow dog lover, I immediately admired that about her – and respected her for it. Roy and I agreed a long time ago we could never like anyone who doesn't like animals.

Tamzin and Ferris live in a house styled like an Italian palazzo in Roedean, an exclusive enclave at the eastern extremity of Brighton – where an expensive girls' school is located. Their house has a sea view to die for, out across the English Channel, and all the toys. Indoor and outdoor pools, tennis court, gym, sauna, steam room, the whole enchilada. She drives a convertible Porsche with a personal plate. I drive a ten-year-old Golf that had 90,000 miles on the clock when we bought it.

But it's not just their house, it's their whole lifestyle. They have a debenture at Wimbledon, which means they go to all the best matches throughout Wimbledon fortnight. They are members of Glyndebourne so they go to the opera regularly throughout the summer season, all dressed up fancy. My envy of Tamzin and her life really came out when they invited Roy and me to see *Carmen*, but at the last minute he had to cancel because a dead body had been found in a park.

So I went alone and was determined to have the best time. We all had way too much to drink, and they invited me back to their house after. Their three kids were sleeping over at the grand-parents'. Tamzin convinced me to stay as it was so late, and we were all so drunk. Ferris went up to bed leaving Tamzin and me drinking a magnum of white.

I texted Roy a drunk message: **Don't wait up, back at Tamzin and Ferris's. Magnum open. Party time! Love you. X**

It was all so hedonistic. We were laughing, spinning each other around and dirty dancing to the music. Then she surprised me by kissing me as we danced, her soft tongue on mine. Everything slowed down. My God, it felt like the best kiss ever. I'm ashamed to say it but I was smitten, I just didn't think of anything or anyone else at that moment. Not Roy. Not Ferris. I was selfishly in lust and out for myself. We ended up making love together on the sofa in the living room then crashing out in each other's arms.

I woke up at 6.30 a.m., with the hangover from hell, my head was thumping, and I was alone with just a blanket over me. As soon as my thoughts allowed, I felt embarrassed. My face reddened as I imagined my parents' reactions. Then more embarrassment at why I cared about my parents' bloody reactions at my age. But this was not my house. What if the kids came back at any moment? I'd outstayed my welcome; I should leave and get back to Roy. I painfully pieced back together the night and snuck out before they got up, closing the front door with almost no sound behind me.

Then came the long walk of shame home, high heels in my hand, clearly last night's clothes. I texted Tamzin to say thanks for a great evening, wink, kiss. Then I vowed to get my drinking under control. Seriously. Sort my life out. My grey boring life. Find happiness in my life with Roy. I loved him and desperately wanted our marriage to work, and still hoped beyond hope that we would have a baby.

But when I think back on it, no surprise, that's when the dissatisfaction with my life really started. I couldn't get that fling out of my head, I'd enjoyed it. I craved it.

The worst thing of all was that Tamzin was so damned friendly towards me afterwards. As well as being genuinely warm, kind, funny, generous and interested in everyone, she never, for one moment, seemed to take her privileged life for granted. She never mentioned our brief encounter, not once. It was as if it had not happened. Not that it could have continued, of course, but, looking back, it was another rejection. And it hit me hard because I had enjoyed it. It took up way too much of my thoughts. What if this, what if that. One thing I knew for certain: Roy must never know about it – it would ruin him. Well, it must never happen again, and I must work harder at my marriage. What sort of a wife was I? I ended up feeling disgusted with myself.

That summer, when I had quit my full-time job with a firm of accountants to work part-time as receptionist at a doctors' surgery – our infertility specialist had advised me I shouldn't do any stressful job – we were invited over to her house a lot. Such happy, fun afternoons around the pool, with some very nice wines from their cellar. Sometimes in the company of their three beautiful and polite kids – with their equally beautiful, and dutiful, nanny. And always with their two adorably daft and soppy golden retrievers, nuzzling us for cuddles and ever-hopeful of treats.

I so wanted her life and that night together had just intensified those feelings. Not that I could tell anyone. And the problem was that I wasn't just envious – Tamzin had made me start to question my entire life. And to be fair on Roy, that wasn't his fault, it was mine. When I met him, all those years previously, my life – and my aspirations – were very different.

Roy is two years older than me, but in some ways it often feels much more. He's so stable, so calm, so wise. I was nineteen when we met, and my life up until that point had pretty much been a train crash. I am an only child, as is my mother who was born to German parents. But, unlike modern Germans I've met, she totally lacks any sense of humour. She's just a cold fish, and bitter at the hand life has dealt her, in the shape of my seriously weird loser of a father.

He worked all his career as a car mechanic in a small garage in Eastbourne, and spends his retirement building scale model Second World War aircraft, like Spitfires, Hurricanes, Wellingtons and Halifaxes, as well as all their German counterparts. He likes to tell the few visitors who come to their home in Seaford these were aircraft his father had flown in the war, first as a fighter ace with seven kills, then a bomber pilot.

He has always maintained – and still does – that his father was one of the Dambuster heroes, whereas in reality he had been an aircraft fitter and had never been posted anywhere near 633 Squadron. Partly on account of the fact he would have been just fourteen years old at the end of the war.

And to make it worse, my mother has always gone along with it. Maybe, when I look back at her in a charitable frame of mind, I wonder if it's because she was traumatized by what her country did in the war, and this was some weird way, in her weird mind, of her assuaging her guilt.

She had been brought up in England and eventually, to her regret (my supposition), met my father and lived unhappily ever after.

I haven't read much poetry, but I did come across a few lines I really liked from someone called Philip Larkin about how your parents fuck you up.

Oh yes. That resonates. I was fourteen when I first decided I didn't want to live a life like theirs.

ONE OF US IS DEAD

COMING SEPTEMBER 2024

When Taylor arrives late for a funeral, he has to stand at the rear of the rammed country church. But, as the service progresses, Taylor notices a man seated on a pew six rows in front of him. At first he thinks he must be mistaken, but the more he looks at him, especially when he glances around, the more certain Taylor becomes that this is his old school friend Rufus Rorke.

Except it couldn't be him, could it? Because two years ago, Taylor attended Rufus Rorke's funeral. And, not only that, he delivered Rufus's eulogy.

Taylor tries to catch this person at the end of the funeral, but he has vanished into the torrential rain. How is Rufus still alive? And how dangerous is it to find out why?

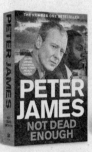
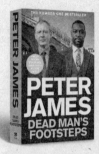

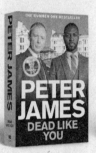
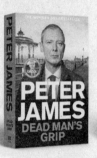

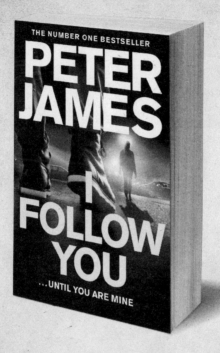

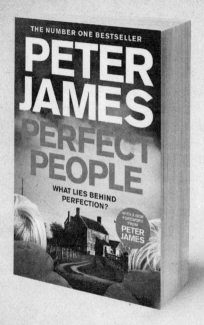

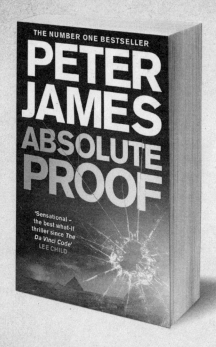

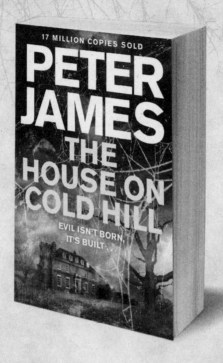